Monster INK Publishing
Presents

FUELED

BY

REVENGE

BB. HUGHLEY

Dedication

This book is dedicated to my mother Claudette Bouttè, and my aunt Sheila "Tia" Bouttè. My mother believed in my dream before I even dreamed it. I grew up writing and she would stand in my doorway and watch me with a huge smile spread across her face. "You remind me so much of Sheila, just always writing." I would just smile back and keep writing. As I grew up, she encouraged me to write more and more and I would also spend time with Tia as she wrote. We would be in her room for hours with me giving her ideas and laughing about the things her characters said or did! Before my mother passed away, she told me to follow my dream and that she knew I was meant to write. It hurts like hell that neither one of them are here to see me fulfill my dream, but I promise to make you both proud!!!! You two were the glue that held us all together and it's not a day that goes by that I don't miss y'all. This first one is for YOU!!!

MOMMA I DID IT

Special Thanks

My Husband: Landon Landon Landon, your patience with me is that of a SAINT. I am constantly writing and that has taken so much time away from us and our quality time, but you have been understanding, loving, and one of my biggest supporters. I literally wouldn't be doing this if it wasn't for you pushing me to finish and believing in me when I was too scared to believe in myself. I love you with my whole heart!

Edvige: You were the very first person to call me an Author. That title means everything to me, and you pushed me and encouraged me to fulfill my purpose!!! You are truly your mother's daughter and I appreciate you so much!! Love you!!

Chantelle: Girl we could inspire the world if our text thread was ever leaked ☺ □!!! You are a driving force of positivity in my life and I'm so blessed to have someone like you in my corner. No one has given me as much unbiased feedback and encouragement as you have. Those "you better be writing" text paid off! I love the way you love me and hold me accountable!! You're everything!

Jewel: I could have told you that I was doing underwater basket weaving and you would have been like "yesss, when do we start"! You support me in everything that I do and that means the world to me! If I even sound like I'm giving up or second guessing myself, you're right there cheering me on, and I love you for it!!

NaVarsha: This all started with us lying in bed as kids, telling "fantasies". We were young as hell telling elaborate stories straight from our imagination. Those stories would go on for days! Once we finished one, we would start on a whole new one, with different boys and cuter clothes! Oh, the memories!! Thank you for sparking my creativity. I went from lying in bed telling fantasies out loud, to sitting at my desk penning them, and now I'm on my laptop publishing them!

Thank you to everyone that has believed in me, poured knowledge and wisdom into me, prayed for me, and encouraged me to keep going. After losing my mother, I didn't believe this was possible. I hit my lowest low and I felt like I couldn't do this or anything else without her by my side. Grief can be stifling but many of you rallied around me and showed me there was light after darkness.
This process was LONG, but it was worth it.
I appreciate and love you all!!

Jaxsyn Blackwell

"Jaxsyn get the fuck in here, now! I came in there and told you my cootie-cat is burning, and I need your fuckin help! That was fifteen fuckin' minutes ago and you still gone lay yo stupid ass there like I ain't said shit?" My mother yelled from the bathroom and I literally wanted to die. The reason I was born into this hell was beyond my scope of understanding. It's like her life's mission is to work my damn nerves. I find myself wanting to super sock her ass constantly but that's still my mother, so I try my hardest to stay semi respectful and not put my hands on her. Lord knows the last thing I needed right now was another case with my name attached to it.

I kicked the covers off of my body and the morning chill that crept through our house sent goosebumps down my arms and legs. That didn't do shit but piss me off even more than I already was from her yelling like we live in a damn mansion.

"What the fuck Kabrina?" I walked into the bathroom and my mother was sitting on the toilet with her left leg propped up on the side of the tub diggin' in her pussy. To most people, this would have taken them by surprise, but she's done far too much shit throughout my life for anything she does to surprise me anymore.

"The discharge is not all the way green this time, and it don't even smell that bad either. You remember how it was last time don't you? We smelled that bullshit soon as I opened my legs, but I think I caught it early this time," her chin was pressed into her chest so she could dig further. She moved her middle finger in a circular motion and when she pulled it out, it looked like yellowish dough. She wiped her findings on a piece of tissue and then went back in.

"Even though I try very hard to forget, I do remember that. I didn't want to see it then, like I don't want to see it now. This shit so foul Kabrina, even for you. Now, what is it that you want from me so I can get ready for school?"

"I still got some of that cream left from the last time. It's in my top drawer. Go in my room and get it for me and grab those antibiotic pills out of my purse too."

"You know this is your own crazy ass fault Kabrina? Keep fuckin' Andre raw and his ass gone keep you in this bathroom cocked open lookin' nasty."

"Bitch call me Kabrina one more time and watch me knock yo ass into tomorrow. I try to be cool with you Jaxsyn and you always over step your fuckin' boundaries *lil girl*. I don't give a fuck how much you don't like me you better find some respect. I'm momma to you bitch and that's what you better start calling me."

"You focused on the wrong shit," I walked out of the bathroom and down our dingy hallway to her bedroom. The smell of dirt, dick, and crack invaded my nostrils but that was the only things that was constant in our household. The stench made me sick to my stomach, but she gave less than a fuck about anything but Kabrina.

I looked through her top drawer carefully and with caution. I wasn't trying to get stuck by one of her dirty ass crack syringes or anything else that could be lurking in her junk drawer. "This green tube?" I asked and started reading the label.

"Well it's the only damn tube of cream in the drawer genius."

Smart mouth havin' ass bitch. I grabbed the cream and then got her pills from her purse. I knew once she fixed herself up, she was going to work on my nerves far more than she was already doing so I rushed back to the bathroom to give her the coochie cream and pills. I needed to bounce before her ass even had a chance to pretend that she was a mother and bark orders about the house.

"Don't tell Andre," she looked up at me while she spread the cream all over the lips of her red swollen twat.

"I don't even talk to that man and you know it," I leaned up against the door and folded my arms.

"Yeah but he damn sure talks to you. I know y'all wish I was a lil bit slower. I see how he looks at you and I see how you be wearing those little ass shorts and shit to get his attention. Don't forget where you get all that ass from heffa. Me! I gave you that body that you around here

6

flauntin' for my nigga. The difference between you and me is that I know how to work it waaaaay better baby girl. How you think you got here? I used to pop this pussy for Brian every night, so don't even try me."

"Clearly you just thought I was one of your friends. You stay on that stupid shit. I'm out," I went back to my room, closed the door, and turned my music on. That bitch swore up and down somebody wanted her nigga but she's in there dabbing pussy cream on herself because of him, yeah, I'll pass boo.

"Aye, what you doin?" I called my sister Zionna.

"Over here trying to get ready for school, but you know how that shit go."

"Bitch, Kabrina on that same bullshit this morning. Hurry up so we can smoke before we go in. She on my nerves."

"Alright. Give me like ten minutes."

"Yup," I hung up and got dressed. Mornings with Kabrina was always unpredictable so I had to make sure that all my shit for school was done at night before she came home. I always take my bath, iron my clothes, do my homework, and most definitely make sure my personal possessions were hidden to the best of my ability. Her ass could steal gum right out of your mouth as you chew on it. I always had to find new spots, or my shit was ghost. She got me one too many times growing up, and I learned from my daddy how to hide my valuables in places her cracked out ass mind wouldn't think to look.

I looked at myself in the mirror and I was the shit as usual. I definitely didn't look like what the fuck I was going through and that was a plus. Growing up in Detroit, anything could get you clowned. Even your mother being on crack as if you had any control over that shit. You always had to be on your A game and for the last few years that wasn't a problem for me or my sister. I loosened the strings on my new Jordans that my boyfriend Black bought me and fixed my Hudson jeans at the bottom that my daddy bought me, so they sat exactly how I wanted them to on top of my shoes. Hudson's always made my ass look plumper and if my dad knew that's why I begged him to pay $98.00 for one pair of jeans he would have never bought them.

I snuck to the kitchen while Kabrina was still in the bathroom and brushed my teeth in the sink. I damn sure wasn't going in there with her while she dug the stank out of her coochie. I crept back to the room and applied my lip gloss. My makeup was light but perfectly applied and I looked ready to shit on hoes.

"I'm gone *Kabrina*!" I smiled. "Make sure you turn that light out when you finish. The bill was high as hell last month and I ain't made of money."

"You a hard head lil bitch huh?" She yelled from the bathroom.

"If I am, I learned from the best Kabrina! Kabrina, Kabrina, Kabrina. Kabriiiiina!" I yelled. She stays worried about the wrong shit. I know her ass better turn that light out though.

I grabbed my book bag and laughed about her silly ass as I walked out. I cuss' like a damn sailor, but she gets pissed when I call her by her first name. It don't have shit to do with her wanting to be a real mother and more to do with her jealousy towards my step mother Rebecca. That ain't my fault tho'. In my world respect is earned and my step mother earned the title of "ma". Kabrina punk ass whose left me home alone for days with no food, steals my shit for her habit, and beat my ass when she's fucked up don't deserve to be called nothing more than a Bitch. Kabrina will do though until I'm eighteen and out of her house. At that point I can't make no promises on what the hell she'll be called. Real talk.

I spotted Zionna at the end of the walkway rolling up a blunt that I desperately needed to hit. When you wake up to your mother diggin' inside of herself and smearing the findings on a piece of tissue, that's definitely a reason to hit the morning L.

"Good morning sis. Did you see Black ride by yet?" I asked as I walked up on her.

"Good morning. I just got out here. You know them nigga's always runnin' late anyway," she sealed the blunt and looked up at me. "You look cute," she smiled.

"Thanks baby, you too."

"Here," she hit the blunt and passed it to me. "I'll call Quan and see where they at. I'm not just about to be standing out here waiting for Freaky Jason to come rape us."

I chuckled and nodded my head as I continued to smoke.

"Nigga I know you not still sleep and we standin' the fuck outside waiting for your ass," she snapped on his ass which was nothing new. He stayed on her last nerve and I never understood their relationship, but it wasn't mine to understand. "Oh… Alright," she rolled her eyes and hung up. "He said they about to pull up now."

"Then why you look like that?" Her face was all twisted and I laughed.

"That nigga plays too fuckin' much. It's too early for all that shit."

I passed the blunt back to her so she could change her attitude before they pull up. We stood out there blowin' for another five minutes or so and then I heard Black's music bangin'

8

before he even hit the block. I couldn't even help the smile that formed on my face. I love his black ass to death and niggas knew they didn't have a chance with me because of him. I didn't see no one else but my baby. He had me wide open and I wasn't ashamed of it at all. I was actually proud of our relationship and how far we've come. Before he was able to put Jordans on my feet, he couldn't even afford to put food in his own mouth, I was by his side. I had been hustling for me and my sister my whole life, so I hit the corner with him and helped my baby grind for everything he has now. When his own niggas wouldn't open the side door and pass him a plate of food on days that the stomach rumbles got the best of him; his rider not only made sure he ate but came up with a plan to make sure he always ate and ate good.

Over the years I became a pro at stealing. It's the only way me and Zionna was going to eat because our mothers weren't shit. I started going into grocery stores outside of my hood and stealing all the good shit. One day I would go for bread and butter and all the necessities and then the next day I was stocking up on chicken, steak, fish, bags of shrimp, and everything else my little body could hide. Once Black came into the picture, I had three mouths to feed and not just two. I would never see him down bad and not help. He's not just my man, he's my best friend.

"Bitch we have two weeks before we out this raggedy bitch for good. I don't know how all this shit is about to play out but we out and that's all that matters." Zionna said seriously. I could tell that whatever bullshit her hoe ass mother Sandy was on today had my sister's mind wandering.

"I feel you. This shit can't happen fast enough sis. I woke up to Kabrina diggin' in her pussy again. I can't keep dealing with her triflin' ass man. I swear."

"Damn. Andre set fire to her ass again huh?" She laughed and I nodded with a smirk "You know it."

"Well Sandy threw scalding hot water on me about two o'clock this morning because she thought I was being too sexy around Gary. How the fuck am I being too sexy in regular ass pajama pants, under the cover, in my room, with the door closed. Man, I been up ever since contemplating slappin' the dog shit out of her stupid ass. My damn back is still irritated so it's probably going to blister if it hasn't already."

"I told you to lock your door Zionna. You can't keep forgetting that shit," I was irritated. I can't be at her crib twenty-four-seven to protect her which means she needs to be locking that damn door like I told her to do too many times before. "Anyway, I get it. I guess I'm fuckin

Andre behind Kabrina's back again or trying to. You know it's always something and I can't keep up with the shit that she makes up in her head anymore. I swear these hoes is nuts and I can't wait to get far away from them and all the dysfunction that comes with them."

"Two weeks bitch. That's all I keep chanting in my head. Two funky ass weeks and these bitches will be left, right here alone, to self-destruct with the rest of these fuckin' people that don't want shit out of life."

"Hell yeah," I nodded my head and agreed. "There they go." We walked to Black's car and got in.

"Hey baby," he looked over at me and my heart smiled.

"Hey, you," I leaned across the center console and placed my lips on his. He smelled like winter fresh and weed. I kissed him deep and as soon as I felt his tongue enter my mouth, I wanted him. He pulled me closer and we kissed for another minute or so and then stared into each other's eyes. "I missed you," I chewed on his gum that I took.

"I missed you too beautiful," he pecked my lips again and then pulled off. He turned his music back up.

Everybody doing them, I'm still scratchin' on the block

Like "damn, I'ma be a failure"

Surrounded by thugs, drugs, and drug, paraphernalia

Cops, courts, and their thoughts is to derail us

Three-time felons in shorts with jealous thoughts

Tryin' to figure where your mail is, guesstimate the weight you sellin'

So, they can send shots straight to your melon wait!

He rapped Jay Z's part on "This Can't Be Life," and I already knew once he threw that song on, some real shit must have gone down at his crib. He was in a zone and I let him be. I never pressured him to talk about what the fuck was going on at home because I didn't need him questioning me about my home life. The streets talked and I know that he knows Kabrina is a crack head like I know that his dad is in jail for molesting him and his sister, and his momma is on drugs too. We all have our own crosses to bare and neither of us like to talk about what was happening behind closed doors. I simply held his hand to let him know that I was here for him if he ever wanted to let me in.

10

"Are we going to school?" Z yelled to no one in particular and Black turned his music all the way down.

"I was hustlin all night so I'm not." Quan spoke up first. That was no surprise since the nigga never went to school. Zionna did all his work for him and I'm sure she's the only reason his ass is even graduating on time.

"I ain't feelin that shit either honestly, plus I'm done with all my classes already," I said and looked over at Black.

"We can go to my brother's crib," he turned the music back up and I made eye contact with Zionna. She used to kick it with his step brother Jared and rather not be around him. She shrugged her shoulders letting me know she didn't care, and I set back in my seat. As long as she was good, I was good too. I didn't want her to get there and then be uncomfortable.

My mind drifted off to thoughts of getting away from my momma and going to college. These days I couldn't think of anything else. I finished all my classes early and now I'm just waiting to walk across that stage and be out. Fuck being average or following in our parents' footsteps. Both me and Zionna want way more out of life than what we see every day and I'm going to make sure that we get it. By all means necessary we will be better than Sandy and Kabrina. Shit, I damn near wanna skip graduation and be out this bitch now.

"Baby I need you to come take care of your man." Black took my hand into his and we went to his brother's room.

"Aye make sure y'all change those sheets! Kim will kill my ass if she come home to stained sheets again." Jared laughed but we knew he was serious. His girlfriend Kim was just as big as his ass and she loved to fight. She had no problem going toe to toe about her man or with her man. That's the main reason Zionna hated being around him. She never wants Kim to find out that they used to fuck around.

Black closed the door and laughed.

"That nigga scared as shit."

"If I was her size you'd be walking around here 'noid and nervous too."

"Nah I'll be fuckin' that aggression out of yo' big ass. He's a pussy," he pulled me into his arms, and we started undressing each other. Black was my first and God willing he will be my last and only. He was everything to me so I gave him everything; my time, my loyalty, my love, my body, my mind, and if he asked, he could have my soul too. I was his for the taking from the very beginning and he's never given me any reason not to feel a hundred percent comfortable in giving all of me to him. We ride for each other hard. From standing on corners together and handling niggas that's trying to take what's his, to simply being there for each other emotionally when we can't even find the words to speak.

"Fuck Jax!" He grunted as I planted my feet and bounced up and down. I don't play no games when it comes to pleasing him. I had to make him remember why he chose me, every time. "Shit, I'm about to cum," he grunted as he squeezed my ass and busted.

I wiped the sweat from my forehead and smiled down at him. "Satisfied?" I leaned forward and kissed him.

"Always baby. You have no comp and that's a fact," he laid me on his chest. "I'm going to miss this Jaxsyn," he said as he rubbed my head and I closed my eyes.

"I know baby. I'm going to miss you too, but we'll still see each other all the time."

"That's bullshit. You should just go to State like I asked you to do man. It's a good school and an education is an education," I could hear his disappointment... again.

"We have to get away Black. It's no way that I can stay in this state for school. We'll only be five hours away tho' baby. Once I get a car, I'm coming to see you all the time. You know I am."

"You say that shit now like everybody that's in our position. Over time the contact and visits will become less and less. Next thing we know it's been years and we randomly bumping into each other smiling about how long it's been and how good it is to see each other. By that time, you'll be with some preppy ass white boy with two kids and I'll have a baby momma that I can't stand but I love my kid, so I deal with her crazy ass."

"First of all, stop watching so many Lifetime and BET movies with your sister nigga. Second, that ain't how we rock. Fuck everybody else that's been in our situation. This is us baby and we can make this work if we try. I wish it was another solution, but I have to go baby. I literally have too. It's so much shit that I'm not willing to keep dealing with here and the only way to overcome it, is to escape it. This is my out Black and I can't jeopardize that for anyone."

"Yeah, not even me. The nigga you claim to be in love with," he mumbled under his breath as he rolled over. I understood why he always got mad when we talked about me going away to college, but I had no other choice. This decision was bigger than me, and him, or us together. I love the ground this man walks on but nothing in this world was going to stop me from breaking out.

Since the age of four, Zionna and I have been taking care of each other because our mother's ain't shit. It's no better way to put it because they're not. We stayed right next door to each other our whole life and we found out that we were actually sisters and not best friends when we were about six-years-old. Our dad is a white man that grew up in the hood with his aunt who is mixed. His love for black women was genuine, plus that's all he's ever been surrounded by. When he crossed paths with our mothers it was a wrap. He started fuckin' with both of them and then going back to the suburbs to be with his wife Rebecca. She was cluelessly sitting at home with my two brothers Jagger and Dawson while Brian was out here doing him.

When he came to the hood, he wasn't coming empty handed. He was bringing pure cocaine with him and they would all get high and fuck around. Unfortunately, both Kabrina and Sandy got hooked on its purity and that addiction turned into crack since they couldn't afford what he was supplying them with once he was gone back home. They had an itch that needed to be scratched so they started chasing that high.

In the process of him just coming through having "fun", he actually fucked over their lives and gave them us. Unlike them, our dad stopped the bullshit and got himself together. He already had two sons and when they got pregnant back to back with us, he knew he needed to get his shit together for his kids. Thank God he did because at least I had one good parent. He comes to get me all the time and I spend time with him, his wife, and my other siblings as much as possible but I always have to come right back to hell and struggle with Kabrina's ass until my next visit.

She refused to give him full custody like he's begged her to do my whole life and will clean up her act anytime he threatens to take her to court. I know she loves me even though she fucks up, but hell is hell no matter how you try to wrap it in a pretty bow. Her and Sandy was shitty fuckin' parents and deprived us of growing up the way we deserved. Every day we didn't know if we would eat, see them, have heat, have to run from their dealers and pimps, or nothing else. No day with those two was easy and now we're going to college and finally catching a real break. Finally escaping our mothers. I couldn't allow nothing to come between us and that kind of peace. I love Black to death, but he'll just have to be mad because I'm out...

Jaxsyn Avery

I slowly crept through my city on my way to Zionna's house with tears streaming down my face. My day started out perfect and now I was in the middle of an emotional breakdown. I finished the decor in one of my clients' homes and when she went to hug me, her pregnant belly rubbed against me. I felt the tears coming immediately and couldn't get to my truck quick enough. I tried my best not to react like that whenever I was around pregnant women or children, but the heart wants what it wants.

I've been yearning to start a family for the last couple years but Black outright refuse. He's not even willing to have a conversation about children anymore. He feels like he wants us to be more established before we bring kids into the world, but I make great money. He claims it's about him being a man and providing, but it sounds like some bull to me. He doesn't mind allowing me to finance our life in any every other way but when it comes to children, he claims to have all of these pride issues.

"I'm outside," I called my sister as I wiped my face.

"Why are you here? You are irritatin' ass fuck man," she hung up and opened the door with an attitude a few seconds later.

"You're entitled to your opinion, now go get dressed," I perked up like I always did to hide the pain.

"What time is it bitch? Damn. I was at the hospital all night."

"It's 12:30 and I don't care. That's what the hell Registered Nurses do sweetie, they work. Now go get dressed so we can grab the rest of the stuff I need."

"Did I mention how utterly fuckin irritating you are?"

"You might have mentioned it," I chuckled as she sluggishly climbed her steps.

14

"Hey Jaxsyn," I turned around and Quan was behind me. The sight of him made my ass itch but she still loves this bum after all this time, so I try to play nice as much as humanly possible.

"Hey," I turned back around.

"Where's Black?"

"Up at the shop."

"Oh okay. Zionna told me you needed me to do the flyers for Black's party."

"Not anymore. That was over a week ago, so I got someone else to do it," I was growing irritated and I'm sure he picked up on it, so he walked away.

He stays on my bad side because of his whorish ways. He's never mastered the art of keeping his penis either inside of my sister or inside of his pants. She's at my house every other week with a new story about some random chick that she's caught him up with or another episode of "what he gave me this time". I've literally lost count on how many STD's he's given her over the years. This nigga is a bum and I couldn't wait for her to leave him for good.

"I'm ready," she came downstairs and I smiled.

"Oh, how I love when you match my fly. I love us so damn much," I blew her a kiss.

"I love us too," she laughed. "Quan I'm gone."

"Y'all have fun and don't do anything I wouldn't do."

We both looked at each other and then at him. "I'm not going to say a word. That wouldn't even be fair," I shook my head and walked toward the door.

"Please don't." Zionna smirked. "I'm not in the mood for it today."

He had a lot of nerve, but he doesn't do anything that she doesn't allow him to do so I was becoming less and less involved in their mess. It was obvious she wasn't going anywhere, and neither was he. If they wanted to bask in a cesspool of nastiness, who the hell am I to stop them?

"Bitch I need a drink so we might have to do that first and then go get everything for Black's birthday."

"Whaaat? The proper princess used real profanity? Isn't that quite throwback Thursday of you. It's still early and your day is going that bad already? Talkin' 'bout *bitch*. Girl who the fuck are you right now and where is my damn sister?" She teased.

"Kiss my ass Zionna. My client rubbed her pregnant belly against me by accident and I freaked," I fought the tears that wanted so desperately to fall again.

"Aww sis. I'm sorry," she grabbed my hand and rubbed it.

"I just don't understand Z. We have everything and he continues to make excuses. Look," I dug in my purse when we got to the light and pulled out a check for $18,000.

"Wow."

"This was just from one of the jobs today, but he wants me to believe that money is the issue."

"Fuck it then Jax, trap his ass. Y'all been together long enough for you to know his ass ain't going no damn where. Do you boo boo!"

"You sound crazy as hell. I'll divorce him before I trap him. I shouldn't have to trap my damn husband just to start a family Z. This shit hurt and it's sad, but I refuse to be dragged down that road."

"Then be patient sis. He's not saying no persè, he's saying not right now. You guys have to be way more careful though. Too many abortions and you won't be able to have a baby when the time comes Jax. I can't stress that to you enough."

"I know," I shook my head just thinking about the abortions he's talked me into over the years. Never again. If I get pregnant again, I'll just take my baby and go. My heart and body can't go through that again and I won't. I drove us straight to the bar because I was serious about getting some shots before we went shopping. I needed to get my mind right.

Zionna Blackwell

Jaxsyn said some slick shit in front of Quan before we left the house and I knew his ass was going to text me eventually. We finished with our drinks and was almost done shopping before he sent me a text. I guess his ass had to sit with it for a minute.

My Headache: *You just let that broad say anything to me and when I say shit back to her, I'm the bad guy.*

Me: *You heard me tell her to chill and for the record she didn't even say anything*

My Headache: *You a fuckin lie! You ain't say shit and you never say shit*

My Headache: *She come in this bitch like she owns the place, but I guess that's cool huh?*

My Headache: *Could you go to her house and talk to Black how you let her talk to me?*

Me: *Whatever Quan*

I sighed heavily and powered my phone off. Everything was an argument with him and like I told my sister, I wasn't in the mood for it today. Shit, I'm never in the mood for it but I just didn't have the energy to put into his ignorance today. She didn't even say shit and actually caught herself before I stopped her. He was trippin' for no reason, once again.

"Bitch I need to smoke," I laid my head back once we left Party City.

"He got you stressed again? What he say?"

"Same ol shit about you, but it's more than that. I just want his punk ass to do right. Why the fuck is that impossible for him? He's using you as a distraction because I caught him Face Timing a bitch in the shower this morning. He didn't expect me to walk in that bathroom, but I didn't work the double I said I was going to work. He dropped the phone because I scared him and when I looked down, she was naked and playing with her pussy. Of course, she didn't know what was going on so she's still moaning and calling his name. He almost had a damn heart attack, but I didn't even have the energy to address that shit. That's how over it I am. I walked out and took my ass to sleep."

"You allow him to slide a couple times and now he's ice-skating sis. He do some bull, you go ape shit crazy, and as soon as he thinks you've calmed down, he opens those legs, bury his face, and all is forgiven."

"The muthafucka's head game is stupid though," I chuckled to myself.

"But he's also given you syphilis, gonorrhea, chlamydia and trichomoniasis. Stop fuckin his dirty dick havin ass Z," I knew she was right. I knew that I should have been kicked his ass to the curb but truthfully, I was scared too. Aside from loving his stupid ass, he's always been there for me when I needed him the most. That shit is hard to just fuckin' pick up and walk away from. The unknown was more petrifying than whatever STD he could give me. As a Nurse I know that's some stupid shit to say but it's my truth.

Instead of taking me to get my weed we did three more hours of shopping for Black's birthday and I was completely over this party shit. Normally she throws all his gatherings at a club but this time she decided to do it at the house and volunteered me to help. I wanted no parts, but I knew she needed my help, so I forced myself to hop on board and pitch in. That was a mistake, this girl was driving me crazy.

"Umm I still need to smoke. I haven't forgotten," I looked over at her and she busted out laughing.

"I know you didn't, but I couldn't have you gettin' all lazy on me. You know how you get when you're high. Let's go holla at Rasheeda. She keeps the hella good greens on deck."

"Yeah she does. Plus, she wants to fuck you, so she gives us a little extra."

"You have no chill whatsoever."

I laughed because she really looked disgusted. I didn't care though; it was the truth whether she liked it or not. She threw on Kash Doll and we rapped word for word until we pulled up in front of Rasheeda's spot.

"My favorite sistas," she was sitting on the porch smiling when we got out.

"What's up Sheed?" I spoke first.

"I can't call it sweetheart. Hey Jaxsyn," she licked her lips and smirked.

"Hey. We need to cop a quarter from you real quick." Jax ignored the flirty shit and passed her the money.

"I'll be right back baby," she got up and we looked at each other.

18

"Don't even say nothin'." Jax shook her head and I died laughing. Her ass knew I was right, and I was tickled pink. Rasheeda has been in love with her for years and she don't try to front about that shit.

"Here y'all go. It's a lil something extra in there for you baby," she passed the bag to Jaxsyn and looked her up and down.

"Thanks, Sheed," I smiled and we both walked away.

"That nigga still treatin' you good Jaxsyn?"

"Of course."

"Nigga's always drop the ball baby and I'll be waiting on the court when he does," she smiled, and we got in the car.

"Bitch roll that shit up right the fuck now." Jax shook her head and I fell the fuck out. Her prissy ass hardly ever cusses anymore, and although she buys my weed for me all the time, she hardly ever smokes. In college she switched up on me. She said she wasn't trying to do shit that reminded her of home, and she didn't, but every now and then I get a day or two out her that reminds me of the old times. Today she's actually going to smoke with me, and I was excited, plus the bitch been cussin' since she pulled up. Honestly though, she didn't even sound right. This girl embodies "good girl" these days and long gone is that ruthless bitch that used to hug the block with Black, beat bitches and niggas asses, and protect me against the evil that lurked in the dark.

"Stop at the store so we can get some backwoods."

"I'll stop but you know I don't do backwoods. I'm trying to smoke, not cough up a lung," she talked shit as she pulled around the corner and The Knights were everywhere. Of course, that caused the birds to flock. The Knights were the hottest new thing in Detroit, and they had the hoes going crazy. Just a group of sexy, get money niggas on motorcycles.

"I'm not getting out alone Z. You already know how this shit is about to go," she looked at me.

"Bitch if yo' ass wasn't so big you wouldn't have to worry about these thirsty ass niggas."

"I'm pretty as fuck too tho'," she stuck her tongue out.

"Now who don't have no fuckin chill, Cussin' Cathy?" We started crackin' up again as we got out of her truck.

It didn't matter how much money a nigga had, they couldn't ever stop themselves from being thirsty and these niggas was no exception. They were trying to holla at us the whole time we were walking up to the store, in the store, and when we left out of the store. As fine as they all were and the fact that they were surrounded by bitches showed just how thirsty they were. How you got twenty half naked bitches in your face ready and willing to bust it wide open but you still yelling at us?

"Hey pretty lady." One of the younger guys grabbed Jaxsyn's arm. "My boss wants to holla at you real quick if you have a minute to spare."

"Tell your boss I'm married so I don't even have a second to spare," she looked down at ol boy's hand and he let her go.

We kept walking and I've never been happier to make it to her truck.

"How is it so many of them? Where the fuck did they even come from?" I stared at the parked bikes and it had to be a hundred of them.

"Giiirl I have no idea. That's crazy though," she started the car and out of nowhere they all got on their bikes and surrounded us. "What the fuck?" She looked around as they all formed a circle around us with their engines revving.

"You have your gun in here?" I asked.

"No. I drove Black's car last night and forgot to get it out."

"Dammit Jax!"

"I know." We looked around but they weren't moving off of their bikes. They were just sitting on them blocking us in and then someone tapped on her window. On my life he was the sexiest man that I've ever seen.

"Roll it down and see what the hell he wants Jax," I nudged her, and she rolled it down.

"Why are y'all surrounding my truck like this?" She said with an attitude probably more out of fear than anger.

"Because I always get what I want, and currently, that's you," he smiled, and his teeth were snow white.

"I'm married."

"I didn't ask you about your relationship status."

"Well I'm just letting you know," she smirked.

20

"I think my brother is trying to get your attention," he pointed, and it was another one on my side of the car.

"Y'all twins?" I let the window down as I looked back and forth between them and then Jax did the same thing.

"Identical." They said at the same time and it made both me and my sister smile. "Nah we fuckin' with y'all. I'm older by a year." The one on my side said with a chuckle.

"Obviously y'all play too much but seriously, y'all are identical. That's crazy."

"We get that a lot."

"I bet, so what can we do for you?" I asked.

"Step out and let me see what you can do for me." The one on my side said and I opened the door. Shit. I wasn't married and these muthafucka's was sexy as shit. Let the games begin.

Jaxsyn

"Step out."

"I can't get out. I told you that I'm married," I was dead serious when I said it the first time to his lil flunky but obviously they were ignoring both me and the ring on my finger.

"And I told you that you're giving me information that I didn't ask for," he opened my door and reached for my hand. I stared at it for a minute since he acted as if he didn't give a damn about anything I had to say. Everything inside of me told me not to give him my hand but I did it anyway and stepped out. For some reason his presence demanded obedience.

"You're gorgeous," he went from looking at me from head to toe to staring directly into my eyes.

"Thanks," I blushed. I hadn't blushed in years and I tried hard not to right now, but it was the way he damn near stared into my soul that caught my attention. I felt vulnerable, special, and beautiful under his gaze.

"So, you live around here?"

"No. I live in Bloomfield Hills."

"Oh okay," he held his hand up and all the motorcycles started to move away from my truck. "Let me take you out," he smiled and what a beautiful smile it was.

"I really don't want to keep repeating myself but-"

"Then don't. I haven't asked you anything that would cause you to give me the same answer twice. Now back to me taking you out. Just say yes. By the way, I'm Messiah," he extended his hand and I smiled.

"Jaxsyn," I gave him my hand and he kissed it.

"Nice to meet you beautiful. So, you'll go out with me?"

"Messiah, I-"

"I should warn you Jaxsyn, I never take no as an answer. Especially when it's something I really want, and right now that happens to be you," he rubbed the side of my face gently and I could feel myself getting moist between my thighs. My husband has been the only man to ever turn me on sexually, and here I was; standing outside, in broad daylight, with this complete stranger, leaking like a faucet. The way he was looking at me was unlike anything I've ever experienced. "We'll see each other soon, that's my word baby," he smiled, kissed my cheek, and then opened my door to help me get back into my truck. I didn't even know what to say to that. I simply waved as he swaggered away.

My mind couldn't comprehend his arrogance or the effect it had on me. I gutted the cigarillo and started rolling up immediately. I was trippin' and this feeling was way out of character. I sparked the blunt while I waited for Z. She was still out there smiling like a damn fool. I looked through my rearview mirror and Messiah was on the phone and chicks was surrounding him just that quick. He wasn't paying them any attention, but they were around, and for some reason, I was jealous. It had to be the weed because I was definitely trippin'.

"Okay. Bye." His brother helped my sister climb back into my truck and then closed the door. She couldn't even wipe the cheesy smile from her face if she tried. "Bitch I like him already. If there was ever a nigga that could make me forget about Quan, it's him. Nashon fuckin' Knight."

"If you don't shut your goofy ass up. These niggas just trapped us into talking to them and we thought we were about to be robbed, raped, or murdered."

"Did we die though?" She busted out laughing. "Don't lie sis, that shit was sexy."

"Here. Just hit the L," I passed it to her and tried to ignore the lingering smell of Messiah's cologne.

"Don't try to shut me up. When was the last time you laid eyes on a nigga that sexy?"

"Every damn night," I wiggled my ring finger.

"The lies you tell. My bro is cute an all but babyyyy those two niggas right there," she pointed to them. "Tuh… that shit is a whole new level. They have to be at least six foot four, serving just the right amount of muscles underneath their beautiful golden-brown skin. Whew, don't even get me started on those hazel brown eyes. Giiirl, what!" She did a little dance in her seat.

"Well, I'm not into braids," I shrugged. Messiah's braids hung to the middle of his back and Nashon had dreads at that same length.

"You reachin' and I see your arms gettin' tired so I'm going to let you make it," she chuckled to herself. "I'm not into braids or dreads either but I've never seen cleaner dreads or crispier braids and neither have you. Anyway, I'm going out with Nashon tomorrow night," she clapped, and I couldn't believe her. I turned Kash Doll back on and sped all the way to her house. She could do whatever the hell she wanted, but I love my husband and I'm definitely not about to jeopardize what we've built and the years that we've put in, for a fling. I don't care how sexy he is or how good he smelled.

****

"Oh my God baby. Yesssss," I moaned as my husband ate the box like it was his last meal on earth. I gripped the sheets as he dipped his fingers inside of me and brought me to another orgasm. My back arched automatically, as my legs trembled from sheer bliss.

"I love you boo," he placed kisses on my stomach and worked his way up. I became wetter as his lips brushed up against my skin gently. He entered me and sent chills all over my body.

"Mmmm. I love you too baby," I wrapped my arms around his neck and inhaled his familiar scent. He brought pleasure to every inch of me and my body quivered from satisfaction. He stroked me slow and with purpose. I rolled my hips as he kissed on my neck causing my nipples to harden even more. Once he started groaning into my ear, I knew he was about to cum. He deep stroked me for a few more minutes and then swiftly pulled out and came on my stomach instead of inside of me. My heart broke into pieces yet again, but as usual, I didn't say anything. I simply looked away to avoid him seeing the tears that threatened to spill from my eyes.

He got up and walked to the bathroom and I turned around to watch. Every curve, scar, and muscle on his body has been kissed by me or touched by me. I was blessed to have a man like Black. His love for me could be felt by anyone in our presence and that gave me a proud feeling. Over ten years together and three years of marriage hasn't changed our undying love one bit. I didn't want me wanting a baby so bad to change how I viewed him. Sadly, it was though. I had a void in me that he was causing, and he didn't even care. Couldn't have cared less actually. I was hurting from deep within' and he chose to look the other way causing me to look at him differently.

Maybe my sister has been right all these years and I have him spoiled with giving in too much and just allowing him to do whatever he wants. Now, what I want doesn't matter. Now my needs came second to his wants and I had to just roll with the punches. I had no idea what was happening between us, but it hurt. I never wanted anything to be able to crack the foundation that we built so long ago but this whole baby situation was definitely doing that. Every time he pulled out of me and released his seeds somewhere on my body was another blow to my heart and another reminder that he didn't want me to bring his child into this world. Another reminder that he doesn't want to start a family with me.

"What's your plans for today?" he asked from the bathroom, giving me a break from my thoughts.

"I have a staff meeting at eleven o'clock and then I have a showing at two," I swallowed my feelings to avoid from having the same baby conversation that would only lead to an argument. Instead, I got up and walked into the bathroom. I stood behind Black and admired his physique in the mirror before wrapping my arms around his waist and placing kisses on his back. "I love every part of you baby."

"That's sweet Jaxsyn. I need your car when you finish doing what you have to do."

"What's wrong with your car?" I put my hands on my hips and looked at him through the mirror.

"Truth?"

"Please and thank you," I already had an attitude and I didn't even know what he was about to say.

"I have Ray coming to pick me up in a minute for work because Quan needed to go see his PO and I let him borrow my car last night to get there."

"Are you kidding me right now Derrick Avery? Quan is going to Ohio in the BMW that I *just* bought you four months ago? Please tell me you didn't really make a judgement call like that without talking to me first."

"Baby I'm a grown ass man if you haven't noticed. I don't need to sit down with my mommy wife before making decisions. He needed help and I helped. Chill out, he's my best friend Jaxsyn."

"Ta' hell with what his bum ass needed help with Derrick and don't tell me to chill out either because I'm not trying to be your 'mommy wife' as you so kindly put it. Right is right and wrong is wrong. I seriously can't believe you right now and you knew you were on some bullshit because you didn't even say anything about it last night. I don't care that he's your friend, you should have told me. He's wrecked four of his own damn cars and been in how many accidents Black?" I turned on the shower so I could get ready for work. I was over the conversation all together. I honestly couldn't believe him. We've sat around and joked about how careless Quan is with cars and he handed his keys to him. The keys to the brand-new car that *I* just got him. Unbelievable. Literally, un-fuckin'-believable.

"I'm sorry baby," he tried to hug me but I pushed him away. He knows that when I get mad, I get quiet before I say something that I'll regret. I tried so hard to be different these days and avoid popping all the way off on people. My temper is ferocious and sometimes I have to concentrate on staying calm to avoid my darker side. I took a few deep breaths and continued to ignore him. I needed space so I hopped in the shower and allowed the water to beat down on my neck and back. I needed this moment of silence and *peace*. My shoulders were tense, and I needed a massage to relax me properly, but the water was definitely soothing my nerves.

"Baby talk to me."

Black followed me around the house as I got dressed for work. That's how I knew that he was very aware of how stupid his decision was. His tone switched up real quick. He was just a grown ass man and now he's talking about some "baby talk to me". I wanted to yell out *fuck you* so bad, but like I said, I'm trying to be a different Jaxsyn. When you know better, you do better, and I was trying my damndest to be better.

"I have nothing to say, excuse me." I stepped around him and grabbed my briefcase. "I'll drop the car off around three when I finish with what I have to do," I walked out and left him standing in his own stupidity.

I wouldn't trust Quan to wash my car and my husband thought it would be a great idea to let him borrow his brand-new BMW like I don't work hard for everything that we have. Like I'm not still paying that car off. Like I'm not going to be the one paying the deductible if he tears it up. Yeah, I needed to calm the hell down because I was seeing red.

"Please tell me you have a minute to talk," I called my sister.

"I have about six minutes for you before my shift starts. Go."

"Black let Quan drive his BMW to Ohio."

"Get the fuck out of here! Quan has the worst luck with cars and why would he let him drive the brand new one? He would have done better just renting him a car."

"Exactly. I'm so pissed right now I don't even know what to do with myself."

26

"I hope you went off on his ass Jaxsyn. You're still paying that bitch off and he allowed someone irresponsible to drive it to another fuckin state. That's too much to just-… Wait a damn minute… When the hell did Quan go to Ohio?"

"He said he gave it to him last night. I guess he'll be back today."

"Bitch Quan didn't go to no fuckin' Ohio yesterday, last night, or today. I called off last night because I was with Nashon again and when I got home that BMW was not at my house and his momma picked him up from work."

"And he was home this morning when you woke up? He didn't have any court dates in Toledo? He didn't say he-"

"Ahhhhhh!" she screamed in my ear. "You are so irritating right now. Where's my damn sister at Jaxsyn?"

"She grew up Z. I don't have to cuss Black out like you want me to do or play these kiddie ass games. Did Quan have a fuckin' court date, yes or fuckin' no?" My heart was racing. If Quan didn't have his car, then who has it, and why did my husband just tell me that bold face lie…

"You can be grown as fuck Jaxsyn and still go upside your lying ass husbands head. It's no age limit or maturity level restricting it. No, Quan didn't have any court appearances to make, yes he was home all last night and this morning before I left for work, yes your husband is a fuckin' liar, and yes I'll be on standby if you wanna fuck his stupid ass up. Your six minutes is up. Bye," she hung up and I seriously couldn't think straight. He didn't just lie to me, he allowed me to get pissed off, argued with me, and really sold this shit. I couldn't believe him. I honestly wanted to hit a U-turn and go spazz on him but these days I'm serious about protecting my energy. Everything that happens in the dark comes to the light and if he's cheating on me after everything that we've been through, I'm done. It's no coming back from him fuckin' another chick and having that hoe in the car I bought. I'll never look at his ass the same so that'll definitely be grounds for a divorce, and he needs me a whole lot more than I need his ass, that's on God.

Derrick "Black" Avery

I watched Jaxsyn as she got into her Range Rover and drove away pissed. I looked out of the window and waited a minute for her to drive down the block before I grabbed my wallet and keys and left out too. I headed in the opposite direction and walked around the corner. I couldn't risk the chance of running into her. I made it around the corner in less than five minutes and hopped in the driver seat of my car.

"I didn't keep you waiting too long, did I?"

"Nah I just got here daddy." Shardae smiled and I kissed her.

"Bet. How was the doctor's appointment? How's my babies?"

"We're fine, but it would have been better if you were there with me."

"I know and that's on me, my bad." I kissed her again and then rubbed her pregnant belly.

"Whatever. I have another appointment on the third and I want you there Black. No fuckin' excuses. Period."

"You look so pretty making demands and shit."

She smirked. "You annoyin'. Hurry up and get me home so I can fuck you right. I know Prude Patty didn't give you no pussy, but I got you," she reached over and started rubbing my dick.

"That's why I love yo' ass."

"I know. I love you too baby," she kissed on my neck and I pulled off. "Damn daddy, I want you right now."

"We'll be there soon," I laughed. Her ass is a freak unlike my wife. I mean Jaxsyn can get that shit poppin' for sure or I wouldn't have married that pussy, but Shardae is a different breed of nasty. She with the shits and is willing to do stuff that would make my wife's goody-goody ass cringe.

"Pull over."

"Baby," she was trippin' right now. I had just hit the freeway.

"Now Black. This pussy is throbbin' for you baby and I'm not waiting any longer. You know when I get like this I can't be put on hold. These hormones are ragin'," she opened her legs, putting one on the dashboard and the other damn near across me and started rubbing on her clit. Her moans filled the car and her juices were flowing. I was trying to focus on the road and see the show she was putting on. I pulled onto the shoulder and hit my hazard lights. Fuck it, she was fingering herself faster than the speed of light and I couldn't resist any longer.

"Get the fuck over here before I get a ticket," I unzipped my pants, and she got excited.

"Hell yeah baby," she climbed her pregnant ass over the seat and slid down my pipe. "Shit!" She yelled out as soon as it was inside her. I laid back and watched her in action. She bounced up and down and filled the car with her screams and sounds of wetness.

"Ride your dick baby," I put my hands on her hips and started going in. "Just like that baby, damn," she had my toes curling inside of my shoes within minutes and I started fuckin' her from the bottom. She was losing her mind and I was damn sure losing mine. Shardae got the A1 pussy and that's why her ass is pregnant now. She had a nigga bustin' in her raw damn near every time. I knew I was fuckin' up and I knew I was fuckin' up bad but pulling out was so fuckin' hard. She got pregnant the first time and got rid of it with no problem, so I really got comfortable after that. Wasn't shit better than knowing I could bust in her and she would take care of the problem. My wife wanted kids, so I had to pull out of her but Shar willingly went to the clinic. Unfortunately, I misread the situation because that second time she got pregnant, she let me know that same day that she was keeping it. I tried everything under the sun to get this bitch to the clinic, but she wasn't having none of that. She literally stood toe to toe with me ready to fight for this pregnancy. Now she's having my baby and I just have to keep her happy and quiet.

"I'm cummin'! Oh God baby I'm cummiiiin!" She sang out and held on to the back of my seat while she released her essence with me and I smiled. I loved watching her cum. It stroked a nigga ego for real.

"Get yo ass back over there so I can get you home and fuck you right."

"Mmmm sounds good to me baby daddy," she licked her lips and climbed back over to the passenger side.

"I need my car back by six today," I said as I was pulling off.

"I know. I just have to make a few runs for my momma."

"Bet. After I give you this dick, I need you to drop me off at work."

"Okay," she sat back and started showing me the ultrasound of our baby from today's appointment.

****

Four years ago, Jaxsyn bought my auto body shop when I got out of jail. I fucked up in college and when I got back home, I didn't have shit and slanging on the corner wasn't my thing anymore. Plus, it didn't feel right not having Jax out there with me. My baby is a muthafuckin' beast and with her by my side out there we were making a killing. My wife is bad as fuck so that might have had something to do with it, but she also knew her shit and watched my back. I was out there doing the best that I could alone and got caught up so when I got out after doing that year, she sat me down and told me that she didn't want me in the streets anymore and if I went back, she was done. She didn't just come at me like that without a solution, she slid the papers for my new shop across the table to me. I swear I couldn't believe she actually made that shit happen for me. I had been talking about it forever and she followed through with my dream.

Unfortunately, I didn't know the first thing about running a business. I was hiring niggas I was friends with just trying to look out and it backfired. I didn't know how to manage my books or people, inventory was a huge issue from the very beginning, and a list of other shit. I struggled with my business for a minute and even though I told her that I would pay her back for it, that hadn't panned out the way I thought it would but thank God things have been looking up for the last six months or so. I was pulling myself out of the hole and starting to see a profit. Well I was breaking even but shit, that was better than being in the negative. I was able to hire a highly skilled manager for little to nothing. He was going through some personal shit and asked can he come work for me because he didn't have a place to stay and he was trying to get his bread up. I told him he could stay in the room on top of the shop if he pitched in and helped me out. He did me one better and taught me everything that I needed to know. I had no fuckin' clue that it took so much to run a business, but he was getting me together and it was showing.

I looked at the clock and I started getting my shit together. I was tired as hell and ready to go home. I had been in the shop since six this morning and a nigga was beat.

"Hey baby," I called Jax.

"Hey. Dinner is almost ready."

"Okay, but I have about two more people before I can leave."

"That's fine. I'll keep it hot for you."

"The food or my pussy?" I smiled.

"I guess both," she was dry, and she had been for a couple days. I hope she wasn't still mad about that Quan shit. That was the best shit that I could come up with on the fly because my stupid ass hadn't even thought of an excuse as to why I would need her car. Most of the time she doesn't question me, so I honestly was thinking she was just going to say "okay".

"You good baby?"

"Yup. Tired."

"Oh okay, well hubby will be home soon to rub your back and that pussy in a few."

"Sounds good. If you take too long though, I'm starting without you."

I smiled. "Better not. Love you baby."

"Love you too." We hung up.

I love my wife more than my next breath. She had my back even when my own family didn't. For a man to know that his woman is as loyal as my wife is and not have to question that shit is everything that we search for. Bitches now days don't have Jaxsyn's kind of loyalty or dedication. They lookin' for come ups and handouts but what I had with her was solid and real and built on genuine love.

"Alright. I'm out y'all."

"Later boss." The guys yelled from the back. They were probably smoking or drinking before they went home to their women. I didn't say shit to them as long as they didn't try that shit when we were open, but after hours they could do whatever they wanted, and Ray was good with making sure everything was locked up after they left.

I stopped at the gas station to fill up my car and grab a couple Slim Jims, a two-liter Vernors, a bag of Dorito's, and a bag of Swedish fish.

"What's up stranger?"

"Wooow, I'll be damned," I turned around smiling so hard it felt like my damn face might crack. "It's been too long Ty."

"Yeah, I know, way too long. How you been?" He barely smiled which was understandable.

"Shit, I can't complain. You?"

"It's all good this way," he nodded. "And how's Jaxsyn?" He looked away for a minute and then back at me.

"Great."

"Right... Well, it was good seeing you Derrick," he waved, and I could tell that he was still bitter about our break up. He had every reason to be mad at me and I would never hold a grudge against him for his anger toward me. I fucked him every day for well over a year straight, maybe two, back when we were in college. We started planning a life together but the whole time I knew that I was lying. I was young, reckless, and having fun but it's no way I could go back to the hood with a fuckin boyfriend, plus I was still in a relationship with Jax. We were at different schools, but she was still my girl and we talked every day. We hadn't skipped a beat other than the fact that we couldn't see each other that often because of the distance.

To this day I haven't forgotten the look on Tyler's face when I finally told him that Jax was actually my girlfriend and not my cousin like I had lead him to believe. Under the same breath, I told him that she was pregnant with my baby and I was going to marry her. He was crushed and that shit hurt me more than he'll ever actually know. His pain quickly turned into anger and he destroyed all my shit in my dorm room then tried to kill me with a pocket knife. I calmed him down and made love to him repeatedly, but the damage was already done. I had broken his heart and I hated to do it, but I knew I could never give him what he wanted or the life he deserved. Either way I was going to have to let him go no matter how much it hurt the both of us, and she was the perfect out.

I finished pumping my gas and watched him get back in the car with a guy. I can't lie, he was looking good as fuck and I felt a little jealous that another man had filled my spot. A spot that was solely mine for so long. A spot that I still thought about from time to time. I had no right to feel the way that I felt so I shook that shit off quick. I caused the friction between us so if that other nigga was making him happy, I had to live with that like he lived with me leaving him for Jaxsyn. I glanced at them one last time before I hopped in the car and sped down Gratiot Ave. I needed to drop this shit off and go home to my wife. I didn't have a lot of time because I should have left work when we first closed.

"I'm outside. Open the door," I grabbed the bag from the gas station and got out.

"Hey baby daddy." Shardae greeted me with open arms and I kissed her.

"You good? How's my baby?" I rubbed her belly.

"Alright but we missed you today Black. Like missed you, missed you," she pouted and then got mad as hell all within seconds. "This is why the fuck I get to flippin' out on you all the damn time," she closed the door and started on her bullshit. "You show up three hours late and now I only have a few minutes with you before you go running off to her when I've really been fuckin' missing you all day."

"Shardae I was at work baby and how the fuck was you missing me all day? Didn't I come dick you down on my lunch break and bring you something to eat? Then when you came to drop my car back off, we chilled in my office for about an hour. You forgot all that?" I looked at her ass like she was crazy.

"I mean, I didn't forget, but you also said when you get off work you were going to chill with me."

"And that's what I'm trying to do right now but you rather fuckin argue," I wrapped my arms around her waist. "I'm about to fix you something to eat, massage your feet, and then suck on my pussy until it's time for me to leave. Don't fuck it up with arguing baby. I have enough of that shit going on in my life and I don't need this drama. Be a nigga peace Shar."

"When are you leaving this bitch Black? It's been over a year and I hate to see you miserable. I wouldn't be bitchin' if you didn't have to leave us all the time and go home to a bitch that can't even make you happy. Baby I want you heeere," she whined, and I stuck my hands in her panties to shut her the fuck up. Every day I regret slipping up with her. This is the shit I have to deal with now. I allowed her pussy to put me in a fucked-up predicament and now she's five months pregnant, moody as fuck, and demanding. We were just good earlier and now she was on my ass about Jaxsyn again. I was honest when I met her, and she was cool with being a side chick as long as I threw her the typical $40 for her hair and nails or whatever she was begging for.

All that changed as soon as she told me she wasn't getting another abortion and we were about to be parents. She switched up on me quick. Now she's asking to whip my ride every day, expecting me to spend every second of the day with her, talking shit about my wife, demanding money, and all kinds of other shit that I wasn't feeling. Everyday it's something else, something different, and a new attitude. I can never allow this shit to get out, so I have to play by her rules as much as possible. There was no way in hell I was going to let Jaxsyn leave me over a fuckin mistake with a random. That's why even on days like today, when I didn't want to be bothered with Shar, I had too. I couldn't just be bothered either, I had to keep her happy and quiet, so I had to play her game.

"Oh, shit daddy." Shardae screamed and I rubbed her clit faster.

"Feel good?"

"Yes. Right there baby. Mmmm, right fuckin' there!"

"You want to keep arguing or you want me to keep doing what I'm doing?"

"I'm sorry. Finish Black. Please, finish baby!" She laid her head back against the wall and started playing with her titties as I finger fucked her. My baby was going to fuck around and come early with the amount of freak shit that we had been doing lately. She doesn't like that soft mushy shit so with the exception of me fingering her now, I'm normally around here breaking her back. She called my phone at three o'clock in the morning last week because she was horny and wouldn't stop calling or begging until I snuck out. I got here and she had her best friend Nedra already in the middle of the bed ready for whatever. I end up calling into work that next day because we fucked until nine o'clock that morning. I didn't even say shit to Jax when I came in later that day so hopefully, she just assumed I left out early for work.

"I'm cummin'. Fuuuuck!" I had three fingers inside of her, my pinky in her ass hole, while I thumbed her clit until she busted all over my hand and started bucking from pleasure.

"Nasty ass. Gimme all that shit," I kept going and she started screaming and moaning. "Bitch whose pussy is this?"

"Shit, shit, shit! It's yours baby daddy! It's yoursssss!" Her body jerked but I wasn't ready to stop yet. I knew she had another one in her that was begging to come out. I started ramming my fingers inside of her hard as hell and she was damn near limp in my arms. "Goddddd," I watched her panties become soaked as she came hard as hell and collapsed against the wall. I squeezed her nipples and then stuck my middle fingers into her mouth. She was struggling to catch her breath, but she sucked them one by one. "You don't play fair. How you make a bitch cum like that with just your hands? That lame you have at home don't know what the fuck she got," she took a deep breath while pushing herself off the wall. "Where's my snacks baby?" She smiled.

"On the table," I kissed her because she adjusted her attitude just that fast.

"You don't have to cook dinner BD, but I definitely need the head you promised," she looked back at me and I smiled.

"You know it's anything for you baby."

"I love you so much Derrick Avery," she climbed into my arms after she grabbed her snacks and started kissing on me.

"I love yo crazy ass too," I said honestly as I rubbed her stomach. She works on my fuckin' nerves and I'm never leaving my wife for her but somewhere along the line I grew real feelings for her. I hated the fact that she was having my first child but it ain't shit that's going to change it now. It is what it is. I chilled for a couple hours, kept my promise and put her ass to bed off some bomb ass head and this dick to her guts. Then I took my tired ass home to Jax so I could do the same shit and go to bed.

Zionna

Once again, Black found a way to be a complete fuck up. This was his new normal these days and I wasn't surprised in the least bit. Jax spent weeks planning his birthday party and this fuck nigga played her. She wants to keep acting like the nigga is so perfect, but everybody can see through his bullshit, except for her. Either she's blindly in love or she's choosing to ignore all the signs that's right in her face. The disrespect was getting way out of hand. She's calling me crying every fuckin' day because he did something, and I know Jax is a private person so she's not even telling me half the shit that he's doing, and it had me wanting to beat his ass for her.

We waited three whole hours for this nigga to get to his own party that he knew about. When he finally showed up, he was pissy drunk and belligerent. I could completely understand if this was a surprise party and he came home late because he didn't know, but he's known for weeks. The whole night he kept shooting her text message after text message about being on his way and to keep everyone "partying" until he arrived. Three hours of fuckin' texting. How the hell is everyone "partying" at your shit, but you…

Then he tells her that he was late and fucked up because the guys at work kept buying him drinks like his grown ass couldn't say no. Like he couldn't have just moved that party to his house where he knew we were "partying". Her feelings were so hurt that I caught her crying in the kitchen. She spent so much time, energy, and money making his shit perfect only for this hoe ass nigga to miss out on all of it. Down to the smallest details she gave it her all and I didn't even hear him apologize, but in reality, what the fuck would an apology do? Nothing. The damage was done and unfortunately, I don't think I made matters any better because when she wanted to talk about it the next day, I stopped her. She's always telling me about Quan, but she never wants to hear shit about Black, but I wasn't letting her off that easily this time.

I kept that shit real with her and maybe my timing could have been better, but it is what it is. All the signs were there and if I don't know shit else in this life, I know a fuckin' cheater. I know cheaters like the back of my hand and his ass was definitely moving how cheaters move. I didn't know who to blame though, and I was honest when I told her that. He's been calling her a prude for years and she laughs it off like he's joking and now he's cheating. Who's to blame in that scenario; the person that told you the problem or the person that chose to ignore the problem. I told her that he didn't marry the barely cussing, barely smoking, barely living, upright citizen that she is now. Yes, people evolve but my sister takes this goody two shoes shit a bit far. I've even told her about herself. Back in the day those two hugged the block together. Shot moves together. Beat asses together. She's the reason any of us ever had shit and now she's home by six pm gettin' her Susie The Homemaker on. Maybe that's not what he wants and found someone more his speed. Hell, she should have found someone her speed too, honestly. My sister deserve someone that's going to treat her like a queen and protect her heart. Black is simply incapable. They're holding on for the same reason Quan and I hold on, history.

She's been depressed ever since we had the conversation and I didn't want that for her but the truth stings like a muthafucka sometime.

"Meet me at the Red Wind," I called her, and she sounded like she was sleeping.

"I don't really feel like it today Zionna. Maybe next week," she hung up and I called right back. "Hello."

"Fuck that. Not next week, today! I want you to get dressed in your cutest lil outfit, do your hair and makeup, and meet your sister for a drink. How many times has Quan fucked up and you didn't let me wallow?" She was quiet but I knew she was still there, so I held the phone right with her ornery ass.

"Fine. What time?" She said with an attitude.

"Eight."

"Bye," she hung up and I smiled. "She's coming," I looked over at Nashon and he texted his brother.

"Y'all too pretty to deal with nigga's that don't appreciate you."

"We met them when we were young. The difference between me and Jax is that I know my nigga ain't shit and I want to leave. She's so head-over-heels in love that she's blind to her husband's bullshit and when he does hoe ass shit it breaks her all the way down. Love got her being Ray Charles to his behaviors and it sickens me."

"That's fucked up. Bro gone fix that though, no worries," he spoke confidently as usual. I looked at his sexy physique as he put his dreads in a ponytail. His athletic build had me in a trance. I could stare at him forever.

37

"I have to go baby, but I can't wait to see you later," he kissed me, and I smiled as I climbed out of his bed.

"Me either," he took me into his arms as I walked him to the door. I turned around and faced him stealing another kiss that we allowed to linger causing him to smile.

"Sexy ass," he pecked my forehead and stepped around me. "Lock the door when you leave baby," he walked out.

Quan had lost and he didn't even know it yet. I was getting the best dick of my life; from the most handsome and genuinely thorough man I've ever had the pleasure of meeting. Nash was showing me how real men move and I was slowly becoming addicted.

****

When Jaxsyn and I step into a room we turned heads and we were very aware of it. That shit came from years of us practicing to shit on bitches when we were teenagers and eventually, we mastered it. That was one of the very few highlights of our younger years and now we're professional room killers.

"I feel better already," she smiled.

"I know. I can tell."

"It's nothing better than dressing up and being gawked at."

We both giggled because it was the truth.

"Oh look," I smiled from ear to ear.

"You didn't," she whispered as they walked up.

"Hey gorgeous."

"Hey Messiah," she smiled, and he pecked her on her cheek.

"Did you miss me?" I smiled at Nashon.

"You know I did baby," he kissed my neck and whispered in my ear that he could still taste me. I couldn't do anything but blush which was exactly what Ms. Jaxsyn was doing a lot of already.

"Our reservation is ready." Messiah grabbed her hand and she didn't pull away. At that point, I knew it would be a good night.

Jaxsyn

I sat across the table from Messiah trying my hardest to avoid eye contact. He had been sending flowers and gifts to my job for weeks and now he was sitting in front of me looking edible. He was staring directly at me, making me nervous. Zionna knew damn well she was wrong for this shit. He was making me moist again and that shit was getting out of hand. I was so disappointed in myself and I felt like I was cheating on my husband. Regardless of what's happening between us right now, I wasn't trying to stoop to his level or compete. Acting out on my current emotions would be reckless and wrong on many levels.

"You need to stop actin' like you not feeling a nigga because I know you are," he was smirking at me and it caused me to smile.

"Cocky or nah?"

"Confident baby," he chuckled because I couldn't hide what I was feeling even though I was trying my hardest. The nigga had swag that you couldn't ignore. He was sitting across from me looking real Zaddyish and was well aware.

"Same thing. You must be used to bitches throwing themselves at you."

"Some. Not all. I mean shit, ain't nothing wrong with knowing what you want and going after it. Right?"

"It's called being thirsty."

"Well call me a dehydrated ass nigga because I'm definitely not stoppin' until you're mine." We all laughed but I shook my head at his persistence.

"I'm married."

"Do I look like I even remotely give a fuck? Be honest, because if I do, I'll change my expression or readjust myself."

I smirked and shook my head *again*. It's really all I could do. He was something else.

"You're a mess."

"I'm just honest baby. You should try it."

"I am being honest," I looked at Zionna who was all in her own world with Nashon. "I'm telling you that I have a husband and I'm telling you that I respect my marriage."

He leaned forward, "but are you telling me that your pussy is wet just off the sight of me and you've been thinking about me fuckin you since the last time you saw me? Are you telling me that you don't soak your panties every time you walk into your office and it's something from me waiting on you?" The smirk he wore was so smug. "Now that's the honesty I'm looking for because that's the kind of truth I fucks with," he stared at me intently with those beautiful brown eyes that was housed under the prettiest lashes I've ever seen. I had nothing to rebuttal with, so I sipped my drink and avoided eye contact, until my phone rang.

"I have to take this," I looked up at him.

"Do you baby," he got up and pulled my chair out. I smiled at his manners and answered my husband's call as I walked away.

"Hello."

"Hey baby. What are you up to?"

"I texted you earlier to tell you that I was having drinks with Zionna," I said dryly. I was still heavily in my feeling about his birthday party and his recent behavior. My feelings were hurt about the party and he tried to down play his actions by saying "but everyone had fun", as if I spent all my time and thousands of dollars planning a party for our friends and family to enjoy *his* birthday. I was pissed and giving him the cold shoulder, but his actions and absence lately showed me that he couldn't have cared less, making his fuck up even worse, and driving the dagger further into my heart.

"Oh. It didn't come through. Well go ahead and tell her I said hey."

"Okay. Where are you?"

"Um, on my way home," I rolled my eyes.

"Alright. See you later then."

"Yup," he hung up and I knew he was lying. His background was way too quiet for him to be in the car and it had a slight echo. It sounds like he was in a bathroom but what I wasn't about to allow, is for him to turn me into Inspector Gadget. I hated watching my sister dig through Quan's pockets and check his phone and social media all the time. I feel like once you get to that point, it's over. If Black is messing around behind my back and honestly at this point, it's highly likely, it'll come to light on its own. He's definitely moving different but I'm not

40

going searching for anything. When it surfaces, which it will, I'll handle it then. Until that moment happens, I didn't have shit to say. I didn't have evidence and I wasn't about to sit through a bullshit excuse as to why this nigga was sneaking out of our bed and coming home in the wee hours of the morning. I'm not stupid, nor blind, and he's going to be sorry he played with a bitch like me.

When I got back to the table Messiah was alone sipping on his drink. I didn't see Zionna or Nashon anywhere. I sat down and he kept looking at his menu with one hand and spinning his tipped lowball glass of brown liquor with the other, as if it wasn't an elephant in the room.

"Umm, where did they go?" I pointed to the empty chairs.

"Home probably," he said nonchalantly as if that was the correct response. He brought the glass to his lips again bringing attention to his mouth. I couldn't peel my eyes away if I wanted too.

"Wow. So, she left me here with you?"

"Damn, so that's the tone you're going to use? You act like she left you with a pedophile without your rape whistle."

"That is not at all how I said it."

"Shiid," he set his cup down at an angle again.

"Well I apologize. It's not how I meant it Messiah."

He flashed a lopsided smile and it made me blush. I hated the effect he had on me.

"Let's go."

"Where?"

"Does it matter? You're with me so you're *safe*. No rape whistle needed baby."

I looked at his smart mouth having ass for a minute and I threw all my inhibitions out of the window. It felt good to get out of the house and be amongst the living since I had been locked away and moping daily. I wasn't ready to go home to a house that I already knew would be empty since my husband is hardly ever there these days.

"Okay," I smiled, and he took my hand into his as we left the restaurant.

"Thanks," he tipped the valet driver and we got into his Infiniti truck. He said he would bring me back later for my car.

"Why me?" I looked over at him as he drove.

"Why you what?"

"Everything. Why am I the one that you want or whatever you've been saying since we met?"

"The timing is right, but you also peeked my interest and that's rare. When I saw you coming out of the store that day it was something about you that immediately grabbed my attention."

"Physical shit," I chuckled.

"I'm a man and an ass that fat damn sure didn't go unnoticed, but it was the way that you carried yourself. You demanded my attention without even trying too. I dig that shit. That's that shit a nigga can commit too. When a woman can hold your attention from across the room without saying a word, you have to lock her down."

I smiled. I did a lot of that in his presence.

"And that sexy muthafucka right there."

"What?"

"That smile is a beast baby," he stroked the side of my face like he did the first day we met. "You make me want to do everything in my power to keep that smile plastered across your face."

"I don't know what to say," I know my cheeks had to be rosy. "Now I can't stop," I laughed and tried to cover my face but he wouldn't let me.

"Yeeeeeah," he laughed too. "I did that," he bit his lip and nodded proudly because he had me smiling from ear to ear and it was beyond cute. Shit, he was beyond cute.

We rode around for hours talking and getting to know each other. Even though I knew he was in the streets heavy I could still see that he was a really good guy. More so than that, he wasn't just into street shit, but he was a well-established business man. I listened to him talk about his companies and the stock market in awe of who he was turning out to be. I was absorbing knowledge that I wasn't even seeking. Unfortunately, the more we rode around, and he made me laugh, the more I couldn't get my husband out of my head. It was getting late and he hadn't even called my phone, which meant he wasn't home, as I assumed. Black was leaving the door open for another man to gain my attention and I didn't like that. Never in a million years did I want to be where I am right now, but this felt good and I needed that right now.

Messiah Knight

I took Jaxsyn to a park that I come to when I need to think or simply have a quiet moment to myself. It was also the perfect place to set the mood and relax. I could tell she had a lot on her mental and this park has never let me down. It's located off of a lake, so the moon and stars glistened off of the water. Although quiet and serene, the nature surrounding us spoke volumes. Wind softly blowing, trees rustling, water slightly swishing, and crickets singing. I looked over at her and she exuded a sexiness that you only come across once in a lifetime. It was effortless and most of the time she wasn't even aware of how sexy she was being. She was more than the eye could see and I knew that shit from the start.

"I have to go."

"Do you have to, or do you want to?"

She looked out of at the water briefly and then back at me.

"I have to." There was a sadness in her eyes that I didn't like but the innocence in her voice caused me to smirk. She didn't want to leave me. I pulled her closer to me with no problem. She had stop fighting me hours ago because she knew she wanted me just like I wanted her. She just felt guilty, which was understandable considering her circumstances.

I stroked the side of her face and covered her lips with mine. I slowly parted them and slid my tongue into her mouth. She didn't stop me and instead she sucked on it. I had her whether she wanted me to or not and I was never letting go. I picked her up gently and a moan escaped her lips.

"I want you," I kissed her neck and watched chills cover her body. I pulled down the straps on her dress and exposed her perfectly round breast. I took each one into my mouth and sucked on her nipples that were already rock hard and awaiting my touch.

"I can't do this Messiah," she was battling with her conscience and I carried her to my car. "He doesn't deserve this," I ignored her as I laid her on the hood of my truck. Without any words spoken I put my face between her legs. She arched her back and grabbed my head. She was soaked and trembling with satisfaction already. I flicked my tongue fast over her swollen bud as my thumbs parted her lower lips wider giving me full access. Her pussy was as pretty as they come, and her natural fragrance mixed with the berries that I was catching a whiff of was intoxicating. I wanted nothing more than to please her in this moment. I hadn't eaten pussy in a minute, but it was just like riding a bike. Her juices were slowly trickling out and running down her ass. I slurped and licked every last drop of her. I knew she would taste as good as she looked and that's why I had to dive in head first. "Messiah!" She softly purred my name after making her cum for the second time. She had a death grip on my braids as she rode her wave and I kissed her pussy repeatedly until she recovered.

"You ready?" I helped her down off of my hood and fixed her dress.

"What?" She looked at me seductively and confused.

"You said you need to go."

She stepped closer to me and pulled my face to hers, kissing me deeper than before. "Make love to me Messiah," she wrapped her arm around my neck, and I picked her up. She damn sure didn't have to ask twice, a nigga was already bricked up and just trying to be respectful. I slipped into a condom as she sucked on my neck and I pushed myself inside of her.

"Shiiiit!" She dug her nails all the way into my back and I swear on everything I love; she had the tightest pussy I had ever been in. If she wasn't married, I would have sworn on any amount of bibles that she was a virgin. "Oh my God," she held me tightly and I knew immediately that she wasn't used to handling dick this big, so I had to fuck the shit out of her and show her a new world. We would have plenty of time for love making, right now I needed to introduce her to some real shit. I put my hands on her hips and plunged into her. She gasped and before she caught her breath, I did it again. Her head went back instinctively, and her words got caught in her throat. I dug deeper and she found her voice. She cried out for me even though she was in my arms. She started squirting and I could tell by the expression on her face that she didn't know what the fuck had just happened to her. She gave a nigga a real waterfall, not just that typical shit.

"This pussy so tight baby. Got damn," I was delivering deliberate death strokes to her guts while her pussy choked my mans like never before. "Let me in Jax," I put her legs over my arms and started murdering her organs. "I said let me in this tight mafucka ma."

"Ohhhh Messiah. Ooooooh my God it feels too gooood. Ughhhhh," she tossed her head back and started grinding into me.

"Hell, yeah baby. Fuck me back. Shit!" Her sexy ass did just as I told her too. She leaned forward and started kissing me wildly. I was bouncing her up and down and she was moaning and screaming my name over and over. This shit was blowing my mind. I put her down and then placed her hands on the hood of my truck. I rammed myself into her and she almost collapsed.

"None of that. Let me see that arch, you takin' all this dick tonight baby," I pulled her back far enough so I could dig into her stomach. I wanted her to feel every inch of me. I grabbed her hair and snatched her head back with enough force to make her yelp but enough passion to make that pussy squirt for me again. "You feel that?" I was in that pussy so deep I bottomed out and was hitting a brick wall. I was hittin' her shit so hard I was trying to break past the barriers her body had setup. She was screaming my name at the top of her lungs, cummin' every couple minutes, and shaking like a fuckin fiend. I loved every minute of wearing her ass out and I didn't stop going full throttle on her until I was ready to bust.

"Throw that pussy back at me Jax," I slapped her ass and firmly held her neck in my hand causing her head to come back. That back was arched to perfection and I could tell she loved being handled with a little force. That pussy got wetter every time I snatched her ass up. "Uhhh huh. Just like that baby, shit, just like that," I slapped that ass again and watched it jiggle. Her thick ass was showing out and I was here for it. "Reach back and open this fat mafucka up. I wanna see you take all this dick baby," I held her waist as she reached back. Seeing her manicured fingers spreading her ass cheeks apart and watching my dick disappear inside of her was more than what I was ready for. I came instantly and she was right there with me screaming from the orgasm that was ripping through her soul. Neither of us moved immediately because we were spent. I can't ever remember a woman having me this fuckin' gone but she had me and I would be a damn lie to deny that shit.

"You okay?" I stood face to face with her and she nodded bashfully. She looked so beautiful. I kissed her and she wrapped her arms around my neck.

"That was amazing," she stared at me.

"Stop pushing me away and you can get that all the time," I smiled and kissed her neck a few times. "Let's go," I opened her car door and she got in. Dick will get a chick together real quick and she was the proof. Her ass was relaxed and chilled as fuck. She grabbed my hand and laid her head on my shoulder as I drove her back to her car in comfortable silence.

This was the start of her husband getting removed from the picture. Fuck that nigga. He was on borrowed time and just to make sure, I gave her the dick again outside of the restaurant that her car was parked at. I get whatever the fuck I want, and I wanted her ass bad, but I told her that from jump.

****

I had been real lenient on niggas lately and it was starting to show. I got a call at six am from my nigga Solo telling me that some nigga's wearing Knights jackets was breaking into the warehouse we keep all of our pharmaceuticals in. I called my brother and he had just gotten the same call. I let bro know I had just got home, and I was tired as fuck, so it was going to take me a minute. He said he was with Zionna and couldn't leave out right away either. I knew that nigga had to be in the middle of fuckin' by the tone in his voice. I told him I was about to send some niggas to check it out and based on what the fuck they report back I would hit him up. He damn near sounded relieved and I laughed. I couldn't even get comfortable again before my lil niggas hit my line and told me it was two of my own nigga's that had broken in and they already had they ass and was waiting for us.

"Pussy ass nigga." My brother slapped the fuck out of Martez with a steel chain. He was pissed he had to jump out of that pussy and come handle this business. I wanted to laugh at him, but this overall moment was nothing to laugh at. Niggas that we've been feeding was taking from us. Ain't no humor in that shit at all. "You stealing from family nigga? Huh?" He yelled before he hit him again. We all stood around and watched as Nash went crazy on these niggas. We play all day, we ride out with these niggas, and it's all love, but once you cross the line, you're done. No coming back from that.

"I swear-" Before he could finish his sentence, I went upside that nigga head with the brass knuckles.
"Swear what nigga? Don't ever lie to my fuckin face. You got caught bitch boy. Red handed," I unscrewed the bottle of one hundred percent alcohol and poured it all over his opened wounds. He screamed until he passed out. He took too long to wake back up, so Nash popped his ass. Immediately Rodney started pissing on himself. He knew he was next.

46

"You don't understand. We were just-" I emptied the clip in his ass. Fuck both of them and their excuses. We look out for everybody on our team and their families. It ain't never a reason to steal from us and in cases like this, when a nigga does steal from us, we had to make an example out of them. A thief will never be tolerated in this camp. I don't care if it's pennies. If they don't belong to you then you're touching some shit that you shouldn't be touching, and the punishment is death. Period. "Call the cleaners and get this shit taken care of," I said to no one in particular, but five people moved at once.

"You try to be nice to muthafuckas and they test you so let them be an example of what the fuck happens when you bite the hand that feeds you. They fuckin' knew better. All y'all fuckin' know better," I looked at the dudes that was there and everybody stared me straight in the eyes showing that they did know better. My brother used to tell me that I was too brutal but now he saw firsthand why I had to be, and he's developed the hunger for blood too. We don't do shit to nobody that don't deserve it and when it's go time; we go!

I went to the back to wash the blood off of my hands and make sure I didn't any get on my clothes, then hopped on my bike. I didn't have no plans on dealing with this kind of shit today and I needed to go lay my ass back down.

"Sih." My brother was walking over to me.

"What's up Brodie?"

"So, what happened last night with ol girl? Was she pissed when she came back, and her sister left?"

"She didn't stay mad," I shrugged with a smirk. "I dropped her off about four this morning," I ain't no pillow talking ass nigga, but he knows me.

"All that shit she was talking about loving her husband," he laughed.

"Oh, she loves the nigga, believe that. Her ass ain't as happy as she's pretending to be tho'. I could see the sadness in her eyes last night when we kicked it."

"Zionna said the nigga treat her shitty. She can't stand his ass but apparently Jax loyalty got her staying."

"Fuck that nigga. He left the door open for a nigga like me to walk right in. That was a mistake."

"You really like this one huh?"

"Yeah nigga. I wasn't bullshittin'. I want her and you know how I get. That ass is mine and it's a done deal."

"What about Mariah?"

"That's drama that I'll deal with when it's time."

We both laughed. "Yo ass... I'll holla at you later bro, I'm on my way back to the crib. I had to leave Zionna there for this bullshit."

"Bet." We dapped and I pulled off headed back home. Jaxsyn had a nigga tired after that last round. I practically begged her to come back home with me, but she wouldn't. It was only a matter of time before I got her to my bed and once she was there, she would decide to stay on her own. Guaranteed.

Black

I crept into the house for the fourth day in a row and tiptoed downstairs to the basement bathroom. I turned the shower on low and washed Ty's scent off of me. After seeing him that day at the gas station, the jealousy I felt wouldn't go away. I kept imagining him with that nigga he was with that night and the shit would piss me off, plus I honestly missed him. I tried not to dip back into my past, but I couldn't resist reaching out to him. I searched Facebook and I couldn't find him, but it didn't take long finding him on IG. I slid into his dm's as soon as I found his page. I kept it real with him about how happy I was to run into him after all these years and how I couldn't get him off of my mind. He was equally happy to hear from me and agreed to meet me for dinner.

I completely forgot just how amazing Ty is as a person. He's smart, funny, laid back, and sexy as hell. When he first got to the dinner table things were very awkward for the both of us because we hadn't cleared any of the dirty laundry from our past that was piled sky high and I also hadn't been with a man since him, so I was tense.

"Can I say that I've missed you without starting an argument?" I broke the silence.

"No. That will definitely start an argument," he sipped his wine. I ordered his favorite kind just to smooth things over a bit and show him that I still knew him.

"I apologize Tyler. Maybe I should start there."

"That's where you should have started four and a half years ago. You broke my heart Black."

"I know I did, and I never meant for that to happen."

"I loved you, and I trusted you, and everything you said turned out to be a lie."

"I have to call bullshit. I know I fucked up, and I made quite a few missteps that I can honestly apologize to you for, but I've never lied about my feelings. I loved you then and I still love you," I reached for his hand and he allowed me to hold it. "I grew up in the inner city of Detroit where you could get clowned for everything and anything. I was young, immature, and I couldn't imagine bringing home a boyfriend. I was scared as hell of the backlash and ridicule that I knew was going to come my way if I even tried it."

"That's an excuse Black. You loved her."

"That may sound like an excuse but it's not and you're right. She was my first love and I never broke things off with her when we decided to go to different colleges. When she showed up for spring break and said she was pregnant, I did what I thought was right."

"And then that bitch aborted the baby and you stayed," he rolled his eyes. "You fuckin stayed Black. I would have taken you back. I swear I would have. All I wanted to hear was that you love me, and you made a mistake and I would have fuckin' taken you back. That's all I wanted to hear, and it never happened." His words faded towards the end as tears ran down his face.

"I love you and I never meant to hurt you Ty," I tried my best to comfort him. It was as if the wounds I caused all those years ago were still wide open. I've always known that I broke his heart, but I never imagined that it was this bad. I felt horrible.

He shook his head as he dabbed his face with his napkin and finished his wine. "Let's get out of here," he tossed some money down on the table and grabbed my hand. The tension was too thick for me to take my hand from him, but I damn sure looked around to see if anyone had peeped it and they hadn't.

He lead me out of the door and into an alley around the corner. "Show me how much you missed me Derrick," he kissed me with a purpose that exposed the passion that was still burning between us. He knew what we had was real and he wanted to show me what I missed out on. I knew him well enough to know that this was a power play. He's always hated Jaxsyn and this was him showing her that he could still have me without actually saying it.

"Bend over," I pushed him forward and he placed his hands on the wall assuming the position. The truth was, he *could* have me. He possessed something that the women in my life didn't, but that goes both ways. I spit on my dick as I gripped his small waist and moaned. He felt exactly the same and more of those old feelings came rushing back all at once. That was what he wanted. I fucked him like I would never see him again because I didn't know if I would. I fucked him like I missed him because I did, and I fucked him like that ass was mine because we both knew it was.

We left the alley and spent the rest of the night at his apartment a few blocks over from the restaurant, making up for time missed. That was about a week and a half ago and now I was creeping into my house again trying to quietly wash off my infidelity. I was supposed to be home at nine o'clock last night but right as I was leaving work, Ty called. I was fuckin' up big time and Jaxsyn deserved better from me. I was playing this shit too close and neglecting home for outsiders. I had to get a handle on all this shit, I couldn't risk losing her. That's my fuckin' baby. No matter how much dirt I do in the streets, she will always hold the key to my soul. I finished cleaning myself and then made her breakfast.

"Good morning my love," I kissed Jax with the same lips that had just been all over Ty's body. Guilt washed over me in a major way and I backed away from her.

"Mmmm. That smells amazing," she looked at the tray.

"You look amazing," I stared at my wife for a moment just taking in her beauty. "I love you so much Jax."

"I love you too," she sat up and I fed her a few pieces of fruit. The sun was shining in the room and it shimmered against her face. Perfection. She had a glow that I had never seen before and I couldn't help but to smile at her. She looked stunning and it was only nine am.

"Come lay with me beautiful," I laid back and she nestled into my side. I stroked her head and she went back to sleep as I dozed off too. I was tired as hell from the night I had.

Wherever I slide thru

I gotta buy two

If I get it in pink, I get her the light blue

Brand new Range Rover, that was for her bday

I just auctioned off some shit

You could get it on e-bay

The Nicki Minaj ring tone Jax has set for Zionna started blaring and I jumped.

"Baby, your phone," I nudged her, and she reached over to get it.

"Hello," she smiled through her sleepiness and then stretched. "I hate you so much Z. Here I come," she got up laughing and went down stairs which was perfect because I needed to check on Shardae right quick.

"Aye momma. How are you feeling?"

"We're good baby. Come see us."

"Right now?"

"I mean, yeah. Nigga I called your fuckin' phone a million times last night and you didn't answer. I guess the wife has been acting right lately huh? I can always tell when that bitch gets her act together. That's the only time you go ghost on me and shit."

"Chill out killa, I was actually at work last night."

"Mm, my bad."

"Stop thinking the worse."

"I'm working on it. Just get over her so you can dive into ya baby momma. I'm wet as fuck and I need you. I might even call Nedra's ass over here to play with us again."

"Do that and I'm on my way."

"See you in a minute."

"In a minute baby," I hung up and got dressed. I couldn't stand her punk ass attitude as of lately, but that pussy stayed juicy since she was pregnant, and she stayed horny. This was the most I've been around Shar since we started kicking it. She couldn't get enough of the kid. I had been pleasing her day and night and she was still popping up at my job fuckin' me in the office and begging for me to come break her off in the middle of the night. This was one of the reasons my household was getting neglected. Shar's pregnancy hormones were running her but I had to be there when she called. She's carrying my child, and now I've put Ty in the rotation and my time was getting spread paper thin. I have to figure this shit out because right now, Shar and Ty was getting more of my time than my wife and I knew eventually she would notice, and the work excuses wouldn't be enough to keep her off my ass.

"Damn. That was quick." Jaxsyn raised her eyebrow because I was fully dressed. "Where are you off to?"

"Work." The lie rolled off my tongue naturally.

"You've been working so hard lately." Her eyebrow was still in the air but she didn't seem mad.

"That's a man's job baby. Yo rude ass can't speak?"

"You walked into a room that I was already in so you should have spoken first. Manners 101, but *hey* anyway." Zionna snapped on me real quick and I knew she was still mad about my birthday party but if my baby was over it, her ass should be too. It was a fuckin' mistake that I apologized for more than once. It was actually the truth too. My niggas took me out and got my

52

ass fucked up. I kept telling Ray and the rest of their asses that I had to go, but they kept the rounds coming and before I knew it, I was faded. Shit happens.

"See you later Jax," I blew Z off before I said some shit that would have my wife mad at me. We had enough tension surrounding us so I waved bye to my baby before I bolted to Shardae's house. I was still riding the high from the night I had with Ty and now I was headed to a threesome that I knew was about to set my day off right. I wasn't about to let my sister in law fuck up my mood. Especially over some shit that didn't concern her habitual line stepping ass.

Zionna

"Alright you nasty lil bitch. He's gone now. I want allll the tea so spill it," I smirked waiting for Ms. Perfect to tell me every nasty detail about her cheating on her ain't shit husband.

"I can't believe he told him."

"He didn't tell Nash anything to my knowledge we just both assumed. Messiah called Nashon about some business shit while we were gettin' it in and he had to leave. When he came back, we were talking about how tired we were, and he was like *yeah, my brother was half sleep too, he had just dropped your sister off.* Umm, that was definitely hoe hours ma'am, so I need this tea while it's still piping hot, and don't leave shit out."

"You aggy." She took a deep breath and shook her head, trying to suppress her smile. "Initially, I was mad as hell when I came from the bathroom and you were gone, but giiiiirl," she couldn't stop blushing and her caramel skin had turned red which caused me to smile. I loved seeing her this giddy. "That man dick is so big it should be framed and put on display in a museum for show and tell Z."

"Ha! Yassss bih. You crazy as hell but I knoooow. Remember they're brothers honey." We both laughed and high fived each other. "Get to the details. You know I'm nosey."

"The sex was freakin' insane sis! We messed around like three or four times and he literally had me screaming his name and trying to run from him. Ugh, the way he grabbed my neck with just the right amount of pressure, the way he gently bit my neck as he came... Girl... I never experienced anything like that in my life but aside from all the nasty bits he's a genuinely nice person. We talked for hours by this little lake where he held me and kissed me tenderly under the stars. You know I love a hood nigga that know how to get his gentleman swag on. It's why I fell for my husband."

"I love it sis! They definitely have that gangsta with morals vibe on lock. Shout-out to their granny, sis did *that*! Nash is so hood but the way he does certain things like open doors, put me on the inside when we're walking down the street, check on me throughout the day, and make me text him when I get home, just makes him everything. Most niggas don't give a damn, but he does, and instead of talking about it, he allows his actions to speak." We both nodded with goofy smiles just thinking about these damn Knight brothers. "Did you feel guilty?"

"You know what, I did feel extremely guilty. The whole way home I was going through different emotions. One minute, I'm still tingling on the inside and throbbing at the mere thought of Messiah and what we had just finished doing and then the next, I was on the brink of crying about committing adultery. I was a mess driving home and then I pulled into an empty driveway. I talked to him at the restaurant and he claimed he was on his way here so what the hell happened between that phone call and me pulling up at four am? This nigga thought he was so slick too, but I played the role right along with him. I heard the nigga when he tip-toed in the house at seven this morning and went straight to the basement. I crept down the stairs and his ass was taking a shower."

"No, he wasn't."

"I wish I was lyin' but nah… He was down there with the water running low hoping I wouldn't hear his sneaky ass. You remember when I told you he used to do that shit months ago and I confronted him, so he stopped? This time I'm not saying shit. I'm going to let this play out how it's going to play out. I know something is going on and I promise you on my life, I'm foolin' on his ass. He better hope like hell my intuition needs a realignment because his ass is going to be sorry."

"Well you know I got ya back baby," she was too good to his sorry ass for him to be stepping out so I would burn this whole bitch down for her if she gave me the word.

"I already know…" She shook her head. "I swear the guilt was killing me Z, then I pull up, and his ass ain't even here. Girl… Now, I just don't know…"

"Sis enjoy Messiah. Real talk. If Black wants to allow another man to fill the time that used to be solely reserved for him, then let that shit happen. Fuck it. This ain't the fifties and sixties and you not about to be waiting around the house with a hot meal ready for your cheating husband. Nah, we living our best lives out here boo. If he can do it, you can do it better."

"Okaaaay bih."

"I see you're still getting back to your roots hood rat."

"I think I am," she laughed. "I was so focused on not becoming the old Kabrina that I lost Jaxsyn," she stared off and then looked at me and smiled. "Thanks for pointing that out."

"I always got you."

"So where has Quan's ass been?"

"Girl somewhere trying to figure me out. I haven't been fuckin' with him at all. I can't risk fuckin' with that dog ass nigga no more. I'm not trying to bring shit to Nashon. Obviously, Quan only fuck with dirty bitches so nah…"

"That's so pathetic. He needs to do better."

"On some real shit, I don't give a fuck what he do. I feel cliché as fuck, but Nash introduced me to real, now I hate lames," I shrugged. "I don't even want him to touch me."

"I feel that on a spiritual level. I had no desire to fuck with Black today. He came in the room trying to kiss me and I kept backing away. I didn't even feel comfortable in his arms. Messiah turned me out and now he has me looking at my husband sideways. God, I hate to say that out loud, but it's all facts." We sat quietly in our thoughts for a minute before we both busted out laughing because we both had these lustful expressions on our faces. These niggas had us giddy and gone. Nashon's sexy ass had me hooked and I didn't want anyone else.

I chilled with my sister for a little while longer, but our sperm donor's other daughters called, and she started making plans so that was my cue. I don't fuck with him or them and I don't pretend too. I told her to call me later and left before she attempted to include me. As if he could feel my time free up, Nash called me and told me to meet him in our old hood. He wanted to see me and that alone made me smile.

See, guys never understand just how simple it is to make a woman smile. I didn't ask Quan for big gifts or expensive trips. I asked him to come home every night. I asked him to not bring his ass in my house smelling like another bitch when he did decide to come home. I said don't bring another bitch's disease to me. I said remember my fuckin' birthday since I've known you since we were fourteen-years-old and it's the same fuckin' day every year. Simple shit. I go to work every day, so I didn't need no one to finance me or my lifestyle. I needed a man that was going to call me in the middle of the day and say, "Come see me lil mama, a nigga missin' yo' face". Yeah. That shit right there, that's going to keep me on my knees and fuckin' Nash every chance I get.

My manager Deena called and asked me to come to work tonight right before I pulled up on Nash and as bad as I wanted to say *hell no*, I told her I would be there. Nothing comes before my coins, that includes good dick.

"What's up baby." Nashon walked up on me looking good as fuck and I hugged him. He smelled like a man and I knew when I caught myself sniffing him that this shit was getting serious.

"Hey," I smiled as he let me go and I waved at Messiah. He was surrounded by groupies as usual along with the rest of The Knights. He wasn't wearing his jacket, but I knew it wasn't far. They all had specialized jackets that looked more like leather letterman jackets than the traditional skulls and bones motorcycle jacket. Hoes ate that shit up but I can't lie, it damn sure added to their sexiness.

"Where you comin' from?"

"My sister's house."

"Being nosey," he smirked.

"I meeean."

"Uh huh. Fuck it. I was the same way, but that nigga wasn't trying to come off the info." We laughed. "He just gave me a look and I knew what was up."

"Y'all need to mind y'all business." Messiah was passing us, and we all started crackin up.

"Come ride out with me baby," he grabbed my hand and walked me to his bike.

"I have my purse."

"Sih! Come get her bag for me bro. We'll be back." Messiah came back and took my purse, put it in his car then locked the door. I hopped on the back of Nash's bike and he looked back at my ass. "Yeah. That's what I wanna see," he bit down on his bottom lip and I blew him a kiss with his sexy ass. I didn't know how long this ride was going to be, but I was hoping to get some dick before I had to go into work tonight. When I'm with him that's all I can think about and this time was no different.

Jaxsyn

I rolled over yet again to an empty bed. All I could do was shake my head and move on with my day, per usual. As of lately I had no idea what was going on with Black. It seemed like one day we were making love, laughing and joking around, lying in each other's arms watching movies, and just doing us. Now, we're like two strangers coexisting under the same roof. He's allowing Messiah to occupy all my time and honestly, I was happier than ever. For the last few weeks Black and I barely spent any time together and neither of us seemed to mind. I was all cried out but luckily, I found something to do other than wait for my husband to slip up and confirm my suspicions.

Any time I wasn't swamped with clients, I was basking in everything Messiah, and he definitely had my nights on lock. I had become a professional liar. Black thought I was with Zionna or my little sisters. He didn't even question me, but how could he? I was getting home at ungodly hours, and he was still coming in after me.

Messiah had my full attention. He was sending flowers to my job daily with cards that either made me laugh hysterically or tear up from how sweet he was. He was buying expensive gifts, taking me to exclusive restaurants, fuckin me like it was going out of style, catering to my every need, and showing me a whole new world. Sih was straight out of a hood fairytale and I was faded off of his very existence.

"Oh God!" I gripped Messiah's head and pushed his face deeper into my kitty. He never failed at bringing me to new heights of pleasure. I arched my back and he palmed my ass in his hands. I couldn't get enough of him. He was well aware and played on it. Whenever my mouth got too slick for his liking, he would stop fuckin' me or fuck me so crazily I would readjust my attitude asap. He was turning me into his own personal freak. He was too in tuned with the control his dick possessed and I was too obsessed to not grant him the control he demanded. He had this pussy on lock, and I couldn't even deny that shit.

"Damn this fat mafucka juicy baby. Feed Daddy his pussy Jaxsyn," I rolled my hips and he held a smug look on his face as he watched my every move. His cocky ass knew just what to do and how to do it. He never took his eyes off of me as I continued to fuck his face like he wanted. His nasty ass licked me from my clit to my ass hole and back. He slipped two fingers inside, instantly landing on my spot. "Mmhm."

"Siaaaah!" I screamed out as my legs twitched.

"Mmmhmm," he wouldn't let up on my spot and his other hand spread my kitty lips wider offering him full access to my clit that was thumping like a heartbeat. His tongue game was lethal, and I showered him with my essence. I've never squirted the way this man makes me squirt. His touch was magical. He kissed between my legs and seductively massaged my thighs as I came down from my high. "Come ride me baby," he said after literally sucking my soul out. He laid back and I climbed right on top even though he knew I didn't want to ride him. This man is abnormally huge, and I still have to adjust to his size, every single time.

"Sssss," I slid down as far as I could.

"Take it all," he demanded and gently pushed me down.

"Ughhh," I moaned, digging my nails into his chest. "Sihhh." My body shook with each inch I took.

"That's right baby. Take all of me," he started rolling my hips and pushing me down further and further. Sometimes he would let me slide without putting it all the way in and then other times, it was almost like an insult to not accept all of him.

"It's too biiiiig," I whined while I tried to work it, but he was just too deep. He sat up and faced me.

"No, it's not," he kissed me tenderly as he pushed me down. I could feel my pussy gushing all over his lap and I tried to wind my hips for him. "Keep doing that shit right there baby... Fuck!" He grabbed a handful of my ass and increased the speed.

"Oh my God Messiah," I bit down on his shoulder as he dug me out.

"You better learn how to take this dick Jaxsyn," he kissed me wildly and pulled my hair. Everything he did turned me on, but nothing was better than him pulling my hair or choking me. "Ride this mafucka *now*," he ordered as he tightened his grip on my hair and I stopped whining like a bitch and took the pain; and oh, my goodness was it pain, but I damn sure wasn't going to punk out like I had been doing. I wrapped my arms around his neck and bounced up and down. I made sure I went all the way to the base and tighten my muscles around his head. I could feel the nigga in my chest, but I showed out for him. I knew when he laid back, I had him right where

I've been wanting him, but didn't have the courage to take him. I planted my feet and I rode him like I had spurs and a lasso.

"Got damnmm Jax," he grabbed my thighs tightly and I knew I was giving him exactly what he was asking for. His head dipped back into the pillow and I took all the control he had been having for weeks. He bit down on his bottom lip and his toes cracked. He was in the zone and I rode him nonstop for over an hour. A bitch was tired as hell, but this kitty was still getting wetter and contracting on his pipe with every moan and groan that escaped his lips. I had more energy than I thought and gave him another thirty minutes. I was driving that nigga crazy with each move I made but I could feel myself about to cum again.

"Fuuuck. I'm about to nut baby," he said and started matching my rhythm. He was going so fast that my juices were splashing everywhere, and I started screaming his name. He was murdering my insides and we both yelled out in ecstasy as we came hard and I collapsed onto his chest. My legs were completely numb, and he could barely catch his breath.

"Is it possible for your pussy to just keep getting better and better? I'm convinced that muthafucka got pixie dust in it." We both laughed hysterically.

"You are crazy."

"For real. I'm about to start calling yo' ass Tinker Bell," I giggled shyly, and he kissed my forehead. He loved when I became all bashful around him, but his compliments always did that to me. They somehow reached my soul and it made me giddy like a school girl. After a few minutes of basking in the moment we just shared, he stretched and got up to go to the bathroom. "I have some shit to do in a minute so I'm about to hop in the shower. You gettin' in with me?" He looked back at me and his muscles glisten with sweat causing me to smile. "What's that smile for baby?" He smiled back.

"Everything about you makes me smile."

"Mission accomplished. Come on."

"But I can't walk," I pouted, and he chortled.

"Spoiled ass," he picked me up and carried me to the bathroom. I kissed his beautiful caramel skin the whole way there. He sat me down on the counter and started the shower. We were supposed to be quick because he had business to handle but when I got the feeling back in my legs the first thing I did was drop down to my knees. When I started deep throating him, he had no choice but to let me finish.

60

"Aye bro. I'm sorry about earlier. I'm on my way," he called Nash. "You got niggas mad at me ma."

"That's you taking forever to cum," I smirked.

"That shit was sexy. You know what that sensual sloppy do to me. I had to relish in the moment baby," he bent down and kissed me.

"Mm I love you," I whispered it to myself, but I immediately wanted to take it back because I could tell by the expression on his face that he heard me. It was way too soon and I'm a married fuckin woman. What was I saying?

"I know. I love you too baby," he responded casually and then kissed me again. I was shocked. "You coming with me?" He continued getting dressed.

"What do you mean *I know*?" Yeah, my priorities were fucked up. That definitely shouldn't have been what I was asking or concerned with in the moment considering the circumstances. Yet here I was, looking at him, wondering something that I shouldn't have been wondering, concerning something that I shouldn't have even said.

"I knew," he shrugged. "Don't worry, I love yo big head ass too. Time don't matter sweetheart. I felt that shit when it happened, and you did too. We spend every day together Jax, and when we're not together we're either talking on the phone or texting. What did you think was going to happen beautiful? I make love to you more than any other woman I've ever been with and I know for a fact you ain't over there giving that nigga my pussy. This shit snuck up on us both, but I told you what it was the first day I met you."

"I'm married though. How can I feel this way about another man? I know we spend all of our time together but still… This is so fuckin wrong Sih," I sat on the side of the bed.

"You fuckin with a real man now baby, that's how. I showed you how you were supposed to be treated and you fell in love with it. I appreciate the Queen that you are. I know how to bow down and cater to you, without tipping my own crown baby." *Jesus!*

"You are everything," I stood up and hugged him from behind like I've done to Black so many times before, but this feeling was different. His bare skin against mine scared me. He felt like an addiction that I don't want to go to rehab for. He rubbed my arms and stared at me through the mirror. I could see the love in his eyes and my heart started pounding inside of my chest. "I feel guilty."

"Guilty for what baby? I make sure you're well taken care of and this nigga don't even know if you're home at night or not. You're a priority in my world and an option in his," he turned around and faced me. "His time is running out and I'm getting tired of sharing you with a nigga that don't even give a fuck about your safety and well-being," he looked at me intently and I didn't have anything to say. I loved him but he was asking me to leave my husband and I just couldn't see my life without Black in it. We've been together for years and no matter what we go through or what we've gone through, I do love my husband. Maybe this is just a rough patch and we need to get some things out of our system. I don't know, but this conversation had me nervous because at this point, I don't want to lose Messiah either. My heart would shatter.

I was so confused; I didn't know what to do and I could see he read my expression like a book. He leaned forward and kissed me deeply. I wrapped my arms around his neck and our bare skin felt perfect against each other. "I'm not forcing you to do shit Jax. You gone come to me on your own. You know like I know that this is where you want to be so I'm going to let you wrap your mind around the moves you need to make," he swooped me into his arms and slid inside of me taking my breath away instantly. "Yeah… you know this pussy is mine." Arrogance had him back inside of me knowing damn well his brother was waiting for him. The way my kitty was gripping him, I knew Nash was just going to have to be mad. "Tell me whose pussy this is Jaxsyn," he looked down at his dick that was covered in my cream wearing a smug expression. I was silent because he was right… I knew. "If I have to repeat myself, yo' ass is going to need a walker to get around," he dug deeper, and I whimpered.

"You know this pussy is yourssss."

"And have you been giving my pussy away Jaxsyn?" Again, deep shots to my organs coupled with his hand firmly around my neck.

"No baby. No! I don't ever want another man to touch me. Shiiiit," I gushed all over him and he smirked.

"Mmhmm. This pussy know who daddy is. I love yo' ass to death baby."

"I love you too," I hugged him as he bounced me up and down. God, I hoped karma didn't come to collect on me for cheating on my husband, but I swear I can't let Messiah go. Even though this was wrong, I prayed it last forever.

****

"Happy twenty-fourth birthdaaaay bihhhh!" Zionna screamed into the phone at midnight and I laughed. We're always the first person to tell each other happy birthday as soon as the clock strikes midnight. I wasn't about to tell her Messiah already told me early and then again through text right before she called. Of course, like every day, we had spent the day together but since my birthday was approaching, he made the day extra special. He flew me out to Chicago where he was handling some club business and we spent the day shopping, eating, and making love. I was on cloud nine and I didn't want to come down. Today was the first day I actually considered spending a night because I didn't want to leave him.

"Thanks love."

"What are you doing? It sounds like you're in the car."

"I am. I'm on my way home."

"From Sih's house?"

"I was with him, but we weren't at his house. He was in Chicago handling Knight business and flew me out. I think he had a stressful day, so he just wanted to see me, unwind, and celebrate my birthday. We just got back like an hour ago."

"Aww bitch you didn't even tell me you were leaving."

"It was last minute. That wasn't even actually my birthday gift. He said he has something special planned for me, he just needed to see me today."

"Y'all are becoming goals right before my eyes. The nigga got money coming out his ass so his something special could be any damn thing. Shit, he flew you to Chicago on some 'I miss you' type of shit. Ain't no telling what the real gift is."

"I know and I'm soooo not used to this Z. Don't get me wrong. Black bought me nice things when he could, but he's never made the grand gestures that have me stuck like Messiah does."

"Bitch, other than Nash, I don't think nobody could. These niggas are two of a kind and they don't know how to do shit if it ain't big."

"After all the hoe shit we've been through, we deserve whatever the fuck they're willing to give."

"Oooo, all this profanity makes me happy. I'm loving what Sih is doing to you. Everyday I'm getting my sister back."

"I told you I was trying to get back to Jaxsyn. I was serious," I laughed at her crazy ass. She was right when she checked me about Black after his birthday. I consider myself a realist, so I didn't get mad at her, I kept it real with myself and took in everything that she said. Truth was, he didn't fall in love with a prude and every day since college that's what I gave him. I could have found balance, but I went all in on changing me, to run from becoming Kabrina. In the process of not trying to become someone else, I lost me.

Unfortunately, we never had a real conversation about it. If he needed me to change something or he wasn't happy, all he had to do was sit me down. I normally just blew him off like it was a joke since he always said it jokingly. Now he's probably filling his time with a bitch that's like the old me. Had this been months ago, I would have cared and showed him that I was getting back to the real Jaxsyn, a better Jaxsyn, but now days it just didn't seem worth it. "Wait. Who the fuck is this on my porch at this time of night?" I pulled into my driveway.

"You got your gun on you?"

"Yeah," I took it out of my glove compartment. "It looks like a dude."

"I'm on my way. Stay in the car."

"Naw don't do that I have my gun."

"Too late. I'm already getting in the car. You know it only takes five minutes for me to get to you so stay in the car."

"Alright."

"What is he doing?"

"Nothing. Just sitting. He has his head down so I can't even see who the fuck it is, and I don't recognize this car that's out here either."

"That's crazy. Maybe one of your neighbors got drunk and wandered to your house again."

"I don't know. Maybe."

"I'm pulling up," I looked back and she was behind me. We both hopped out with our guns drawn.

"Who are you and why the fuck are you on my porch?" I racked my gun so the nigga could know I was serious.

"It's me Jaxsyn. Tyler. Black's college roommate."

"Oh," I took a deep breath. "You scared the hell out of me." We both went back to our cars and turned them off. We had left them running in case we needed to make a clean break for it.

"Come on in. Is Black expecting you? It's pretty late and he didn't mention anything to me," I asked as we all walked in to my house.

"I can guarantee you that he's not expecting me to be right here, right now, with you, inside of his home. This is *nice* by the way." His tone made both me and Zionna turn around and look at him.

"What's going on Ty?" I folded my arms, pressed my lips firmly against each other, and stared at him with a raised eyebrow.

"I'm tired. That's what's going on *Jaxsyn*. I'm sick and muthafuckin' tired. Tired of the lies, broken promises, more lies to cover the original lies, and now a got damn baby! Reeeeally? A muthafuckin baby."

"I'm so confused," I looked at Zionna and she was just as clueless as me. He was rambling on and on and none of it was making sense to me. I didn't know if he was drunk or not but why the fuck would he come here with this drunk shit? I was about to walk over to my purse and grab my phone to call my husband, but he spoke again.

"How are you still confused?" he yelled, stopping me dead in my tracks, as he stepped into my personal space. Now I could see that his eyes were blood shot red like he had been crying and he wasn't drunk at all. This whole scene was going left, and I definitely needed to call Black so he could come home quick and get his friend. This nigga was not about to be in my house yelling at me.

"Wake! The! Fuck! Up!" He clapped as he spoke. "Damn! Are you really this dense? I've been fuckin Black since college you stupid bitch. He was my boyfriend for almost two years, but he was scared to come out of the closet. Then here you come, bringing him a belly full of baby. He wanted to do the right thing so he broke my heart for you but that didn't stop us from fuckin' until the day he married your ass. I literally sucked his dick in the parking lot of the church before the ceremony started. I still can't believe he went back inside and fuckin' married you," he threw his hands up and started crying.

"Quick FYI boo, we've been fuckin' for months now. Know why? Because his ass was never over me to begin with. We were in love Jaxsyn, we're still in love Jaxsyn, and we're always going to be in love Jaxsyn! Still confused? Well let me help you out. *My man* doesn't leave my house until he's thoroughly satisfied which is normally when the sunlight beams through my bedroom window. *My man* hasn't gone one day without hittin' this since we reconnected months ago. What kind of marriage do y'all really have if he's in my bed more than yours? He may have loved you first, but it's me he's actually in love with! It's me that holds his heart. Y'all shit is a facade," he was boasting, and my insides were shaking. Gay? *This* is who the fuck he's been sneaking around with?

"Now, the got damn plot has thickened because he has a young hood rat bitch on the east side pregnant and he's promising this bitch the world to keep her quiet. Lord forbid his precious Jaxsyn finds out even though I know about the abortions you've had. Yeah… we pillow talk sis," I was floored. Actually, stuck and unable to move. Zionna had tears streaming down her face but I was completely fuckin' numb. It felt like the organs in my body were shutting down one by one and it wasn't shit I could do to stop them.

"Look in my purse and get my inhaler Z," I said through shallow breaths and she grabbed my handbag from behind her. This man just told me that he's been fuckin my husband for years and as if that information wasn't damaging enough, it's also a bitch in the equation that's pregnant. Pregnant? My life with my husband flashed before my eyes and all of a sudden, a wave of delayed emotions hit me like a ton of bricks. My skin got hot, my head started pounding, my eyes filled with tears, and my heart rate sped up as it shattered into pieces. I snatched the gun off my end table, dropped the clip, flipped it around, and swung at him with every inkling of strength I had inside of me.

"Bitch!" I screamed and completely blacked out on Ty.

66

Zionna

I sat in the lobby of the police precinct for over two hours waiting for Jaxsyn to be booked and then released. I was a complete and utter mess. I literally cried the whole time. Her bail had been posted but her legal issues were far from over. If Ty or Black decided to press charges against my sister, she could go to jail for up to five fuckin years and I didn't know how to accept that information. I was so hurt for her; I couldn't imagine walking in her shoes right now. Ty delivered a blow to her heart that even knocked the wind out of me. With all the drama we've been through, Jax has never lost control like she did tonight. Tonight, she even had me scared.

"Zionna," I heard my name and turned around. Nash and Sih were standing behind me and I ran to Nash like we were in an airport and he just got back from war. He held me tight as I cried hard against his chest. He wrapped his arms around me and kissed my head.

"What happen to her Z? What's going on?" Sih was genuinely concerned and that's the energy my sister was going to need to get through this.

I started telling them what happened from when I called her, until Ty started spazzing. Their facial expressions changed drastically as the story progressed. "Y'all she went completely silent and then she said she couldn't breathe. Next thing I know, she grabs her gun, drops the clip, and start pistol whipping the shit out of him. I'm screaming and yelling and trying to pull her off of him and she's completely zoned out. She's swinging over and over and I'm trying to guard myself and stop her at the same time. Absolutely nothing was working. He was bloody and unconscious before she stopped on her own and then she jetted out of the front door. She went to her husband's shop and did the same thing to him. I didn't even know where she was going when she ran out of the house until one of the dudes that works for him called me and told me the police had been called and she was about to go to jail. I rushed over there, and I swear, in twenty-four years I've never saw her like this. He broke her and she snapped," I started crying again as Nash held me. "She wouldn't even talk to me before they took her away. She looked dazed, and that light that's normally in her eyes was gone."

"Damn man." Messiah sat down. "That shit is deep."

"I know," I wiped my tears and Nash and I sat down too.

My Headache: *Man, what the hell is going on? Somebody told me Jax beat Black's ass and ain't none of y'all answering the phone.* I didn't feel like being bothered with Quan. I had too much on my mind right now to repeat what happened to another person.

"There she goes." Nashon pointed and Messiah hopped up.

Unfortunately, she still had that blank look on her face as the officers were talking to her. I instantly wanted to cry again but I had to be strong for her because she couldn't be strong for herself right now. I wrapped my arms around her as soon as she came through the sliding plexiglass door. She hugged me back and took a deep breath. "I have your inhaler baby," I passed it to her, and tears were streaming down her face. "Please talk to me Jax. I know it hurts but you're scaring me. What can I do? How can I help?" She just looked past us, and I don't think when I called Messiah and Nashon that they knew exactly what they were walking into.

"I had three abortions," she was still struggling to breathe, and her tears fell more rapidly. "He made me abort three of my fuckin babies because he wasn't ready. It crushed my fuckin' soul but I followed his lead like I thought a good wife should... do... A good wife..." Her words trailed off and she shook her head as if she was trapped in her thoughts for a moment. "I held him down when he went to jail and people didn't even know the nigga was gone for a whole year. I kept money on his books, bought his business so he wouldn't go back in, and fronted him the money to get everything he needed for it. I haven't seen a dime of my money back that he insisted on repaying me. I paid for his stepdad to be buried, and his mom to go to rehab three times; the whole time he was fuckin a nigga behind my back and now he got a bitch pregnant?" She gasped so hard that it looked like her chest was going to cave in. "The whole fuckin' time?"

"Please hit your inhaler Jax. I'm begging you."

"That's what I deserved for my devotion, loyalty, and dedication to him? Every meal he ate was cooked by me, I bought that nigga everything from the brand new car he's driving to the briefs his boyfriend is tugging at. I washed and ironed all of his clothes, his house is thoroughly cleaned daily, I was fuckin' him every day, I made sure all of our bills were paid in full and this is what the fuck I deserved in return Z? This..." Her words got caught in her throat as she cried harder. "He got her pregnant Z. He fuckin' got her pregnant."

68

I hugged her tight and my world shattered with hers. I didn't know what the fuck to say. What the fuck could I say... I just held her as she cried so hard that her body shook in my arms. This shit was so sad man and I knew that even if the words found me, they still wouldn't be enough to bring her comfort in this shit storm she was dropped into.

"I need to get my clothes from that house. I'm done with him. Completely. This nigga really-" She was gasping for air as tears continued soaking her face. I pushed her hand to her mouth and made her hit her inhaler. It barely helped and I was seriously nervous that she would have an asthma attack or hyperventilate.

"Okay baby, calm down," I wiped her face and rubbed her back. "We'll get them, but you have to stay calm. I'm worried about your breathing."

"I'm okay." Her eyes were filled to the brim with tears making me hug her again. She laid her head on my shoulder and started boo hooing all over again and I started crying too. This reminded me of when we were kids sitting in one of our houses all alone while our mommas were gone on another binge, leaving us to figure shit out. We would hold each other and cry until we both fell asleep under the bed or in the closet. This was the other half of my heart and when she hurt, I hurt.

"Come here baby. You want me to go with you?" Sih took her into his arms and she looked up at him.

"Yeah. I do," she nodded sadly, and he wiped her tears before kissing her. She placed her hand on his face and held their lips together for a few seconds longer before she laid her head on his chest. He rubbed her head and look at us.

"Y'all go ahead and ride together, let me talk to her," I hugged her one more time before we all dispersed and went in different directions. Nash told me he would send someone to get my car since he wanted me to ride with him. I was in no condition to drive. As we approached his car, he stopped me and just took me into his arms. I broke down crying and he held me closely and stroked my head.

"She gone be straight baby. My brother is not going to let her spend no real time in jail and she's going to bounce back from this whole shit."

"You think so? I've never saw her like this Nash. Ever. I hope she doesn't hurt herself. She's the strongest person I know and he just... he..."

"Come on baby. If she's as strong as you say she is, then you know she's going to bounce back better than ever. She gone shake this shit off and glow up on his ass," he placed his hand under my chin and started drying my face, then he pressed his soft lips against mine. I closed my eyes and got lost in every morsel of him. He pushed me back against his car and slipped his hand inside of my pajama pants. I didn't have time to get dressed when I rushed to Jax house and now I was thankful for it. The minute I felt his fingers sliding through my folds I quivered and gave in to his touch.

"Mmmm," I moaned against his lips as he took his foot and opened my legs more, giving him enough access to please me right there in the parking lot of the police station. "Shit, Nash," I laid my head back against his car and he started kissing on my neck.

"I don't want you to worry about anything baby. You hear me?"

"Yessss."

"Do you really?" His fingers went deeper, and his thumb slid across my clit faster.

"Yes baby! I hear yo-" I came all over his fingers within seconds as he kissed me through my orgasm.

"She gone be straight and in the meantime I don't want you worrying," he pulled his fingers out and licked them. We both smirked and my whole mood was better. He kissed me one more time and then opened the door for me to get in. I watched him walk around to the driver side and I silently thanked God for blessing me. This man had me all the way gone off of him and I felt God's favor by just being in his presence.

"I need you to give me directions baby so don't take yo' ass to sleep."

"You know me so well."

"I do," he kissed me and pulled off. I laid on my left side and stared at him like I always do. He used to call me a creep but now he's used to it. I loved to just look at him, studying every inch of him. He rubbed my leg as he whipped through the streets of the city he ran and the more I watched him the hornier I got and before I knew it, I was on my knees, leaned over the center console, suckin' dick. I just couldn't get enough…

Messiah

We walked out of the precinct hand in hand and she was quiet as a church mouse. She didn't even look my way until we got into the car.

"Come here," I pulled her into my arms and held her. She cried and I just let her go in. Her heart was broken, and she needed to get it out. Wasn't no shame in that. She didn't stop for almost a half hour and I texted my brother so he could tell Zionna why we wouldn't be there for a while. I didn't want her worrying about Jax more than she already was.

"I'm a mess but I can't fuckin cry to you about him. I apologize. This is so disrespectful," she raised her head and wiped her face.

"Yes, you can and no it's not. You know I live for that smile baby so if this is the tears that has to be shed to get back to that smile that I love so much, then let them flow freely."

She leaned in and kissed me. I took her face into my hands and caressed her cheek deepening our embrace. "I love you Messiah."

"I love you too baby," I ran my fingers through her hair, and she laid her head on my shoulder.

"I don't know how to live without him. He's been the man in my life for as long as I can remember."

"He's never been a man baby. It was all smoke and mirrors. Y'all went from being kids that understood each other's struggle, to kids in a long-distance college relationship, and y'all carried that familiarity into adulthood. He never grew up, but you did. You were ready to be a wife and mother after your career took off, while he was still out here playing kid games. You're worth more than what he's put you through."

"I really wanna believe I am," her voice cracked. "But if I was then-"

"Nah. Don't do that. This ain't on you. This is all him and I'm not about to let you carry that nigga's burdens. He was out here on bullshit. Ain't no way in hell he should have ever let that nigga run his mouth to you if that's how he been gettin' down and he damn sure shouldn't have a baby on the way that's not coming from you. Don't try to make sense out of his bullshit. That nigga is going to regret the day he fucked you over. Watch."

"You are my sanity Messiah Knight," she kissed me again before climbing back into her seat and I pulled off.

This nigga really had his wife in the clinic aborting his seeds but let the random bitch on the side keep it. Where the fuck they make these lame ass niggas? I don't give a fuck if he had to kick that bitch down the stairs until she choked on that got damn baby; she was never supposed to be able to have a leg up on his wife. No cap. Especially the wife that was begging to have a baby. He was going through life ass backwards, literally and she wasn't about to doubt herself in front of me or try to take any blame. He's a bitch and moved how bitches move.

We pulled up to the house and for the caliber of woman that Jax is, I wasn't all that impressed with where he had her living. Then again, she's been footing the bill for both of them. He got all this shit going on and he can't even afford to take care of himself. This nigga priorities was fucked.

"You want us to come with you?" I asked before we got out of the car.

"He's here," she wiped her eyes as they landed on the car in the driveway.

"You want us to come with you?" I didn't give a fuck whether he was home or not.

"Messiah."

"Baby I told you I was tired of sharing anyway. This nigga was going to be out of the picture sooner than later, and we both know that shit. Stop frontin'. You're mine and you have been for months now. You were trying to hold on to him solely based on y'all past, but your heart already found its way home. Everything from the top of your head to the bottom of your feet is mine." We stared at each other and she bit down on her bottom lip causing my dick to jump. "Once again, I'm asking *my* woman, does she want me to come inside or not?"

"Come on," she didn't hesitate as she reached for the door handle. I hated when she tried to downplay what has happened between us. I know it's hard to accept that she fell in love with another man, but it is what it is. Jax ain't no low-down female. If ol' boy was handling his home like he was handling his side pieces, I wouldn't have been giving his wife the world. She's been with me every single day since the first night we messed around. Not only did I tell her off rip that I wanted her, but I've showed her repeatedly and showered her with the love and affection that she was missing. Yeah, I felt bad about how all this shit went down but this muthafucka was on his way out of the picture anyway.

As we all walked up to the door, I could tell she was feeling a plethora of emotions, but we all had her back. Her head was hanging low and I corrected that as soon as we were standing on her porch. I placed my index finger under her chin and made her look at me.

"What yo' head down for?" I asked and she shrugged with tears in her eyes. "Whose burden is this Jaxsyn?"

"His," I kissed her.

"Damn right and you ain't carrying no bum ass nigga burdens on my watch," she nodded and unlocked the door.

"You need me to help you pack?" Zionna asked as we walked in.

"Naw. I got it. I'll be right back," she looked back at me and I nodded my head letting her know we would be right here.

"Jaxsyn!" He called out to her as she was going up the stairs and she stopped.

"I can't do this," she turned around and came running into my arms.

"Baby what do you need from here?" I asked as I held her.

"My clothes and shoes. Purses. All my personal items."

"You have any sentimental things, keepsakes, jewelry or anything like that, that can't be replaced?"

"No. I don't want any of these pictures or memories, or nothing that he's bought me. I'm done with this part of my life."

"Then I'll replace all that material shit." We all turned to walk out of the door.

"Jaxsyn!" He came running down the stairs. "Man tell me what the fuck happened? You attacked me and didn't even say shit. That's what the fuck we on? I been calling every fuckin' precinct in the city trying to find out which one they took you to. What the hell is going on?"

"Fuck you Black. Like seriously. Fuck. You!" She turned around and he grabbed her arm.

"I would let her go if I was you," I stepped into his face.

"And who the fuck are you supposed to be?" He looked at me, over to her, and then back to me.

"Her man and you need to let her arm go before I break your fuckin face my nigga."

I looked his ass dead in his eyes, and he let her go. I could tell he had heart, but he wasn't fuckin' with a nigga like me and the way he let her go showed that.

"Wow," he stepped back and looked her up and down. "Your *man*?" He laughed. "That's funny as hell. Does he know you're fuckin *married*? Shit, do you know you're fuckin married while you're standing in front of your husband letting some random nigga claim you?" He seemed shocked, like he had any room to be.

"Fuck boys ain't allowed to question her in front of me. Nigga do you know you're fuckin married while you around this bitch playin' with nigga's assholes? You ready Tinker Bell?" I looked at her and she smiled.

"Yeah, Bae. I am." We turned around to walk away and he grabbed her again.

"This nigga thinks I'm bullshittin'." Both me and my brother stepped into his space ready to drop this clown.

"Sih," she placed her hand on my chest to stop me. "Don't touch me Black."

"You allowing this nigga to come in my house and disrespect me? Where the fuck we lay our heads? Then turn around and tell your own husband don't touch you? Don't fuckin' touch you? Everything on you is mine. Fuck you mean?"

"Everything like what my nigga? That access was revoked months ago. You were so busy neglecting home for random's that you didn't even notice your wife stopped fuckin' you." He cocked his head to the side with confusion written all over his face.

"So, you fuckin this nigga Jax?" He was pissed and me and my brother just stared at his hoe ass waiting for him to make a move based on the hurt that I could see swelling in his chest. If she wasn't standing right in front of me, I would have dropped this nigga. I was growing more and more irritated by his audacity.

She took a deep breath as she shook her head and eyed this nigga with nothing but hate radiating from her. "Every chance I get, and suckin' his dick too. You say you want the old Jax back, well here the fuck she is," she stole on that nigga so hard the impact echoed through their house. He looked like he wanted to fade her ass and I wanted him to try it. "You're exactly what the fuck is wrong with the world. Out here fuckin Ty and the lil Eastside bitch you got pregnant and then coming home fuckin me raw, like it ain't shit. Just thinking about yo' snake ass got me wanting to fuck you up again. Good thing since he's been around, I haven't fucked you once or I'd let him kill your nasty triflin' ass right where you stand. You're pathetic and I'm sick I

74

wasted so much time on your worthless ass," she stepped in his face. "Stay the fuck from around me before you catch a hot one hoe," she mushed that nigga and turned around. "Let's get the fuck out of here y'all before I seriously catch another case tonight," she was in rare form and he wanted to say something back, but between the heat radiating from her and me and Nash still grilling his hoe ass, he just kept his shit on mute.

"Yasssss Jax! That's what the fuck I'm talking about sus! Never in my life did I think I would hear you tell your husband you out here suckin' your boyfriend's dick but bitch you did *that*!" Zionna started clapping and we all busted out laughing hysterically at her crazy ass. Zionna is a whole fool and Nash had his hands full with her. She definitely changed the mood just that quick though and I appreciated her for it. That's what Jax needed right now.

"You so crazy." Jax playfully pushed her. "The sun is coming up, I'm sleepy, it's my Birthday, and my whole life just made a huge shift." Jax nibbled on the corner of her lip. "More shit for my stepmom or another therapist to deal with when I'm older," she shrugged.

"You'll be over that nigga this week," I kissed her. "Now wake yo' sleepy ass up and let's go take some shots. We about to get fucked up. I got some shit planned for your sexy ass too," I put her over my shoulder and carried her to the car as she giggled. "It's a fuckin' celebration baby!" I yelled out and she continued to laugh and blush. I waited a long time for a woman that made me feel the way that she makes me feel. She was about to get everything that she didn't even know she wanted. This was the beginning of what we both needed, and she was the perfect woman to make this shit happen with.

Black

I couldn't believe how my life had went from sugar to shit in a matter of days. Jaxsyn knew about everything and love turned into hate real quick, but how the fuck did she know? No one knows about Ty, so who the fuck could have told her everything? This shit was blowing me. I couldn't wrap my damn mind around the pain in her eyes, the boyfriend, or the fact that she knew about the baby too. Never in a million years did I want her to find out about Shardae. Never. I would have taken that shit to the fuckin' grave with no problem but that definitely explains her erratic behavior at the shop.

Jax hit me with her gun so many times that one of my guys in the shop had to call the police on her. She was swinging so hard and fast that I couldn't grab her hands. All I could do was block the hits that she was delivering and pray that her ass stopped before she knocked me out cold or worse. I had to get eleven stitches behind that shit. I thought she was just on some emotional female shit because I had been neglecting her lately. I had no fuckin clue that it was because of my secrets getting exposed. She had every right to snap.

"Don't hang up. I know you're team Jaxsyn, but I need answers that she's not giving me. I guess she got me blocked or something," I called Zionna.

"You damn right I'm team Jax and hopefully she does have you blocked. Nigga you played her, and I've never seen her more broken in my life."

"Well define broken Zionna because she damn sure didn't look broken when she walked in our house with a nigga she admitted to fuckin', while she's still wearing my ring and last name."

"Cry me a fuckin' river Black. You were fuckin a man behind her back since college nigga. College! You have no room to talk about shit you pushed her to do. Then to add salt to an open wound, you're pillow talking with, and allowing a side bitch to have your baby. She pleaded with you the last time she got pregnant. She was literally willing to quit her fuckin' job to dedicate herself to motherhood. She begged you to let her keep the baby and get on board with the thought of becoming parents, but you flat out refused. You stopped talking to her and treated her like shit. Threw a whole fuckin' fit and drove her to the clinic yourself to make sure she did it. You made her lay on that table knowing good and well that your side bitch was already pregnant with your first born. That's fucked up on so many different levels it literally disgusts me."

"It is. I battle with that shit every fuckin day and for the record, I tried to get her to have an abortion, but she refused. I never wanted to hurt Jaxsyn with this baby shit. Ever. I fuckin' love my wife Zionna. I messed up by cheating on her, but I swear I wouldn't hurt her like this purposely," I didn't even want to talk about Ty. "Is she really with this dude?"

"You love you Black, not my sister. Keep it all the way real my nigga and what I'm not about to do, is get into her personal business with you. Are we done?"

"I have two more questions."

"Ask your questions so you can get up off of my line."

"I caused her some pain but is she happy Z? Regardless of how this shit look, I do love my wife. I know you not gone speak on her and ol' boy business but if she's happy then I'm happy for her."

"Nah, you don't love her and yes, she's very happy. Now, last question."

"How did she find out?"

"Really?" She laughed.

"I have no idea Zionna. All I know is she came barreling into my shop like someone had set her ass on fire and she started swinging."

"Mmhmm well your beloved boyfriend or boy toy or your bottom, whatever he is to you, came to the house on her birthday screaming it at her like she had did something wrong to him. He told her all about the baby and how you're only with her because you're too much of a bitch to come out of the closet to be with him," she hung up.

What in the entire fuck? Ty was behind all of this shit? I paced the floor as my mind raced in a million different directions. He came to my house? This nigga really lost his fuckin' mind. I had so many emotions running through me, all I could do was dial his number and wait anxiously for him to give me some answers.

"Oh, now you wanna call? Two weeks has passed since that bitch assaulted me, and now you call?"

"Assaulted you? What?"

"Yes! Assauuuulted! Is she so perfect that it's too hard for you to believe?"

"What the fuck are you even talking about Ty?"

"Your fuckin wife attacked me Derrick! That's what I'm talking about. I had to get stitches and I was in the hospital for two days. That crazy bitch fractured my eye socket and oooh yes, I'm definitely pressing charges against her ratchet ass too. Believe that!"

"You ain't doin' shit. You asked for whatever ass beating she gave you. Why the fuck did you come to my house?" I was pissed hearing him confirm what Zionna had just said.

"Okay, that was wrong. I was pissed. When I saw you with that young pregnant bitch that I've been hearing about for weeks, I lost it. I had a few drinks and got into my car. Next thing I know, I'm sitting on your porch. That still gave her no right to put her hands on me though, and you can't stop me from pressing charges."

"You're not and that's not up for discussion! You gave her every right! You didn't even say shit to me about it, but you thought it was a good fuckin' idea to come to my house and scream it at my wife nigga?" Every time he opened his mouth, I could feel myself getting angrier. How couldn't he see how bad he fucked up? There was no justifying this shit.

"She needed to know," he said nonchalantly further pissing me off.

"And you needed that ass whoppin' she gave you. I can't believe you did that bullshit. Then you yelled at her like she was the wrong one, when she's the only one in the fuckin' equation that didn't know what was going on… That was a bitch move Ty. Real talk."

"I just told you I was mad and slightly intoxicated Black. I apologize, damn."

"It ain't enough apologies in the world to make up for this. She went to jail on her birthday because of you!"

"You really need to bring it down a notch or two and take some got damn responsibility. You were fucking me and the young bitch behind her back. It was all bound to come out eventually sooo…"

"So, what? So, you take it upon yourself to be the messenger of my fuckin business? She fuckin left me Ty. My *wife* is gone because you were jealous over some old shit."

"Well… Then there was two," he laughed. "I don't have shit to be jealous of and we both know that for a fact. You've been lying to yourself for so long, you're actually starting to believe your own bullshit Derrick Avery. You loved what she represented more than you actually loved her. It all may have come out the wrong way, and for that I honestly apologize, but don't keep

78

frontin' Derrick. I did you a favor and you're welcome," he hung up and I felt dazed. I was completely fuckin' out of it. I fucked my baby over for two people that I was now questioning everything about. Shar has good pussy and that's a fact, but that bitch is a nineteen-year-old thot. She was never anything other than ass, but I chilled one too many times and feelings started to develop. Now I have to deal with her ass for the next eighteen years. Then there's Tyler, yeah, I love his ass and he's very aware of it, but would I ever go out in public with him as my nigga? Nah, I won't. He did all of this and he's still not going to get the version of me that he was hoping for. This shit was crazy…

      Me: *I need your login for IG* I texted my sister. I had to just see Jax. I was missing the fuck out of my baby.

      Asia: *She has me blocked too bro. Y'all might really be done this time.* I read her message and went straight to the liquor cabinet. This shit was unreal and coming at me fast.

Jaxsyn

I woke up to Messiah staring at me and I blushed as I covered my face with the sheet I was wrapped in, then peeked at him over the top.

"Why do you stare at me like that?" I smiled.

"You're beautiful, and you're mine, and you're an unexpected blessing that I always knew I needed but didn't know how to get my hands on."

"Awww baby." My eyes filled with tears, but he thumbed them away before they could fall. "Thank you Sih!"

"You're welcome baby. Now come feed me my breakfast," he smiled and displayed his bright white teeth. I was so head over heels in love with this man I couldn't even think straight. I ran to the bathroom to brush my teeth and freshen up, then climbed on top of his face. My baby was a soul snatcher and it was nothing better than waking up to the royal treatment. I rolled my hips and bounced on his face like I was riding his pipe. He liked it wild and nasty so that's what I gave him every single time. He held my waist making me stay right where he wanted me.

"Ughhhhh," I could feel myself oozing and I gripped his head while quenching his thirst. I was spent off of the first orgasm, but he wasn't done. I came so many times he had me in tears from sheer pleasure.

"Perfection," he kissed my throbbing bud and then helped me down. My legs weren't shit for giving out the way they did. "I have to go baby. I have to make a run to Chicago with Nash. I'll be back tonight though," he stood on the side of the bed and I pouted causing him to smile. "When did you become a brat?" I shrugged and crawled over to the edge of the bed where he was standing.

"Are you going to miss me Bae?" I kneeled in front of him and wrapped my arms around his neck.

"I always miss you when I'm away from your spoiled ass," he stuck his tongue into my mouth, and I could taste the remnants of the head he just gave me. I got turned on all over again. It didn't take much around him at all. I increased our kiss and he laid me down.

"Freak."

"You made me this way. Now come here," I smiled and pulled him on top of me. I mean I had to give him the kitty before he hit the road. That was a given.

I didn't have any real plans for my day, so I got up, showered, and headed to the mall. Slowly but surely, I was getting my wardrobe back but with all better shit. Sih spared no limit to the amount of stuff that he gave me. I was walking around with his credit card like it was mine and wads of cash bigger than I've ever seen before. As long as I was happy, he said he was happy which made me even happier. This nigga was seriously like a hood fairytale come true and I've been telling him that from the start. Most days I couldn't even believe my life.

After I left the mall, I figured I would be productive and make the most out of my day, so I grabbed some color swatches for work and ran a few errands. I was dealing with a client that had me more stressed out than I'd like to be, but I knew I was going to win him over eventually. He's one of those guys that doesn't respect women until you prove yourself and I had no problem with that. When it comes to interior decorating and staging homes for real estate showings, I'm a pro. My business is the one thing in life I knew no one could take from me. Along with that confidence comes amazing results to support it. He'll see. My work will speak for itself.

When I pulled up to Zionna's house I was instantly pissed. She was standing in front of her house talking to Black and they both looked my way as I got out of the car. She knew I was on my way, so I didn't understand why the nigga was even present.

"Why is he here?" I needed answers.

"They about to go sis." Z looked at me apologetically.

"Baby I just wanted to see you."

"Bitch fuck you. I got my gun in my purse, so I suggest you make your next move, your best move," I walked into the house and went to the kitchen. I poured a glass of wine, sat at the table, and texted my baby. I was missing him already.

Me: *Hey love. You never said what time you would be back, so I made plans*

My Heart: *What plans?*

Me: *Bailey's with my girls.*

My Heart: *Watch how you dress before you make me catch a case like yo hostile ass lol*

My Heart: *My nigga's will be there too…*

Me: *That's not funny baby* ☹□

Me: *To check on me? Lmao! So, you're crazy, crazy, huh?*

My Heart: *Sorry baby. Too soon? Lmao*

My Heart: *Lol nah. It's G's baby momma Birthday or some shit*

Me: *Definitely too soon!*

Me: *Oh, okay. Love you bae. Be careful*

My Heart: *Love you too Tinker, Always…*

I smiled at the nickname he gave me. He had been completely amazing since all the shit with Black went down. He's nurtured my soul in a way that I didn't even think was possible. Aside from how much he's given me emotionally, he's also granted me full access to his home and what a fuckin home it was. He had a full staff and that shit blew my mind. I knew he had money, but I definitely didn't think it was like that. We had been going to his condo in the city since we met but when everything happened, he brought me to his actual home and I'm still in awe of how beautiful it is.

When we first pulled up, I literally thought it was a joke. The stone and brick exterior made it look like a modern-day castle and my mouth was wide open as we drove up. He laughed and lead me inside where I was immediately greeted by a warm and inviting feeling. Not at all what I assumed it would be from the outside. His housekeeper Tabitha was the first to greet me and I immediately fell in love with her. Her aura went with the feel of his home. She was so welcoming and nurturing. He told her to assist me with anything I needed and as we made small talk, she showed me around.

Chandeliers, swimming pools, theatre rooms, sauna, whirl pool tubs, state of the art kitchen, and walk in closets that were the size of normal people's bedrooms. I was in awe and he really gave me access to it all. Even though I told him I wanted this move to be temporary until I found something else, I could truly see myself living there. I think it's all a part of his plan too.

He bought me a custom-made Harley Davidson bike for my birthday with a dope ass pink and black leather "Lady Knight" jacket. I cried in his arms as I made love to him on top of it. The very next day he started talking about how we needed to expand the garage for our motorcycles and cars. I peep everything he says and it's always "our", "we", or "us". Shit like that matters to me and it's another thing that I was missing and didn't realize it. My Siah is all about *us* and I couldn't ask for more from him.

"What could you possibly be in here smiling about when I'm out there stressed the hell out, trying to get your ex to leave?"

"My baby."

"Figures. You so sprung," she laughed. "Just smiling and shit for no reason. That nigga got you."

"I am and I can't even fuckin lie, he does," I was blushing so hard I covered my face to hide it from her.

"Oh my gosh Jax. You are a mess. Look at you," she was crackin' up. I couldn't stop the giddy feeling inside of me from boiling over. Sih had me around here walking on cloud nine and I will forever be grateful. I was supposed to be at home crying about how my life was falling apart but instead he had me around this bitch grinning and glowing.

"When I tell you, he treats me like a Queen Zionna, I can't even fully put it all into words. He waits on me hand and foot, buys me whatever I want, gives me full body massages daily, whispers the sweetest affirmations to me as I lay in his arms; I still get flowers delivered to my office every day, and every morning when I wake up he tells me to feed him his breakfast. I climb on his face and he feasts. Sometimes, like today, it's for hours bitch."

"Wow."

"I knooow. I feel like I'm dreaming."

"Awww. I'm loving it boo. They don't make 'em like Nash and Sih anymore. Speaking of Nash, he gave me a fuckin ultimatum and I couldn't believe it," she poured a glass of wine and sat down.

"When?"

"Yesterday. Well last night before we left each other. We were at the club house chillin' with The Knights and he called me back to his office. He was lookin sexy and shit, so I get down on my knees and give him a lil lip service. We been on one all week. I don't know what's been going on with us, but we can't keep our hands off of each other. Anyway, when I get up, he's just staring at me so I'm like *what?* He stands up and gets in my face and say *you must think I'm a hoe ass nigga.* Girl he shocked the hell out of me, and I was all confused and shit. I mean, I just gave him head that I knew was fire okay, and now he's all in my damn face. He's like *how long do you think I'm about to be your side nigga? How long you think I'm going to let you keep laying my pussy next to that nigga at night?* Girl I shook my head slowly not even knowing how the hell to respond to that or where the hell it was stemming from. He took my face into his hands and said, *get rid of that nigga or we're done. I'm too selfish for the bullshit that you're on. Girl,*" She rolled her eyes. "Like how do you just go from zero to a hundred like that?"

"First of all, if the head was as fire as you, that's what sparked it. You ain't about to be suckin' dick that good and going home to someone else. Tuh... You got bro fucked up." We both laughed hysterically. "I ain't surprised at all though. I told you that's how Sih was starting to act. When that nigga said he gets what he wants, he was not bullshittin' and I'm sure Nash is the same way."

"But here's the thing, Quan has really changed in the last few months that I've been messing around with Nashon. Now I'm confused. I don't know-"

"Unt uh. Let me stop you right there. Nash is in, Quan is out. You know damn well Quan hasn't changed in real life. He probably just noticed you're not checkin' for him so he's trying to be on his best behavior before you drop his ass. How can you see that I deserve better, but you can't see that you do too?"

"Aww that was sweet Sissy Pooh," she smiled and blew me a kiss.

"Whatever. Just tell Nash that Quan is done. Secure your position in Nashon's life," I sipped my wine. "So, I ran into Porsha at the mall today and she invited me to Bridget's party, wanna go?"

"I'm good luv, enjoy."

"Don't do that. I really want you to go. Why do you act like that?"

"Because you always bringing random hoes around and we always end up beatin' they ass. You annoyin', say I'm lying Jax," she put her hands on her hips and pressed her lips together challenging me and I smacked my lips.

"Who Z?" I laughed.

"Shanae, Talitha, that one chick from college Preena, Jay, April-"

"Oooookay!" I was in tears from crackin' up. I really hadn't thought about it like that and she make me sick for reminding me of how friendly my ass can be sometimes. People used to swear I was mean but that wasn't the case at all. I just had a resting bitch face; I was always bringing chicks around though.

"Bitches be fake, and we don't roll like that."

"That's facts but they not new, so just come to the got damn party with me Z. Damn. Funny actin ass."

"What time bitch?"

"I need a drink, so I want to go early. Be ready around nine."

"Okay."

"Alright boo. I'm about to get out of here. I need a nap first. You know my ass ain't used to going out," I hugged her and left.

Zionna

I went upstairs and grabbed my phone so I could call Nash to tell him where my head was. After talking to my sister, I knew for a fact that she was right. Quan's ass was never going to change for real. He gives me just enough to keep me and then fucks up again. I've been down this road with him far too many times to pass up on Nash, who is showing me what a real man is. I love Quan, I really do, but we're toxic and at this point in my life, I need more, and more is something that he can't provide. There will always be another bitch, another lie, another disease, another disappointment, and that's not hardly what I need more of.

"Hey baby. I'm riding my bike, hold on." His background was loud. "Hello," he got back on the phone.

"Baby what did I tell you about riding on the bike and talking on the phone?"

"I made everybody pull over for you ma. That's why I put you on hold."

I smiled from deep within. "Thanks. I needed to talk to you, but it can wait."

"We already on the side of the road now baby. I'm listening."

"I'm going to tell him it's over today. It's you that I want, and I didn't mean to make you feel like a side nigga at all. I hope you know you mean more to me than that Nash."

"I do. I also knew what I was getting myself into when you said you had a nigga but what we're building is real and I can't have another nigga that close to what's mine. Feel me?"

"Yeah baby, I get it."

"Good. You might as well do what Jaxsyn did and leave all that shit there and come stay with daddy."

"Umm it's too soon for all that na," I laughed.

"Says who? Baby you should know by now that I don't live by everyone else's rules. I make my own."

"What if it doesn't work Nash?"

"What? Us? This is it for you. You ain't going nowhere else. Who yo ass tryna' get killed baby?" He laughed. "Fuck you mean?"

"You are crazy."

"I'm dead ass serious too. Pack whatever the fuck you need or leave all that shit there and I'll see you at *home* tonight when I get back. You still got the key right?"

"Yeah."

"Bet, I'll talk to you later baby."

"Alright. Be careful."

"Always," I hung up and jumped up and down. I had my reservations but waking up next to Nash everyday was an ideal situation for me. Of course, his morning wood came to mind first, but there was no denying that I was falling for him. We don't talk feelings and shit, but I knew he was feeling the same way. His actions always proved exactly how he was feeling.

Coming from the piss poor ass projects and low-income housing that me and my sister grew up in, we were actually doing great and living our best lives. Once we left our mommas house, I vowed never to live like that again, and so far, both me and Jax has stuck to that promise we made many years ago. We knew we never wanted to allow history to repeat itself and we were succeeding. We had careers that we worked our asses off to secure, men that adored us, clothes that we could only dream of back in the day or had to steal, money in the bank, and our health. We were winning and this move with Nashon was my reality check. He was moving me into a mini mansion and showing me that he wanted a future with me. After all the pain that I suffered throughout the years, I was finally getting my happiness. God is good and I was ready to celebrate with my sister.

****

I heard Jax blowing the horn and I ran down the steps. I was running late as usual, but I needed a nap before going out too. Overall, we hated clubs and sometimes, it was hard to even stay awake unless it's really hype. There's no way we could survive the night without our nap.

"Hey boo," I sat down.

"Hey. You look cute," she smiled and pulled off.

"Thanks. Okay, soooo I talked to Nashon and he wants me to move in with him," I looked over at her waiting for her reaction.

"Girl they move so fast. Sih wouldn't even let me say no. They give you the mean dick and then get you to say yes to whatever the fuck they want."

"That's exactly what it is. You think a nigga with no meat can make demands? Girl bye. I woulda slapped his shrimp dick havin' ass down like you did Black." We died laughing. "I'm dead serious, but listen, Zaddy say pack so I'm packing my shit bihhhh."

"Yesssss! So, when does he want you to move in?"

"Tonight. He ain't playing no games with me. He said you might as well do what Jaxsyn did and leave all that shit there."

"Might as well. It's working for me," she beamed.

"You already know I am. We're celebrating the level up tonight!" We high fived. "I have a few things I'm keeping but girl, out with the old and in with the new. Speaking of old, I told Quan already."

"What?" She looked shocked. Hell, I was shocked too.

"He came home after I got off the phone with Nash and I told him. He said he's been hearing shit, so he figured it was coming. He was calm and I kinda felt bad. He wished me well and that was pretty much it. No fussing, no questions, no nothing."

"See," She started shaking her head and her nose flared. "He ain't no better than Black's no good ass. He got a bitch somewhere off in the cut and you just made shit easier for him to do him. That was way too fuckin' calm for me. Y'all been together 10 years and all the nigga can say is 'okay, have a great life'?"

"I didn't even think about that but you're right. He didn't trip at all and I was so happy not to argue with him that I didn't even give a shit about the reason why," I chuckled to myself as we got out. "I can't even lie and say I care. Oooo you look really pretty," I was able to take in her whole outfit and sis was shutting shit down tonight. Her body was killing these industry thots and she was all natural. Kabrina came through on the genes. She was wearing an Angel Brinks body suit that hugged her body like a glove and the Loubs she was rocking matched perfectly. Jax hair has always been long and it was bone straight hanging past her bra strap. The beat was light and flawless, and she kept her accessories simple since the outfit spoke for itself.

"Thanks baby."

"You're the only chick I know that can kill one pieces the way that you do. You a whole fuckin' hourglass out here sis. I wish I had that fuckin body," I slapped her on the butt, and it jiggled. I wasn't struggling in the body department at all. I'm what people call slim thick. My upper body was slender, but I had a nice bubble butt and thighs that fit my frame. My sister on the other hand was thick-thick. That ass was serious, and she didn't have no stomach or waist which accentuated her ass and thighs even more. She used to hate that shit because when we were kids grown ass men were checkin' for her constantly, but she embraced it in college and I'm happy she did. She's a beast and she needed to own it.

"You're perfect exactly the way you are," she nudged me, and I smiled.

We didn't go out often, but we're known enough that when we go out, we don't have to stand in lines or pay. Jax waved to the bouncer and we walked right in. The vibe was nice and we both started bobbing our heads to the music. She looked around for her friend Porsha that she ran into earlier in the mall and I heard her before I could even see her. Porsha is one of those people you either love or hate and I hadn't decided where I fell in that category. She's a sweetheart but she's annoyingly loud and that's irritating. I was so happy that she made our drinks, pointed to Bridget, and then went back to entertaining the people that was in their section.

"Happy Birthday Bridget!" Jax yelled and we all exchanged hugs.

"Thanks Boo. I was so happy when Porsha said she ran into you. I haven't seen y'all since high school. Y'all bitches still flawless."

"Thanks Love. What you been up too?"

"Nothing. I have a three-year-old daughter. Y'all probably know my baby daddy Gert. He's a Knight or whateva."

"Nah, we don't," I shrugged. Ugh… That was so tacky. *'He's a Knight'*, giiiiirl bye!

"Oh okay. Well he'll be here tonight. They should be pulling up soon. She looks just like him, they so cute y'all. Soooo cute, and he loves her lil butt so much," she said proudly and Jax was eating it up but all I heard was this bitch bragging not knowing that we're fucking the President and Vice President while she's trying to stunt. This is what I mean about the randoms. I just can't with them…

"Awww, I'm happy for you Bridge." We both smiled.

"Thanks, y'all. Let's go turn up. Don't just be the pretty barbies on the wall, it's my birthday so we gotta show out," she grabbed our hands and pulled us to the dance floor. I had no desire to dance but fuck it, I'm celebrating. We both threw our hands up with her and danced. Porsha brought us another drink and after a while I was tipsy enough to unwind and have fun.

"Get it bitch," I laughed and cheered Jaxsyn on. She had hit Bridget's blunt and she was tipsy too. Her ass was cuttin' up on the dance floor. I hadn't saw her uptight ass this relaxed in years. I loved everything that Sih was bringing out of her.

Jaxsyn

Reality hit me while I was on the dance floor and I got really excited. For the first time in my life I was genuinely happy. No pretending. No acting. No fake shit. My career was soaring, my family loved me, I had money in the bank, and Sih made me feel like the only woman in the universe. Everything about my life was authentically aligning and I felt blessed. *Cheers to new beginnings!*

"Ayyyeeee!" Zionna yelled as I bounced my ass to the beat. I was living in the moment and not caring about the crowd that was gathered around us. Life was good and tonight that reality hit me hard. "Yeeeeah Jax! My baby unfuckwitable," I laughed at my sister and the best hype girl ever. She always gasses me, and I love her for it. Right when I was about to take a break the DJ threw on our boo Kash Doll and it was no sitting us down.

Cause man, now days, hoes hatin' so hard
But live in a small ass crib
With a ham ass nigga
And some bad ass kids
With a shitty ass car
Drive that bitch every day to your shitty ass job
Haaa
Yeah, Boss up bitch

Me and my sister was going hard as hell rapping her lyrics word for word in each other's face like we were at a concert. We honestly hadn't had this much fun in years.

"I'm tired y'all and my baby daddy just got here," Bridget interrupted our vibe.

"Okay hun," I waved to her and she walked away. "Does she seem a little clingy to you?" I asked Zionna.

"Very, but she's always been that way."

"Oh. I never noticed."

"I bet," she rolled her eyes at me. I laughed and pushed her playfully. I guess she had a point with the randoms, so I'll fall back on the new friends and shit.

I felt my phone vibrate so I checked it.

My Heart: *Don't make me fuck you up Ma!*

Me: *What?*

My Heart: *Get yo ass over here… Daddy's home*

I smiled and turned around. "Awww my baby is here sis. Come on," I pulled Zionna and she was just as excited. She knew if Sih was back, then so was Nash. They had us out here jonesing over their asses.

"Hey Jaxsyn." Bridget grabbed my arm as I was walking by. "This is Gert. My baby daddy."

"Oh. I do know Gert. I couldn't put the face and the name together bro. We just always call you G."

"Y'all know it's all love ladies," he chuckled and hugged us both. "Y'all good?"

"Yup, let me get up here to him before he spaz. You know how he gets," I smiled.

"Who?" Bridge asked.

"Messiah," I walked away and left her standing and wondering.

"Thank you. She deserved that with her bragging ass."

"I peep *some* shit, but I play the game and let bitches embarrass themselves," I winked at her and walked up to my baby.

"Hey Bae," I smiled as he looked me up and down.

"Get yo' sexy ass over here Tink." Sih pulled me closer and hovered over me looking good as hell. His light brown eyes were sitting low from smoking and he was biting down on his bottom lip. He had a black NY fitted cocked to the side, resting on his freshly braided hair and I was salivating. My horny ass can't ever get enough of him and my kitty instantly started throbbing. I wrapped my arms around his neck and started running my fingertips through his braids. The sex appeal this man possesses is insane. I brought his face closer to mine and kissed him like I hadn't laid eyes on him in years. I couldn't resist those smooth pink pillow soft lips. I wiped my lip gloss off of him and he turned me around, placing my back around his chest. His strong arms circled my waist and I melted into his embrace.

"Hey Sih!" Two randoms said in unison and he threw a head nod their way as he grabbed my neck causing me to look up over my shoulder at him. He placed an amorous kiss on my lips, and we stared at each other for a moment, escaping into our own little world, while he stroked the side of my face. Damn I loved this man deep.

"I love you so fuckin' much Tink," he said as if he read my mind and I smiled.

"I love you too Baby," I pecked his lips again before we tuned back into the party. We looked out at all his people and a sense of pride filled my chest. When I was with him, I got so much respect. He was the King of his world and people treated us like royalty. He elevated me so much and I was starting to relish in all of our glory. I was embracing this lifestyle again but this time it felt good.

"Aye, we 'bout to get up outta here." Nash and Zionna walked up about an hour later and her intentions were written all over her face. She was horny and ready to go.

"Yeah we are too." The guys dapped each other and we hugged.

"Do you feel what's happening Jax? I'm scared. This feels too real," she whispered.

"I feel it and it's definitely real hun. Embrace it Z. Go home to your new house and fuck that nigga like he's the last one on earth. Talk to you tomorrow," I kissed her cheek and waved.

"I didn't know we were about to go."

"How long you expect my dick to stay hard without sliding inside of you?"

"Mmmm since you put it like that, let's go then nasty," I smiled and took his hand into mine. We went around the section and told everyone bye before sliding right out of the back door. He doesn't like going to clubs either, but he always tries to show his face and support his people. It's one of the things that I adore about him. He has so many layers and he gives me access to them all. I couldn't wait to get his fine ass home.

****

Sih and I spent the whole night making love only for my mother to call my phone repeatedly at six am for me to take her to work. By the time I answered, her ass had already called me nine times, sent fourteen text messages, and irritated the hell out of Messiah. His face was barely dry from my nectar when that first call came in and he grunted in his sleep. By the time that last call came in he was all the way annoyed, but he didn't say anything. He turned his back to me and threw the covers over his head like a kid. When you're in love with someone every damn thing they do is cute because that made me smile from ear to ear and it probably shouldn't have since I knew he was really tired.

I was damn near seeing double I was so sleepy, but I got up and got dressed for her anyway. She's changed her life and I promised no matter what happened in our past, her efforts within the last two years will always mean more to me than those prior years. It didn't matter to me that she waited so long or failed previously. All that mattered is that she's changed now and it's a change that I can believe in. This was very different from her brief ninety day in and out of rehab stints that she's done my whole life. She was two years strong and baby girl is very serious about her sobriety.

When I pulled up to her house all I could do was shake my head. Her and Zionna's momma Sandy went from pals on the pipe to outright enemies. Kabrina can't stand Sandy's ass and Sandy is still heavily in these Detroit streets doing her thing so her level of petty when she hasn't had that hit yet, is like no other. They literally stay into it.

"Kabrina!" I yelled. "Let her hair go." Just that quick my momma had yoked Sandy's lil frail ass up but instead of her trying to fight back, Sandy was crackin' up and doing some leg wiggle shit that she's been doing since I was a kid.

"Now why would you call this bitch over here? What, y'all about to jump me or something?" All the shits and giggles were over with. Sandy's never liked me, and she didn't try to pretend too. She doesn't acknowledge me as Zionna's sister just like the rest of our siblings, and she damn sure hates that I wouldn't allow her random John's to touch my sister when we were growing up.

"Bitch jump you for what? I'll dog walk yo' ass by my damn self, right here, right now."

"Kabrina, let's go. I thought you had to go to work," I was prying her hands out of Sandy's hair.

"Bitch get a job and think she's the shit. I see it all the time with you fake ass hoes. Were you the shit when you were shoving that pussy in my face Brina?" Sandy laughed and started snappy her fingers like the best song she ever heard came on. "Mmhmm. Tell your child that you think you love more than I love mine, all about our white slave master ass baby daddy making you ride my face while you sucked his dick! Oooooo wee, but you so high and mighty now huh sista Brina? I wonder if the people in your new congregation wanna know how that pussy taste." She raised her hands. "Thank ya for the nourishment Lawd!" She moved her feet like she was doing a praise dance but my momma still had her hair. This shit was wild and she was crackin' up the whole time but Kabrina's face had turned fifty shades of red. I didn't have time for this shit, and I saw Kabrina balling up her fist ready to lay hands on Sandy again. I pulled my momma so hard she didn't have no other choice but to let Sandy go. This was the fuckery I moved away from and why I wanted no parts of this life. I've had enough of this dysfunction for a lifetime. I guess Sandy doesn't remember telling this same story a million times when we were younger. Both Z and I are well aware of the threesomes that used to take place between her, my mother, and our father. Shit, she's even told my step mother Rebecca about it. We're all "in the know" now, thanks to Sandy.

"I fuckin' hate her." My momma slammed her body down into my passenger seat. "Who plays with God like that with her stupid ass? Ugh! Do you know she cut my fuckin' spark plugs Jax? Now that's some more money that I have to spend when I didn't budget for it! I have to go buy the part and then pay Rahlo to fix it. All because this hoe is jealous. Jealous! I ain't even got shit to be jealous of. Hell, I'm struggling like everyone else. That damn house is so old it's falling apart and she's out here cutting my spark plugs like I ain't got enough shit to worry about," she went to light a cigarette and I pointed to the window. I hated that smell more than anything and she knew it. There was no argument she just hit the button to roll the window down and then lit it.

"You need to move out of that house and away from her."

"With what money baby? I'm doing the best that I can right now and look," she threw her hands in the air and slapped them down on her thighs. "Now I have more shit to spend money on that I didn't plan for, but whatever man. Karma don't skip over nobody and I'm overdue for mine." It looked like she wanted to cry, and I felt bad for her. She really was trying, and I wanted to help. I knew it was going to be a struggle though. Since the beginning of her sobriety she's struggled with guilt when it comes to her parenting. She really beats herself up and it's nothing anyone can say or do to change how she feels. It probably killed her just to call and ask me for a ride which is another reason I didn't mind getting up and coming.

We've had a million bad days but there were a few good ones in there that I'll hold on to forever. I tried explaining that to her, but it goes over her head. She's far more hurt about her behavior throughout the years than I imagined she would be. My concern is her hurting herself or turning back to drugs to aide in the pain she feels. She came too far and worked too hard to allow the past to haunt her the way that it does. Hell, most of the time she can't even look me in my eyes and it's sad.

"It doesn't look like many people are here," I said as I pulled into the parking lot.

"It's not. A lot of people are off on weekends but a few of us are going into the community today so it'll be more that show up a little later. Thanks so much Jaxsyn, I really appreciate this baby," she dug in her purse and pulled out a ten-dollar bill. "Put this in your tank Love."

"Kabrina," I stopped her. Instead of allowing her to give me money that she didn't have to spare, I dug in my bag and passed her a wad of cash that Sih had given me. "I don't know exactly how much this is, but it should be at least five thousand dollars there. Get away from that toxic environment and get your car fixed."

"Hell no! You know I can't ta-"

"All I know is that you need to take this money and do what I just said do. You deserve a break, and this is the first step in getting one. Move away from that negativity and fix your car," she looked away from me. "Just please take it," I grabbed her hand and put the money inside.

She started crying. "I can't Jaxsyn. This puts me further in debt with you. I've depleted you after everything I've done, and my main focus now is to make sure-"

"Stop Kabrina. Despite everything, I turned out alright. On your highest days you made sure I was clean and ready for school. I mean, if you were home, and not bitchin', but you know…" I smiled to lighten the mood. "Everything wasn't all bad all the time, and I'm straight. You didn't deplete me, drain me, or anything else. Yes, shit was bad sometimes, but we made it. Both of us. Go get a place and get that car fixed lady."

"Thank you so much!" She hugged me tightly and then wiped her face. I watched as she gathered all her stuff and opened the door. My mother was still gorgeous after everything she has put herself through. Smooth peanut butter skin, long gorgeous jet-black hair, and the weight she gained had her body sicker than ever. Now more than ever we looked just alike, and it brought a smile to my face. "Call me Kabrina again and I'm going to slap you the fuck down," she got out and we both laughed hysterically.

"Kabrinnnnaaaa!" I yelled out the window as I drove off, still crackin' up. Some shit doesn't change while other things change completely.

Messiah

Out of all my businesses, the Motorcycle Club is the one that's nearest and dearest to my brother and me. The Knights have two faces and we cater to both. On the back end we're pushing more pharmaceuticals than actual pharmaceutical companies, and then on the surface we're a legitimate Motorcycle Club that rides through the streets of our city, serves the best drinks out of our club, and looks out for our community. Everyone in The Knights play a role and that means a lot of niggas don't know about what's happening on the back end. That's exactly how we want it. We have city officials in our pockets but it's always a do-good ass cop lurking and hating. I'm a twenty-five-year-old black man with several well-established businesses and a net worth of more than most cops will see in their entire life. They hate our black asses and pray we fuck up. That's why it was important to have people throughout my entire organization that didn't know shit about shit and just ran our business legitimately.

To whom much is given much is expected so we make sure that we're doing what needs to be done in the community too. We weren't always selling pills to rich white people and we didn't want to be like other niggas that fuck over their own people and then move out to the suburbs and forget about the lives that was ruined. People are grown and they're going to do whatever they want to do so if they weren't coppin' from us it would be someone else and we get that, but we were products of a drug addict and we weren't about to let little kids grow up like us. The blocks we grew up on are the safest in the city, we give kids book bags filled with all the school supplies they could dream of, we donate to their schools, kids have toys for Christmas and birthdays, we give turkeys out for Thanksgiving, throw block parties; one is coming up pretty soon. We make shit happen and looked out for everyone.

That's one reason that the shit that went down with Rodney and Martez a few weeks back had me lookin' at niggas sideways. I never had to doubt the people we had around us because my niggas had been solid for years. One bad move made me realize how much you really don't know muthafuckas. We do everything for people and that was how they returned the love. No matter what, Nash and I look out for our niggas and the hood in general, so it just seemed like this shit was bigger than them just stealing from us. This was bigger than greed and I could feel it. I had been wrecking my brain over this shit since it happened and kept coming up short. This type of drama is why I wanted to focus more on our legitimate businesses and back away from this pharmaceutical shit completely. Nigga's been sleep on this pill industry for years and we were able to stack millions off of it but now they were getting hip to selling more than Percs and that made us a target. Nash wasn't ready yet and I would never leave my brother alone with these niggas, but we definitely needed to come up with an exit strategy. Niggas was showing their true colors and I wasn't feeling it.

I left the warehouse pissed than a bitch because Mariah's punk ass had called my phone eighty-one times and drained my fuckin' battery. I'm in the middle of handling business and this bitch is in her feelings, texting and calling my phone over and over on some petty shit. I hadn't even noticed that my phone died until after the meeting I was holding, was over. I knew my girl had called and since Mariah's stupid ass was doing the most, Jax was probably worried about me. It didn't take much.

I plugged my phone in and as soon as it powered on, I called my baby. "Hello," her voice was angelic.

"Hey baby. My phone died."

"I figured that, but I was still worried about you Bae."

"I know. My bad sweetheart. What you into?"

"I'm with my little sisters."

"Little sisters?"

"Yeah, Lyss and Syd."

"I just thought it was you and Z."

"Nah, she wish though. Me and Zionna have the same dad and different mothers. My daddy has four other kids with his wife Rebecca who he used to cheat on with our mothers. We have two older brothers Jagger and Dawson, and two younger sisters, Alyssa and Sydnee."

"Jagger and Dawson though?" I chuckled at how corny and lame they sound.

"Shut up. They're white. My father and his wife are white, he just grew up in the hood because he has black people in his family. He got swag and shit, so he thinks he's cool," she giggled. "I love them all the same as I love Z though and she hates it."

"Damn. That must make shit real uncomfortable since y'all so close."

"You have no idea baby. Her mother never acknowledged them as her siblings, and she would never let Zionna go over their house. When my dad came to pick me up her mother would make her go in the house and shit. Just dumb. Z really doesn't know them at all and the times that she was around, she acted a fool. My dad still loves the ground she walks on though; he's just a really dope ass father like that. He'll never stop trying with her."

"Real man shit right there. Ain't neither one of my parents worth shit. My OG sent us to live with my granny because her ass wanted to do her and who the fuck even knows who our dad is or was. I don't know if the nigga is dead or alive."

"Some parents just ain't shit. I'll share my father with you baby."

"I appreciate you Tinker Bell but I'm too old for all that now." We both laughed.

"You're never too old for genuine love Sih."

"Yeah, I hear you sweetheart."

"Well, I stepped away from the table to take your call and I'm being rude, but I'll see you later."

"Bet. Have fun."

"I will. Love you baby."

"I love you too beautiful." We hung up and I shook my head. Mariah had called me nine fuckin' times while I was talking to Jax and another call was coming in now. "Man, what the fuck do you want?" I yelled at her stupid ass.

"What do I want? Are you fuckin' serious right now Sih?"

"I'm dead ass serious. What the fuck do you want Mariah and make that shit quick before I hang up on you."

She sarcastically chuckled to herself. "You could have been anything in this world Sih and you chose to be a fuck nigga, huh? Congratulations, you're a clown."

Now it was my turn to laugh. This bitch had to be as crazy as everybody kept telling me she was for years. Man… Good pussy can be blinding but when those fuckin' blinders come off and these hoes get exposed, it's no going back. "If I'm a clown why are you trying to be a part of my circus Riah? That says a lot about you. My fuckin' phone battery died because you decided to call my clown ass a hundred times today. I told yo' ass we were over and here you are, still on this fuck nigga line."

"We ain't never going to be over so let's not act brand fuckin' new. I told you I was sorry, so just let this shit go Sih. Damn… I fucked up when I slapped that bitch and I know it. In my defense though, I was pissed off at your ass once again. As usual you were trying to play me, and I hopped in my bag. You know I don't like people questioning me and all in my personal space when I'm mad. I've been at your house enough for Tabitha's ass to know when we're going through something, I need to be left the hell alone."

"So, you slapped her because she should have known better than to be in your space? That's whack as fuck, especially when all she was trying to tell you was that I left a message for you. I wasn't home because I was out planning something special for your unappreciative ass. Our vibe had been off for weeks because I was working so much, and I left a note upstairs that I told her to make sure you got. She tried to tell you about the note, and you slapped her down like she wasn't shit. The people that make my house function may just be staff to you, but they're fuckin' family to me. You violated and I'm done."

"You're not done, you're dramatic. We have too much history for you to just throw us away like that. I'll apologize to her again baby. Stop fuckin' trippin'. This is the longest we've gone without each other and I miss your stupid ass Messiah. I know you miss me too baby. Let's wave the white flags and get back to being us."

"Nah. Actually I don't miss you and I'm completely done this time so it's no need to wave shit. Fuck our history and fuck you. No more games, no more bullshit, no more dumb ass arguments, no more of you thinking you run shit. I'm with someone else and I'm happier than I've ever been. Enjoy your life," I hung up and blocked her.

Mariah's problem is something I created. I allowed her to get away with thinking she was running shit when she wasn't. I fucked with her heavy for years, but she's always been toxic and since her pussy was good, I gave a lot of her behaviors a pass. She's used to clowning and showing her ass but this time her actions got her replaced. Over the years, when we fell out, after a few weeks or sometimes a couple months, she pops back up and all is forgiven. She gets rid of whatever bitch I may be fuckin' around with and we go right back to the same dysfunction that we're both accustomed too. Seeing her hand print on Tabitha's face changed that. When I told her to get the fuck out of my crib, I meant forever. That same night I had all the locks and key codes changed. That's when Nash really knew I was serious this time and I wasn't just pissed on some temporary feelings type shit. Mariah played herself.

While other muthafuckas chose to spend their money on material shit like cars, shoes, and clothes, I chose to get a crib and a staff. We grew up poor because my granny took care of most of her children's kids. She worked her ass off taking care of nine growing boys in a three-bedroom house. When the bread started coming in, we bought her house and I started saving for mine. Growing up sharing one bathroom with that many people made me desire space and a lot of it. The people that take care of my home, essentially takes care of me, and I'll never allow them to be disrespected by anyone.

My brother hit my line right before I got on the freeway to head home and told me to fall through. He was in the hood chillin' with a few of our niggas and since I knew Jax wasn't home yet, I told him that I would fall through. I was tired as shit though, so I let him know quick that I wasn't staying long. I didn't have the energy to pull an all-nighter with these niggas plus that posted up hood scene was getting old to me anyway. I've hugged the block enough over the years to learn to appreciate the solitude and peace that my home brings. Especially now that Jaxsyn has been staying with me. It's nothing better than chilling with my lady, laid up all day watching movies and making love. She rolls over riding my dick at will or giving me head. That's something that I'll trade this block shit for in a minute.

"This nigga stays saucin' on muthafuckas." Solo, our second in command dapped me as soon as I walked up. Nash and I don't see each other as number one and number two, we do shit equally so we call him our second and everyone respects him as the second.

"Shid nigga, I don't know no other way." We laughed and I dapped the rest of my niggas and then walked down to where Nash was standing. He looked pissed off, so I was immediately ready for war. "What's up? Some shit happened?" I asked.

"Man naw. I'm good," he hit the blunt hard as fuck and I chuckled to myself.

"That wasn't an 'I'm good' pull nigga. Fuck wrong with you?"

"Toya's stupid ass just left from over here. You already know how that shit go."

"She showed her ass huh?"

"Doesn't she always? I told that bitch she was really forcing my hand bro. I ain't never wanted to slap fire from a bitch so bad. She better be glad I didn't pay lil Tiffany crazy ass to fuck her up. Look at this shit," he held his phone up and his screen was shattered.

"Damn. What she do that for? I thought you wasn't fuckin' with her like that?"

"When the fuck has that ever mattered to her or Mariah?" His nostrils flared and he hit his blunt again before passing it to me. "She pulled up on me talking about I was acting brand new like she didn't hold me down when I did my bid."

"What?" I started cracking the fuck up. Three years ago, this nigga did five months in county before our lawyers got him out on a technicality.

"Bro you already know I looked at this broad like she was stupid. She in her feelings about Zionna. One of her hatin' ass friends sent her some pictures of us out but like I told her; I'm single as a dollar bill and I don't have to answer to no fuckin' body. Fuck she thought this was?"

"Real talk," I passed the blunt back. "You and Z ain't gone make shit official tho'?"

"Hell yeah, that's my fuckin' baby but we both just got out of some shit and I want to get this shit right with her. Plus, I need to know that nigga is out of her system before they make me catch a couple bodies."

"On God." We dapped. I felt him on that shit. We play about a lot of shit but our money and our pussy ain't one. Once I stake claim to a female every other nigga she ever knew before me is a non fuckin' factor in her life. Jax's pussy ass ex used to hit her line but she never answered and then she blocked his ass. I wanted to see how she handled it before I said anything, and she did exactly what I wanted her to do without me saying a word. That nigga don't have no reason to hit her line and I better not find out he's in her dm's and shit either.

I told Nashon about Mariah and the nigga told me he was proud of me. I couldn't do shit but laugh it off because not only did Mariah get used to the back and forth shit between us, but everyone around us did too. Every time I said, "fuck her" everybody would be like "here they go again."

"Ain't that her on the corner?" I turned around and looked behind me. She had just hit her blinker to come our way. I shook my head and told Nash I would hit him later. I hopped in the whip and burned out before she could even make it all the way down the block. I said I was done, and I meant it.

Black

Drinking had become an everyday thing. I couldn't remember the last time I had been to my shop or even left my house. Ray texted and left voicemails with updates, but I was focused on other shit. Like how much I was missing and craving my wife. I needed her touch, her love, her mere existence. I don't know where she's living, if she's still hurting, was she still with that nigga, was he touching her body that used to solely belong to me… the unknown was fuckin' with my head. I wanted to go up to her office to hopefully catch her coming or going. I thought about it for days, but knowing her, she'll call the police on me if I show up there. Never in a million years did I imagine having to live my life without her. I missed my baby so much it physically hurt.

Yeah, I was dead fuckin' wrong and the list of shit I've done wrong while we were together is longer than most are even aware of and damn sure too much for me to get into, but damn man… I didn't think she would leave me. Hell, I didn't think she would ever find out. I played some dirty ass games over the years, but I always hid the shit well. I guess I got too comfortable. Too used to doing her dirty, and now karma was here to collect. My life had become the living proof that what happens in the dark, always comes to the light. My shit came to the light and my baby left my ass in the dark.

"You're not even getting hard Black. Are you thinking about that bitch again?" Ty raised his head from my lap, and I pushed him away from me. I got up with my limp dick still swinging and went to the kitchen for another drink. I hated watching him walk around me and Jaxsyn's house freely, but I also didn't want to be alone. The loneliness and quiet was killing a nigga softly. It was either go over Shardae's house and deal with her poppin' her gums and irritating me, stay in this bitch and be lonely, or allow Ty to come over and try to mend my broken heart. Obviously, I chose the latter.

"So, you're just going to ignore me? Are we going to do this every day until that bitch is out of your system?" Before I knew it, my right hand was firmly wrapped around Ty's neck and I had him pinned up against the refrigerator. The fact that he was here after the shit he pulled

104

should have had his ass walking on eggshells, but this nigga was hell bent on trying to make me hate my wife and secure his spot in my life.

"Watch your fuckin' mouth when you're speaking on her and I'm not going to say it again," I said through gritted teeth.

"Oh, you mean the wife that was cheating on you? The wife that brought a nigga into this very home that y'all shared? The wife that walks around like she's perfect but is dating the biggest drug dealing gangster in the fuckin' city? That wife Derrick? I just want to be clear about who we're talking about?" He pushed me away from him. "I think fuckin' not! Fuck her and whatever raggedy bitch that birthed her cheatin' ass. How is she mad at you when she was playing the same damn games, and how are you this hurt about losing someone that you ain't never been faithful to? You admitted that you weren't even faithful in high school sooo, tuh..." He rolled his eyes and neck. "You're around here drinking and smoking your life away when I'm standing right in front of you. I'm telling you it's okay to stay in the fuckin' closet as long as you need too. I'm telling you that all the fuck I want is you. I'm even telling you that I'll accept your fuckin' child that you're having by a nineteen-year-old gold digger," he pushed me up against the refrigerator like I had just did to him and snatched the ice cold bottle of Henny from my hand, slamming it on the table behind him.

"Focus on what's important." His tone had me getting hard. "Focus on me. Please Derrick. This is finally our time to do us. No guilt from having a girlfriend in a different state. No creeping behind anyone's back or dipping around corners. Just you..." He kissed me. "And me..." Another kiss. "Doing what lovers do," he dropped to his knees in front of me. He stared up at me and I needed this moment. I did exactly what he asked and focused on him. We went round for round, pound for pound, but as soon as I busted my last nut and put his ass to sleep, I was right back in my feelings, right back to thinking about my wife, and right back on the couch with my Henny in my hand, wallowing in my fuck up. As much love as I have for Ty, he could never replace Jaxsyn.

****

I stared at Shardae as she paced back and forth in her living room gossiping on the phone to her momma and her best friend Nedra. I hadn't been over in a few days and I knew if I didn't get my ass over here soon, she was going to throw a fit. Much like the one she was throwing now but thank God it wasn't directed at me. They had some hood drama poppin' off and her pregnant ass was amped up and going in. As I listened to her and watched her prop the phone between her ear and shoulder to punch her hand repeatedly, I regretted even fuckin' with her. Every day since Jax left me I've been really realizing that the shit I was pulling behind her back wasn't worth it.

Jax is classy and educated but still has the right amount of hood in her and a savage that she keeps hidden well. My baby was everything I needed, and I threw what we had away. I wanted the more hood version of Jax because that's what I was used to but what didn't register at the time was that she was elevating us. I was stagnant, and for what? We came from syrup sandwiches and sugarless Kool-Aid that she stole from the grocery store and when I got out of jail my baby was cooking us shit like butter poached lobster and asparagus for dinner. Hindsight is definitely twenty-twenty.

Momma Brina: *Please stop calling me boy. I just saw I had five missed calls from you. That's ridiculous Derrick!*

Me: *Ma please. I love her and I just need to see her!*

Momma Brina: *You don't love my daughter. According to your side nigga she was just a place holder. Keep that same energy.*

Me: *I fucked up and I can admit that, but I need my wife and I'm sick as hell without her*

Momma Brina: *Get well soon… Have that nigga to nurse you back to health. I'm sure he's able and willing… stop calling and texting me Derrick!*

I shook my head and laid back. Once again, I took in the scene around me much like I did this morning before I left Ty at my house. This wasn't what I wanted. I would give anything to walk into my crib and see my Jax cooking dinner for me naked with nothing but stilettos on. Dropping to her knees on sight just to welcome me home. I called her a prude for taking care of home and staying out of the way. I left her at home, alone, and chose random bitches over our Netflix and chill nights. I made my bed and now she was making my dog ass sleep in it.

"I'll be over there in a minute. I want that bitch to say that shit to my face." Shardae ended her call and snatched her keys off the table.

"Man, who is your pregnant ass trying to pull up on?"

"This one bitch that used to stay with my momma! That hoe is over there tal-"

106

"I don't give a fuck what she's over there saying or doing. You need to sit the fuck down and act like you're carrying my fuckin' baby that you wanted to keep so bad."

"Nigga you-"

"Get fucked up in this bitch today," I cut her off again and stared her down. I didn't want to hear shit she was talking about. "Come sit the fuck down Shar and I'm not playing. How you look taking your big pregnant ass across town to check a bitch? *Think dummy!* If some shit pop off she's not going to aim for your fuckin' stomach first!" I yelled and she jumped and so did her nieces and nephews that she was babysitting. She saw how mad I was, and she didn't say shit back. She came and sat next to me and put her keys on the table. Her phone rang and she looked at it, looked at me, and then back to her phone.

"Hello," she answered. "Nah. Baby daddy said no so we're about to chill. I'll hit you back later," she hung up before whoever it was could say anything else. She curled up in my arms and laid her head on my chest. "Sorry. You're right. I never want to endanger our baby."

I didn't even respond to her blatant lie. Had I not yelled at her pregnant ass or been here she would have been right there at her momma house ready to throw hands with a bitch that was probably going to kick her in her stomach. Stupid young shit.

Ty: *Divorce papers just came baby! They thought I was you. You ready to start our journey?* ☺☐☺☐☺☐☺☐

A fuckin' divorce… Wow. I definitely needed a drink!

Zionna

"Man, what the fuck!" Nash was squeezing the shit out of my hand and I was crackin' up. "Aye this ain't funny and as soon as I get on the ground, I'm stretching you across my knee." His eyes were closed tightly, and it made me laugh even harder.

"Awww don't be like that handsome," I said in a baby voice. Sih looked back at us and laughed. "Look bae," I said just at the right moment and he opened his eyes as we plunged three hundred feet at ninety-three miles per hour.

"Ahhhhhhhh! Ahhhhhhh! Ahhhhhhh!" he yelled at the top of his lungs and I can't lie, I was screaming loud as hell too. The Millennium Force at Cedar Point Amusement Park ain't no hoe and as much as I ride rollercoasters, when that free fall hit you baby, it really hits you.

I needed this two-hour road trip to Ohio more than anyone knew. Well Nashon knew how stressed I was which was why he invited me on the trip they planned for the neighborhood. Every summer The Knights rent about fifteen buses to drive to Cedar Point which is a must if you're a Detroiter. We hate Ohio State football team but will go to Sandusky Ohio dripping in our Detroit gear every summer for their amusement park. I loved that he wanted to relieve me of my stress and told me I was coming no matter what. Thank goodness he did too. It's a racist white bitch at my job driving me insane. I know she's trying to get me fired and it was taking a toll on my nerves. This was exactly the break I needed.

"Damn bro. Was that you screaming like a female on that bitch?" Sih cool ass was crackin' up and fuckin' with my baby hard.

"Aye shut yo' ass up. I told y'all I wasn't feelin' that shit. Got a nigga woozy and shit. Unless yo' ass got wings ain't no way in hell you supposed to be that high up in the air." Nash looked sick and I tried to hug him, but he pushed me away. "Nah... keep the same energy you had on that ride from hell. Talkin' 'bout some 'look bae' as we're falling to our death."

"To our death?" Jax was in tears laughing so hard. "This nigga said he woozy! You so extra bro. That shit was fun as hell. Come on we gotta get the pictures y'all."

"Nah. The last thing we need to do is remember this shit," he had us weak with knots in our stomachs from laughing so hard and of course we got the pictures anyway. We were never letting him live this one down. He showed his ass on that ride and the picture made it even funnier. His big thugged out ass walks into rooms and make nigga's shudder, but he's on an amusement park ride screaming at the top of his lungs. Classic moment.

My baby needed a break from riding rides plus Jax invited her siblings and I wasn't in the mood for being around them. I keep telling her not to force them on me and according to her she wasn't this time. She claimed she asked them to come before she knew I was coming. Jagger even brought his girlfriend so that was probably true but either way, I opted out of being around them.

Growing up, when Brian came over to get my sister, Sandy would never allow me to go. She stressed the fact that Brian had a white family that he loves, and I wasn't a part of it. She said he had a wife and kids and Kabrina was forcing Jaxsyn on him. She made it very clear that she wasn't going to be one of those weak bitches that had to beg a man to build a family with her. I was never allowed to go to him and Rebecca's house, therefore I didn't really know them or their kids. Then when I got older, I wasn't interested. When Sandy finally started letting me go over there with Jax it was a boring weekend with strangers. Everybody except Rebecca was trying to be black and it was annoying. Not because they have a lot of black people around them, mean they get to talk and act like us, and then Brian would try to push them on me and shit. Hell, I barely knew his ass so why the fuck would I want to be bothered with four other people? Easy pass. I wasn't interested and I'm still not. Sandy made it very clear that they weren't family and it stuck. I mean she said the same thing about Jax, but we looked alike and we lived right next door to each other, so she was going to be my sister regardless. The Brady Bunch was not.

I bit into my elephant ear and before I could wipe the powdered sugar from my face Nash had it covered. He gently wiped my face and I blushed. I swear he was doing something to me that had never been done before. He was loving me properly. Just that simple. I've never had a man to love me without reason. Quan and I were just used to each other. The other niggas wanted to fuck. My father was forced when my mother wouldn't abort me, but Nash simply loves Zionna for Zionna and that's major.

Granted, he's never uttered those words to me, but it's in his actions. From the start it's consistently been this way. He's about showing and proving and not talk. How he moved proved to me that his feelings were right where mine is and has been for a while. It's in the way that he looks at me, the way he touches me, and the way that he carries me. This was the real thing. I felt this man in my soul, how could it be anything else but real.

"You gone let me bite that shit Baby or I gotta go get my own?"

"I'm sorry Boo. Here," I passed him the plate and he passed me the cherry icee he was holding. We killed our snacks and then went to play some games. His ass was trying to do everything in the park except ride the rollercoasters and I was okay with that. I was enjoying just being with him and away from my stress in the D.

It started getting later and it was almost time to go. He won three big ass stuffed prizes for me; a huge Stewie from Family Guy, a big ass pink heart that I was obsessed with immediately, and a stuffed Goofy that was damn near as tall as me. I was cheesing from ear to ear and he teased me by calling me a big ass kid.

"You ready to stop bullshittin' baby?" We stood by the bus waiting for everyone to come out of the park.

"What you mean?" I asked curiously. I didn't know what he was talking about.

"I want you to be mine. I know we've been taking shit slow but I'm ready if you are beautiful. You know a nigga don't be on that lovey dovey shit so I ain't about to turn this into no long ass speech. I fucks with you the long way and I'll body a nigga behind you baby. This is it for us," I smiled as my heart fluttered in my fuckin' chest. He definitely wasn't the lovey dovey type but when he did hop into his feelings, I loved that shit. I leaned forward and kissed him deeply. He made it sloppy and gripped my ass.

"I love you."

"Here you go already, making shit hella deep," he shook his head and we both busted out laughing. "I love yo' rock head ass too girl," he pulled me closer and placed his index finger under my chin. "So, you mine forever baby?"

"Forever and always." We kissed again and I felt like I wanted to cry. I wanted what I felt in this moment my whole life and here he was, serving it to me on a silver platter. He held my waist and played with my tongue as I enjoyed every minute.

"Y'all cute or whateva." We turned around and Jaxsyn was holding a Snoopy that was almost as big as her and Sih had his arms draped over her shoulders lovingly. They were the epitome of goals.

"Thanks boo."

"Sih where can we put our stuff?" Jax little sister Alyssa asked.

"Under the bus. I'll put them under there for y'all."

"Thanks bro." Alyssa, Sydnee, and Meka, Jagger's black girlfriend passed Messiah the stuffed animals they were holding. Jax said that Messiah was on a roll and winning back to back so after he won her a few things he won some stuff for them too. I guess that was nice, but I didn't care. I took Nash's hand and walked away.

"You gotta stop being like that beautiful," he kissed my neck.

"I didn't even do anything."

"Yup. That's a lie," he bit me, and I popped his arm.

"That was not a lie," I pouted and folded my arms. He moved my arms and started sucking on my bottom lip that was poking out.

"It was and you better stop acting like that. Sandy was wrong baby. Those are your siblings, just like Jax; and you may not like sharing her, which is really your bratty ass problem with them, but you're old enough to know that they don't deserve for you to treat them like that."

"I-"

"I'm not trying to hear shit you about to say. Take yo' ass up there so I can play in my pussy on this ride back with your mean ass," he slapped my butt and I smirked, not saying shit back. I turned my horny ass around and did what daddy said do.

I'm still not fuckin' with them but I get what he said.

Jaxsyn

"Shit Siaaah," I whispered as his fingers dipped in and out of me. We were in the back of the bus and unlike the ride to Sandusky Ohio, the ride back to Detroit was so quiet you could hear a pin drop. Everyone was sleep or doing their own thing and I'm sure I heard a few moans throughout the bus, but I didn't want mine to be a part of that orchestra.

"I can't wait to get you home," he tapped against my spot causing my words to get caught in my throat. His shirt was balled up in my hand as I rolled my hips. "Gimme that shit Jax. You squeezing the fuck out of my fingers. Just let that shit go." His thumb went over my protruding bud faster and I buried my face in his chest as I let go on demand. My body jerked and he kept going bringing me to tears as orgasm after orgasm ripped through my soul. "I love the fuck out of you Tink," he kissed the side of my face as I regained my breath.

"I love you too Bae," I slowly raised my head and brought him closer to kiss him. I felt like a teenager again from the butterflies swirling in my stomach.

The whole two hours back to Detroit were filled with me and Messiah exploring each other. We couldn't keep our hands to ourselves and for some reason I fell deeper in love with him on this trip. He's taken me out of town before but this cute little trip to Ohio made my heart skip a beat. This was the shit that I watched on TV when I was kid and wished that I could do, and he was giving it to me. The whole day was magical and no matter what the future holds for us I'll never forget holding his hand while we rode every rollercoaster in the park or him carrying me on his back while we waited in the long lines to ride. We had a fast lane pass but on days like today you still had to wait. I know people hated the PDA, but our love was on full blast and we kissed and hugged the whole time. I couldn't believe how happy he made me with little effort. I was head over heels and falling deeper by the second.

"Pooh call me and let me know y'all made it home," I hugged Alyssa and then Sydnee.

"I will Shugga. Thanks again for everything Messiah."

"You welcome lil sis. Y'all don't forget to hit her line when y'all get home. It's late."

"We won't." They waved as they got into Alyssa's car.

"Alright y'all. Thanks again for everything. It's been fun as hell but I'm tired." Dawson dapped Messiah and then hugged me and then Jagger followed.

"It was nice meeting you Meka. Hopefully Jagger stops keeping you all to himself and you can come to some of my game nights."

"It was nice meeting you too and he's stingy so hopefully." They both smiled brightly at each other, and I thought it was too cute. I loved seeing my brother happy. His ex did a number on his heart, but Ms. Meka seemed to really be into him and according to my brother it's been almost eight months. That's good because now days, relationships barely last eight days.

We waited with Z, Nash, and a few Knights as all the parents picked up their children and all the buses were emptied. The guys planned this event so they had to make sure everything was okay before we could leave. After we said our goodbyes, we hopped into Messiah's Infiniti truck and hit the Lodge freeway headed home. I couldn't wait to get there so he could stick to his word and bend my ass into a pretzel. He brought the freak out of me and there was no turning back from where we were.

****

I stared at Frank Daniels as he walked through his newly built home. I swear, to date, this man is the most difficult client that I have ever had. Messiah has had to get in his ass twice for calling my phone in the middle of the night when an idea popped into his head. He makes all kinds of demands and changes his mind every two seconds. One moment he'll call my office a million times just to tell me that he changed his mind about a cabinet or a doorknob and then turns right around and calls a million times more to go back to the original idea. He was driving my ass crazy, but not only was the commission insane on this project, but I also wanted the satisfaction of making him eat his words. He's a chauvinistic ass hole who I needed to show a thing or two just for my own pleasure.

"Mrs. Avery."

"Ms. Blackwell," I reminded him *again*. No, my divorce hadn't been finalized yet, but his bitch ass didn't know that, and I wasn't about to keep allowing him to call me something that I told him not to call me weeks ago.

"Whatever it is-"

"No, not whatever it is. Mr. Daniels, I do not call you Mr. Jones, Mr. Smith, or Mr. Williams. I call you Mr. Daniels. That's your name and I wouldn't call you anything else. My name is Ms. Blackwell and that's what I want to be called."

"I'm impressed with the work you've done," he ignored me as he looked over his glasses at the kitchen cabinets that he bitched about for five days in a row. "This home is everything that I've dreamed of and I know my wife will love it," he nodded as he continued to comb over every detail. Wife though? All this time and he never mentioned her. Who the hell would want to deal with this man for a lifetime? Lord. Bless her heart.

"I'm happy I could meet your standards *Mr. Daniels*. I aim to please. This has been a long process but, in the end, everything worked itself out. I'll go ahead and get out of your hair. Thanks so much for your business."

"You're welcome, *Ms. Blackwell*," he looked at me over his shoulder and we both wore a small grin as I nodded. "By the way, you didn't just meet my standards, you exceeded them," he walked away, and I walked out of his new home smiling from ear to ear. I was jumping for joy on the inside. Not only did I kill that shit like I knew I would, but his ass admitted it and finally called me the right name after I spoke my mind. Hell yeah! This was huge.

When I got in the car, I called Zionna, but she didn't answer. She was probably at work like always or with Nash. I would normally call her again, but I didn't want to bother her, so I called Sih instead.

"What's up beautiful?"

"I killed it like you said I would Bae. He loved everything and even called me Ms. Blackwell."

"Because you're the shit Tink. Let's celebrate. Anywhere you want to go. I'm in the middle of something right now, but I'm about to wrap this up and head home."

"Aww thanks baby. I'll figure something out and be dressed by the time you get home."

"Okay. I love you."

"I love you too," I hit the button on my steering wheel and ended our call. I couldn't wait to celebrate with my love. My day was made!

Right before I pulled up to our house my mother called my phone and I didn't want to answer but I hadn't talked to her in a few days and I know she likes us to check in with each other. It's some new shit that came along with her sobriety, so I try to participate since she's trying.

"Hello."

"Hey Jaxsyn. You busy baby?"

"Nah. Just coming from work, pulling into the driveway."

"Oh okay. I didn't want anything. I was calling to tell you that I got my car fixed and since it's just me now, I didn't need a big house, so I found a nice two bedroom in Oak Park. It's closer to my job too."

"Well you did call for something Kabrina, that's great! I'm so happy for you. Did you need someone to help you move? My boyfriend has plenty of people that could help."

"That would be great. I was hoping to get everything moved tomorrow since I don't work on Sundays."

"It's short notice but I'll definitely see what he can put together and I'll let you know."

"Okay. Thanks so much Jax."

"No problem. I'll call you later."

"Cool. Don't call me Kabrina again heffa," she hung up before I could say anything, and I smiled. I loved where our relationship was. We came a long way, and we had a ways to go, but we were definitely getting there.

Tabitha had the house smelling like warm cinnamon and fresh apples. All it took was me telling her that cinnamon and apples was my favorite scent when we first met, and she always makes sure that the house was permeated with it. I loved her so much. It's not even the big things that she does that makes her special. It's those small details that she picks up on in basic everyday conversations. She holds on to them and then out of nowhere, she's integrating something you've said into your everyday life. She's absolutely amazing.

"Good evening Ms. Blackwell."

"Jaxsyn, Tabitha. Just Jaxsyn."

"Oh no Ms. Blackwell. Mr. Knight is Mr. Knight and you're Ms. Blackwell. Nothing else," she said in a thick Spanish accent and I playfully rolled my eyes.

"Fine. Good evening Ms. Garcia," I teased, and she smiled brightly. I chopped it up with her for minute about her day and then made my way upstairs. Before I could even turn the shower on my baby was stepping into the room looking heaven sent. My kitty instantly started throbbing.

"Nasty ass. You got that look on your face," he towered over me and I leaned my head all the way back to receive his kisses. I wrapped my arms around his waist and held him there as my tongue weaved in and out of his mouth. Shit! This man, this man.

"I missed you."

"I see that. Daddy missed you too Tink," he pecked my lips again. "Aye, the block party is today, and I completely forgot. I don't know how but I did. You mind if we hit that first and then go celebrate?"

"The block party is good enough baby. That'll be too much trying to do something afterwards. Question, my momma is moving tomorrow, you think you and some of your people can help?"

"I can make that happen for her, but I won't be moving shit. I supervise my baby," he slapped my ass. "Get dressed so we can go."

"Come help me get dressed," I said seductively, and he willingly followed me into the bathroom. I stared at him in the mirror as I slowly undressed, and he watched attentively. I love when he stares at me while biting his bottom lip with his sexy ass. We'll get there when we get there. I needed the head that I was about to give him to blow his mind. He deserved nothing but the best from me and even though this day was about me celebrating, nothing makes me happier than seeing my man happy.

Messiah

By the time we pulled onto the block it was packed. My brother and the rest of the squad had left enough room for my bike, so we were able to ride down the sidewalk and park but people driving cars had to park blocks away and walk. I'm glad I told Jax to ride with me instead of her riding the Harley I bought her for her birthday. She wouldn't have had anywhere to park.

Every year the block party got bigger and bigger. The Knights' name was on the banners and flyers because we paid for everything, but Ms. Londa started this tradition when we were younger. She knows everybody in the hood and has raised damn near every crack head's child over here. She wasn't about to see any kid go without and that's why we started sponsoring the picnic a few years ago. She won't allow us to get it catered because she said everybody wanna taste her cooking, but we don't take no for an answer, so we told her we'll at least buy all the food she's going to cook.

"There's my baby," Ms. Londa smiled, and I opened my arms, but she pushed me out of the way.

"I'll get to your big butt in a minute. I'm talking about this baby," she pulled Jax in for a hug and rocked her from side to side. "I missed you so much pretty girl. How ya' momma?"

"I missed you too! She's good. Clean and working every day."

"God is good. Didn't I tell you? I saw it in her years ago. That wasn't her. She made a bad choice and life got away from her." They hugged again. "Wow that's good. I'm happy for y'all. Where's that sister of yours?"

"Around here somewhere."

"Momma Londaaaaa!" Z came running up.

"I just asked about you." They hugged.

"How y'all know each other?" Nash asked what I was thinking.

"Nigga this is our hood. I don't know how we didn't know y'all, but we grew up two blocks over."

"Damn for real?" They all nodded.

It became abundantly clear that Jax and Zionna was known in the hood when everybody started coming up to them for hugs and showing love. Jax supposedly was a bad ass back in the day and used to run the streets with that hoe ass nigga she married. I didn't feel like hearing people constantly bringing him up, so I stepped away.

"Ol' jealous ass nigga." Nash came to where I was, talking shit.

"Whatever. I ain't jealous of no nigga," I hit the blunt and passed it to him.

"Keep that. Yo' day just got hella bad," I followed where he was looking, and Mariah's ass was headed my way. I looked over my shoulder and Ms. Londa had just passed Jax and Z a piece of steak. I had a few seconds to get this bitch out of my face before my baby could assume this was anything more than what it was.

"You think I'm a joke huh?"

"I actually don't think about you at all. Move around Riah."

"I ain't going nowhere nigga. You been duckin' and dodging me for weeks and that's some bullshit. Especially after I apologized to yo' punk ass about Dora The Explorer," her and her girls giggled at her joke about Tabitha.

"Mmm Dora, huh? You out here showing off for your homegirls, but you were singing a different tune on the phone a lil minute ago."

"It was a joke Sih, damn. Ain't nobody out here puttin' on shows but you my baby. You actin' real brand new," she stepped closer to me and tried to stand between my legs, but I moved her.

"Fall back. I told you I have a girl."

"Consider that a warning." Jax came out of nowhere and Z was right behind her mugging the fuck out of Mariah.

"Can we help you?"

"Ain't no *we* when it comes to y'all two and *you* can't help me with a muthafuckin' thing." Jax snapped real quick and I already could see this shit was about to go left. "Don't try me," she looked at me like I had did something wrong.

"Baby you know me better than that. Mariah walk away. I'm not about to say that shit again."

"Baby? Oh. This is the chick that I keep hearing about?" Riah laughed. "You play so many games nigga. They never last so dismiss this bitch so we can get back to doing us."

118

"Jax don't catch another case sis. Please," I could hear Z whispering to Jax even if Riah couldn't.

"Messiah tell your bougie ass lil friend don't get fucked up because you know I'm about that life." Mariah kept going.

Jax turned to Z and said, "He's worth it plus I got the bail money on deck. You know my codes to my accounts." Z nodded and Jax turned around and punched Mariah in her face so got damn hard blood gushed everywhere. Riah stumbled backwards but Jax wasn't having that shit. She grabbed her hair and snatched her forward delivery blow after blow. All face and head shots. Each hit sound like freight trains colliding. "What life are you about bitch? Tell me that. What life?" Jax hit her again. "Huh bad ass? I can't hear that smart mouth shit no more." Riah was trying to block Jax hits and cover her face but she didn't have no answers for my baby. I was stuck in shock at Riah gettin' her ass whipped but also at Jax doing the whipping. My baby was manhandling the fuck out of her.

"Jax that's enough. Please stop."

"Fuck her Z. I tried to let the bitch make it, but you know I don't do that slick talking shit that bitches be on," she was holding Riah's head in front of her with a death grip.

"Get off my friend you stupid ass bitch. That nigga ain't shit and he gone play you for her like he's done the rest of the bitches that thought they could take her place."

"She better go train with Mayweather before that happen. If I even think he's fuckin' with this bum ass bitch, I'm going to kill this hoe with my bare hands," she slapped fire out of Toya's mouth, and out of nowhere Zionna followed up with a two piece and they started fighting.

"Come on baby. That's enough. You know me better than to believe these bitches," I pried her hands out of Mariah's hair while my brother pulled Toy and Z apart.

"You a hoe ass nigga Sih. You let these bitches jump me? I swear you're a bitch." Mariah yelled at me as she started crying.

"Disrespect my nigga again and get your ass beat again." Jax stood in front of me and I swear a nigga dick was hard. My baby goes hard as fuck for her man.

"Nashon I need some tissue." Toy's mouth was leaking.

"Just leave Toy. Take ya' girl and go. Y'all embarrassed y'all selves enough out here, and for what?"

119

"Over my nigga! Fuck you mean Nash? I was just *sis* but now it's 'take ya girl and go'? Y'all niggas pros at playing roles for new bitches." Riah had tears streaming down her face. "Sih keep this shit a buck and tell this hoe how much you love me. You can stop all this bullshit right now with the fuckin' truth. Tell her that it's me that will *alwaaaays* have your heart nigga. You got her out here looking stupid by fighting over you when we both know you coming back. We have history baby girl. A history that new pussy can't compare too. Other bitches tried to take him too, but he always comes back no matter what," she yelled and we both continued to stare at her with everyone else that was outside. "We have a bond that's irreplaceable. Ask him, if he's the real nigga he claims to be, he'll tell you what it is."

"Move the fuck around Mariah. I told yo ass I had a lady and blocked you after you hit my line a hundred times in one day. I ain't thought about yo' ass since then. We solid as fuck over here so chill with the bullshit." Jax looked like she was itching to lay hands on Riah again, so I grabbed her hand and lead her to where my bike was parked. "We were supposed to be celebrating," I kissed her knuckles and then stroked the side of her face. "I'm sorry about this baby."

She looked down at her scratched-up arms from Mariah trying to claw her way out of Jaxsyn's grip. "If you ever ch-"

"Never. We ain't even got to go there baby. Like I said, our shit is solid as fuck and ain't neither one of us going nowhere. This is forever. I love yo' ass to death Tink and it's no woman out here that can compare. They can't give me what you give me or love me the way that you do. I put that on my life baby."

She simply nodded and I hoped she really understood, because I meant every word.

****

After Jax really sat down and let the night of the block party play out in her head she got pissed at me. She hasn't fucked with me for almost two weeks. We're walking around the house literally not saying shit to each other. I bought her everything that I could think of and her ass was still pissed and sleeping in one of the spare bedrooms. She said I should have walked away when Mariah first walked up and then when Mariah went on her rant, I didn't deny anything that she said, and it made her feel like it was some truth to what was said. I tried to explain to her that

120

I tried to get that bitch to go away and that bullshit Mariah was yappin' about was just that, bullshit, but Jax wasn't trying to hear me. She was all the way in her bag and what I was saying to her fell on deaf ears.

I was on the block with my brother and I saw my baby pull up and my chest swelled with pride watching niggas try their hardest not to look her way. Her body is vicious, and I bricked up as soon as she started strutting my way. She came to drop something off to Zionna, but she walked straight pass me like I'm not her nigga. I snatched her ass backwards so quick it got everyone's attention. I was tired of not having my baby because of a bitch that didn't even matter. I understood that Mariah trying to stand between my legs wasn't a good look but Jax was draggin' this shit and I wanted my baby back.

"Cut this shit out Jaxsyn."

"Let me go," she snatched away, and I snatched her ass right back into my arms, this time holding her tighter so she couldn't get away from me.

"No. Stop fuckin trippin' ma. You're the one that I love. You! It's not a bitch walking around this muthafucka that can take your place and you know that shit so stop trippin' over nothing."

"According to your ex, she got your heart and I'm just new pussy, right?"

"Man chill out. You know damn well this shit is real as fuck between us. Don't let no bitch that don't matter fuck up what we got going on."

"You did that when you didn't check that bitch on sight. She said it and you didn't deny it," here we go…

"Okay. I should have shut the bitch up, but you still know what the fuck this is between us. I don't fuck with her, at all! She's the past and you're my present and future. I don't want nobody but you. I been kissing your ass for weeks and you about to chill the fuck out," I pulled her closer. "I fuckin love you baby and you know it. I give you all of me Jaxsyn and that's something that no other woman has ever had."

She looked away.

"Tell me you love me Jax. I need to hear you say it. You've been treating me so cold ma."

"I love you," she finally looked up at me and I smiled. "But I won't be disrespected again Messiah. Hoes like her need to be shut down immediately by the guy in the situation so they understand their place. That bitch was talking about how much you love her and all you said was move around."

"Baby I never meant to make you feel disrespected and you have my word that it will never happen again," I kissed her, and everybody started clapping like some lames. I would have done anything to see her smile again and all they asses knew it. I had been in a shitty ass mood without my girl. "I love you so much baby."

"I love you too," she smiled and just like that we were back to being us and I was happy because I couldn't go another day without her talking to me.

"Aye bro we have to go handle that business in a minute." Nash reminded me but I hadn't forgot.

"Yeah. I know. Give me like twenty, thirty minutes," I looked over my shoulder at Jax and he shook his head.

"Make that shit quick Broddie," he smirked. "None of that I miss you long strokin' type shit."

"That's why I love you bro," I laughed. "You know me too well," I walked back over to Jaxsyn. "Come ride with me real quick ma."

"Okay. I have something to tell you anyway," she smiled as she looked up at me and I knew that she was relieved that we were back on good terms just like I was.

We got in my car and I drove a couple blocks and turned down the quietest street I could find. She was already unzipping my pants because she knew what was about to go down.

"Climb on top," I threw the car in park and she moved swiftly from her seat to mine.

"Mmmmm," she moaned as she slid down. She leaned back against the steering wheel, exposing her freshly shaven pussy to me. Fuck I needed her. She was wet as hell and had my dick glistening.

"Damn Tink, I missed being inside of you." My left hand massaged one of her titties while my right hand swept across her clit.

"Ughhh, I missed it too Bae," her moans were sexy as hell and driving me crazy. Her skills were unmatched without a doubt and she was riding me like a fuckin pro. I gripped her ass and started moving her faster while I was still playing with her pussy. Watching my dick go from shining with her juices to snow white from her creaming had me harder than ever before. She leaned forward and kissed me wildly. The passion that filled my car was exactly what I needed from my baby after two weeks of being cut off.

"Who dick you ridin' Jax?" I locked my fingers in her hair and pulled.

"Miiiine," she whined.

"Don't you ever in your life forget that shit," I dug deeper, and she whimpered. "You understand me?" I started destroying her guts.

"Yessss baby. I understaaaand."

"Shit Tink, I'm about to bust," I gritted and squeezed her ass with both hands.

"Mmmm, cum baby," she sped up and I grunted loudly. Using her cheeks for leverage I sped up with her and we went stroke for stroke. I could feel her muscles contracting and I knew she was close too. I kept going until she had a nigga weak and my toes curling.

"Fuuuuck!" I yelled out and gave her my full load as she drenched me with her essence. I laid my head back and she smirked.

"Mmmhmm, you really missed your Tinker Bell huh?" She laid her head on my shoulder.

"More than your ass knows gorgeous," I bit her neck and she squirmed then giggled. She had no fuckin' clue how much I truly missed her and all the things that makes her, *her*. Yeah, a nigga can definitely admit to being whipped. She got me.

"I have something to tell you," she was still sitting on my dick and I could feel myself getting hard again but I was trying to focus on what she was about to tell me, plus my brother would be on my head if I didn't hurry up and bring my ass back to the block.

"What's up ma?" I smiled at how pretty she looked on my lap.

She reached over and looked through her purse. She pulled something out and passed it to me like we had just made a drug transaction and we both laughed. I opened my hand and it was a pregnancy test.

"I'm pregnant Bae."

I stared at the test and my heart sped up in my chest. Nothing in this world could have prepared me for how happy I was in this moment. My baby was having my baby. "You just made my fuckin day Jax," I hugged her tightly and she giggled. "I'm going to be a daddy for real?" I couldn't hide my excitement if I tried but I wasn't just happy for me. My baby had been through so much with pregnancies in the past that this moment was major for her.

"You're going to be a daddy for real baby and I'm going to be a mommy," she beamed, climbing back into the passenger seat and reaching for her wipes to clean us off.

"When did you find out?"

"Yesterday. I was sick and I've been throwing up for a few days, so I decided to take a test and it came back positive."

"I'm so fuckin happy baby. I can't believe this."

"Me too and I can't either. We're going to be parents Siah."

"The best and flyest parents ma," I kissed her deeply and then kept pecking her lips until she was chortling again. "Aye so did you file for divorce like I told you to do?"

"Weeks ago, baby. I didn't waste any time. I'm beyond ready to close that chapter of my life."

I nodded and drove off. I didn't want that nigga to have no parts of what's mine and it felt good that she didn't want it either. She already legally changed her name back and all I needed was that divorce finalized. "I have to go handle some business with Nash but we're celebrating properly tonight so get dressed and I'll be home around eight," I kissed her tenderly, savoring this huge moment we were in. "Plus, I'm still trying to celebrate Mr. Daniels appreciating my baby and you killing that assignment like I knew you would," she looked over at me. "Nah, I didn't forget," I grabbed her hand and kissed it. "I'm really sorry baby. I didn't mean to make you feel no kind of way. You know you're my Queen, right?"

"I know and I'm over it baby. I accept your apology and I apologize too. The thought of another woman being in your space or taking you from me puts me in a bad head space and I showed my ass because of it. You know that's not even me anymore."

"Don't ever let your mind even take you there beautiful. When I say this is forever, I mean it with my entire soul. They can't compete where they don't compare," I kissed her hand again. "Don't ever doubt me baby. I'm all about you."

"I won't and I know you are. I was trippin' hard. I'll be ready at eight baby. Be careful."

"Always," I parked and after a few more kisses and I love yous she got out. A nigga was on cloud nine for real. A couple minutes later my brother opened the door.

"Have that pussy ready for me when I get back. My granny fucked my nut up this morning with all those calls, but I still need that." Nash and Z were hugged up in my passenger

124

side door which wouldn't have been a problem until I looked over and saw her grabbing this nigga piece.

"Man get the fuck on with all that. Y'all niggas have zero chill," I said causing both of them to laugh.

"I love you baby," he slapped her ass and she bent over and started to twerk, and his ass got behind her and started acting like he was hittin' it from the back. These two play all day. They're a good look for each other and it was good to see bro this happy.

"I love you more daddy," she giggled, and they kissed.

"Remember what I said Z."

"I stay ready Boo."

"You ain't lyin Ma," he got in and stared at me. "Nigga you long stroked that shit."

I laughed. "Naw that's just what a quickie is for us."

"You were gone like forty-five minutes. Ain't shit *quick* about that. Let's go," he shook his head.

"Well that's how the fuck we do what we do. Anyway, I got good news," I checked my side mirror and pulled off.

"What?"

"Jax is pregnant."

"Get the fuck outta here. I'm going to be an uncle?" His excitement matched mine.

"Hell yeah nigga. She just told me."

"I'm geeked as fuck bro. Plus I know how bad you've been wanting to do the family thing. This shit is major. I'm happy as hell for y'all."

"Thanks man, this shit is definitely major. Life couldn't be better right now. My baby ain't mad no more, she's giving me the seed I've been ready for, and the money is rolling in faster than we can count it. Nigga we good out here."

"Salute to that shit right there my baby! This is what we've been busting our asses for our whole lives and it's happening. Life is good. Finally."

"Finally," I smiled and dapped him.

"Love yo' ass bro. You gone be the best fuckin' father ever and it don't matter that our hoe ass donor didn't stick around to teach you how. You got this shit Sih, and I'll have your back when you think you don't."

"I love you too bro and I appreciate that more than you'll ever know."

He nodded as I sparked a blunt and we headed to the money feeling good as fuck.

Zionna

I couldn't believe my ears and I couldn't even think straight. Everything was moving in slow motion but too fast at the same time. I could see everything that was happening, but my mind had gone absolutely blank. I was shaking like a leaf from head to toe and my heart was pounding out of my fuckin' chest.

"Hello." Jaxsyn answered and hearing her voice made me cry harder. "Z what's wrong?" She panicked when she heard me crying.

"He…" I gasped for the air that my lungs were desperately in need of. "He…" I couldn't get the words out.

"He, who? Zionna you're scaring me honey, please tell what's going on? Talk to me. Who is he?"

"He's gone Jax," I gasped again as my heart sank into an unfamiliar abyss. "He's dead."

Now she was gasping. "Who's dead?" She yelled.

"My baaaaby. Nashon is gone. They took my fuckin' baby Jax. They took him from me." *Lord why him?* My mind couldn't fully comprehend it. I was just with him and now he was gone…

"Huh? What? Where are you? That can't be true. Who the fuck told you that Zionna? Where the fuck is Sih? Zionna where the fuck is Messiah?" She started screaming and crying hysterically.

"Here Jax. The hospital. He's been shot too."

"Noooo," I heard the phone hit the floor but I could still hear her screaming at the top of her lungs. *"Jesus no. No, no, no, no, no. Please Lord, don't do this,"* she was crying uncontrollably. There wasn't much I could do for her because I couldn't do shit for myself, so I hung up and texted her the hospital info. Hopefully Tabitha is there or someone else that works for them, to make sure she could get here safely.

People from the hood was filling the lobby one by one to show their support and respect but it was probably one of these hoe ass niggas that set them up. That's normally how this type of shit works. One minute they're all homies and brothers riding their bikes and shooting the shit at the club house and then the next minute, niggas turn into whole hoe ass snakes. That's why I don't trust muthafuckas.

"Lord my grand babies." Grandma Knight walked up, and my heart broke all over again. She's their whole world and vice versa. I got up and hugged her and she wailed in my arms. Everything that she was, and her legacy was in all of her grandsons and she was crushed. "Somebody please tell me what's going on. I just saw my babies this morning Lord. Tell me what's going on."

Their cousin Wayne got up and grabbed her. "Granny I'm so sorry. I know how much they mean to you, but they said Nash was covered with a sheet at the scene Big Ma. They saying he gone, and it's not lookin' good for Sih. We have to pray."

She fell all the way out and he held her. It was all too much for her and the cries that came from the lobby showed it was too much to take in for a lot of people. I was overwhelmed and had cried so hard that my head was banging but the tears were still rolling.

"Where's my Sih?" Mariah ran into the lobby and everyone's eyes fell on me. I didn't even have the energy for this bitch and her shenanigans. This wasn't the time or the place. "Where is he?" She yelled and one of the girls in the crowd of people whispered something in her ear and hugged her. She started crying hard and called Toya. She wanted her conversation to be heard but regardless of how much she tried to provoke me, I couldn't give her what she wanted. She could call whoever she wants and act like a damn fool as much as she wants, today was her free pass. I had zero energy to give to her or her friend. I was dying a slow agonizing death internally. Never in my life had I felt pain in its rawest form and so deeply… so immensely. I could barely breathe, and my chest had shooting pains that I could feel all the way to my back. My world was rocked and shook to its absolute core.

Tabitha and Jaxsyn walked in about twenty minutes later and Jaxsyn looked like she should have been admitted. She was weak as hell and Oscar from the hood sat her down next to grandma Knight. She was shaking and her leg bounced rapidly.

"The doctors haven't said anything about Sih yet baby." Grandma Knight rubbed her leg and she nodded but she was clearly out of it. I got up and went and sat next to her but for about five minutes she hadn't even noticed that it was me. She looked over like she was shocked to see me, and I hugged her tightly and we both cried.

"I…" She took a deep breath. "I… I just can't," she buried her face in my shoulder and I did the same. "Why Z? What happened? We were just with them, he was just in my arms."

"I don't know. I have no idea." We continued to cry together.

"I'm so sorry he's gone baby. I'm soooo sorry," she rubbed my head as I cried on her shoulder harder than I had cried the whole night. They stole the best thing that ever happened to me and all I wanted to do was die with him. I never wanted to experience life without Nash again. "I got you sis. Always," she continuously whispered in my ear until all I could do was allow my silent tears to soak her shirt.

We sat in the lobby for hours before the doctor came out to tell us that Messiah was still in surgery and Nash in fact was gone. I was hoping, wishing, and praying that it was all a rumor but hearing "deceased on arrival" from the doctor was all too much. I fell the fuck out and my soul cried out for him. This was not supposed to happen. Not to him. To us. We had plans and our whole future ahead of us.

"The family of Messiah Knight." A different doctor came out an hour later.

"That's us." Everyone jumped up.

"Mr. Knight was shot six times and two bullets are still lodged inside of his chest. We did everything that we could to get them out, but the location would cause more injury and possibly internal bleeding if removed. He's currently in a coma and on a ventilator. At this time the ventilator is doing one hundred percent of the breathing for him so his body can heal. The next few hours will be critical, and we just have to wait and see if he remains with us. His body has been through a lot. If Mr. Knight pulls through the next forty-eight-hours, then his days ahead will still be touch and go but we'll be more optimistic about a positive outcome. We ask that only the immediate family be allowed in the room. His body needs as much rest as possible if he's going to make it," he pulled their grandmother to the side and asked her a few questions and then wrote something down.

"Their mother will be here tonight, so she'll be on the list, myself, and Messiah's girlfriend Jaxsyn. Everyone else, I'm sorry. I know Messiah has lots of love in this room right now and we'll keep you all posted." Their grandmother announced and then went to the back with the doctors.

"You!" Mariah hopped up yelling at my sister. "Bitch I've been around for years and she picked you. I've stuck by that nigga side through the right, the wrong, the clean, and the dirty, and she picked you? Oh, I got you and that old ass bitch too," she cried as she left the lobby with everyone else and we all ignored her. My sister was so dazed she probably didn't even hear that girl. Like I said, this wasn't the fuckin' time.

The fact that Nashon was gone broke my heart and what broke my heart even more was the fact that I didn't even get to tell him that I'm pregnant.

"You can go back there sweetie. I can't take it." Their grandmother came out and gave Jaxsyn the green light to go visit Sih. She looked back at me before going through the double doors, and my heart broke for the both of us. Selfishly it broke a little more for myself because now I'm carrying a child and its father was just ripped out of my life. My thoughts became too heavy, and the pain became unbearable, all of a sudden everything started to fade to black.

Jaxsyn

I was at the hospital more than anyone else. I stayed with my man morning, noon, and night. He needed to hear my voice and know that I was right there beside him. He needed to know that he was stronger than this and that he could pull through no matter what the doctors were saying. He had to pull through. There was no way I could live without him and raise our baby alone. I made sure that I told him how much his unborn child needs him daily so he would have a reason to come back to us. A reason to fight.

About three days after Messiah was shot the police came and put cuffs on his wrist and sat outside of his door. He made it out of the critical stage of his recovery and they didn't waste any time with their punk asses. They said him and Nashon had several drugs in the car, but I know them, and I know how their operation works. From the start, Messiah kept it real with me about his legal and illegal businesses. One, they haven't sold "drugs" since they were teens so the coke they claim they found doesn't belong to them. Two, they get their pharmaceuticals shipped straight to the warehouse directly from the big pharma companies. It was clear they were set up and it was no doubt about it.

I called his lawyer immediately and had him on standby. I told him everything that was going on and he advised me to call him as soon as Messiah opens his eyes. He also told me to make sure that all Messiah's purchases were accounted for, so I spent days combing over his books for the Knights club house which operates as a bar, and all of his other legitimate businesses that him and Nashon co-owned. He was way smarter than what he portrayed to the world. My baby was at the top of his game and that's why niggas was hatin'. He owns several legit businesses that he washes his money through, and every single dollar down to the last coin was accounted for legally. I was proud of him and it only made me love him more.

I didn't trust the nurses to wash him and I didn't want him to get bed sores, so I washed him from head to toe and lotioned his whole body twice a day. Some of these people were in here smelling like their own feces and that shit was ill to me but I wasn't surprised at all. Most of the nurses are young, straight out of school, and getting burned out by the long hours. I had my sister to show me what to do and tell me what I should be asking and from there I took over. I spent one hundred percent of my days making sure my baby was cared for properly. His visits were few and far between but as long as he had me, the fact that other people didn't visit wouldn't bother him.

I started bringing my laptop with me when I visit so I could take care of both of our businesses from his room. I explained my situation to my current clients, and they were willing to communicate via email and FaceTime or Skype. Some even sent flowers and cards to my office. I was also happy that my staff stepped up for me the way that they did. They've been going on sites taking pictures and recordings for me and together we were still running Jaxsyn's Creative Interiors & Design Studio, like a well-oiled machine. I was getting pulled in several different directions, but I was handling it all and I had a great support system.

Kabrina: *Hey baby. Just checking on you. Make sure you're taking care of yourself and I'm praying for him.*

Me: *Thanks! I am. I'll call you tomorrow so we can reschedule our lunch.*

Kabrina: *Don't worry about that girl. We'll figure it out. I love you Jaxsyn*

Me: *Love you too Kabrina!*

Kabrina: *These hands stay ready heffa. Stop playing with me!*

"Ms. Blackwell someone is here to see you?" I looked up from my phone.

"To see *me* or him?"

"You were asked for by name so I'm not sure."

"Oh. Okay," I got up and kissed his forehead. "Someone is here so I'm stepping out for a second baby, but I'll be right back," I whispered into his ear and walked out of the room. I never leave him without letting him know where I'm going and that I was coming right back to him.

We kept the restrictions on Messiah's room so anyone that came to check on him had to wait in the lobby until the staff called me. The couple times that Solo came by they would just say Messiah has a visitor and they gave me his name so I can say yes, or no. Mariah ass tried once, and that shit was laughable. Hell no I wasn't approving that request and she should have known better. No bitch that fucked my man before, is going to be in his presence sick or healthy. Plus, this hoe busted out both me and Grandma Knights windows after she wasn't allowed access that first day. She had a lot of nerve even showing up after that and if the circumstances were different, I would have dog walked that hoe.

"Hi. I'm Sih's auntie Lydia."

"Nice to meet you. I'm Jaxsyn," I smiled. Nash and Sih looked a lot like her. I thought she was their mother.

"You too. My sister, their mother, is on her way up. She was finishing her cigarette. We just got here this morning."

"That's great. He doesn't get many visitors."

"It's times like this that expose people."

"I couldn't agree more," I nodded. She might as well throw her own name in that mixing bowl of exposed people right along with their mother but okay sis…

"Hey, I'm Charlene. You must be Messiah's girlfriend Jaxsyn?" She extended her hand and fought back her tears.

"I am. I didn't know you two were twins."

"I'm a year older than her." Lydia said with a half-smile.

"Oh. Okay. The resemblance is uncanny just like with Nashon and Messiah. Well come on," I lead them to his room.

"Wait." His mother pulled my arm and I turned around.

"Does he look bad? I'm so scared. That's why it took so long for me to get up here, honestly. I've been getting updates from my momma but I'm a wreck," she started crying and I hugged her.

"He looks like he's sleeping. There are a couple tubes attached to him, but he looks handsome and peaceful. You can't see any of his wounds, they're under his gown," I held her hand and we all walked in together.

"God why would they do this to my babies?" She kissed his forehead and rubbed his face. "He does look peaceful. Lord I know I've done things that I'm not proud of and I've let my boys down more times than any mother ever should, but please don't take my baby. He's all that I have left," she stared at him and his aunt whispered something in his ear. I do that all the time so hopefully it's a memory that brings him back to us or something motivational.

"He smells good." Lydia looked at me.

"I wash him twice a day."

"Doesn't he have a nurse?" His mother looked concerned.

"He does, but I rather do it, so I know it's done correctly." They both smiled and sat down.

We talked for hours and his mother reminded me a lot of Kabrina. She had recently gotten her shit together too. Who knows how long that will last though? I've been down that road one too many times with Kabrina for me not to know the drill. They go in with high hopes, come out with even higher hopes, and then surround themselves with the same damn people and start doing the same damn things.

Charlene told me that Nashon never got to see her this sober so she was praying hard that Messiah made it so he could. She has a lot of guilt and now that she's loss Nashon and Messiah is lying in front of her in a coma, she's really feeling it. Hopefully it's enough to keep her clean.

"Are you the one fighting the plans for the funeral?" She asked me.

"I don't want to talk about that in front of him. Let's step out." We all got up and went out to the hall way. I walked pass the officer that was posted outside of his room and rolled my eyes. "I have no authority to fight Nashon's funeral arrangements but yes, I am the one that told Grandma Knight that she should wait a little while longer. Messiah loves Nashon more than anything in this whole world and all they've had for years is each other. I don't want Sih to open his eyes and not only is his brother gone and never coming back, but already buried too. He deserves to say goodbye to Nash more than anyone else."

"I agree sweetie. I hadn't thought about it like that." Lydia said.

"Yeah I guess you're right. I get it now too."

"I wasn't trying to over step. That's not who I am at all. I'm just looking out for my man's best interest, and it's in his best interest to be there when his brother is put to rest," I shrugged and walked back into the room.

They stayed for about thirty more minutes and then left. They said they were tired and would try to come back tomorrow. I was exhausted too but there was no way I was going to leave his side. I couldn't.

****

"Hey sis," I called Zionna to check on her after I washed Messiah and prayed over him. Every day when I wake up, I immediately jump into caring for him, then checking on our businesses. After that, I call my sister. She had me on pins and needles when they told me she fainted in the lobby. We've never experienced death this close to us before and she was struggling.

"Hey Jaxsyn. You good?"

"Baby I should be asking you that. How are you?"

"I'm alright, all things considered."

"I feel so horrible that I haven't been able to be there for you like I really want to Z. I swear I do."

"Stop. I completely understand. I would be right there with Nashon if that was him lying in that bed."

"I love you."

"I love you too. How is he?"

"The same. He's been breathing over the machine for the last couple days and he squeezed my hand last night, but they said it was just his reflexes. I know it was him though. I said something that made him react."

"What did you say?"

"I'll tell you face to face, but I know he squeezed my hand so I'm hoping he opens his eyes soon."

"Me too. Losing both of them would be incomprehensible."

"I agree." We both got quiet for a minute.

"Well, go ahead. I'm praying for y'all. I'll talk to you later."

"Okay. I'm praying for you too and even though I'm here Z, if you need anything, and I mean anything at all, just call me and I'll come running to you. Even if it's just for me to hold you. I promise I'll come."

"I know you will."

"Be strong sis."

"I'm trying," she hung up and I cried. She was so hurt, and I was hurting for her. Losing Nashon has been hard as fuck and I know it's even harder for everybody because Messiah and Nash were practically identical. He's going to be a constant reminder of Nash.

"I need you so much right now Messiah Knight. Baby soooo much is going on and so much has happened," I cried on his good shoulder and after a few minutes he squeezed my hand

135

again. "Open your eyes for me baby. They don't believe you're squeezing my hand. Baby please just open them for me. I'm begging you. Force them open Messiah. I swear I can't handle all of this on my own. I'm trying my best, but I need you with me daddy," I repeated myself over and over as I stroked the hand that he was still squeezing. I cried until all I could do was gasp for air and when I looked up, his eyes were open. "Oh my God! I knew you could do it Bae. I fuckin' knew it," I was unhinged as I cried hard and placed kisses all over his face. "Listen to me closely. I'm going to get the doctors, but the police are outside, and you're cuffed to this bed. I know you're confused right now and I'm going to explain everything to you, but I have to call your lawyer first. You already know not to say shit to anyone," he nodded and pointed to the tube in his mouth. "Let me just make this call and then I'll have them to come get that out," I called his lawyer and told him to come now, waited about five minutes, and then I called the nurse and told her that Sih opened his eyes.

Within seconds doctors and nurses came rushing into his room and fussed over him for about twenty minutes. He didn't know what the hell was going on but as long as he had those eyes open, I was good. His lawyer showed up just like I needed him too and everything was playing out how I wanted. I didn't want him waking up with no lawyer present.

"I need a moment with him really quick and then you can discuss business with him," I told the lawyer after all the hospital personnel left out.

"No problem," he walked out to give us some privacy.

"What happened Jaxsyn?" he said weakly and his voice was raspy from the tube that was down his throat for so long.

"So much baby. I need you to try to remain as calm as you can for what I'm about to tell you daddy."

"Okay."

I kissed him and then sat on the side of his bed. "Nashon didn't make it baby."

"What?" Tears instantly welled in his eyes and a mug covered his face.

"Someone sprayed your truck. You got hit six times and Nashon was only hit twice but one of the bullets hit his lung and he bled out before the ambulance could make it to y'all."

He closed his eyes and cried harder than I had ever saw a grown man cry before. I held him tight but that's all that I could do. His heart shattered right before my eyes and I knew he would be this hurt when he found out.

"What the fuck, man," he wiped his face, but the tears kept coming. "Not my muthafuckin brother. Nah man. My other fuckin' half baby," he held me tightly and I cried with him. I couldn't imagine losing any of my siblings, so I wasn't even about to pretend that I understood his pain but seeing him hurt made me hurt for him. "This shit cut deep baby. I swear to God I ain't never felt no shit like this in my life. My fuckin' brother gone?" He laid his head back. "Awww man, this ain't right. This shit ain't right," he looked at me. "I don't wanna live without him ma," he broke down again. "How the fuck am I supposed to live without him?"

"Baby," I wrapped my arms around him and his whole body shook from him crying so hard. He held me so tight I could barely breathe and as strong as I wanted to be for him in this moment, I couldn't get my shit together either. We held each other and cried hysterically for the longest time and when we stopped a few minutes passed and he was starting back up again.

"How long have I been out Jax?" Messiah's eyes were bloody red and swollen. My heart broke for him as I wiped his face.

"A little over three weeks baby."

"Y'all buried him already?" Fresh tears streamed down his handsome face again.

"I made them wait baby. I knew it would be too much for you to miss seeing him. I have your lawyer working on you going to the funeral as well as everything else."

"Why is he even here? Tell me everything that's happened baby and don't leave shit out," he continued crying while I told him everything from the moment, I got the call from Zionna to the very moment that we were in. I told him what Solo said the streets were saying and what the police were saying. I knew it was all too much for him to take in, but he needed to know everything, and he needed to hear it all from me.

"Fuck," he hit the side of his bed with his free hand and I thought that bitch was going to fly off. He kept shaking his head and I knew his wheels were turning.

"Messiah you can turn this shit around. You can't bring Nashon back, but you can beat whatever they're trying to charge you with and handle shit from there," I gave him a look. "I need you focused, and I need you ready to face all this shit head on. Cry to me daddy and no one else. These niggas cannot see you sweat baby. Not right now. They already know losing Nash is going to throw you off and they're going to play on that," I kissed his hand. "Our baby needs you on the outside of that cement wall and on this side of the dirt. You are going to have several moments baby but have your moments with me and show them nothing but the beast that you are."

"You right," he wiped his face and told me to send his lawyer in. I kissed his forehead, then his lips, and did what he asked.

Messiah

I held Jaxsyn's hand as I watched my brother get lowered into the ground. One of his Knights jackets was laid across his casket and something changed inside of me. A part of me died with him and was getting lowered right along with his body. It was an emptiness in my heart that I never felt before and the lower his casket went into the ground the emptier I felt. The colder my heart became. Something dark was brewing in the depths of my soul that I couldn't quite describe. We've spent our whole lives protecting each other from ever having to do this shit. Yet here the fuck I stood, watching my big brother get lowered into the ground. Somebody had to shed blood for this, and a lot of it. Someone's mother had to feel how my granny felt if I didn't make that bitch leak too for giving birth to a bitch ass nigga. My blood was running ice cold through my veins.

"You okay baby?" Jaxsyn rubbed my hand and looked up at me.

"I'm alright," I responded. She's the only person that held me down like she should have. Well Solo had been trying to be there for me, but I didn't feel like fuckin' with no one but my girl. The rest of the Knights was gone have to see me too. I heard a few of the niggas that's handling business on my illegal side was out here making moves like I was gone and for that they'll be handled accordingly.

We all looked away from them throwing dirt over my brother's casket, to look at the street. The Knights lead a brigade of several different motorcycle clubs. It was easily two hundred niggas showing my brother love. This was a tradition when one of our brothers fall no matter how he went. The Knights started the burnout and the smoke was orange. No matter how mad I was at a lot of them, that shit touched me. It was Nash's favorite color. Tears rolled down my face from under my glasses and I tapped my fist over my chest to let Solo know I felt the gesture. The rest of the burnouts continued until the whole street was smoked out and I gave them a head nod and salute to show my appreciation. My brother was going to genuinely be missed and no matter how many snakes were around us, it was definitely some real love amongst us too.

The police hauled my ass in time I was discharged from the hospital so I couldn't make the moves that I wanted to make. My lawyer was able to immediately get me out on bail and I have a court date in exactly one month, so I had to make shit happen in a small amount of time and quietly. He said that I could serve up to five years for possession of the gun I had on me, but they couldn't get me on the drugs they found. He subpoenaed a video from the bank across the street that showed someone walking up to the car with something in his hands. That put an end to all the drug charges but my finger prints were on the gun so it's not much he can do about that except try to get me the least amount of time possible. Had this shit happened in a jurisdiction that I controlled, I wouldn't have even gotten charged, but this was niggas that I wasn't familiar with. I was going to find an in though. It's no way in hell I'm serving five years.

Everyone went back to my granny's house after the funeral and it was good to see that my brother brought our family together, it's just bullshit that it had to be his death that did it. I still couldn't believe this shit and I've spent many nights crying over my nigga. This hit hard and left me sick as fuck. My mother cried and showed her ass, but I didn't buy her bullshit for a second. She's clean now but who the fuck knows what six months from now holds for her. She's called us before, telling us how she was clean and sober and she was going to come get us from granny's house so we could be a family and next thing I know, my niggas in NY is hittin' us up telling us how they saw her suckin' dick for rocks. I'm not about to act impressed until she has some time under her belt. I wasn't in any mood for pretending with people. Those days were over and done with. Fuck her and her sobriety. We barely even knew her ass. She did drugs her whole pregnancy with me and then shipped us out to keep her habit. You don't get no respect for that.

"Boy you look just like yo' daddy boy." My oldest uncle said, and my mother shot him a look.

"Unt uh. Don't go there."

"Hell, shit, the boy do. It ain't my fault that-" Before he could get his words together, she slapped the dog shit out of him, and my grandmother didn't say a word. Obviously, he was about to let some family secrets rip.

"I said don't and I fuckin' meant it," she got up and stormed out of the room. She was pissed but within seconds the conversation changed, and everyone was back to talking about my brother. Jax looked at me from across the room and I shook my head.

"Can I talk to y'all outside for a minute please?" Zionna asked me and I waved Jax over.

"Absolutely."

We moved through the house and followed her out of the front door because people were everywhere in the backyard.

"What's up sweetie?" Jaxsyn asked as she hugged her sister. Zionna really took it hard and I felt bad for her. She looked like she was going to fall out at any minute, and I made sure I kept an eye on her throughout the day. Her and my brother was building a life together and she's all he talked about. This was hard for the family, but we also didn't discount that this shit was killing her too.

She started to cry and Jaxsyn continued to hold her and rub her head. My baby held everyone down, but I know her and Nashon were close too and she hasn't had a moment to herself to grieve for him which broke my heart. After we cried together in the hospital, she's been all gas, no brakes. She went from helping my grandmother with the funeral to doing it all herself when it became too painful for granny. She had the food catered, bought Nashon's clothes with instructions from Zionna. She contacted the family that hadn't been contacted, ordered the flowers, contacted the funeral home, and had his obituary made. She was stretched thin for us and my grief made me fall short on giving her what she was giving everyone else.

"I'm sorry y'all. I'm really trying to stop. Especially for you Messiah. For real," she got choked up.

"Let it out sis," I wrapped my arm around her. "I know how much y'all meant to each other."

"We were everything to each other. This shit don't even seem real," her lip trembled. "I should have told him," she took a deep breath. "I'm pregnant." Jaxsyn and I looked at each other and we busted out laughing. It was a laugh that I needed, and it was a blessing that me and my whole family needed.

"So am I." Jaxsyn smiled.

"What?" Her eyes bucked.

"Yes. I told Messiah before they left that day."

"Sis I know from how excited he was for me when I told him that he was going to be an uncle, that even with him not being here, death couldn't stop his love for you or this baby."

I hugged her and she cried uncontrollably in my arms. She was broken and this is the most powerless I've felt in my life. "I got you. On bro, I do. You not in this alone Z. That's a promise," I whispered in her ear and she nodded her head. In my mind I had two kids on the way. It's no way in hell my nephew or niece would want for anything. Ever.

Zionna

Every day was a struggle for me to get up and get out of bed but every day I was forced too. I hadn't gone back to work yet so Jaxsyn was toting me around on her jobs and annoying the shit out of me daily. She means well and I love her, but some days I just wanted to lay in the bed I used to share with the love of my life and reminisce. I just wanted to go back to that day so I can stop him from going with Messiah and tell him about this baby or make love to him just one more time. I wanted him back and I couldn't shake it. Then it's ten times harder because Sih has his face. When he walks in the door, I want to run to him and hug him but he's not my baby. As much as they looked a like, they were completely different.

"Did y'all talk to the lawyer?" I asked Jaxsyn as she packed her stuff up so we could leave for the day.

"Yeah. Max is five years and the minimum is three to six months."

"Five years?"

"Yup. All I can do is pray Z," she fought back tears. "It's so much going on right now, that's all I can really do," she shrugged. "Are you coming over for dinner? You know Messiah is going to stalk you if you don't."

"I don't know why he think I don't eat. What have you been telling him?" I put my hands on my hips.

"Nothing," she smirked, and I knew her ass was lying.

"Yeah right. You not even a good liar Jaxsyn. I eat all the time."

"Now who's lying? Anyway, he has Chef Blank at the house. He's our new chef that specializes in cooking healthy foods. He wants me eating better for the baby and he wants you eating the same things."

"He's so over protective. How do you deal?" I rolled my eyes. Sih was team too much and working on my nerves. This girl been cooking her whole life and she's damn good at it. I'm sure if he told her to cut back on the salt and butter she would have. A whole new chef was so extra to me.

"I'm used to it now and you will be too."

"I'll never get used to that shit," I shook my head. Sih was annoying, I just could say that out loud. The chef wasn't the only extra shit he was doing. He also had her taking all kinds of pregnancy classes, getting pregnancy massages to relax her and his baby, and all this super white extra shit that was causing me to side eye the fuck out of them. She was two seconds pregnant and none of this shit was called for. He was becoming a dadzilla already and she loved every minute of it. That's not how Nash and I were at all. Well, this would have been his first child too so maybe he would be right along with this maniac Sih. I don't know, but I can guarantee if he tried that chef shit on me, I would have cussed his ass out, unlike my sister who is basking in her man's bullshit.

I started thinking about the fun Nashon and I used to have and how much I was missing simple shit like laughing hysterically at inside jokes or just chillin' at the club house together. I excused myself and went to the bathroom and cried. This pain is my chest wouldn't go away but at the same time I was completely numb. I had breakdowns like this all day every day. I couldn't stop the memories of him from crowding my mind or surround myself with enough people for the loneliness to go away. Nothing filled the void in my heart or eased my aching soul. I yearned for another moment with Nash even if it was brief. Realistically, I knew it would never happen, but I craved it anyway. I was struggling.

"Have you told your momma yet?" I came out and sparked up a conversation so my sister wouldn't feel obligated to comfort me through another breakdown. She had been amazing, but she was stretched thin between Sih and I, and it wasn't fair.

"I haven't told anyone but you. I'm trying to wait until I'm out of the danger zone."

"That's smart. I was going to tell mine tonight when I see her, but I probably should wait too."

"I would but it couldn't hurt telling her. I guess. She is your mother."

"I haven't been around her in so long I don't know if she still runs her mouth or not. I mean I talk to her, but you know. Once her ass start working on my nerves, I'm hanging up, which is our usual routine."

"I forgot how much she used to run her mouth. I don't know how I forgot with the way I told you she was going off on Kabrina that one day and yelling about their threesomes with daddy," she rolled her eyes and I felt her on that. Sandy stay doing the absolute most. The day

144

Nashon was taken from me she was trying to tell me about a sexcapade, and she was on speaker, so she killed whatever vibe we had going. Then his granny started calling for him to come have breakfast with her, Sih, and the rest of her grandsons so we never got to make love. My eyes watered thinking back and I shook it off.

"Girl. Everybody knew everything and she gives unnecessary details that takes all her stories too far," I blinked back my tears so she couldn't see me slipping into another moment.

"Facts. Nope, don't chance it. You can always tell daddy though."

"Fuck him."

"It's been years Zionna."

"You heard me," I shot her a look and she dropped it. I didn't give a fuck about that man or his kids and I was tired of fuckin' saying it. No one can tell me how to feel when it comes to them. I understood Nash when he told me to let it go and blame Sandy, and yes, she played a big role in me not knowing him but at the same time, it's still fuck him. Brian was the reason that our lives were so fucked up to begin with and instead of Jax hating him like I do, she became a got damn daddy's girl. They talk all the damn time and she hangs with her siblings and they all love her which his great, but how Sway?

Brian didn't force Kabrina and Sandy to do drugs, but he damn sure supplied it in quantities that they couldn't afford on their own and then went back to his cushy life in the burbs every night while they went scouring the fuckin' city for more drugs. It was his ass that didn't give a fuck about also admitting them into that fancy ass rehab center that he admitted himself into. He claims he stopped because he had children that needed him, but he didn't think the mothers of his black kids needed the same kind of treatment and to get their shit together for us too? He didn't give a fuck just like Sandy said.

He fucked them like they weren't shit but ass, got them hooked on the purest fuckin' coke that he could get his hands on, and then said fuck them and us. Yeah, he came to get Jax every weekend or whenever she called him but what about the everyday check in. We would be in the house hungry as fuck and hadn't laid eyes on Sandy and Kabrina in days before he showed up for a weekend visit. Before he brought Jax back to his suburban home, he would buy me fast food but leave me right there in that empty ass house alone. Why not boss up on Sandy if you really fuckin' wanted me and not take her shit? Instead he was a pussy and allowed me to stay in a house where niggas were trying to rape me constantly. If it wasn't for Jax I would have been ran through and damaged. She's seven months younger than me and was more of a parent to me than both of my parents. So yeah, it's fuck them both. All day every day. The only reason I even talk to Sandy is because even in her drug induced state the bitch was still there and that's more than what I can say about him…

Jaxsyn

I literally hated discussing my daddy with Zionna and I should have known better than to bring him up. No one made our mothers do drugs and he was doing them too, they just got hooked and he didn't. Well he did, but he went to rehab and they refused. If she ever talked to him, she would know that. He offered to pay and everything, but they didn't want the help. Kabrina and Sandy were young, pretty, and high as a kite. They weren't ready to give up their carefree lives that they were living.

My dad is amazing. He's always come around and he always made sure that we were taken care of. He used to come get me all the time when I was a kid and bring me to his home. His wife Rebecca was sweet, and I couldn't understand how or why, considering the fact that I was his illegitimate child, but she was and still is. Over the years I've grown close to her and she's like a mother to me, more than Kabrina, actually.

My dad is a great father and man and I won't sit back and allow my sister to play him like he's not. Period. He calls me every single day to check on me, he's never missed a birthday and plastered in his house are pictures of me and him from my first birthday and Christmas to the most recent. He's been my backbone my whole life so when she disrespects him over a half ass story that Sandy told her, it's offensive to me and her hate is so strong towards them that she don't give a fuck how it makes me feel, which pisses me off even more.

I also love my brothers and sisters very much and she doesn't want anything to do with them either, which is fine. No one is forcing her too, but why? They all used to ask why she never comes around and I never knew what to say and then they just got used to her not coming. She blames my dad, but she should blame her crazy ass mother for never allowing her to get to know the other side of her family. Blame her for putting stupid shit in her head, like daddy not loving his "black family". That was complete and utter bullshit. Shit, if we didn't live next door to each other I wouldn't have known her either because of Sandy's stupid ass logic. I had the best times of my life going to my daddy's house and it was a breath of fresh air to get away from

Kabrina's ass for a little while when we were kids. Her mother played her by keeping her away from him, but she places all the blame on him, and I hate that shit.

We rode the whole way to my house in silence. I had too much on my mental to argue with my sister over some old shit. If she didn't want daddy to be a part of her life, I had to let that shit go just like all of our siblings has. He won't because she's his daughter but that's between them.

I walked into my home and Chef Blank was in the kitchen cooking and Sih was in the living room on the phone. I could tell that he was talking business, so I didn't even bother going in there. We spoke to Tabitha and Chef and went to the basement.

"Let's watch a movie," I suggested.

"No. I just wanna lay here Jaxsyn. *Please*." She snapped.

"Fine," I left her alone to wallow. That's all she wanted to do and no matter how much we told her that it wasn't good for the baby she ignored us and sulked anyway. Last week we had to rush her to the hospital because she blacked out and they said it was stress and dehydration, but she continues to do her. It's hard to tell grown people how to be grown so that's some more shit that I'm going to have to back away from.

"Hey Tink." Sih was in the kitchen.

"Hey baby," I smiled.

"Why you didn't come see your man when you got home?" He rubbed my little pudge and kissed me.

"You were on a call that seemed important."

"Yeah, that was my lawyer. They pushed my court date back three months. The shit pissed me off because the further they push my shit back the more likely it becomes that I'm going to miss my baby being born. He said he was going to see what he can do but when he says shit like that, it's nothing he can do."

"Well at least we get more time together now Bae. I'll just have someone record it," I laughed.

"Who? I don't want nobody lookin at you like that but me."

"Not even your granny?"

"Especially my granny. She's a freak." We all died laughing.

"You a damn fool. I'm going to change."

148

"Okay," I went upstairs and took off my work clothes. My pudge was too cute, and it made me smile. I wanted so badly to share my excitement with my sister, but she wasn't excited at all about her baby or mine, so I called my little sister Alyssa.

"Hello."

"Hey Pooh."

"Hey Shugga. I miss you. How's Sih?"

"I miss you too. He's much better. He's home now and in physical therapy daily. One of the shots caused some damage to his arm but he's almost one hundred percent."

"God is good."

"Girl ain't he! I prayed and prayed, and he pulled through."

"Now what's going on with the case?"

"They pushed it back, so we still don't know anything yet."

"Oh okay."

"I have some good news for you, and I want to tell you face to face."

"I like good news sissy. I can come down there this weekend."

"Perfect. I'm off so this will be fun. I haven't saw you in forever."

"Girl you saw me a couple months ago when we went to Cedar Point."

"Well it seems like forever so sue me." We both laughed.

"Daddy said he's been trying to call and check on you."

"I called him back this morning. Maybe I'll stop over there tomorrow after work."

"Oh okay. Yeah, they miss you and want to make sure you're good. You know how momma get when she's worrying about one of us. She's probably driving daddy crazy over there."

"You know she is. I'll go check in."

"Okay Sissy. See you this weekend."

"Alright Pooh. Be careful driving down here."

"I will. Love you."

"Love you more," I hung up and continued changing my clothes. Alyssa loves me so much and she used to try to be just like me when she was younger. She was my shadow, hell she still is, she just can't follow me around like she used because she's in college. I still keep her fly and up to date on the latest trends. Our other sister Sydnee hates it. She thinks Alyssa is spoiled and all they do is argue. I gave up trying to be the peacemaker between them a long time ago so now, for the most part I just deal with them separately just like I do with them and Zionna.

"I'm starving," I went back to the kitchen and Sih was still talking to Chef Blank.

"It's ready. Your timing is perfect."

"Great," I smiled. "Come on Z," I yelled downstairs and Blank made all of our plates.

"Hey Zionna. I didn't even know you were here."

"Yup," she dragged and sat down at the table.

"Anyway. Baby my little sister is coming this weekend."

"Alyssa? That's great."

"Yeah. I know. I can't wait."

"You two together are going to be a giggle fest and that shit is going to annoy me."

"Probably but I want you here. I'm going to barbecue."

"The chef will barbecue. I don't want you inhaling that smoke beautiful."

Zionna laughed. "Are you going to piss and shit for her too or can she do that alone? Jax you need a wiper because I'm sure Sih got you?"

"Zionna," I looked at her like she was crazy.

She slammed her fork on the plate, got up, and walked away.

"Here," I got up and followed her. I held out my hand that was holding the keys to my Range Rover. "Go home. You don't want to be here, and I don't want him feeling like he has to walk on eggshells in his own home. We'll leave you alone since that's what you really want."

She looked at me with her nostrils flared and one eyebrow up, then snatched the keys from me. I knew she was hurting but I refused to let her disrespect my man in his home. We're all grieving but she was going too far, and if alone time is what she wanted, she was definitely about to get a lot of it. I could only be so nice, and she had just blown it.

Black

Bad news travels fast and I was aware of Jaxsyn's new nigga almost getting killed and them actually gettin' his brother. Shit didn't surprise me one bit from the way that them niggas came at me. If they were out here on that type of shit, then a nigga probably called their bluff. Quan said he knew of the niggas and supposedly they run a motorcycle gang or some shit. I ain't never heard of them or "The Knights" and I grew up over there. Then again, I haven't been in the streets in years. Funny how my wife wanted more for us and demanded I leave that street shit alone, only to turn around and leave me for a nigga doing the same shit.

I stared at myself in the mirror and this was as good as it was going to get. Today was my divorce hearing and I had rescheduled and prolonged this shit for long as I could. Even with everything that's happened between me and Jax, I still didn't want to hear the judge grant this divorce. I tried to force mediation and everything but thanks to Ty petty ass that wasn't happening. He had been in boxing and texting Jax since their altercation. He was mad that I wouldn't let him press charges and the charges got dropped. She had plenty of proof that I had been cheating on her including pictures of me and Ty laid up in our bed. I should have kicked his ass to the curb for that petty ass shit but Shardae had just given birth to my daughter and couldn't fuck for six weeks. Plus, I love him, so he lucked the fuck up playing with me like that.

I grabbed my keys and wallet and took a deep breath. Damn I didn't want to do this shit, but I didn't have a choice. I had to be a man and face this noise like one.

"Finally. You were taking forever."

"Fuck you mean, finally? You ain't coming with me Ty," I looked at this nigga sideways like he was purple with two heads. What the fuck be on his mind is all I really wanna know? He's fucked with Jax this whole time and now he wanted to come face to face with her with police around? Nah. That was a recipe for disaster.

"Ooooh no, we're not playing that game anymore mister. If you don't want to hold my hand and kiss me in public, fine. I agreed to that. Stay in your safe little closet where you're comfortable. That's fine too. What we're not going to do, is pretend that I'm just a nobody. I'm your boyfriend and you're going to respect me as such. You're fuckin', suckin', and telling me you love me daily. I deserve respect and I'm not settling for anything other than that. I'm ready to go," he fixed my shirt and tie as I stared at him. He had been really trying me lately and I didn't know how to react to none of this shit. On one hand, I understood him, but on the other hand, I been told this nigga I was straight on this gay shit and on him. I tried to push him away so he could find someone better than me, but he won't let go of me. Now he's pushing me to be the man he wants me to be and that shit is weird as fuck.

"When did we establish that you're my boyfriend Ty? How the fuck does that even sound?"

"It sounds like I'm living in your house, fuckin' you regularly, cooking all of your meals, praying you through this tough time with your cheating wife, helping you pay bills, and everything else that a boyfriend does. You're in denial. Your heart belongs to me and only me. It has for years and we both know it. You couldn't even see me with another guy when we ran into each other at the gas station without getting mad. You hated that shit so much it wasn't even a week before you were sliding into my DM's and then inside of me. What's happening between us is real Derrick. I'm your man and you're my man and you love me unconditionally," he placed my face in his hands. "And I love you too baby," he kissed me, and I pulled him closer. I did love Ty. I loved the fuck out of him. Even when he pisses me the fuck off, my heart still reacts when I'm near him. He was right, I was fighting him because of what us being together would look like to friends that hadn't called me once and checked on me since I was going through this shit with Jax. He gave me a real quick reality check.

"Get your shit and let's go," I said, and he smiled as he gave me a slight nod before grabbing his jacket and phone. We walked out and I reached back for his hand after he locked the door. I shocked myself but it felt right for some reason. I needed to grow up and this was the first step.

"You don't have to do this. I'm not trying to for-"

"I'm a grown ass man and I'm well aware of what I don't have to do. You in this shit with me or not?"

"Are you admitting that I'm your boyfriend no matter how strange that sounds out loud?"

"You're my boyfriend Ty. No matter how much I hate how that shit sounds and for the record, I hate the fuck out of how that shit sounds. This is not going to be easy, but you deserve more respect from me and I'm going to do my best at giving that shit to you. I swear yo' ass get on my fuckin' nerves sometime but I can't deny that I love yo' sexy ass and you always have a nigga back when I can't even have my own shit. Be patient with me though. That's all I can ask."

Tears fell from his eyes. "I've waited years for this very moment Derrick. I love you so much," I stepped closer to him. This was huge coming from me. We were outside in the open, but I hated seeing him cry and instantly went to him like I would have if we were behind closed doors. It was second nature. I've protected him since the first day we met years ago, and I would protect him and care about his feelings until the day my casket drop.

"I'm sorry for what I put you through Ty. This shit is hard for me man, but I love yo' ass to death too. Never give up on me okay?" I wiped his tears and he nodded.

"So, this you now?" Quan walked up and Ty instinctively backed up. Watching fear wash over him like we were wrong, made me hop in my bag. It was me that had him feeling like that. Ty is openly gay, and he doesn't give a fuck who likes it and who doesn't, but me hiding who I am had him back in the closet and that shit wasn't right.

"Yeah. It is." The words left my mouth as if it wasn't shit for me to tell my best friend that I was gay, and this was my nigga.

"Bet. So, you ready to do this shit or what? Is she taking yo' ass to the cleaners or she's acting like she got some got damn sense?"

"The cleaners bro but she ain't asking for shit that ain't rightfully hers so I'm not trippin'. She already got the car repoed a few weeks back. Ty sent her pictures of us in the crib and she added the house to the motion, which is in her name, she wants the other car that neither of us drive, and a few other things. My lawyer pushed me to ask for spousal support, so she'll have to pay me alimony."

"Damn nigga." Quan shook his head. "I never thought this shit would get this ugly. I mean I knew she was going to divorce your confused ass, but I was hoping she didn't rake you over the coals and shit."

"It's all good. We about to head to the court now, you coming?"

"Yeah I'll ride with y'all. I haven't saw my baby in a minute and she'll probably be there with her."

"You know her nigga got killed and shit."

"Yeah. The hood held a candle light visual for him when it happened. I heard he was a good dude. That shit was fucked up."

"Yup…" I left it as that. "Ty this is Quan, one of my best friends."

"I think we met years ago."

"Probably." Quan gave a reverse head nod and we got into the car. We all made small talk and I couldn't tell if Quan was uncomfortable or not, but I was trying not to focus on that. Ty deserved me trying and that's what I was on right now. Today was a new day for us. We held hands the whole way to the court and I got out and opened his door for him when we got there. Same shit I would have done if we weren't in the inner city or if Quan wasn't with us.

We were earlier than I thought and end up waiting damn near forty minutes and a recess before Jaxsyn and her mother walked in with her lawyer. They both looked our way and Kabrina rolled her eyes. Even when she was high, she loved Jaxsyn and I together. She used to tell me all Jax favorite things to make sure I got her everything she wanted for gift giving holidays and her birthday. She tried to be a good mother to Jax even though she was fucked up and jealous most of the time. She was definitely a complex woman but her love for her daughter never wavered. Jax used to say she was only happy about us being together because she was scared Jax and Andre was going to fuck but I think it was because back then we were genuinely happy, and she knew Jax deserved that.

"All rise. Court is now in session. The honorable Jennifer Tolliver presiding," she walked in and after she sat down everyone else sat down too. My hands started to get sweaty and my heart sped up. My lawyer walked in as the judge and the bailiff discussed her next case. Ty placed his hand on my knee as my lawyer started whispering to me and I didn't hear shit. I looked over at Jax and her lawyer was in her ear too. How the fuck did we get here when we were so in love? On God, Jax was a nigga soul mate and I never thought we would end up in divorce court and committed to people that weren't each other. This girl has literally hugged the block with me and put niggas down to save my life. Now here we are, on two different sides of the aisle. She looked over at me and we locked eyes for a brief moments before she looked at Ty and shook her head. I saw the sadness in her eyes even if she tried hard to hide it. I hurt her and regardless of how many times I think about her cheating and being with another nigga, I knew I pushed her into his arms. I knew without a shadow of doubt she was only with him because I was giving all my time to Shardae. I didn't take care of home how I should have.

154

Two hours later our divorce was finalized by the judge and I was awarded $1,762.00 a month in spousal support based on her income. Jax looked like she wanted to spit in my fuckin' face but it is what it is. It wasn't my idea but I damn sure could use it. Especially since she was awarded everything else. The house, cars, and even my business was given to her. She had proof that she bought it and I hadn't been doing what I needed to do so they granted her request, but it backfired too. That was also proof that she had me living a certain lifestyle which aided in the judge granting the spousal support.

"So, we're moving into my apartment?" Ty asked after Quan left.

"If you don't mind," I kissed on his neck. He's all I had right now, and I needed him. He moaned and told me how welcomed I was to live with him. I turned him and unbuckled my pants just as Shardae was calling. "Be quiet, I gotta get this," I answered the phone.

"Hello."

"Are you coming to see your daughter or not?"

"Oh, I can see her today? You not on that bullshit?" I made Ty arch his back more.

"I was mad, and I apologize. I shouldn't be playing games with our baby. My momma cussed my ass out and told me I was wrong."

"So, when I said you was wrong it didn't mean shit, huh?"

"Are you coming or not Black?"

"Yeah I'm coming. Give me like forty-five minutes."

"Okay. I'm hungry too. I need you to take us out to dinner."

"I can do that."

"Thanks. After that I'm suckin' your dick to apologize. I really didn't mean to keep her from you baby daddy."

"Don't do that shit again Shar. What we go through is what we go through, but my baby can't be something you hold over my head to be petty."

"I won't daddy. Come let me apologize."

"I'll be there in a few," I hung up. "Fuck!" I was about to cum.

"Tell me you love me Black. Oh God, tell me."

"I love you baby. Shit! I love you so much!" I nutted and he was jerking off to cum with me.

"Mmmm," he collapsed, and I kissed his neck.

155

"I'll be back."

"Okay. Kiss lil mama for me," he closed his eyes and I ran upstairs to shower. I didn't want to cheat on Ty the same day we made shit official but Shar's childish ass is reactive to everything, and if I don't give her what she wants then she'll play games with my daughter. I love my baby girl already and if I gotta give Shardae dick and dinner to smooth shit over then that's what the fuck I'm going to do.

Katrina: *You just crossed my mind and look what happened.*

Katrina: Picture Message

Katrina: *Come plug this leak for me Black*

See how shit happens? My phone been dry as fuck for weeks and now bitches were trying to come out of nowhere. I stared at the picture and shook my head.

Me: *So thinking of me did all of that huh?*

Katrina: *You already know! You coming over? I'll be naked and waiting.*

Me: *I still got the key. I'm on my way. Start playing with that pretty mafucka for me. I wanna hear moaning when I walk in.* I damn near ran out of the door to get to Katrina. I started fuckin' her years ago. She was married and that shit was perfect. We both fucked each other whenever we could and when we couldn't, it wasn't a big deal. She got hooked on the dick and gave me a key to her crib. I was sneaking in that bitch while her husband was in the basement playing 2K and shit. The thrill had us gone. I was twenty-two-years-old and reckless.

I remember one time I fucked her during a family barbecue. Their people were everywhere, and I showed up. She spotted me from across the room and I wanted to die laughing at the expression on her face. I went to the basement and ten minutes later she came running down the stairs scared as fuck. It didn't stop her from riding me on that nigga weight bench though. I had her ass in the basement for two hours fuckin' her ass silly and then walked out of the backdoor leaving her knocked out on their basement couch.

Me: *Gimme a hour baby my sister got a flat and I have to go help her*

Shar: *No problem baby daddy*

Katrina freak ass was exactly the stress reliever that I needed and then my baby momma was going to finish me off like only she could. Today was rough and I needed them to clear my head. I didn't want to start this shit behind Ty's back but I'm going to always need a shot of pussy on the side. I'm addicted to that gushy shit.

Messiah

Jax was pissed the fuck off when she came back from court and I didn't know whether it was because she was finally divorced from this nigga or if something happened. She had Tabitha to run her a hot bath as she laid across the couch. I kissed her lips and left her alone. Her pregnancy emotions were running my baby and I didn't want to be on the receiving end of whatever was happening.

About an hour later Jax came into my home office and straddled my lap. She looked gorgeous and her skin was glowing. I ran my fingers down her back and she pulled my dick out of my jogging pants. She knows my shit belongs to her and don't mind taking what's hers. I loved that shit too. Women be on that shy shit and a nigga always gotta initiate sex but not with my baby. She'll climb me like a fuckin' tree to get to this dick.

"Shit," I leaned forward, and her titties were in my face. I sucked on each of them circling my tongue around her hardened nipples. "Yes baby," she stroked my head as her pussy suctioned my dick. She felt too fuckin' good.

"Damn Tink."

"You like that Daddy?" She rolled her hips and I sat back to watch the show.

"Hell yeah," I held her waist and let her do her thing. We stared at each other making the lust and passion between us more intense. Love consumed us. Her head dipped back, and she played with her titties as her hips were still working slow and sensually. The sight before me was nothing but perfection. My free hand traveled to her stomach and I felt more blessed than ever before. "Shit baby." I grunted. My nut was building, and she leaned forward and started increasing her speed. She was showing out and within seconds she started squirting all over me making me go crazy in her shit. I gripped her ass and plunged in and out of her. She started screaming my name and after a few more shots to her guts I was releasing hard as fuck. Had she not already been pregnant that load would have gotten the job done.

"I love and appreciate you so much. I love the man that you are and everything that you stand for. I love that you don't mind proving how much you love me when I'm feeling insecure and how you do it so effortlessly. I'm even in love with the smallest of things that you do for me that may seem like they go unnoticed, but I notice baby, and it makes me love you so much more. My life is more blessed than ever before because you're in it. Sometimes I cry just thinking about the future and the fact that I get to spend it with someone so fuckin' remarkable. You're the proof that somewhere along the line I did something right in my life," her eyes were filled with tears. "Can you just hold me for a minute?" She swallowed hard and I wrapped my arms her. Her head was on my shoulder and she broke down crying hard as hell. I didn't say anything. I allowed her to have her moment because I knew this moment was needed. These were tears that she should have *been* shedding for many different reasons. I ran my fingers through her hair and kissed her repeatedly as she purged her soul. After a while, she raised her head and smiled as she wiped her tears. "I'm good now," she got up and went to the bathroom in the hallway and cleaned herself and then came back and cleaned me.

"You wanna discuss what just happened baby girl?"

"It's nothing to discuss. I simply appreciate and respect the man that you are. I love you Messiah Knight."

"I love you more baby," I pulled her close and kissed her before she walked out leaving me to my own thoughts. I had a lot on my plate, and it was comforting to know that I wasn't dropping the ball with her like I thought I was. I handled a few more orders for the club house and a couple more for a few of my other businesses before I shut down the computer. I went through the house looking for Jaxsyn before I found her in our bed sleeping peacefully. I stared at my blessing and quietly thanked God for her. I kissed her head a few times and inhaled her familiar scent before walking out.

Since I was so close to this shit with my brother and running off of pure emotions, I went to extreme measures and called my cousin from New York to come help me sort this shit out. I was still healing, fighting for my freedom, and trying to find the niggas that did this shit to us. My head wasn't fully in it and that's how niggas get themselves killed. I couldn't take any chances.

Gizmo used to do business for us a long time ago when we were deep into the street life and we stopped using him because he started charging us like we weren't family. We were on some young shit and instead of paying him what we both knew he was worth we went with someone else. Giz never took that shit personal and said several times that business was business. That's just how he is. A real stand up nigga that's about his shit and that's exactly what I needed right now. I don't give a fuck how much this nigga wants, I'm willing to pay it. Somebody took my brother from me and tried to take me from my unborn child. Niggas had to pay for that, and they knew I was out for blood, so I needed him to snuff these niggas out.

"Cuz." Gizmo hugged me tightly.

"What's good my baby?"

"Shit man. I just heard about Nash a day before you called nigga. You know I don't even be around the fam like that B. Had I known I would've been here."

"Yeah I know. I need you to handle this shit for me tho'. Get the information I need to get these bitches. I don't care what it takes cuz, who gotta get that dirt nap, or how much it cost. I need these niggas heads."

"I got you and it ain't gone cost you shit. Nashon was fam."

"Thanks man." We hugged again and I ran everything down to him. I told him about the meeting and all the nigga's that's looking at me sideways, surprised I fuckin pulled through at all. I didn't give a damn how bloody this shit had to get, what methods had to be used, or how long this shit would take. I needed answers and I'm not stopping until I have them.

Jaxsyn

Messiah didn't allow me to do anything to prepare for my sister's arrival, instead he ran Tabitha and Chef Blank like slaves. I apologized to both of them repeatedly, but they kept saying that it was their job. I guess I still had to get used to being pampered and waited on daily by other people. I didn't grow up like this and Black damn sure wasn't getting me a chef or maid. Speaking of his stupid ass; wow... Just fuckin' wow! Spousal support and the nigga showed up with his fuckin' side nigga! I swear I hated that man with everything inside of me. Ty had been in my inbox for weeks and he thought it was a good idea to bring this bitch ass nigga to court with him. Then Quan fake ass sitting there smirking the whole time like our life falling apart was his entertainment. I was just disgusted with the whole scene. Black had no fuckin' respect for me and it made me realize he never loved me at all. I was a cover up and that shit hurt no matter how much I love Sih.

"Ms. Blackwell your sister is here." Thankfully Tabitha snatched me away from my thoughts because I was getting pissed all over again.

"Yay," I hopped up and ran downstairs. "Oh," I stopped dead in my tracks. "Hey."

"Yeah. Wrong sister huh?" Zionna looked pissed.

"That's not at all how I meant it Z."

"Yes, you did," she said with an attitude. "So, you invited all of them here and didn't think to invite me? The bitch that always has your back?" Something was off with her, but I couldn't place my finger on it. She doesn't talk to me like that and I was looking at her ass like she was crazy.

"Why would I invite you when you don't like any of them Zionna? When we were at Cedar Point you wouldn't even speak to Jagger's girlfriend who don't have shit to do with nothing so why would I subject them to that again?"

"I didn't speak to the bitch because I didn't hear her and I told you that then," she rolled her eyes. "And just because I don't fuck with them doesn't mean you just get to not invite me to shit you throw. Let me be the one to decide whether I want to decline the invitation or not."

"Zionna, I know you're hurting right now, but you're being a real bitch and I'm not in the mood for that shit today. I've done everything that I could to help you cope and it's still not enough so…"

"I'm being a bitch? You invited our sperm donor, his wife, and all four of your siblings over but didn't say shit to me and I see you damn near every day. But I'm the bitch Jax? Me?"

"I said Alyssa was coming over when we were at the table Z. You remember? The day you snapped on Messiah in his own home."

"I apologized to him yesterday for that Jaxsyn."

"Good. You should have been apologized," I shrugged. "I don't mind you staying Zionna and you know that, but we all have fun when we're together and you don't like any of them, so I don't want you ruining what we've put together."

"Well I'm staying."

I shook my head with disappointment. "You're staying just to be a bitch, but you know what, you're more than welcomed to make an ass out of yourself, yet again," here we were arguing over our family again and I didn't feel like doing this shit with her. Sandy really fucked her head up and instead of her grown ass righting the wrongs of the past, she's holding on to it like a child who doesn't know any better. This bullshit was old and annoying.

The doorbell rang and I walked around her.

"My Pooooooh!" I opened my arms and Alyssa ran to me.

"My Shuggaaaa!" We rocked back and forth and then laughed.

"I missed you so much," I played in her hair like I always do.

"I missed you too sissy. Where's Sih?"

"He'll be back soon. The rest of the family will be here in a few too and Zionna is in the living room."

She rolled her eyes and I smiled. "Great."

"I know right."

"So, about this news you have; is it for the whole family or just for little old me?"

"Just for you and you cannot say a word," I held out my pinky and she wrapped hers around it.

"She's pregnant. Hi Alyssa." Zionna came from the living room.

"What a bitch move Zionna," I couldn't believe her ornery ass. "Wow," I shook my head in disbelief. Losing Nash really had her on one.

"Well at least I spoke this time, right?" She shrugged her shoulders.

"Congrats sissy." Alyssa hugged me and ignored Zionna just like she ignores Sydnee when she acts like that. I swear for two people that don't know each other they were two of a kind.

"Thanks. I'm so happy but I'm not telling anyone until I know the baby is safe."

"I'm happy too. You're going to be a really great mommy Shugga and this baby is going to be blessed because of you and that heart of yours. You went through so much to get to this point in life but you're with the perfect man and everything is finally happening the way it's supposed to happen. I can't wait to be an aunt."

"An aunt?" Zionna laughed.

"That's right. She's no more your sister than she is mine Zionna." Alyssa said sarcastically.

"Stop. Both of you. Zionna if you're going to act like this, I told you, you can go boo. I'm not playing."

"I thought I was invited to stay."

"You are and forever will be but not to insult them or to be rude. I'm not having that," I rolled my eyes.

"That was far from rude but okay Jaxsyn," she was working on my damn nerves and I wanted to snap her neck.

"Look who I found." Sih walked in with my parents and the rest of my siblings.

"Daddy," I hugged him.

"Hey baby girl," he kissed me and then went to Alyssa.

"Hey Ma," I hugged Rebecca and she rubbed my head.

"You've been through a lot and we need to unload some of that baggage baby," she whispered in my ear and I nodded. "I'm not playing around Jax."

"I know and we will," she kissed my cheek and I hugged my big brothers.

"Sydnee you better hug me before I slap you down to the ground."

"Didn't I tell you?" She looked at Sih and he laughed.

"Baby she said, 'my sister is so violent watch', and I'm like not my Jaxsyn. I guess I was wrong huh?" We all laughed.

"She brings it out of me with her spoiled bratty butt. Get over here Syd," I hugged her tightly and she continued laughing. Zionna had wandered off to the kitchen so I ushered everyone to the backyard.

"This home is beautiful Messiah."

"Thanks. You know your daughter had to redecorate, so this is all her doing."

"It's really beautiful baby." Rebecca smiled as she took it all in.

"Thanks Ma," I looked around with pride.

We made small talk once we made it to the backyard and Zionna finally made it outside but her whole attitude had changed. Alyssa and I looked at each other and didn't know what to think. She went from snappy and rude to pleasant.

"Hello everyone," she smiled and waved.

"Hey baby." My dad got up and hugged her but no one else moved they all just spoke back.

I kept staring at her while everyone was talking, and it finally hit me. This bitch was drunk. I could see it all over her face now. My blood started boiling. Was she fuckin' serious right now, sitting amongst my nigga while she's drunk and carrying his dead brother's baby!

"Hey Zionna, let me talk to you really quick sweetie," I whispered and we both got up. "We'll be right back y'all," I smiled, and everyone continued their conversations.

"Bitch I know damn well you are not fuckin drunk?"

"I had one drink so pipe the fuck down Mother Theresa, maybe two drinks," she laughed. "I don't know, but not enough for you to call me drunk bitch."

"Nashon is dead Zionna. The baby that you're carrying is the only way to hold on to a piece of him and you're fuckin' drinking? I don't care if it was one drink or a half of a drink, you're wrong! If Sih notices he'll kill you with his bare fuckin hands. Literally," I pushed her. I was pissed. "I can't even believe you Z. How fuckin' selfish…"

"Whatever Jaxsyn and fuck you for judging me. You don't know what the hell I'm going through. The hell I'm living in every day. You don't know how it feel to be in a room full of people and still feel lonely. It's real easy to fuckin' judge when your man is still out there loving on you and mine is in the ground. Gone! Never coming back to me. You don't know the pain I feel every single second of every fuckin' day," her eyes filled with tears. "I'm about to go," she said calmly and as bad as I wanted to feel for her the liquor on her breath shut down those feelings and I didn't care about her tears. My niece of nephew's life was being toyed with and I didn't appreciate it. I've offered to be her shoulder to lean or cry on and she turned to liquor instead.

"Go pick a room upstairs and sleep this shit off. I'll have Alyssa to drive you home when everyone leaves."

She walked away without saying anything and I didn't feel bad that I had yelled at her. She was fuckin losing her mind right before my eyes and I wasn't about to pacify that behavior. Yes, I know she's hurting over Nashon, and no, I don't know that pain and pray I never do, but I know how much love I have for my unborn child. I know that she's carrying precious cargo and acting recklessly with it. There was no excuse good enough to make up for drinking while pregnant. Period.

We had a great day and my love for my family grew even stronger. The setting that we had tonight out on our patio was what I always wanted and needed as a kid. This was the life I dreamed about and once I was out of Kabrina's house. When you're growing up in the slums, and scraping to survive, your dreams become big, but the older you get they become far-fetched and you give into your surroundings. Not me. I prayed for days like this and even if Messiah hadn't invited me into his home, I was well on my way to obtaining this dream.

"Where's Alyssa?" Sih asked.

"She went to take Zionna home. She didn't feel that well."

"Man, I feel so bad for her. When you don't feel good you have me to rub your belly and run around for you, but my bro is gone and she's alone," he shook his head and I brought him into my arms and held him. He always has moments about Nashon and I'm always right there to console him through them. I wouldn't want it any other way. I tried to do the same for my sister, but she called me annoying and started pushing me away.

"I love you Bae."

"I love you too Tink," he kissed my pudgy stomach and we continued to hold each other tightly. We were blessed and we knew it.

Messiah's court date had been shuffled around several times over the last couple months and tomorrow was finally the day, but neither of us made a big deal about it. Rebecca's birthday dinner distracted us well enough that we laughed and danced all night. No stressing about what will happen tomorrow and no sulking. We really enjoyed our time with my family, and we needed that brief mental break. He's been grieving, going to physical therapy, running the streets with his cousin, and worrying about everything under the sun. It was good to see my baby breathe for a minute.

"Look at your stomach baby," he smiled and hugged me from the back while we both looked at my reflection in the mirror. I had just undressed and was standing there practically naked.

"I know. I'm getting so big."

"And beautiful Tink," he kissed my neck. "You have a glow that draws me to stare at you sometime baby. I hope it's from being happy."

"It's you, it's our baby, it's our life, and most of all, it's our love. Of course I'm happy," I turned around and kissed him. "Whatever happens tomorrow I'll be right by your side."

"I know you will," he ran his fingers through my hair and forced a smile. I knew that he was trying to be strong for me, but I could tell he was stressed to the max. The last thing he wanted to do was leave his pregnant girlfriend and his unborn child.

"I love you," I kissed his chest.

"I love you too Baby."

I continued kissing on him until I lowered myself in front of him. I unbuttoned his pants and took him into my mouth. Pleasing him is all that I wanted to do, and I planned on doing just that, all night long.

I stared at Messiah until his alarm woke him up so we could get dressed for court. We didn't know what was coming our way and the fear of the unknown had me awake for hours.

"Good morning baby," he smiled, and my heart skipped a beat.

"Good morning."

"Let's get dressed so we can face this shit."

"Let's."

"Baby I need to know that if they sit me down you can hold this shit together."

"You know I can. I got us."

We got up without another word being spoken about court or his future and got dressed. I wanted him to know that I would be good so I fixed my somber attitude and we spent our time loving on each other and laughing hysterically like only we could do.

"We have to go baby."

"Okay," I got up from my vanity and followed my man downstairs. He looked delicious in his suit and I quickly rolled up the partition to give him some lip service in the back of the Maybach on our way to court. His ass couldn't do anything but smile and shake his head when I straightened my clothes and crossed my legs when I finished. I'm his freak in the sheets and his lady in the streets. He'll never find another that has this shit down to a science like I do.

We heard case after case and then they called his name. My heart was in my stomach, and I know he was shitting bricks, but we held our heads high and remained composed. Even if he had to serve six months that would be huge for us, so we were both lost in our own thoughts but maintaining a dignified front.

The judge's words were a blur just like both lawyers' words were a blur. All I wanted to do was fast forward to the judgement. What was about to happen to our lives? We had been waiting months for this moment and here we were still waiting and debating.

"Hey sis." Alyssa sat next to me and I smiled. She was home for Rebecca's fiftieth birthday and stayed an extra day just to support us.

"Thanks for coming," I fought back my tears and she held my hand. I needed her so bad in this moment. I hadn't talked to Zionna in almost two months and I didn't have anyone else, so having my little sister next to me in this moment meant more to me than I could ever explain to her.

We both sat there and waited impatiently for the judge to hand down his ruling.

"What's the plea agreement that they keep talking about?" She asked me as we watched them all walk out together; the prosecutor, our lawyers, and Sih.

"I don't know." We got up and followed. They went into a small room across the hall from the court room and came out thirty minutes later.

"What's going on Messiah?"

166

"The prosecutor was pushing for me to serve the whole five years and pay $1,300 in fines and fees. I pulled a few strings and got them down to eighteen months with the possibility of early release and $10,000 in fines baby."

"Oh God," I hugged him. He was going to miss the first year of our baby's life, but it wasn't five years which made this agreement bittersweet.

"We good ma. It could have been the whole five and I can't lie, that shit would have killed me. My connections could only get it down so far, but we can do eighteen months apart baby. We're mentally solid enough for that."

"I know."

"Alright Messiah. I have everything taken care of, and you turn yourself in on Monday afternoon."

"Thanks for everything." They shook hands and smiled but all I wanted to do was cry. "Let's see if we can get this ultrasound done ma. I want to see what we're having before Monday. Thanks for coming lil sis. She needs you," he hugged Alyssa and we all walked out.

I made several calls to different doctors and they all told me that sixteen weeks was ideal, and I was only fourteen weeks.

"I got someone, and they can do it today." Alyssa smiled and held up a piece of paper. "We have to leave now. I told him that we would be there before his lunch break."

"Okay." We said excitedly and rushed over to the clinic that she found.

"Hey Dr. Messer. This is my sister Jaxsyn and her boyfriend Messiah. I went to school with Dr. Messer's daughter," she smiled, and I could tell off rip that she fucked him. I was irritated and pissed off. I mean this nigga was fine as hell, but he was also way too old to be touching my sister sexually.

"Hi Jaxsyn. Right this way. Why the rush?" He looked back at us.

"We're excited and we want to know. Plus, I read online that you can see the sex as early as thirteen weeks."

"That's true. Sometimes you can. It all depends on your baby."

"Well hopefully this baby cooperates. We really want to know," I smiled at him and a nurse took my weight, vitals, and talked to us about my diet.

"Let's take a look," he squeezed a cold gel on my stomach and moved his instrument around.

"Wow," he smiled.

"What?" We all looked at him and then at the fuzzy black and white image on the monitor. I've never been good at looking at these things. When chicks used to show me their ultrasound pictures I would just smile and congratulate them.

"I'm unable to see the sex unfortunately and you will have to wait a little while longer but that's because you're having twins."

"What?" I sat up and stared at the monitor harder trying to see what he was seeing.

"Twins." The doctor pointed to them.

"Messiah Jr. and Nashon." Messiah smiled from ear to ear. He was over the moon happy.

"They might be girls' punk," I smiled just as hard as him. Black put me through a lot when it came to having children, so this moment meant everything to me.

"Or, that's my sons in there," he kissed my forehead. "Thanks doc. We appreciate you," he shook his hand and I cleaned myself off with the paper towel Dr. Messer passed me.

"The blessings keep pouring in sis." Alyssa hugged me. "I'll be right back."

"Yeah I bet," I shot her a look.

"We'll talk later," she seemed disappointed that I peeped what was going on, but she already knows I peep everything.

"You happy baby?" Messiah asked as if he was unsure about how I felt.

"Happier than I've ever been about anything in my life. I'm hurt that I have to do it alone for a little while but other than that, of course I am. I get two parts of you instead of one. Honestly, nothing is more perfect than that." We stared at each other for a moment before he kissed me deeply. I couldn't believe I was this blessed.

Messiah

I spent the whole weekend shooting moves and getting shit together with The Knights and my other businesses making sure when I leave the money would still move. I hated leaving my pregnant girlfriend in charge of everything, but I didn't trust anyone but her and I knew even if she didn't want to run shit, she would on the strength of her love for me. I gave her a crash course on shipping and receiving pharmaceuticals, and the warehouse that we store them in. I also left her access to everything that was mine and my brothers. She was sitting on millions and I had to believe that she would do the right thing. I didn't tell her about one of my stashes on some just in case shit but I'm one hundred percent sure that I can trust my baby with everything that I have.

Last night I had the whole mansion covered in red and white rose petals. When we walked in, it felt like plush carpet under our feet. As laid back as I am, I've never been a romantic nigga but since I've been with Jax she brings that shit out of me. It's always been something about her that made me want to step my game up. Maybe it's her smile that I fell in love with the first day I met her. I've always told her that I would do anything to keep that smile on her face and I meant it.

I allowed the staff to leave for the night and we at dinner in the sun room that's completely made of glass. We could see the stars so clearly that it felt like we could reach out and touch them. I wanted to do it at the lake where all of this started for us, but it was too chilly outside. I was happy the sun room turned out to be a great alternative. She was crying from the gesture, so my mission was accomplished. In the whole time that we've been together, last night was as mind blowing as it gets. We explored each other in a way that let me know I was making love to my wife and there was no denying that. My love for Jaxsyn was deeper than I even realized and last night catapulted us in ways I didn't expect.

"Aye meet me at granny house." Gizmo called.

"Alright," I hung up. "I have to shoot a move real quick Tink. I'll be back."

"Okay. Be careful Bae," she waddled to me and I smiled. She wasn't huge but she damn sure couldn't continue to hide it like she had been doing.

"You have to take videos and pictures every day, all day. I don't want to miss any minute of this process ma."

"I promise," she kissed me deeply and I could feel the love she has for me radiating off of her.

"I love you so much Jaxsyn," I kissed her and then my babies.

"I know you do, and I love you too."

My cousin was sittin' on my granny's porch when I pulled up and I waved for him to come to the car. This wasn't a social visit and if she came outside and saw me out there, she would make it one.

"Nigga every time I see you, you in a different whip."

"Stop it," I chuckled slightly. "What's up?"

"You know a nigga named Tone?"

"I know a bunch of Tone's."

"Damn."

"Why?"

"This nigga's name keeps gettin' dropped."

"I know about six or seven Tone's just from this hood alone, three more from the east side, and that's just the niggas I can think of off the top of my head."

"Then I need to write down all info you know on each one of them nigga's and I'll weed out the nigga that I'm looking for. If you think of anything else let me know."

"I got you," I took out a piece of paper and wrote down everything he needed.

"What should I do once I find them? You want me to handle it since you goin' in?"

"I wanna know who it is before you do anything because it might be more of them and my girl is out here pregnant. You know I told you about them niggas stealing from us and that shit felt like it was more to it. Then we got shot. Some shit not adding up."

"I feel you," he nodded. "You know I don't mind keepin' an eye out for Jax, but that's definitely going to cost you."

"That's no problem. Keep her safe twenty-four-seven cuz and help her run shit until I get back. She'll pay you weekly."

"What's the ticket?"

"I'll let her decide and let you know. She runs the show you're just her muscle cuz. I don't want her feeling like I don't trust her or some shit."

"I got y'all."

We dapped it up and he got out. I knew that I could trust him to do exactly what it is that he does and that's murk niggas. I don't know why I didn't think to pay him to watch out for Jax sooner. She may not like it, but her ass was going to have to deal with it. I had to make sure she stayed safe while I'm away.

"Jaxsyn," I called out to her when I got back home.

"Yeah Baby?"

"I need to talk to you. Hey Chef," I tossed a head nod his way. "Meet me in the basement Tink," I grabbed a plate of food and went downstairs. "Listen. I need to make sure you and the kids are safe while I'm gone. I'm not saying anything will happen, but I still don't know who shot me and killed Nash. Nigga's actually threw drugs in the car so obviously they want smoke and I need to be able to knock these eighteen months out without worrying more than I'm already going to do."

"Okay."

"I'm putting my cousin Giz in charge of being your personal security. I don't want you doing shit if he's not right there by your side. I don't care if it's simple shit like you going into work or just a quick grocery store run. I still want you to stay strapped too but also let him protect you. I don't even know who I can trust in The Knights other than Solo so ain't no riding with them niggas without him or no shit like that. Every move you make until I get out, I want Gizmo somewhere near you. I told him that you would pay him weekly."

"How much?"

"Whatever you see fit baby. I have the guys from the security company coming tomorrow to put cameras everywhere and the gate will be closed from now on because they're fixing the security monitor on that too."

"Damn baby. Is someone really after us?"

"We just need to be prepared at all times. I was trying to get these niggas that shot us before I went in, but I don't have any more time for that. Now I'm left with making sure whoever the fuck it was can't get close to you. If you hire a nanny, she has to go through the same process that Tabitha, Blank, and the rest of the staff went through which takes about two weeks. Do not just let anyone in here because they seem nice Jax. It's a lot of shady ass bitches out here that go hard for they niggas and play games. They'll befriend you in the humblest way and before you know it, you're having coffee at Starbucks with the enemy."

"Yeah, I know better. I'm not the innocent Jaxsyn that you may think I am."

"I know you're not but I'm just sayin' ma."

She stared off quietly for a minute before looking at. "I'm scared baby. When it was just me back in the day, I had a heart for this shit like this, now, I'm about to be a mother."

"It's okay to be scared. I'm nervous too baby. Niggas shot me six times and I don't know who it was. I'm definitely noid around this bitch baby but we can't let it stop us from living. We talked about this in the beginning and I'm sorry that you fell for a nigga like me, but you can do this Jaxsyn. I know you can baby. It's only for a few months and then I'll be right back home to take this shit off of your back."

"I know. I got it. I really do," she took a deep breath.

"I know you do. I did my research," I smirked at her.

"I bet you did punk. I was much younger back then Messiah."

"Yeah but you were in these streets heavy and you know how this shit goes baby. I need you to be that girl that I heard about for your family until I get back."

"Anything for us Daddy," she came closer to me. "It's us against the world."

"Til this bitch blow Tink," I kissed her, and she gave me the best head of my life. She made it so hard to leave her ass but I had to and in just a couple hours so I took her upstairs and enjoyed her thoroughly and talked to my babies for the rest of the night.

Zionna

Jaxsyn still wasn't talking to me for drinking while I'm pregnant and I made it worse cussing out her sister when she dropped me off at home that same night. At first, I didn't give a shit, but lying in this hospital bed alone as my mind wandered more than usual, I realized that I was wrong. Dead wrong. I turned to drinking instead of being honest from the beginning; at least with Jaxsyn. I've never really lied to her and that's all I've done for the last few months. There's no way in hell I was going to keep this baby if Nashon hadn't been killed. That's the God's honest truth. I had no intentions of telling him that I was pregnant like I told everyone I was going to do. Literally and unequivocally, no intentions.

We were nowhere near ready for a move so big. We were both living our best lives, fuckin' in random places and doing spontaneous shit. We weren't ready for a fuckin' kid and I didn't want to bring one into this world. Not to say we would never have a baby or that we wouldn't be great parents. Shit, I couldn't imagine spending my life with anyone else and I knew we would start a family at some point, but we loved our three am motorcycle rides. We would ride through the city, then park somewhere random, blow L's and talk about everything and anything. That was us. We stayed doing impulsive shit and I loved it. A baby would have changed that, and I selfishly made a decision to abort our child without him knowing. The only reason I even told Jaxsyn and Messiah is because this baby was all that was left of Nashon and I wouldn't have been able to live with myself knowing I aborted his offspring, and this was a piece of him that no one could get back. This decision was made for other people, not for me. The appointment had already been scheduled.

Guilt was ripping through me and my tears wouldn't stop falling. I missed my sister so fuckin' much it didn't make any sense and I needed her so bad. I should have listened and that's all that I could keep thinking. Jax has never lead me down the wrong path and I allowed my grief to push her away repeatedly. I was wrong on so many levels and for so many different things.

"Ms. Blackwell are you sure you want to do this?" Martha Bigsby asked as she handed me the papers in her hand.

"I wouldn't have had you to draw them up if I wasn't. Don't let these tears fool you. I want this more than I've ever wanted anything in my life. I explained my situation and my emotional state. It would be dangerous to leave a child in my care. Where do I sign?" I wiped my face and took a deep breath.

"We're ready for you Ms. Blackwell." The doctor and nurses came walking in.

"Okay. One moment," I looked over the papers and she showed me where to sign. "Thanks so much for this," I forced a smile and passed the signed papers right back to her. She was bending a few rules for me, but I needed this to happen.

"You're welcome. Just for the record, that was Zionna Jenise Blackwell signing over her rights to said daughter to her sister Jaxsyn Briana Blackwell and the minor child's uncle Messiah Mauricio Knight. Zionna Blackwell is of sound mind and she has decided to give full custody of her female child to the names I stated. She is not able to care for this child and is committing herself into a rehab following delivery. This matter has several witnesses present and has been processed by myself and my office," she turned off her recorder. "In this document it states that you have no rights to this child after today Zionna due to foreseen neglect. I have to ask again."

"I'm sure. I don't want her, and I have a drinking problem. I wouldn't trust her with anyone but my sister and her boyfriend Messiah Knight."

They wheeled me away to have my C-Section. Jaxsyn warned me about drinking and had I listened, this baby wouldn't be coming right now but I didn't and now this kid was coming early. Far too early. Of course, I knew better, shit I'm a fuckin nurse, but the pain from losing Nash was too hard to cope with and too strong to handle sober. I refused to touch drugs, but I swear, now more than ever I understood why people did them. I understood wanting to make the pain go away. I understood the need to feel numb.

Going home to an empty house that only held memories and not my man, clouded my judgement. All I have left was the smell of his shirts and pictures of us happy and loving each other without a care in the world. Nash was the first man to love me genuinely and when I lost him, I lost a piece of myself too. I can barely function daily without a drink. I could barely get myself to the hospital because I was drinking before my water randomly broke. I guess this little girl couldn't take it anymore of my shit and decided to make her appearance.

"You'll feel pressure Zionna but not much pain."

"Just get it out."

I could hear everything that they were doing, and the squishing sounds of my opened stomach was nauseating. I knew it was the alcohol that had me feeling this way, but it was horrible. A couple seconds later I heard her little cry and I felt nothing. They took her away as soon as she was out and sewed me back up. She's premature so I did want to know that she was okay, but a deal was a deal. I gave up my rights to ask them questions about her and sadly I didn't really care much. Hopefully she'll be alright.

They brought me to my room and told me that they were going to discharge me in the morning, and they would call my sister then. I didn't want to cross paths with Jaxsyn because I knew she would guilt trip me into a different decision or go the fuck off on me for being weak. All I wanted to do was hop on a plane to Arizona and escape everything and everybody in Detroit. Nash was no longer here, and I didn't want to be either.

Jaxsyn

My phone started ringing at five am and I could barely reach over and get it. My stomach was huge with these damn twins and I still had two and a half more months. The doctor put me on bed rest, but I was still working from my office and occasionally going out into the field. Gizmo was driving me around like Ms. Daisy and he was such a huge help. An absolute life saver on some days. I loved having him around and paid him well for it. Plus, it was cool to have someone to talk to other than Tabitha, Blank, and the gardeners.

"Hello," I groggily answered.

"Hi, may I speak with Jaxsyn Blackwell or Messiah Knight please?"

"This is Jaxsyn," I turned the light on my nightstand on.

"Ms. Blackwell this is Martha Bigsby. I'm a lawyer that your sister Zionna Blackwell hired. I'm here with-"

"A lawyer? For what? Is she okay? Is she in jail? What did she do? What happened?"

"She's fine Ms. Blackwell, please calm down. Can you meet me at Mt. Sinai hospital?"

"Sinai? Now? Is she okay ma'am? I seriously can't handle any surprises right now. I swear I can't," I was already in tears and this woman hadn't even told me what was going on with my sister yet.

"I can assure you, I just saw her, and she's fine."

"Okay. I'm on my way."

I waddled out of bed and got dressed as quickly as my swollen body would allow me too.

"Gizmo," I called out.

"I'm right here ma, what's good?"

"Do you ever sleep?"

"Sometimes. What's the word?"

"I need you to take me to the hospital."

"It's time?" he panicked.

"No. Not for me. I think it might be something wrong with my sister."

"Oh okay," he helped me down the stairs and into the car. Simple tasks like getting in the car was a process without help. I can't wait until my munchkins are here and they give their mommy her body back.

"What's going on?" he asked.

"I have no idea. Some lady called and asked me to come down there."

I laid my head back as he kept telling me not to worry but that's all I could do. For the first time ever, I cut my sister off and made her reap the benefits of her actions and now a hospital is calling me. I was just trying to teach her a lesson about owning up to her actions and it may have back fired. I picked a fine time to teach her a lesson though, she's pregnant and she just loss the best boyfriend that she's ever had. She must hate me. I tried to fight the tears that wanted so badly to fall.

"Let me help you out." Gizmo hopped out and ran around the car.

"Thanks."

"No problem. I'll be in the lobby."

"Okay," I walked in and told the front desk who I was looking for and they sent me to the maternity ward.

"I'm looking for Martha Bigsby," I told the nurses station.

"I'm Martha. You must be Jaxsyn."

"I am. Is my sister really okay?"

"Yes, she is. Come this way," I followed her to an office where a white man was already seated and we both sat down too.

"Jaxsyn this is Ryan Miller with CPS. Your sister came to me a couple weeks ago and said she was unfit and couldn't care for her baby. She's been heavily drinking and wanted to sign her rights away. I drew up the papers that she asked me to prepare and she had the baby last night. She thought she was going to have more time to talk to you and Messiah Knight, but she went into labor prematurely," she turned the papers around to me. "You are now the legal guardian of this female child and your sister surrenders her rights." Tears streamed down my face. I couldn't even pin point one reason they were falling because it was so many.

"She what?" I said barely above a whisper as I eyed the papers in front of me.

"I know this may be a lot to take in, but it's what your sister wanted."

"Where the fu-" I stopped myself. "Where is Zionna right now?"

"I can't disclose any information other than what we're talking about right now."

I took out my phone and called her, but her phone was disconnected. "Are you fuckin kidding me Zionna?" I said out loud and wiped my face.

"You do have the right to say no Ms. Blackwell, but the child would then be sent to a foster home and placed up for adoption. That's why Mr. Miller is present."

"Never," I said with an attitude and picked up the papers. Right there, big and bold as shit, was my sister's signature. What the fuck was I going to do with three newborns?

I continued reading the papers and she had both Messiah and I listed. She literally wanted no rights to this child at all. What had gotten into her? Was she really this hurt over Nashon or did she have some other shit going on that she wasn't telling me about? I was so confused my head started to hurt. I didn't even want my mind to wonder about drug usage, but it went there anyway. We grew up around it and vowed to never touch it, but you never know with people. Kabrina was a straight A student in high school and had her whole life ahead of her. No one would have guessed that she would go down the path she went down. This really seemed like a crackhead move to me, but I just didn't know...

"I'll sign," I said in a defeated tone because I had no other choice. Ms. Bigsby passed me a pen and I was sad and pissed as I flipped through the papers signing my name under Zionna's. What type of bitch gives away a child that they can take care of? My sister was financially stable and this I know for a fact so there was no excuse. Drinking? There are rehabs for that. How did she become an alcoholic in just a few short months? We were just laughing and joking about the kind of father Nashon would have been a few months ago and now all of a sudden, she was a full-blown alcoholic who couldn't care for their baby? I swear I couldn't wrap my head around this, but I knew for sure that I would die before I allowed my niece to go into the system.

"I signed but I need my lawyer to read over this as well. Is that okay?" I asked.

"Of course. This process is far from over," she started explaining how I was getting emergency custody of my niece and we would still have to go to court. The more she talked the more pissed I became. My sister was on bullshit and when I called Messiah's lawyer, I made sure to tell him I want everything iron clad. She fucked up with this move.

"Ready?" Ms. Bigsby asked after I got off the phone and I gave her a slight head nod. "Right this way. I'll take you to the NICU."

"What's wrong with it? Her."

"She's premature and underweight by a pound or two I believe. The nurses and doctors are very optimistic, and they'll explain everything to you better than I can."

I smiled. I thought it would be more serious because of her drinking but I was relieved.

"This is Jaxsyn Blackwell. Baby Jane's mommy," she introduced me to the nurses that was in the room. I looked at her because I hadn't thought about it like that, but I was her mommy now. In the matter of minutes, I had become a mother. Just like that I was on the verge of crying yet again. These babies I was carrying had a bitch on an emotional rollercoaster.

"Right this way." The nurse told me all about her as I washed my hands. She was gorgeous with a head full of hair. I was completely and fully in love with her immediately.

"Can I pick her up?"

"Absolutely. She's yours," her words echoed through my mind. She brought me a rocking chair and placed her in my arms. She had a couple tubes connected to her, but she assured me that I wouldn't hurt her. Her little face was angelic and everything about this baby girl was perfect. She looked up at me through sleepy eyes and all the bull that was happening all around us no longer mattered.

"How long before she can come home?"

"She only has two more pounds to gain before we can release her, so I'd say in just a few weeks."

"Awww okay," I placed kisses on her face and held her tightly. I texted Gizmo and told him that I would be here for a while. I asked him to transfer the calls from the house to my cell so I wouldn't miss Messiah's call. I didn't know how long I was staying but I didn't want to miss his call.

I stayed with lil mama for hours and even fed her a couple times. I asked the nurses was there some kind of time limit and they said no since she was in the NICU. They actually got me a foot stool so I would be more comfortable as I chilled with her.

"Hello."

"Hey baby."

"No recording?"

"I'm using someone's cell phone," he laughed.

"That's funny. So, I have some news."

"What's going on?"

"Zionna gave birth to a beautiful baby girl."

"That's great news baby. I bet she's beautiful. Wait, she came early?"

"She is beyond beautiful, she's premature, and she's also ours."

"She's also what?"

"Yup. My sister signed over all of her rights and bounced. Her phone is disconnected, and I don't even know where to start looking for her."

"What the fuck is wrong with her Jax? What would have happened if we didn't take her?"

"She would have gone into foster care, so I signed on the dotted line. The paper say that she has zero rights to her the moment I signed my name."

"Then we'll raise her as ours baby. She's my brother's legacy. She's the only piece of him that I have left. We have no other choice."

"I know Daddy and we're going to make him proud. She's good now."

"Are you going to be okay?"

"I don't know. I was scared to take care of our two and now I'll have three babies."

"Hire a nanny. Background check them and go from there."

"I'll see how it all goes. I also have your lawyer coming to read over the papers and make sure everything is iron clad."

"Good. She's definitely not about to be in and out of her life. She made her decision and now she's going to live with it. Send a picture of her to this phone. I'll have this for a while, so I'll be able to talk to you."

"I'll definitely need to hear your voice. I'm still on bed rest so this shit will be interesting."

"Listen, I love that little girl already, but you can't jeopardize my son and daughter's health. Okay?"

"I won't bae. They'll all be fine."

"Did she name her yet?"

"No. She literally had her and left."

He exhaled and I could picture the disappointment on his face. "What are you going to name her?"

"I've been looking at her and I think Nevaeh would be beautiful. It's heaven spelled backwards and fitting for the situation."

"That's perfect Tink," I smiled at her. "Alright baby. I have to go. I love you so fuckin' much baby and don't overdo it."

"I love you too and I promise I won't. Talk to you later." We hung up and I sent the picture of Nevaeh to him.

3135551478: Damn she's beautiful ma. She looks just like she could be ours. Talk to you soon. Love y'all deep

I smiled and put my phone away. We're going to be the parents to three children and that was so crazy to me. Zionna forced us into this without a call or a heads up which was whack as fuck, but I loved Nevaeh already, so it is what it is… I guess.

Messiah

These niggas in jail was weak as fuck and everybody was looking for someone to lead them. The dudes that was around this bitch actin' hard was pussy and I called they asses out within the first week of arriving. I had built a fuckin team around me and was gettin money on the inside just like I was doing on the outside. I had to fill my time with something other than missing my family, looking at the walls, and lifting weights. Why not make money. Shit, this life was all Nash and I knew from our early teenage years. Before the legit businesses and the motorcycle club we were foot soldiers doing whatever it took to make sure granny's bills got paid. She was busting her ass taking care of a house full of boys and we didn't like that shit and changed it. We hit the block hard and worked our way into an empire. This right here was light work.

I had Gizmo to send this lil bitch from the hood to visit me with all the pills from Solo that I needed every week. I could have used the guards but some of them niggas start getting the big head and thinking that you really need them when they ain't shit but a pawn on a chess board. I placed them where I needed them, but I didn't want their hands too deep in my shit. She knew exactly how to get pass them and I knew what to do from there.

I structured the perfect operation and the shit was effectively moving just like on the outside. I guess nigga's thought since I was in jail that I didn't still have eyes, ears, and killa's on the outside but they found out real quick that shit would still get handled. I had Gizmo to make an example out of the first nigga that tried to hit one of my shipments thinking shit was going to be easy and since then none followed but I knew there would be more sooner or later and when they feel frogish enough to leap, they'll get handled too. The gloves were off, and no mercy was given.

"Here boss. Jermaine said his people pay the bill every month so this would be the best phone to use for business."

"Tell him good lookin' out," I took the phone and had my hackers to check it for wiretaps and anything else slick a nigga may try to pull. Once they gave me the word that it was good to go, I texted Gizmo with the new number and subliminal instructions on some shit I needed done.

Every day I worry more and more about Jaxsyn and her stability. She's trying to take care of my brother's baby, carry my two, she's still working, and I know she's lonely without me. Plus, no matter how pissed she is at Zionna, I'm positive my baby is worried sick about her sister. Gizmo says she cries herself to sleep every night and it ain't shit that I can do for her in here. I hated putting her in this predicament. She's becoming harder every time I talk to her. Gone is the soft-spoken girl who barely even cussed that I fell in love with. She's now all business with me; pretty much like *what do you want I'm busy*. It's almost like I annoy her, and I never wanted her to have so much on her plate that she starts to resent me for not being able to help. I can't even remember the last time she called me bae or daddy and I ain't no soft ass nigga, but I swear I miss that shit. I own my part in some of her bitterness, but Z is a major factor and Jax is taking it out on me. I just have to take that shit for now and fix it when I get out. I miss the fuck outta my baby though. I can't lie...

Jaxsyn

"Push Jaxsyn!" My sister yelled at me and I was trying my hardest. I swear I was trying. My son had already come out with ease, but my daughter was giving me hell. It felt like her lil ass was holding on to my damn uterus and refusing to come out.

"Come on Jaxsyn. One more big push sweetie. Just one more!" The nurse encouraged me while my sister recorded this horrendous scene.

I gathered every bit of strength that I had inside of me and pushed.

"It's a girl." The doctor held her up and she looked just like Messiah Jr. I cried and they passed her to me. I had never felt the type of love that I felt in the moment when they passed my babies to me. I hysterically cried as I stared at my blessings. Every pain that I felt, every struggle that I faced carrying them, all the uncomfortable nights, none of that mattered. My loves were here, and they were the best parts of myself and their father. I felt so blessed and appreciative. Love consumed me.

"We'll get them cleaned up and give them right back to you Mommy." The nurse took them from me, and Alyssa followed her with the camera. I told her not to miss anything and she didn't. She followed me everywhere with that damn camera whenever she was home from school.

"They are so beautiful Shugga."

"Thanks. I'm bias but I think so too," I smiled.

"They look like both of you. Those hazel eyes are nothing to be played with. They are going to be spoiled rotten. You hear that Sih," she turned the camera around. "Spoiled rotten bro," she laughed and turned the camera back to me. "So how do you feel?"

"Sore, tired, happy, overwhelmed with love, and tired. Did I mention tired?" I smiled and waved.

"Okay. I'll turn it off now."

"Thanks."

She bent down and kissed my cheek. "I'm so proud to call you my sister."

"That was really sweet. Thanks, Pooh," I smiled.

"I'm going to tell the rest of the crazy people in the lobby that our babies are here before they lose their minds."

"Send momma in please."

"Okay," she walked out and moments later Rebecca appeared.

"Congratulations baby," she smiled and hugged me.

"Thanks ma. I need that talk now."

"You've been needing that talk Jaxsyn."

"I know... You're right..."

"You have so much going on Shugga and I wish I could take all of your pain away and give you the peace that you deserve but I can't. All I can do is try to walk you through the pain and come up with some strategies to make all this crazy shit make sense like I did when you were a kid."

"Then let's start there. It worked then and it'll work now. If it wasn't for you, I wouldn't have even thought about college, but you told me that I was smart and it was my way out, and you were right. I need that kind of help and support right now," she wiped the tears from my eyes.

"You got it. Don't ever feel like you're too old to call me and daddy," she hugged me, and we talked about everything that I had been dealing with mentally and emotionally until the nurse came in with my babies. I unloaded some of the emotional baggage that I needed to unload and of course she gave me the best motherly and professional advice that she could give.

"Oh, my goodness," she gasped. "They're gorgeous Jaxsyn. Absolutely gorgeous."

"Go wash your hands and grab one granny," I pointed to the sink and the nurse passed my son to me.

"Hi Lil Daddy. You look just like your father handsome," I kissed his tiny face.

"These are the most precious moments Jaxsyn. Don't ever let life get too hectic for the precious moments. They go fast so be present in all aspects," she placed kisses on my daughter.

"I will be, I promise."

****

Having three infants wasn't as bad as I thought it would be. I had already gotten accustomed to Nevaeh's schedule, so I focused really hard on getting the twins on the same schedule. Everyone gets fed, changed, and bathed around the same time which means everyone sleeps around the same time too. That completely worked for me. I had figured out a method to the madness and I didn't need a nanny after all. Tabitha was a big help as well so I would let her go home more often and in return she showed her gratitude by giving me breaks from the babies. We had a system that worked for both of us.

"You didn't even tell me you had the babies Jaxsyn." My mother called me.

"I called you three times Kabrina. You didn't answer."

"Well you know I work all the time baby. Did Zionna come back for her child yet?"

"Nevaeh is no longer her child. I've signed the papers and been to court so I'm raising her as Messiah and Jeniah's sister. She's one hundred percent mine."

"That's a shame that she would do you like that but granny's going to love on all her babies."

"I know you will, and I guess such is life… Becca's been helping me cope with everything."

"That's right. The psychologist," she laughed.

"Don't start Kabrina."

"I'm not starting, that's what she is right?"

"Yeah. Anyway, when are you coming to visit your grandchildren?"

"Probably Sunday. I'm off and I can't wait. I want to spend the whole day with them."

"Okay. That works. Call me."

"Alright baby make sure you're getting enough rest. If you don't take care of you, you can't take care of them." We said our goodbyes and she hung up. Time definitely doesn't change some people. Well not completely. She has so much to be thankful for when it comes to Rebecca, but she refused to give her props. Kabrina has changed a whole lot when it comes to not doing drugs and trying to be a better mother to me but for some reason, she still harbors ill feelings towards Rebecca. Both her and Sandy, which makes me think it's more to the story that no one is saying because how the hell are, they mad at this woman when her husband was cheating on her with them? She's a victim in their twisted threesome having drug induced saga.

"Jaxsyn. Mr. Knight is on the phone for you."

"Okay," I got up and ran to the house phone. "Hello."

"Hey baby."

"Hey. Why you call the house phone?"

"Your cell was going straight to voicemail."

"Oh. Damn. Well, what's up? How are you?"

"I'm alright. How's the babies?"

"Beautiful and perfect," I knew that if Sih could be with me he wouldn't be anywhere else in this world, but his absence still hurt, and it still made me angry. Talking to Becca was helping me cope and have less of an attitude about things that are out of his control. Things that I knew if he could change, he would in a heartbeat.

"Send some more pictures baby. Jeniah looks just like us and she has those hazel eyes like us too."

"Yeah they all look exactly alike," I laughed. "Messiah's little personality is showing; he's going to be a mess."

"If he is, he gets it honest." We both laughed. "How's Nevaeh?"

"Same as them. Since she was a preemie, she's exactly the same size as the twins and everyone thinks they're triplets. I just let people think what they want."

"I would too."

"I love them so much Sih. I can't wait until you can meet them."

"Me either baby. How are you handling everything?"

"I'm alright."

"You're not."

"Well I have to be, so I am Messiah. I don't want to argue this time baby. This is not us and I never want it to be. Let's just talk about something else."

"I'm not letting you run from how you feel ma. Fuck that. I know you're mad at me and I'm mad at myself. I should be there and I'm not. I get that. Just be mad at me and stop frontin' like you're not," he snapped, and I busted into tears. "I'm sorry Jaxsyn. I didn't mean to make you cry baby," he sighed.

"Don't be sorry. You're right," I continued to cry. "I'm so fuckin pissed sometime Messiah. I thought I could do this shit but it's way harder than I thought. Every day I feel weak and out of my element. I'm trying to raise three children and not fuck it up. That's a lot of pressure on me."

"You could never fuck it up Jaxsyn. Give yourself more credit than that. Baby you're way stronger than you think you are and you down play that shit all the time. I know who you used to be and she's still in there. Become the fighter that I know you are and grind this shit out with me baby. It's eighteen months and we were preparing for five years ma. We got this shit. I'm handling my shit in here and I need you doing the same out there. Refocus Jaxsyn."

"I have to keep reminding myself."

"Then do that shit everyday if you have to and I'll remind you too. This is our life baby. Grind it out with me Jaxsyn. Please. I can't do this shit without you Tink."

"I got this Messiah. I really do. I just have bad days."

"Don't let a couple bad days break the warrior that you are beautiful. You're successful at everything you touch, you walk into rooms and shut them down, you're smart as hell, wise beyond your years, and tough as nails. Look at how much shit you went through growing up and look at where you are now. You carried you and your sister on your back through the mud and came out clean as a whistle. You're the fuckin' shit baby."

I smiled. He believed in me when I couldn't even believe in myself, and that was everything to me in this moment. Literally, everything.

"I'm on it daddy. I swear I'm going to get my shit together and refocus."

"That's my Tink. I love y'all so fuckin' much ma. I swear I do."

"I know and we love you too."

We hung up and I had a fire burning in my belly to step up to the plate like he needed me to. He was right. The Jaxsyn that I made myself in college, was me escaping the Jaxsyn that had been through the mud, but at the end of the day I am who I am, and I've been through what I've been through. I was going to step up and handle business like I needed too. Between Messiah and Rebecca, they had me feeling like I could conquer anything, and deep down inside, I knew I could. Shit, I have before…

Zionna

Arizona couldn't have been more amazing. I said fuck rehab and found a job almost as soon as I got here and healed from my C-Section. I started working my ass off to keep myself busy. It's really the only thing that I have to look forward to everyday so I throw all my time and energy into being the best nurse I could possibly be. Getting away from the city as well as the hospital I was working at with that racist ass bitch was exactly what I needed. I've always loved helping people and now that I didn't have distractions in the work place, I was able to flourish the way I needed too.

"Hey ma."

"Zionna where the hell are you, and I'm not letting you ignore me this time? Kabrina is going nuts about how you played Jaxsyn."

"I didn't play Jaxsyn ma. I left her niece with her that hopefully she will raise as her own. People raise their siblings' children all the time. This is no different."

"First of all, you should have never left that baby with a bitch that's not related to us. You could have left her with me. Real blood. Second of all, that girl's plate was already full, and you made shit worse."

"Leave my baby with you so you can leave her alone to go on your binges like you did me? I'm good on that crazy lady and Jax is about as real as it gets. I know she can handle it."

"Three babies are too much for anyone Zionna. It was a selfish ass decision and I don't even like that bitch, but I know that. Her baby daddy goes to jail, then a lawyer wakes her up at an ungodly time to tell her she's a mother to her half-sister's baby. Chile'... I would be on yo' ass like white on rice. You already know that bitch Kabrina was talkin' all kinds of shit, pissin' me off too," her words were slurring.

"Three babies?"

"She was pregnant with twins and on bedrest when you left that baby."

"Oh my God," I literally had no idea. We hadn't been talking so how would I know that?

"Yeah. Feel guilty now huh? Well you should. Leaving my grand baby with a fuckin' stranger that's under a lot of stress. What if she starts beating her?"

"Momma stop."

"I'm just being honest. You know a bitch like me don't know how to do shit but keep it real my baby."

"Bye Sandy," I hung up on her high ass and immediately debated on calling Jaxsyn. I felt like shit now. I didn't know Messiah was in jail and I damn sure didn't know that she was pregnant with twins or on bedrest. I'm not sure I would have changed my mind about giving up my daughter, but I definitely would have gone about everything differently.

I sat in complete silence staring at my phone for over two hours contemplating whether I should call her or not. What would I say? What would she say back? How could I make shit better? I finally got enough courage together and I called her phone private. I took two shots of Tequila while the phone rang, and I hoped that she wouldn't answer so I could leave a voicemail.

"Hello," she sounded chipper. "Hello?"

"It's me."

"Zionna?"

"Yeah. I'm so sorry Jaxsyn. I swear I didn't know you were pregnant with twins and I didn't know that Sih went to jail either. That must be killing you to be away from him. I'm sooo sorry. I can't say that enough. I couldn't keep her Jaxsyn. I just couldn't. I hated her and I didn't want anything to do with her. I wanted an abortion from the moment I found out I was pregnant but then he died, and I felt trapped. I lied when I said I was going to tell him the day he died. I never planned on telling him or anyone else. I had already scheduled the abortion and was trying to figure out how to hide it from him. Then he was taken from me. God... He was taken... The guilt I felt for even thinking about killing his kid broke me down even further than I was already broken down. I was confused about how to feel but then grief kicked in and I really started to hate her. I hated that she made me feel guilty for wanting to get rid of her and I hated her for making me feel guilty about drinking. I needed to drink. I literally needed it to cope with losing Nashon. I've never loved and loss like that Jax. Ever. I was depressed and I needed an out from the lie I told, and you were it. When Alyssa said that you were going to be a great mommy that day at your house, I knew then that I had to make the decision I made. She was right, and I wouldn't have wanted her with anyone else but you. I was selfish and I'm so sorry Jaxsyn. I

190

swear I am," I rambled and rambled. I didn't know if she had hung up or if she was still listening, but I had to get it all out while I had the courage to do so. "Hello?"

"I'm still here."

"Can you ever forgive me?"

"I'm sure at some point in life I can because you're my sister and I love you but no time soon. You literally have no idea how hard it was taking care of a new born baby, while being seven months pregnant, on bedrest, and worrying about my fuckin' sister that went M.I.A. You are a coward Zionna, but you were completely right about one thing, she is better off with me. I rather raise her to be strong and see things through than to be a coward, and bitch out at the first sign of trouble like you," she spoke to me in a tone that she's never taken with me, but I deserved everything that she said. I deserved the anger and disappointment that I could hear in her voice.

"You're right. I am a coward and I knew she would be better off with someone that wasn't me."

"Did you know that if I declined, she would have gone into the foster care system?"

"Yes. I knew you wouldn't allow that to happen tho'."

"You give me too much credit," she said and for the first time since I walked out of that hospital, I realized that my baby was left in limbo and I actually owed her more than I thought.

"It felt like the right thing at that time, but I get what you're saying. I was irresponsible and careless."

"That's the understatement of a lifetime but we can use those words for now. What do you want Zionna?"

"I needed to apologize."

"That's it? To fuckin' apologize? You don't want to know her name, how she looks, how big she's gotten, what her personality is like, what size she wears, her favorite toy, her favorite food, what makes her happy, what makes her cry, nothing?" She said with an attitude.

"Of course, I do but I didn't know if you would tell me Jaxsyn."

"Why wouldn't I?"

"I don't know. I don't know how to be or what to expect in this situation Jax. I really don't, but I do want to know those things. All of those things. If you don't mind, can you tell me everything about her?"

191

"Her name is Nevaeh and since she was a preemie, she's the same size as her brother and sister."

"You had one of each?" I smiled.

"I did. Messiah and Jeniah. People think they're triplets. She's such a sweetheart. All she does is smile. She's happy and that makes me happy daily. She looks just like Nashon and they all have really gorgeous curly hair that I assume they got from their daddies."

"Nevaeh... Heaven spelled backwards. That's perfect," I wiped my face that was drenched in tears.

"We think so too."

"Thanks, Jaxsyn. I knew you'd be a great mother to her and give her everything I can't."

"I am and I'll continue to be. I love them more than my own life," she paused. "I have to go," I heard one of them crying and I smiled.

"Okay. It was-" She hung up before I could finish my sentence. I guess I deserved everything that she was dishing out. I put her in a very fucked up predicament and then walked away and left her to figure it out alone. We've always had each other and now she was literally by herself. The guilt that I felt was from the decisions that I made was much stronger and deeper than the grief that still lingered around. I grieved for Nashon, but I also grieved my daughter; she no longer belonged to me and this shit definitely didn't feel like I thought it would feel. I should have just aborted her in the beginning and kept my mouth shut because knowing that I brought a life into this world that I walked away from is hard and almost impossible to cope with. The pain in my heart plagues me daily. I grabbed my bottle of tequila and went to my room to lay down. This was my normal routine, if I wasn't at work; it was Tequila, tears, and TV.

Jaxsyn

"Keep it real with me Gizmo. I know he has you looking for the person who took Nash from us and I know from how you're stalking my phone for his call that you have some information. Tell me."

"You ain't ready for this type of noise ma. Stay in your lane."

"You don't know shit about my lane or what I'm ready for."

"I know more than you think I know. Who you think gave Sih that information on you? That's not you no more. Stay in your lane, like I said. He got you living in the mansion on the hill so stop trying to revert back to the piss in the projects."

"Fuck you Gizmo. Tell me what I need to know. He left me in charge for a reason so regardless of where I reside now, he knows how I'm cut and what I'm capable of. Just spill it."

"Damn you can be annoyin' as hell. This lil bitch he used to deal with set him up without knowing she was setting him up. Her brother Tone was already plottin' on my cousins and her running her mouth gave these niggas the in that they needed. The business Messiah and Nash were about to handle that night was real, but they were also being followed. Tone had someone to ram their car and they ran up on cuz and the rest is history."

"Mariah?"

"Yup."

"She knew they did it?"

"She found out a few days after it happened. Now they all laying low. I feel like it's more to the story, but this info is major."

"Let's take care of their asses."

"You crazy as hell," he laughed at me like I was a joke and then stopped. "Aye, I heard about you kicking that door in the other day. Don't let these nigga's get you fucked up out here ma. Sih is going to go apeshit crazy when he finds that out so be prepared."

"Fuck that. I did what had to be done. I beat that nigga ass and got my man's money back. Y'all wanted the old me back soooo bad, well, here she goes. This is how I used to operate, and this is how the fuck I'm operating now."

"We'll see what he says baby bad ass," he started laughing again.

"Whatever. Let's handle they asses."

"*Whatever,*" he mocked me. "Nah, *we* ain't handling shit. This one has to be cleared by him. I'm not gettin' involved in y'all bullshit. That man is serious when it comes to you and now you have his kids. I wouldn't even ask that nigga no shit like that if I was you, but to each its own baby girl."

"You're right, to each its own," I walked away, and he followed me. "I'll tell you when he calls," I looked back at him and he smiled.

"You serious about this shit huh?"

"As a heart attack," I turned back around and went upstairs.

Something clicked inside of me weeks ago and everything changed for me. Everyone wanted what my man has, and Gizmo is only one person going against many. These niggas needed to know that it wasn't a free for all on my nigga's shit and the dudes that he left in charge wasn't handling business like they were when he first went in. That left me no other choice but to kick into action and handle my business. His down fall is my down fall and I can't have that. My children depend on every dollar that comes into this house and I be damn if I let all Nashon and Messiah's hard work, and money go down the drain because I didn't step up when I could have. Fuck that. If I could hug the block with a nigga like Black all those years to help pay for his college education and to keep all of our heads above water, than I can damn sure do it for my man and my babies.

I paced the floor for over an hour waiting on Sih's call, yet again. He hadn't called me in three days and that wasn't like him. I was scared that he may have gotten in trouble or something worse. I needed to hear his voice and know that he was okay. He was in there running shit and it's always going to be someone that wants what you have. Just like out here, he was walking around with a target on his back.

I looked at my caller ID and it was finally him.

"Hello."

194

"Have you lost your muthafuckin mind Jaxsyn?" His voice boomed through the speaker. "You know what; don't even answer that fuckin question because I know you have. So, you a thug now? That's what you are? I leave you for nine fuckin months and you become a muthafuckin' thug? Really?"

"Messiah calm down. Shit is not going as planned out here. Nigga's is going against the grain and shit needed to be taken care of. G can only do so much, so I stepped up. I'm not trying to be a fuckin thug; I'm out here holding shit down for my family so if you can't understand that shit, I don't know what to tell you."

"Listen to you. Just fuckin' listen to you. You don't even sound like the same person Jaxsyn. Don't make me fuck you up when I get out of here. I swear on everything I love including you, I will. You need to sit the fuck down and be a mother to my children. Fuck all that other shit. I asked you to handle the business, not kick in got damn doors and pistol whip niggas." Oh, he was pissed. He's never talked to me like one if his friends or went all the way hood like that with me either. I had to reel him back in right quick.

"You need to pipe all the way down Messiah Knight. I am a fuckin' mother to *our* kids and a damn good one at that! Did you fuckin' know a nigga got one hundred bands off of you the other day? Or how about the twenty stacks the week before that? Did they tell you that a couple niggas making drops got robbed?"

"What?" I know that information shocked him.

"Right. That's my point. That's what's been going on out here. Nigga's think the coast is clear to run your shit and the nigga's that you thought was holding shit down, Ain't! Solo and a few of The Knights do what they do, but shit, with so many niggas jumping ship and coming at the same niggas they were calling family a few months ago, it's hard for them to do it all. Plus, a lot of your Knights don't even know about the shit that's happening on the backend so Solo has to play close. I don't."

He got quiet.

"Did G know?"

"Gizmo was busy on his other mission which he has info on, and I want to handle it with him. You may not like the shit that I'm saying, and you may want to protect me and shelter me, but you brought this beast out of me. You wanted me to step up and now I've stepped up and reverted back to my old ways to do so. Deal with it."

"You blowin' my fuckin mind right now Jaxsyn," he took a deep breath. "Completely fuckin' blowin' me right now," I could tell that he was pissed and frustrated with me, but I was stating facts. The streets are ugly, but I grew up on them. I was slinging crack on the corner at fourteen years old and only did three months in Juvie for it. I'm about this life when I have to be, and I was hoping that I was completely past this stage but now the shit is calling me back and I have to answer.

"Here talk to Giz."

I went down stairs and passed him the phone. I had no desire to hear their conversation, so I went back upstairs and checked on my babies. They were still napping and looking like angels. I prayed over them daily. I want more for them and that's what pushed me back into the life that I said I was done with years ago.

"He wants you." Gizmo passed the phone back to me and I walked away.

"Hello."

"I do not like this shit for one second Jaxsyn, but you're the only one out there that I can trust. I swear I don't like this shit and when I get back it's a done deal. A complete fuckin' wrap time I hit that pavement."

"I know baby but it's my job to hold you down until then."

"You right and I'm sorry for yelling. Do whatever needs to be done and be careful out there. Please fuckin' be careful Tink. I would lose my fuckin mind behind these walls if something happens to you Jaxsyn. All I have left is you and my kids. Play shit close to the chest and don't trust no-fuckin-body."

"I got this baby. Trust me."

"I do. I love you Mama."

"I love you too Bae," I hung up and smiled. Now that I had his approval for real; shit was definitely about to change and these nigga's is not going to like it, but fuck'em. They should have stayed solid.

Messiah

I talked with my lawyer every single day trying to get released early. Too much shit was going down on the outside and I needed to get the fuck out and protect my own family. Jax was moving like a nigga and I couldn't sleep worrying about my baby. I needed this nigga to make some moves and make them fast. We went back and forth about the best plans of action and then I think the nigga started seeing that he could trust me more than he thought he could initially. One day he came to visit and said he wanted to strike a deal. I didn't know where the hell the conversation was going but I was definitely willing to hear him out.

This nigga was as crooked as they come and told me that if I gave him $150,000 in cash and as soon as possible, he could get me out. He told me that he works with a lot of people and they needed to know that I could be trusted before any offers could be made. He said "they" had been watching me since I got locked up to see how I handled myself and now everything is a go. I instantly felt two ways; I was relieved because I know I have the money and I can walk out this bitch if he's telling the truth, but I was also pissed.

I've served damn near the whole fuckin' sentence when the nigga was sitting on connections that would have had me out in time to see my kids be born. He should have known when the prosecutor dipped off for fifteen minutes and came back offering eighteen months instead of five years that I was that nigga, and some shit was going on behind the scenes. I didn't show any emotion as to how I felt about this hoe move but I definitely was in my bag. This nigga knew for sure that he could trust me so he should have been able to convince his counter parts based on our relationship, but the nigga didn't, and I won't forget it. I simply told him to go get the money from Jaxsyn.

That was two days ago, and he just got back to me today. He told me I would be free to go in twenty-four hours. Money talks and bullshit walks every time. Had he done this shit months ago I would have paid way more than $150,000. I would've given him anything to see my kids born but that's the past now and I'm out this bitch for good. Now that I know his ass is crooked and he deals with other crooked niggas in the judicial system, I'll never be back to this bitch again. Not even for a day. Me and my bro lived for niggas showing their hands and he showed his and I was going to use him at will.

Jaxsyn

I knew exactly where to find Mariah and Tone. My problem was the other guy, Ollie, that was working with Tone. It took me a lil minute, but I think I have his bitch ass located, finally. Tone is a wannabe and he's the type that will hitch a ride to whoever bandwagon he thinks will put him on. That's definitely why I needed to know who this Ollie nigga really is for Tone to be attaching himself to him.

I knew once Messiah gave me the green light and I could really get into these streets that everything that I needed would fall right into my lap. I had his shit back running like a well-oiled machine and even Gizmo gave me props for the moves I was making on my man's behalf. I had finally gained his respect and Gizmo ain't the nigga out here handing out free points, you had to earn your shit with him, so I knew I was really on my shit.

"What's new ma?" Messiah asked and it sound like he was in a good mood.

"I found what we were looking for."

"It's taken care of?"

"It will be. I wish you could see your daughter right now," I laughed.

"Which one?"

"Jeniah. This girl is a clown and we're going to stay at the school because of her. She's a little diva too."

"No, we not. She going to get her butt whipped."

"Yeah right. They're going to have you wrapped around their pinky fingers and you better not try to be extra hard on my son either."

"I'm not," I could hear him smiling.

"Yeah whatever," I laughed again. "I miss you daddy. Let me come visit."

"This ain't no place for you to come visit me. I send you plenty of pictures and hopefully since you paid this nigga, I'll be out this bitch soon."

"I hope so."

"Me too baby. This nigga could have been shot me that word and got me the fuck up outta here but I ain't even trippin'."

"Yeah, that was some bullshit but at least you'll be home for the kid's birthday's and that's a blessing so I can't even be mad at his whack ass if I wanted to be."

"Facts. I've missed out on enough of their life. At least I get their first birthday's. A nigga can't even stop smiling." We both laughed and then he got quiet. "So, what's this I'm hearing about you choppin' it up with your ex?" He completely went left field on me.

"What?" I smacked my lips. "People should really try minding their business."

"You not answering the question baby."

"He came on the block while I was over there and that's it. I barely said shit to him Messiah."

"*Barely* means something was said though and I'm not about to keep questioning you. This shit should have come from you so you might want to be forthcoming ma."

"I'm not trying to withhold anything from you Sih. I don't have to. Is this why you've been acting shitty towards me for the last couple days? The nigga is a bum and you know that. Don't get in that muthafucka and start doubting me Messiah. He walked up on me while I was on the block and I told him to get the fuck away from me, for the record. What we share, our children, and our future is everything to me. You better remember that shit the next time you try to talk reckless to me about a nigga that don't matter," I hung up on him before he could respond. Nigga's stayed telling him shit and he stayed letting that shit affect him. I couldn't believe he thought that I would really fuck with Black after what he's put me through. I told that nigga if he ever approached me again, I would blow his fuckin' head off and I meant every word.

Sih called me right back and I wanted to shoot his call to the voicemail so bad, but I couldn't bring myself to do it.

"Hello," I answered with an attitude.

"I apologize ma."

"Good. Don't ever doubt me again Sih. If you can't believe shit else in this world you can believe my love, dedication, and loyalty to you is unshakeable."

"I know that. These fuckin walls play tricks on your mind baby. I can't imagine another nigga touching you."

"Imagine it for what? This pussy is just how you left it, with your name written all over it."

"I love you so much Tink. I swear I do."

"I know you do. I love you more Daddy."

We hung up and just like that, shit was good again. He ain't have shit to worry about, these niggas couldn't fuck with him on their worst day. I would have to be crazy to fuck up what I got.

Zionna

My baby's birthday was slowly approaching, and I wanted to see her so bad. I wanted to see how big she was, and I wanted to be a part of whatever celebration Jaxsyn was planning for her. I decided to call her and see if I could attend. I knew it was far-fetched because she barely answers my calls, but it was worth a shot. If I didn't try, I would regret it forever and I have enough of those for a lifetime.

"Hello."

"Hey sis!"

"Hey. What's up?"

"Nothing much. Are you doing anything for Nevaeh's birthday?"

"Of course."

"Do you mind if I attend?"

"Let me talk to Sih."

"Well she's-" I stopped myself.

"Your niece and I said have to talk to her father. I'll call you back," she hung up. The coldness in her voice was familiar and becoming more of a norm than a phase. I shook my head and waited for her to call me back.

In the meantime, I helped straighten up Sandy's house. She claimed that she was clean and sober when I talked to her in Arizona but that was a lie that I shouldn't have believed. She's been lying about getting clean my whole damn life and the shit last for all of two seconds and then we're right back to the same shit. At least Kabrina would stick to her word. She would get clean for decent amounts of time before relapsing, but Sandy didn't last more than a week. Her ass used to be in rehab stealing pills and finding all the people that was smugglings drugs in that bitch.

"How long will you be here Z?"

"I don't know yet."

"Kabrina is going to *our* baby's birthday party, you goin'?"

"I don't know. I'm waiting for Jaxsyn to call me back with an answer."

"Excuuuuse me?" She rolled her neck and grabbed a cigarette. "This bitch has a lot of nerve and she's really pushing her luck with me. I'll break that lil bitch neck if she thinks she's about to keep our blood away from us. See, this is why you shouldn't have ever signed over your rights to a fuckin' stranger. Now she thinks she run shit. You know that's how she's always been. She gets that from her raggedy ass momma."

"Stop ma. I left Jax with a baby and no explanation, she deserves a little more credit."

"Fuck giving that bitch credit for anything. Our baby should have been with family from the get-go. She ain't doin' us no damn favors. She's doing charity work to make herself look good. My baby could have been right here with granny."

"Here we go. She is family!" I yelled. "We have the same man's blood running through our veins momma! The same fuckin' blood," I rolled my eyes.

"That's why I never let you go over there. You too easily brainwashed. That girl ain't no more family than the bum at the end of the damn street. I see you've let her get into your head. She changed you and I'll hate that bitch forever because of it."

"Whatever ma. It's no getting through to you," I put the last clean dish in the cabinet and walked away from her. She was too much sometimes, and I couldn't handle her in this moment. All I wanted was to see my daughter on her birthday and nothing else mattered.

"Where you goin'?"

"I'm just sitting on the porch Sandy," I walked out of the screen door.

"I was just asking, with your fucked-up attitude havin' ass. I'm not the one that sent my kid to stay with strangers and I was the one on drugs, bitch. Take that shit out on them, not me!" I ignored her and rolled up a blunt. I had started smoking heavy again a few weeks ago. Without weed and alcohol I wouldn't know how to cope throughout the day.

My phone vibrated and I silently prayed that it was Jaxsyn. I flipped it over and it was.

"Hey. What did he say?"

"He said it was up to me and I don't want you here."

"What?" Tears instantly filled my eyes.

"But I can tolerate you for one day. The first time you get out of line with my family your ass is gone though. You've disrespected Alyssa for the last time. Not just her, but all of them. Whether you want to believe it or not, they love you like I do and if it wasn't for them, I wouldn't be able to care for my children as well as I do. I will not allow you to show up and make my baby's day about you and your juvenile ass emotional baggage. Get your shit together before you cross the threshold of my home or don't show up at all. Period."

"You have to tolerate me now Jaxsyn?" My feelings were crushed.

"If that's all you got from what I just said, maybe it's best that you don't come."

"Answer me!" I said through shallow breaths. I couldn't regain my composure.

"You're a coward to me Zionna. You left a new born baby at the hospital without even knowing what was going to happen to her. I couldn't imagine my life without these three human beings. Three perfect, innocent lives and you just left her like she wasn't shit. I am blessed for her, but she could have ended up anywhere and that makes a part of me hate you. You know the foster care system because we lived it in before daddy came and got us. Just the thought of my daughter being there breaks my fuckin heart," her voice cracked.

"I admitted that I was wrong."

"Yeah well, Kabrina and Sandy did too. Remember?" She said nonchalantly.

"Low blow. What can I do to change how you look at me Jaxsyn? I love you so much and life is hard without you. You're pushing me away and I want things to be okay with us."

"Nothing. I love you too and I miss you every damn day Z, but I'm so fuckin hurt that you made a decision like you made without even kickin it with me. We tell each other everything and you didn't even come to me, didn't say a word. At the same time, I'm so happy because I love her more than myself. I don't know how to feel about you though. Give me time."

"I gave you time Jaxsyn. Tell me what I can do! I hear hate in your voice, and it breaks my heart," I cried again.

"Then I need more time. I'll text you the info about her party."

"Do you hate me?"

"Sometimes I really feel like I do, but in reality, you're my fuckin' sister, my best friend, and no matter how much stupid shit you do, I could never hate you for real."

"Then that's enough for me. Text me."

"Will do," she hung up and I felt slightly better. Jaxsyn saved me from a lot of shit and she's meant more to me than anyone in my life. The fact that I let her down was what hurt the most. I continued to smoke my blunt, sip from my flask, and try to relax my mental.

Jaxsyn

I sat down directly in front of Mariah and she was shaking from one hundred percent unsaturated fear and rightfully so. I had Gizmo to bring her to "The Spot". I knew a place in the woods I found long ago that I used to do business out of and the best part about it is, it's no people around for miles. It's tucked off deep in the woods and perfect for this type of shit.

"I swear I wouldn't hurt a hair on Sih's head. I love him," she repeated herself as tears poured from her eyes and I laughed.

"Bitch you sound silly. Not only did he get shot six times but Nashon is gone!" I slapped her across the face with the butt of my gun and blood flew across the room. I had been torturing her, Tone, and Ollie for hours. Mariah was a mess and scared out of her mind. She started on some tough shit. Talking about how she flattened my tires and fucked my nigga, but all that smart mouth shit faded real quick when I started laying into this hoe. Tone didn't know shit and was just a pawn like I assumed from the jump. Ollie definitely knew something, but he was tight lipped. This situation was just as I assumed. Tone is a flunky ass nigga that ride other people's wave and Ollie was who he was attaching himself too, but why.

I went in on Ollie's ass while Gizmo sat back and watched. His ass wouldn't budge on the information no matter what, which let me know two things, he was really about this life, and he was working for someone that we needed to find fast. You don't stay that quiet for small fish. He worked for a shark and knew better than to run his mouth even when faced with his own demise.

"Messiah is calling your phone baby girl," he shook my phone and then passed it to me.

"Hey ma where you at?"

"Finishing something up real quick."

"I'll be ready to come home in about forty-five minutes."

"Forty-five?" I said excited.

"Yup. Come get your man baby."

"Mmm on my way Daddy," I smiled and hung up. "Alright kiddies. Fun is over. Y'all ain't saying shit so this is going nowhere fast," I walked up to each of them and put a bullet in their head at point blank range."

"Damn Jaxsyn." Gizmo hopped up.

"Fuck'em," I grabbed my handbag. "Have Sih's cleaners come take care of this for me. I have to go."

"New found respect my nigga." Gizmo gave me dap and smiled. "I'm going to see what I can find on that nigga Ollie too. I know you peeped how he carried this shit."

"I did and you read my mind. It's someone far bigger than we expected."

"Yup. This shit might get ugly."

"I agree."

I left and sped home. I hadn't seen my man in months, and I couldn't show up dirty and sweaty. I hopped in the shower and threw on something simple and sexy.

"I'm going to get their daddy," I smiled, and Tabitha clapped. I kissed my babies and ran out the door.

I didn't care about a cop or a ticket. My baby was home early, and I was flying down the Lodge freeway to get to him.

Messiah

I saw my baby pull up and I felt like a bitch. I wanted to run to that mafuckin car so bad. I had spent too much time away from her and we had a lot of making up to do.

"My muthafuckin' Tink," I smiled, and she jumped in my arms and cried. How could I ever doubt this kind of love?

"I missed you so much Bae," her face was buried in my neck and I could feel the warmth of her tears. I knew they came from a wave of different emotions and I felt every last one.

"I'm never leaving your ass again Baby. Ever," I kissed her wildly as she continued to cry. I wanted nothing more than to just relax and chill with her and my babies. A nigga was finally home.

"You better not," she wiped her face and finally flashed that million-dollar smile that made me smile with her.

"Never baby. Now, let's get the fuck out of here." We both laughed and hopped in the ride.

As soon as we pulled up to the house, I got anxious and nervous. I had missed so much of the kid's life already. They didn't even know who I was.

"What's wrong?" Jaxsyn asked without me having to say a word.

"They don't know me."

"Yes, they do. You're their father."

"I've been gone since before they were even here," I looked at the house, but she turned my face toward hers.

"You better know who you're fuckin' with because I'm not about to keep reminding you that I'm the shit," she smiled and kissed me. "Come on," she got out and waited for me. I didn't know what she meant but I would follow that smile to the edge of the earth, so I got out.

We walked up to the door and I couldn't keep my eyes off of her. That ass was lookin' juicy as fuck and she had a nigga bricked up and ready. My kids turned their mother into a fuckin' master piece. I couldn't wait to explore her all over again. I grabbed her ass and kissed on her neck. I couldn't help myself. She leaned her head back and let me steal a few more kisses before she opened the door.

"Tabitha I'm home honey," I loved their relationship.

"Here we come." Tabitha came from the back carrying the twins and Nevaeh was walking.

"You didn't tell me she was walking baby," I looked over at her.

"It was a surprise. We've been working with her nonstop for her party," she clapped. "Come here lil momma."

Nevaeh giggled and waddled to her.

"Hi mommy."

"Hey baby girl." Jaxsyn kissed her. "Who is that?"

"Daddy," she laid her head on Jaxsyn and tears came to my eyes. Jaxsyn made sure that they knew who I was. Nevaeh looked just like me and she belonged to my brother. This moment meant everything to me. I would never let that man down when it came to her. I'm her daddy until they lower me into the ground.

"Go to daddy." Jaxsyn tickled her and she reached for me. I tried not to hug her too tightly, but I didn't want to let her go and the best part was her hugging me back just as tight.

"Here's Jeniah and Messiah Jr." Jaxsyn and Tabitha held my babies and she wasn't exaggerating when she said they were triplets. Pictures didn't do them justice. My babies are gorgeous, and my heart fluttered.

We went to the living room so I could spend time with them, and it was exactly what I needed. They were all over me and in an instant, I had become dada to the twins and daddy to Nevaeh. I couldn't imagine being anywhere else in this world then right here in my living room with my kids and my girl. I prayed for this moment and God delivered.

Jaxsyn

My feet and back were killing me but I decorated every square inch of the back yard for my Princess. She loved watching Mickey Mouse Club, so I went Mickey crazy for her. I know she's going to flip out over everything, and the thought of her reaction motivated me. Making my kids happy will forever be at the top of my list of priorities. If I could go into work every day and decorate other people's homes for a living there is no end to what I'll do to keep a smile on the faces of my babies.

"You are fuckin' amazing." Sih hugged me from behind, making me blush like he's always had the ability to do. "Look at this backyard baby. You killed it," he kissed the side of my face and gave me butterflies.

"Thanks baby." A sense of pride washed over me as we both stood there taking it all in.

"Can we talk inside?"

"Of course."

He took my hand and we went to the basement.

"Tell me what happened?"

"I don't want to talk about it baby. It's done."

"That's not the relationship that we have Tink. I don't want secrets between us, and I learned in jail that I don't want to hear shit about you from anyone else when I can hear the truth straight from you. I've rested enough and now I need to know everything."

"I made Gizmo bring Mariah, Tone, and Ollie to this house I used as a kid to kill Zionna's step dad and a couple more niggas tried to rape her. I tortured them for hours trying to get more information because Ollie pulled the trigger on y'all, but he didn't work alone, and Tone was just a pawn that was used for the information that he got from Mariah. When I couldn't get any information, I started toying with them, but you called so I popped they ass and came and got you from jail. Ollie was eerily solid, and it was abundantly clear that he knew more. A lot more. Giz felt it too so he said he was going to look into who Ollie's working for."

"Wow," he sat down. "You just let all that shit roll off of your tongue like it was nothing to you."

I sat down on his lap. "Baby, Sandy bitch ass was far more reckless than my mother ever was, and I had to protect my sister by all means necessary at a very early age. Then I fucked around and met Black and he was in deep shit, both in his personal life and the streets. I was already knee deep in my own shit, so I helped him get out of it. I vowed that I would leave all of that shit here when I went to Illinois for college. I prayed for a better life. A different life. I did everything in my power to change who I was. All my life I had to be tough and I just wanted to be different for once. When you went in, I had to do what I had to do to hold you down. I kicked in a couple doors, beat a few asses, and got rid of some low lives that changed the course of our lives forever. I know you want to keep me on this perfect pedestal but I'm not perfect bae. I never was and I never will be."

He laid his head back for a moment and then looked at me. "You're more perfect today than ever, and on a higher pedestal now than you were before. I hate the hand you were dealt in life and I don't like you getting your hands dirty like that anymore. I've said that plenty of times before, but I love the hell out of you for holding me down like that ma. I can't thank you enough," he kissed me. "Go get dressed."

"Help Tabitha get the kids ready for me."

"I'm on it," he smiled, and we went back upstairs.

Since Messiah's been home, he's fully emerged in his role as a dad. He wants to feed them, bathe them, play with them, teach them, and everything else. He's so adorable it's almost too much for my heart to take. I walked into the room two days ago and he had all three of them in the bed sleeping with him and I cried real tears. My heart was full, and that moment was everything to me.

"Look at my baby," I picked Nevaeh up and swung her around. I had her in pink and white Minnie Mouse from head to toe and I had the twins in red and white Mickey. She had real diamond Minnie ears on her head, and I shook my head at Messiah. They were cute as hell but definitely too much for a one year old. I didn't say anything though, I let him do him. "Happy Birthday mommy's big girl."

"I could watch you be a mom forever." Messiah walked into the kitchen holding the twins.

"Vice versa Daddy," I smiled, and we shared a moment. He leaned down and kissed me and those damn butterflies got my ass again.

"Smile." Alyssa walked up and we both turned around. We smiled and she snapped a picture. "Bro I have so much footage for you to catch up on; Nevaeh in the hospital, when we first brought her home, the twins' birth, every moment of her pregnancy that you missed. I have the whole nine yards."

"Damn. Good lookin out sis. I can never repay you for that."

"That's what family is for. Welcome home," she hugged him, and we took the kids to the backyard. I had a few of the girls I was cool with to bring their kids, and Messiah invited the few Knights he could trust that has kids, so we had about twenty kids in total plus my family. Nevaeh went completely nuts when she saw the backyard and it made Messiah and I fall even deeper in love. He chased her around and she giggled constantly. I couldn't have asked for a better moment to share with him.

"Can you hold them?" I gave the kids to my dad and Becca.

"Of course. Grandma can't get enough of these faces," she smiled and tossed Messiah Jr. in the air.

"You better not drop my grandson heffa." My momma chimed in as she walked up looking cute as hell and carrying two handfuls of gifts.

"Kabrina," I shook my head and walked away. I went to play with Messiah and Nevaeh in the bounce house and we had a ball. She was the happiest of all three of our children. Messiah Jr is a meany pants, and Jeniah is a sweetheart but very funny acting. I loved their personalities already.

"Hey, Zionna, just texted me. She's in the front let me go get her."

"Okay." Sih kept tossing Nevaeh and the other kids around.

I ran to the door and she was standing in front of the house.

"Hey," she smiled.

"Hey," I extended my arms and we hugged. I had a long talk with Sih after the kids went to sleep last night and he told me to cut her some slack. Nevaeh is a blessing and we wouldn't have her if it wasn't for Zionna, so in short, he told me I should be happy that she's weak.

"I missed you Jaxsyn."

"Missed you too. Come on," she passed me the bag she was holding and when we got to the backyard, I put it on the gift table with the rest of Nevaeh's gifts. "Look who's here." We walked over to the table that the family was at and once again everyone waved when she spoke, and my daddy got up and hugged her. He loved his kids and even though she's never reciprocated the love, he'll never stop giving it.

"How are you baby?"

"I'm good," she smiled. "Jaxsyn they're beautiful," she complimented the twins and I peeped that my momma had taken Messiah from Rebecca. He was eating up his granny's love, so I didn't say anything, but I definitely noticed.

"Thanks. I'll go get Nevaeh."

"Okay."

"Here she is." Sih walked up with her on his neck.

"Oh my God. That is insane," she looked at her and then looked at the twins and tears formed in her eyes. "Can I hold her?"

I looked over at Messiah and he was already looking at me.

"Sure," I said reluctantly, and Alyssa shot me a look, so I changed my attitude. "I'll be back," I went to the house to breathe and Messiah followed me.

"You're her mother baby and no one can take that from you. I see you look at her and it's no different than how you look at Jeniah and Junior. You don't have to feel what you feel right now Tink," he held me, and I cried into his chest. He read my mind as usual. He stroked my head as I calmed down. I loved that he had the ability to bring me a peace and comfort that no one else could. I fixed myself and we both rejoined the party.

"Daddy." Nevaeh climbed down Zionna and waddled to Sih. He tossed her in the air and they both giggled.

"She talks." Zionna smiled.

"Girl yes, from the time those chubby little toes hit the floor in the morning until we tuck them in at night. She says juice, play, mommy, daddy, babies for the twins, and TT for Alyssa and Syd. Those come out clearest, but she babbles gibberish all day," I laughed.

"That's adorable."

"Yeah."

"Baby she wants you." Messiah came over.

"Mommy," she reached.

"What's wrong baby girl?"

She laid her head on my chest and squeezed my nipple and my ear.

"This girl is crazy. She's hungry and wet," I laughed. "She definitely knows how to tell me what she wants. We'll be back," I walked away, and, in that moment, I truly realized what Messiah had just said. I had no reason to be intimidated. I had a bond with her that was unbreakable.

Zionna

Sitting next to my dad was hard for me but I wanted the relationship that he has with all of his other children. I don't know where that feeling came from honestly. Maybe it was giving birth to my daughter or maybe it was all the time I've spent alone in AZ thinking about my life or maybe it was me realizing that Sandy was on bullshit.

Jaxsyn has the best of both worlds. She has Kabrina that's clean, sober, and healthy now. She's trying to be the best person and mother that she can be. Then she has my dad and Rebecca who adores her completely. My mother always told me that they weren't real family and kept me away but they damn sure look, act, and sound like a real family. Jax used to tell me that I was missing out and as of lately, I've been hearing the truth of her worlds loud and clear.

"How you been?" I asked Brian once everyone was into their own conversations.

"I can't complain baby and if I did no one would listen," he smiled. "How about you? I know everything that has happened had to take a toll on you."

"Yeah. Losing Nashon, giving up the baby, moving away, it's all a bit much. I'm still trying to sort through it."

"Well this is what family is for. When you fall, we're here to pick you up? That's what your sister did by taking full custody of Nevaeh and whatever else needs to be done you just let me know and I'm all over it. Even if it's just a hug on those bad days."

"I appreciate that."

"No problem baby."

I looked over at Messiah and Jaxsyn walking out of the house with Nevaeh and my heart broke a little. Sih and Jaxsyn are everything in her world and I was slightly jealous. She's beautiful and smart and a part of me. I didn't want her back, but I loved her so much. I never knew love like this until I laid my eyes on her today. Before, I just wanted to know everything about her, but I didn't expect to feel what I feel right now. The love and the guilt were intense.

I needed to shake the feelings off, so I reached for my niece and Alyssa gave me a look that I didn't appreciate but she has every right to feel that way about me because of our last interaction. I was drunk and very mean to her. I had some apologizing to do, may not be today but I definitely had to smooth things over with her.

"Hi Jeniah," I bounced her, and she smiled. I could see all of us in her and it made me smile harder. She's gorgeous but I could tell she was definitely going to be her mother's daughter, a definite diva.

"Alright. I need these babies. They have to be changed too and then we can sing happy birthday to big sissy," she clapped and Jeniah mocked her. I passed her daughter to her and watched her play with her. She was built for motherhood and there was no denying that.

"You want me to help you?" Rebecca stood up and went to reach for Messiah Jr.

"I can help you Jax," I stood up too.

"Okay," she looked at Rebecca and then me. "Granny can help next time huh," she made a baby voice as I took my nephew from Kabrina who had been hogging him.

"Auntie Z's going to help mommy clean this butt. Yes, she is," she laid them side by side and tickled their stomachs.

"This room is beautiful sis."

"Girl we have four baby rooms in here. This room is like a play room slash changing room. I went a little overboard."

We both laughed.

"I'm going to let you change Jeniah because Messiah will spray you if you're not quick. I'm starting to think he does it on purpose. Mommy's meany pants," she kissed him, and we started changing them. I felt more like myself just standing next to her and I hadn't felt like myself in months.

"Can I see Nevaeh's room?"

"Sure, you can."

"Thanks, Jaxsyn."

"Yup," she kept playing with the babies.

"I don't want her back Jaxsyn. I really don't. I wouldn't do that to y'all."

"You couldn't do that to us if you wanted too. Our lawyer assured me that the papers are iron clad."

"She's your daughter Jaxsyn. I love her but I know that she's yours."

"Love? Oh God Zionna. Please don't provoke me. I'm really trying so hard today," she shook her head and I felt her mood completely shift within seconds.

"Provoke you by saying that I love a child that came out of me?" I was taken aback by her response. Now I can't even love her? Ain't this a bitch.

"Love is staying up with her from two am to seven am while she cried nonstop because of an ear infection, love is placing her on your bare chest to bond so she can hear your heartbeat, love is knowing every single cry and what they mean, love is waking up every day tired as hell but putting a smile on when she crawls into the room because she's worth it, love is putting her first even when everything in your life is falling apart, that's love. What you feel is guilt sweetie, and that's a whole different monster. The guilt you feel is seeing her and seeing every bit of Nashon through her. Guilt is watching how amazing she is and knowing that you're missing out on precious moments, guilt is hearing her call Messiah and me daddy and mommy, guilt is knowing that you didn't see her or your niece and nephew for a whole F'n year of their life. It's not love baby, it's definitely guilt. You can try to convince yourself that you made the right choice and it was for her own good, but the fact of the matter is that you know you F'd up and it eats you alive. You better learn to love her as auntie Zionna because that's who you are. Wrap your head around that and come rejoin the party, TT Z," she looked me up and down, grabbed both babies, and walked out. "Oh yeah, her door has her name on it. Feel free to check out her living arrangements if that'll help you sleep at night," she said sarcastically and kept going.

I was floored but I swear it was all the truth. I did feel guilty and I did fuck up. I couldn't even say shit back to defend myself because she was right… rude, but very right. I was thinking like a mother and I lost all rights to feel that way. I had to learn to love her as an aunt or Jaxsyn would definitely cut me out of her life completely.

I went to her room and smelled her things. Everything was perfect and in its rightful place. Of course, Jaxsyn had her room fit for a princess. There were pictures of Messiah and Nashon on her dresser, but I didn't make a big deal about no pictures of me being anywhere since I had the choice to be here and he didn't.

"Hey." Messiah walked up.

"Hey," I forced a smile. "This is amazing."

"You know your sister."

"That I do," I nodded.

"She just loves her Zionna. Your presence is like a threat and she's being a momma bear over her cub."

"I fucked up Messiah," I started crying and he hugged me tightly. "Nashon would be so disappointed in me," I looked at the picture of him smiling on Nevaeh's dresser and broke down.

"Listen to me. I knew my brother like you know Jaxsyn and I know for a fact that he could never be disappointed that his baby girl is with me. Real shit. It didn't get no closer than us. I can give Nevaeh something that no one else can give her and that's an Uncle and Dad at the same time. You made the decision that was right for you and even though it pissed me off at the time, I can assure you we're never going to let you or my brother down. Have you seen how Jaxsyn looks at her? It's pure unsaturated love. She would die for a child that you brought into this world Z. That's the ultimate kind of love for you and Nevaeh," he wiped my tears. "It's all raw emotion right now because it's your first time seeing her, but you'll adjust and slide right into auntie duties like Alyssa and Sydnee. She's in good hands and I know you well enough to confidently say that you know that without a shadow of doubt. It's why you put our names down."

"Bro I couldn't love you anymore than if we had the same blood coursing through our veins right now," I hugged him firmly.

"I love you too sis and thanks for giving us one of the biggest blessings of either of our lives. I'll work on Jaxsyn for you too. She'll come around and be the sister that I know you miss. Give her a little time, she's also been through a lot these last few months."

I smiled and cried at the same time. He had changed my world in just one talk.

"Let's go sing happy birthday to Nevaeh and eat that $500 cake her momma bought."

"She didn't," I laughed.

"It's her daughters first birthday. You know she did."

We both laughed and rejoined the party.

Messiah

Gizmo and I hit the streets with a vengeance. I was back and I wanted niggas to feel it in a major fuckin way. Between the information that I got from Jaxsyn, through word of mouth, and Gizmo, I had some scores to settle and that's exactly what I was doing. I do too much in my hood for nigga's to ever try me. I don't just do charity shit like the block party or the Cedar Point trips, we help pay past due bills, look out for the kids who parents are on drugs, we donate to the community and rec centers, we bring supplies to the schools, pay hospital bills, put niggas on both illegally and legally, and then for a muthafucka to then turn around and try to bite the hands that's literally feeding them is a slap in the face. I'm not the nigga you wanna slap either.

"I swear y'all nigga's like Bonnie and Clyde cuz. Jaxsyn ain't no fuckin' joke. I didn't want to geek her up too much B but she's a force." Gizmo nodded as I hit the blunt and passed it.

"Why you didn't tell me everything about her past?"

"I gave you what I knew at the time. After her ass turned into GI Jane and started kickin' doors, I went back and dug deeper."

"She's definitely my equal," I laughed.

"Cuz you talkin' from what you heard. I watched her torture them three muthafuckas and I couldn't believe she was the same person that I originally met. That bitch Mariah kept saying 'I love Messiah, I would never set him up'. Nigga Jaxsyn slapped fire from that dog face bitch with the butt of her gun, hit her in both of her knees with a crowbar, then stabbed her in both shoulders. It happened so quick that bitch didn't know what the fuck was happening to her. She said that stupid shit again and she hit her so fuckin' hard her blood sprayed across the room."

"Damn," he passed the blunt back.

"She a real one. Any female that will do that type of shit and still have dinner cooked and the kids clean, deserves a nigga to have her on the pedestal that you have her on."

"You right. I can't lie cuz. She got me. I would burn this bitch down to the ground for her."

"As you should."

"That's why I got this," I showed him the ten-carat diamond ring that I bought her."

"Damn B. Who the fuck you tryna' marry, Jax or the whole got damn hood? This bitch right here is crazy." We both laughed.

"She deserves it."

"You ain't lyin'. Congrats fam. You already know the answer," he dapped me and I felt a sense of pride.

We rode around until about twelve am and I dropped Gizmo off at the hotel that he was staying at. He was leaving to go back home in the morning, so we said our goodbyes. I knew he wouldn't stay long after I came home which was fine. The nigga gets way more money in New York, plus that's home for him. He did offer to help me track down whoever was working with Ollie, but I told him to go ahead and take his ass back to the crib. I was home now, and he had already looked out in a major way.

"Hey baby," I walked into the house and Jaxsyn was walking around with Junior."

"Hey Daddy. Our little cranky butt wanted to fight his sleep. Let me go lay him down and then I'll fix your dinner," she whispered and then pecked my lips before disappearing up the stairs.

I went to the kitchen and hung my jacket on the back of my chair. She had gotten rid of Chef Blank and started cooking again which was far better than that healthy shit. I let Reno our regular chef goes for Blank but now that she's not carrying my kids, I needed salt and fats and shit.

"How was your day baby?" She kissed my neck and walked over to the stove.

"Come do that again," I smiled.

"Anything for you," she smirked and came right back to me. She straddled me and placed kisses all over my neck. I started undressing her wildly and ripping shit off. She had aroused me to the point that my dick was threatening to bust out of my pants. Her sexy ass knows how to press all the right buttons.

"Come on," I lead her to the basement and as soon as we hit that bottom step, I swooped her into my arms and walked her over to the bar. I craved the taste of her, and I had a thirst that needed to be quenched. I placed her on top of the bar, and she opened wide for me. I smirked because she wanted me there as much as I wanted to be there. She was glistening from how wet she was for me, so I slid two fingers inside of her and watched her body react. She leaned back on her elbows and allowed her head to dip back. The visual of her awaiting me was sexy as fuck.

"Mmmm," she rolled her hips against my fingers and I covered her clit with my mouth. Her body shuttered and I took my free hand to spread her lower lips even wider. "Baaaae," she looked down at me as she grabbed one of her breasts. I licked faster and watched her body convulse. Everything my baby did was sexy, and she had me even harder than I was upstairs.

"You taste so damn good baby," I slapped her thigh and kissed her clit over and over as she came down off of her high.

"I'm cummin' againnnnn Siah, shit," I smiled because I wasn't even trying, and I had my pussy spraying.

"Who?" I asked as I started licking again.

"Daaaaddy! Daaaaddy! Ughhhhh," she rolled her hips on my tongue until she was completely drained, and my thirst was more than quenched. "Hit it from the back," she said breathlessly.

"Oh, you trying to be a big girl tonight, huh? Daddy about to make you cry Tink."

"I know you are. Bully," she bit down on the corner of her lip and then licked her juices off of my face. "Fuck me baby," she whispered as she stared in my eyes and I planned to do just that. I helped her down off the bar and turned her around. She assumed the position and I shook my head. Her arch was insane, and that pussy was dripping wet and smiling at me. I rubbed my dick around her hole, and I knew it was going to be tight to get in as usual, but since she was talking shit, I wasn't taking my time. I played with her for a minute until she was whining for me and then I forced my way right in. Before I could even bottom out, she started leaking like a faucet.

"Ahhhhhh," she moaned and gripped the bar stool. I secured my hands around her little waist and plunged all the way inside of her and she screamed. I didn't ease up in the least bit, instead each thrust was deliberate and deeper than the previous. I had been gone too long not to fuck her like this every single time. She was begging me to stop and keep going all at the same time. Her juices flowed down her legs and my nuts, and unfortunately for her pussy, that made my pipe harder with each splash.

"Shiiiit," she started playing with her clit and I knew she was close to orgasming again, so I banged her harder and watched the water works start. She looked back at me and told me how much she loved me.

"I love you too Tink," I sped up and she whined my name repeatedly. I swear this was exactly what I needed after the day I had.

"Ugghhhhh," I slapped her ass, as I spread her cheeks wider to release my load deep inside of her. I didn't give a fuck about her gettin' pregnant again. No way in hell was I going to pull out of the pussy that I was planning to marry. Fuck that.

Jaxsyn

Messiah handled me in such a way when we we're making love that he makes me want to pull my fuckin hair out strand by strand from the insane amount of pleasure he gives. I can't contain myself and I damn sure can't stop showering him. He drives me fuckin nuts. That's why I'm not married now. Yeah that nigga Black played me but with Messiah fuckin' me like he was, he put Black at a serious disadvantage. He called that shit from the start and I was simply in denial.

"I'll go make your dinner baby," I kissed him.

"Okay," he smiled and then got serious all of the sudden. "Wait, you can walk?"

"Barely."

"I'll have to fix that next time. I want to have to carry yo' ass around after I'm in them guts."

"You are crazy, but it's a date," I stuck my tongue out and slowly went upstairs. I had been making all of his favorite foods since he's been home, and he's been loving it. I wanted to please him in every way that I could since he was back on the outside and I hear the way to a man's heart and soul is through his belly. I was testing that theory.

I scooped his collard greens out of the pot and onto his plate.

"Marry me," he wrapped his arms around my waist and opened a box in front of me.

I gasped so hard I needed to go grab my inhaler. My mind went blank and I almost dropped his plate. "Oh my God Messiah," I instantly started crying. I faced him and he kissed me tenderly before I could speak.

"I love you more than my next breath Jaxsyn. Everything about you since the day I had my Knights block you in at the store has been prefect. I couldn't walk away even knowing that you were married already. I had to have you, I got you, and now I'm planning to keep you forever. I can't live without you and I never want to imagine having too. Will you marry me Tink?"

"Of course, baby," I buried my face in his chest and cried from the depths of my soul. He held me tightly and we shared the deepest moment that we've ever shared. I kissed him and he put me on top of the countertop.

"I love you so much baby. I promise to always be the man that you fell in love with. I promise to always give you the very best of me."

"I love you too Messiah. So fuckin much Bae. I can't even put it into words and just when I think I can't love you any harder or deeper, you find a way to outdo yourself and make me love you even more," he kissed me again and then placed the ring on my finger. It was absolutely beautiful and absolutely massive. I stared at it and then smiled. "You did goooood."

"Did I?" He smirked.

"Mmmhmm. You sure did," I hopped off of the counter and lowered myself in front of him. Fuck dinner! I took him into my mouth and sucked his dick like someone was about to cut me a check in this bitch. My man is everything in my world and I really had to make sure that I was giving him my A game every single time because he damn sure was giving his to me.

"Damn baby," he gripped the stove to balance himself and his toes curled. I sucked faster, deeper, and made it wetter while juggling his balls. I deep throated him and massaged the tip with the back of my throat. He almost lost his mind and I wouldn't let up on his ass. I turned him into a bitch, and I loved every minute of it. I stayed on my knees for well over an hour and then when I was ready for him to cum, I kicked that shit into overdrive and made his knees weak.

"Fuuuuck," he grunted and grabbed my head. I sped up and he started fucking my mouth. That shit turned me on, and I stroked his balls again. He was bustin' within seconds and his whole body seized up. "Maaaan, where the fuck did those skills come from?" He was weak and sweaty.

"Those were reserved for when you put a ring on my finger. That's what head will be like from now on, so I hope you're ready."

"Shit if I'm not, I'll get ready," he wiped his forehead and I finished making his plate. He sat down and ate while I put everything away. I looked at his dick and he was hard again from watching me walk around our kitchen naked.

"You need me to handle that?" I pointed and he looked down.

"You still have energy left after that?"

"For you, I'll find some," I said seductively.

223

"Come here."

Without another word spoken, I walked over to him and sat on his lap backwards. I made round two better than the first one for my future husband and his ass fell asleep right at the table. We had fifteen months to make up for plus a proposal. My A game was fully activated.

Zionna

The relationship with my sister had gotten a lot better and I guess that had a lot to do with Sih. He said he was going to work on her, and she was definitely coming around. Since I had gotten back to Arizona, I've talked to her at least once a week and for her that's huge because she was barely answering any of my calls before. I was able to tell her about Quan reaching out to me and me actually considering going on a date with him. She told me about the altercation she had with Black and how he had his daughter in the car with him at the time. That nigga was really crazy as hell. We discussed me coming to the twins' birthday party and some days we just talked about our day and I couldn't have asked for more.

I've had time to seriously think about the conversation that Messiah and I had as well as what Jaxsyn had to say. They were right and I checked myself. I prayed and I also stopped at Nashon's grave before I left to come back home. I found the closure that I needed, and I was able to make peace with myself and my decisions. I know that's one reason my relationship with Jaxsyn is better and I can truly say that I accept Nevaeh as my niece just like Jeniah, without a second thought. The right decision was made, and I have absolutely no regrets.

****

The twins party was just as fabulous as Nevaeh's. There's no surprise that Jaxsyn is as successful at her business as she is because her attention to detail is insane. She themed their party Dora and Diego and actually had the characters there. All the kids went crazy and it was the cutest thing I've ever seen.

I finally got around to apologizing to Alyssa and she forgave me within seconds. It was time that I got to know my other side, so I invited her out to AZ, and she accepted. Sydnee over heard the conversation so I invited her too. I couldn't wait to get to know them better and spend some quality time together. My dad looked happy, but he didn't interfere. It was long overdue and since it was me that has been the bitch all this time, it's me that has to fix it.

"Hold her." Jaxsyn passed Jeniah to me and ran across the backyard. I didn't know what was going on but whatever it was she was pissed when she came back.

"What happened?" I asked as she took Jeniah back and she laid her head down.

"I heard my baby crying. One of the bigger kids pushed her down and was over there trying to get her to be quiet. I hit other people's kids, so they better stop playing with me."

"Damn, I didn't even hear anything."

"Me either." Alyssa chimed in.

"I swear I know their noises like the back of my hand. Soon as they make a sound, I'm like that's my baby what's going on," she laughed.

"TT." Nevaeh came over with tears still in her eyes and went to Alyssa.

"Awww TT's baby," she picked her up. "What they do to my Sweet Butt?"

"Boo boo," she pointed to her knee and we all smiled at how cute she was.

"Oh no! Let me kiss that baby and make her feel better." Alyssa walked away with her and within seconds she had her giggling.

"She's good with them huh?"

"Great. She's closer to Nevaeh and Junior because Jeniah is getting more and more spoiled as the days go by. She only wants me or Sih. If I had left her with you longer, she would have started crying for us. Oh, surprisingly she'll stay with my momma too, but that's it."

"Do y'all hold her more?"

"Nope. We try not to hold any of them that much now that they're walk to avoid this. She's just a brat," she kissed her forehead.

"Leave my baby alone." Messiah walked up. "Come to Da Da Lil Mama," he reached for her and she went right to him. She snuggled into his chest and went straight to sleep.

"Daddy has the magic touch," he went and sat down with her.

"Mmmhmm." Jax smirked and he smiled at her. They were too cute. I swear. She turned her attention back to me. "So, what's up with the date?"

"I told him I'll call him after I leave here."

"Oh okay," she raised an eyebrow.

"It's just dinner and drinks. Nothing more."

"I didn't say a word," she rolled her eyes and walked away. Quan and I have played this game before and I'm not willing to settle for anything less than what I had with Nashon. He exposed me to what real love is and I can't go backwards.

After the party was over Jaxsyn asked the family to stay. We didn't know what was going on, but the twins had fallen asleep again so Messiah and Jaxsyn went to put them in their beds and made us wait.

"They better not be moving." Rebecca said.

"I would be crushed." Sydnee pouted.

"Beyond crushed. I don't even want to think like that y'all. At all." Alyssa shook her head and continued playing patty cake with Nevaeh.

They really loved Jaxsyn and they all had a real bond that I chose to ignore until recently. Well I noticed before, but I was still rolling my eyes and denying what was happening right in front of my face.

"Thanks for staying a little while longer, but we have some news to share with y'all." Messiah said.

"Y'all not movin' are you?" Sydnee blurted out.

"No." They smiled. "But we are getting married tho'." Jaxsyn held out her hand and flashed the biggest diamond that I've ever laid eyes on.

"Oh my gosh." We all jumped up in excitement and hugged them. Even Kabrina moody ass was happy.

Jaxsyn smiled from ear to ear and told us how it went down. Messiah said he couldn't wait to plan anything fancy he just wanted to hear her say yes and that was beautiful in its own right.

"Congrats. I love y'all," I hugged them both.

"Thanks. We love you too." They both said.

"I knew you would love that ring." Our dad said as she laid her head on his chest.

"You knew Daddy?" She looked up at him.

"Of course, I knew. You thought he was going to marry my baby without asking me first?" He rubbed her head.

"I love you so much," she smiled."

"I love you more baby girl. He's a good man and I'm so happy for you two. Now, we have to get out of here so Becca can get some rest. She worked today."

"Okay." They hugged and I watched the interactions closely.

"I prayed that you would find this kind of happiness baby." Kabrina kissed both of her cheeks. "Umm," She cleared her throat. "You did a really good job with her," she looked at Rebecca and we all got quiet. Rebecca literally started boo hoo crying and Brian hugged her. "I have to go, but congratulations y'all." Kabrina seemed sad and for the very first time in my life, I understood her pain and where her anger stemmed from when it came to Rebecca. She had to watch her daughter love another woman more than she loves her and it was all her doing. My eyes watered at the familiarity.

"*We* did a good job." Rebecca hugged her. "It takes a village Kabrina." They shared an unspoken moment and then Kabrina walked away.

"Wow. I'm sorry y'all but I'm speechless. Congrats to you both." Rebecca kissed both of them and then hugged Jaxsyn for a long time while she whispered something into her ear. Jaxsyn began to cry and then she smiled.

"I love you more than you'll ever know." Jaxsyn hugged her again and then they left.

I was jealous but not of anyone in particular. Their bonds were built from childhood and I couldn't go back in time. I couldn't change the things I've said to them, how I've treated them, or the love I missed out on. What I did have is now, and all I could do was allow my walls to come down and become a part of my family that I was deprived of.

"I'm out too sis," I smiled.

"Text me and tell me how it goes."

"I will," I hugged her and then hugged my other sisters. "Bye, bye Nevaeh."

"Boo boo," she showed me her knee.

"Awww it still hurts?" I kissed it and she hugged me. "TT Z will see you later," I waved, and she waved back.

I hopped in the car and texted Quan. He sent me his address and I took a swig from my flask. I headed toward his house with Nashon heavily on my mind. I never thought I would entertain another man, but life threw me lemons, so I guess this was me making lemonade, again.

228

Messiah

I rode around the hood with Jaxsyn riding shotgun and it was almost like riding around with my brother again. We cracked jokes, talked shit, and blew trees. Baby girl was literally my best friend and my woman wrapped into one. I hated that she resorted to her old ways for me, but I loved this shit at the same time. I hadn't really saw this side of her until recently and I can't lie and say I wasn't feeling this shit.

"There's Paul stuttering ass." We laughed and chucked the deuces.

"I remember when we were kids, he used to try to fuck Zionna."

"That's nasty."

"As hell," she passed the blunt.

"I bet chicks go through that shit all the time huh?" I looked over at her.

"Hell yeah. That's why I had to do what I had to do for my sister when we were younger. Nigga's don't care about age, looks, size, nothing. I had a big booty my whole life and dealt with grown men offering me the world."

"Man, I swear on everything I love, if a nigga even try that shit with my babies I'm killin' they ass on sight."

"Period," she nodded her head. "Zionna used to be weak and Sandy ain't never been shit so if a nigga had a few dollars for her, she was letting them in the door on Z."

"Word?" I had no idea.

"Yup. That's why to this day I don't really fuck with Sandy like that. You ain't never seen me invite Sandy to shit or even kick it with her triflin' ass."

"I hadn't paid attention, but you right."

"It's always gone be fuck her in my book. She kept Zionna away from my dad and that whole side of her family and she still feels like I'm not really her sister because we only have the same daddy. Her logic is stupid as hell, but she believes that shit wholeheartedly and so does Zionna. For so long she used to call me her best friend instead of her sister."

"That's the dumbest shit ever. When did she start calling you her sister?"

"After I saved her fuckin life. At that point it wasn't shit else to call me." We both busted out laughing.

"She got some deep-rooted issues man and Sandy cracked out ass is the cause."

"Deep rooted issues are an understatement baby. You don't know the half," she shook her head and took the blunt I was passing her. "Z loves me as much as she does for a reason and it damn sure ain't because I'm her sister."

"Parents be out here fuckin us up man. You know I haven't talked to my moms since we buried Nashon. Her ass be pump fakin' and then get mad when I don't believe shit she says."

"Yeah. She's a character. Did you ever find out what that shit was about between her and your uncle?"

"Nah... I asked her about it, and she said she didn't want to talk about it. She doesn't never say shit about our sperm donor so it ain't no telling what that shit was about. I didn't even press her."

"I wouldn't have either."

"A nigga got the munchies like a muthafucka. You hungry Tink?"

"I can eat. I don't like stopping this late but I damn sure don't feel like cooking."

"Let's just grab some Coney Island. I can go for some wing dings."

"Hell yeah, and some Chili cheese fries."

"With bacon." We said in unison and laughed with our high asses.

I turned around and went to our favorite spot.

"Lock the doors Tink. I'll be right back," I kissed her.

"Alright."

I got out the car and went into the Coney. Of course, the one we like the most doesn't have a drive thru, but I was strapped so I wasn't worried.

"What up doe Ali. You good, my baby?"

"My friend. How have you been Sih?"

"Good man. I can't complain. Let me get the usual."

"Two wing ding snacks, a chili cheese fry with crispy bacon?"

"Yup. You know it."

"I got you my friend. Coming right up. Tell Jaxsyn I put extra ranch in bag just for her," he said in his thick Arabic accent.

230

"Good lookin' out," I laughed. She was constantly on his ass about not giving her enough ranch, so I guess he finally got the point.

I looked back to check on her and she was looking my way. I smiled and she blew me a kiss. I didn't know what was going on with her lately, but she was throwing her pussy like a porn star and giving me head that was mind blowing every single time. I was impressed with her skills but I'm like where the fuck did all this come from. Shit, before I got locked up, we were gettin' it poppin' like crazy, but this shit is different. My baby was showing the fuck out and had a nigga pussy whipped like a muthafucka. These bitches couldn't even get a second glance from me and maybe that was her plan. She had my head gone.

"Here you go Sih. Have a good one and be careful out there Buddy."

"Thanks, you too," I grabbed our bag and walked to the car.

"Don't fuckin move nigga." A voice came from behind me and I was sick. The bag was in my right hand and my gun was on that side. These niggas in The D is ruthless and will murk me and my baby for the lil bit of cash I had on me. My mind raced on how to get us out of this shit alive.

"Take that fuckin watch off and come out of them J's nigga. Tell your bitch I'm taken the whip too so she can step the fuck out."

"His bitch already stepped the fuck out," I heard Jaxsyn and then I heard her rack the gun and I could feel that nigga stiffen up behind me. "If you don't get that fuckin gun out of my nigga face, I'm going to blow your fuckin brains all over his new Balmain shirt."

"Just calm down baby girl."

"Bitch this is calm. Grab his gun Bae."

I turned around and she was standing behind him with her gun against his temple. I was impressed, pissed at the situation, and turned on all at once. Gizmo was right. She's a force to be reckoned with.

"Kirby," I looked at the nigga like he was crazy. He used to be one of my workers years ago, so he knew exactly how I got down.

"Awww man. I didn't know it was you Sih."

"Bullshit," I felt him down for weapons and put his weak ass in the trunk.

We got in and I looked over at Jaxsyn. "Thanks Baby."

"You don't have to thank me Daddy. What the fuck was I going to do, let the nigga rob us?" She laughed nonchalantly like that shit wasn't a big deal. "Did he give me extra ranch?"

I smiled at her crazy ass.

"Yeah baby, it's in there," I pulled off. "Where's this spot in the woods that you go to?"

"Hop on 75 North," she turned up the music and fed us both while I drove us to her spot, so we could handle this nigga properly.

Jaxsyn

"Yessss!" I screamed. "Fuck me Daddy. Ughhhh!" I was bent over with my hands against his car while he pounded me relentlessly. This sex was every bit of sadistic and it made it that much hotter.

This was our first time killing someone together and while we waited on the cleaners, we got horny and started fuckin' a few feet away from the body. I didn't know what had gotten into either of us, but we were turning into Dr. Jekyll & Mr. Hyde. We were picture perfect parents, great friends, loving family members, but we fuck like porn stars, blow loud by the ounce, and roam the streets late night. Just the thought of us made my pussy wetter.

"Shit, Tink," he came hard and long inside of me. He was serious about not pulling out, so I stayed on birth control. That's probably the only secret that I have. We already have three busy ass toddlers. The last thing I need is a new born on top of that. Leave it to Messiah, we'd already be on our sixth child by now. I'm not against giving him another baby because I know he wants to experience the whole thing, but we have to at least potty train the kids we have, first.

"You are everything Mr. Knight," I sat on the hood of his car and hugged him from behind.

"And so are you Mrs. Knight."

I kissed his neck and I could see him smiling from the side.

"You never get enough, do you?" He laughed.

"Hell no. Stop making me cum so hard and giving me orgasms that stay on my mind for days at a time and then I'll stop being such a fiend," I licked his neck and rubbed his muscular chest.

"I can't do that," he looked over his shoulder at me.

"Then I'll never get enough," I turned him around and kissed him passionately. Our tongues made love to each other like we had just done, and I wanted him again.

"They're here Baby."

"I'll be in the car," I hopped down and waved. They waved back as I got in the car and Sih walked over to them. He's been doing business with them since he moved to Detroit and he doesn't trust anyone else when it comes to cleaning up the messes that he makes.

I looked down at my phone and Sydnee was calling me.

"Hey sis what's up?"

"Are you going to Arizona with us?"

"No ma'am. I think she just wants to bond with y'all."

"I don't want to go if you don't go. I said yes before I really thought about it. We don't even know her for real. This is what I get for being nosey. She wasn't even talking to me," she was serious, and I didn't want to laugh but I couldn't help it.

"I feel you baby but just give her a chance. She's finally trying so y'all can't shoot her down just yet. Well I mean you can, but I know y'all have wanted this for a while. How about I talk to her and see what you guys will be doing and I'll let you know what she has planned."

"Thank you so much."

"No problem Baby."

"Alright bye." We hung up and Sih got in the car.

"They worth every penny man."

"I know."

"Ready to head home?"

"Absolutely," I smirked, and he shook his head.

"Freak."

"Yup. Just for my man tho'," I reached over and grabbed his dick.

"Don't grab him if you don't plan on doing nothin' to him."

"Tuh," I unbuttoned his pants and topped him off as he struggled to make it out of the woods, we were in.

"Get naked as soon as we get home. I'm tearing that ass up. Got a nigga moanin' like a bitch and shit. You about to get punished," he was wearing a devilish grin that I knew far too well. It was on and poppin' as soon as we hit that door.

When I woke up Messiah was gone, and my phone was ringing. I reached over and it was Zionna.

"Hello."

"Sorry. Were you sleep?"

"Yeah. It's okay though."

"Do you go into the office at all anymore."

"Yeah like two or three times a week. I hired a general manager so I can work from home now that the kids are here and just go out into the field when I have too," I yawned.

"Oh okay."

"I was going to call you anyway. What's the plan for the girls when they get there?"

"Who's trying to cancel on me?"

"Neither. I was just asking because you really don't know them so I don't want you to plan something that they may not like."

"Oh. It's a couple really nice restaurants and museums around here, maybe check out the social scene, and just chill."

"Okay. Sounds cool. Alyssa doesn't really do clubs, but she might loosen up for you."

"I was kinda calling you about the same thing actually. Umm, did you want to come out here when they come? I didn't invite you because of the kids but Sih has help. We can all bond and you can kinda mediate for me."

"Yeah you can use me," I laughed. "Let me run it pass hubby since it's last minute and see what he says, but it shouldn't be a problem."

"Yay. This is going to be great. See y'all tomorrow."

"Okay," I hung up with her and called Sydnee back to tell her the news. She was as excited as Zionna and I shook my head. They were all a mess in their own right.

"Where are you?" I called Sih.

"Handling business."

"Okay. I'm about to go get the kids and take them to see your granny."

"Alright. I'll probably meet you over there."

"Okay. Love you."

"Love you too."

"Oh. Hello?" I tried to catch him before he hung up.

"Yeah?"

"Can you watch the kids this weekend so I can go to AZ with my sisters?"

"You deserve a real break. How about I send y'all somewhere else? It ain't shit to do in Arizona."

"You would do that?" I smiled.

"Of course, I would Baby. Get with them, pick somewhere, and let me know so I can get it booked for y'all."

"Thanks bae."

"Anything for you." We hung up and I called all of my sisters on a conference call.

"I just talked to Sih about me going to Arizona and he said he'll send us on a real vacation wherever we want to go."

"What?" Zionna said. "Is he serious?"

"Wow." Both Syd and Lyss said in unison.

"I know and yeah, he's dead serious so let's pick somewhere so he can book it."

"Hawaii." Zionna blurted out and we all got excited.

"That's perfect. Hawaii it is. Let me call him and I'll talk to y'all later." We hung up and I told him our decision. He agreed that it was the perfect place to really get away and unwind. He called his travel agent immediately and booked the trip while I shot to the mall to grab some new swim suits. I was excited for this time away with my sisters. I just hope everything remains peaceful.

Jaxsyn

Every second away from my babies was hell and I had called Sih at least fifty times. I didn't mind leaving them with my parents, my sisters, or Kabrina when we're all in the same state but I was hundreds of miles away and I wasn't used to being that far away from them.

"Hi mommy's babies," I FaceTimed them.

"Mommy." Nevaeh waved and then looked at her daddy like what the hell. We both laughed because she didn't understand how mommy was on the screen, but she was so happy to see me. The twins couldn't have cared less but as long as I got to see them, I was content. Nevaeh turned the phone back on her and was talking like crazy. I guess she had some shit to get off her chest because she was going, and I could only understand "Daddy" and "I said" which had us rolling. She finally got her story out and passed him the phone.

"So, I pissed her off and she's telling on me?" He smiled.

"I think you did baby. You better leave my Princess alone, she's sick of your shit." We laughed. "It's so beautiful out here Bae. We have to come back."

"It's a date Beautiful. Well go ahead and enjoy. I got this Tink. I want you to unwind and have fun. They're fine."

"I know they are," I pouted. "I miss them so much."

"You don't miss their father?" He smiled.

"Of course, I do."

"You better because I miss yo' rock head ass."

"Awww I love you."

"Love you too baby. Now, go enjoy."

"Okay," I blew him a kiss and hung up. All my sisters were already dressed and waiting for me. Sih got us a suit with two rooms so I made Alyssa and Zionna room together. They needed it. Although there isn't any more tension and the flight was amazing with us just laughing, joking, and drinking, I still wanted them to get a better feel for each other.

I slipped into my bathing suit and whipped my hair into a messy bun. My Ray-Ban aviators brought my whole look together and just like that, I felt a million times better and was ready to enjoy the day.

"I'm ready. I had to call the babies."

"You know they're fine." Zionna put her hand on her hips and leaned her head to the side. "Stop trippin'."

"I know. I know. I FaceTimed them just to see their little faces, not to check on him," I smiled. "I'm not going to do it again today tho'. Maybe in the morning."

They all shook their heads, but I didn't expect them to understand. A year ago, I probably wouldn't have understood either but as a mother I had to know my babies were okay at every second.

"You better trust that man with his kids like he trusts you. Don't keep calling him Jaxsyn." Zionna pointed to me. "I'm not playin' heffa."

"I hear you and it's dually noted," I said honestly, and we all walked out.

The hotel was located right on the beach, so we walked out of the door and straight into the sand. Hawaii was simply breathtaking. When we stepped off of the plane, we knew this trip was going to be amazing.

My little sisters played around with some guys that was at the pool while Z told me about her and Quan's new friendship. I thought it was dope that he was more mature now and just wanted to see her happy and healthy. People change and he was the proof.

"I'm hungry." Alyssa said and we all agreed. We asked the bartender where was the best food and he pointed us in the right direction. We could smell the food before we even reached the place, and once we saw the selection, we knew we would love it.

"This is beyond amazing," I bit into my freshly caught Mahi Mahi fish tacos, and they were heavenly. I closed my eyes and savored the moment. Everyone was enjoying their meal and the ambiance, which was simply breathtaking.

"Can we have a real talk? No arguments. No bickering. Just sisters talking." Sydnee looked around the table.

"Oh Lord. We can definitely try," I shook my head.

"I'm just sayin'. We're all here trying to bond right? It's the point of this whole trip. We have to be able to put what we feel on the table and address the issues without conflict. We're all grown."

"You're right. Go ahead." Zionna responded.

"Why do you show favoritism when it comes to them?"

"Who me?" I was genuinely shocked and taken aback by Sydnee's question.

"Yes. Alyssa is your *Pooh* and you're her *Shugga*. It's always one big love fest when y'all get together. Zionna has gotten all of your time and attention because y'all grew up like best friends and then there's me. The odd sister out. You never show me the same love, affection, or attention that you show them."

"Oh my God Sydnee. I never ever in a million years meant to make you feel like that. Like ever. Even momma calls me Shugga though, and if you can remember, Alyssa was like my little shadow when we were younger. You used to be with Jagger and Dawson all the time."

"Yeah because I felt left out. You're always buying her shit and calling her all the time with your secrets. How many times have you talked to them this month and how many times have you talked to me? That's all the proof you need Jaxsyn. I'm not trying to make it a big thing, but it hurts my feelings."

"It is a big thing Syd. It's huge actually. I apologize for hurting you. You're my sister and I love you all the same. No favorites, no differences. I'll do better. I swear," I got up and hugged my little sister because she was right, and I felt shitty.

"And what did we ever do to you?" She looked at Zionna. "Jaxsyn may have made some mistakes but you've never even attempted to connect with us on any level. I really need to know what we did?"

"I knew this was coming," she took a sip of her drink and looked at them both. "Absolutely nothing and that's why I wanted to spend this time with you. I feel like I missed out on so much. My mother has everything to do with why I didn't come around as a kid but now that I'm grown there is absolutely no excuse. I hate that I've missed out on so much and sometime my attitude comes from feeling out of place," she started to cry, and I wasn't expecting that. "I watch all of you together and it's such a family bond and then there's me, the outsider that everyone has to tolerate. I hate that shit so the kid in me lashes out and for that I apologize," she wiped her tears and I reached over and hugged her. Alyssa and Sydnee followed suit and before I knew it, we were all crying and having a genuine moment that we all needed more than we thought.

"I love y'all," I smiled.

"Love you too." The all said in unison and we enjoyed the rest of our dinner catching up, telling old stories, and they all got to know each other better. I couldn't have asked for better sisters or a better place for this moment to happen.

Messiah

I missed Jaxsyn ass so much it was sickening. I should have planned a romantic getaway for the two of us. After being away from her for over a year I didn't want us to spend any more time apart. I did enjoy my one on one time with my children tho'. I seriously take my hat off to Jax because they ran daddy like a got damn slave. I owed her the world.

"Tabitha I'm going to pick up Jaxsyn. Nevaeh is playing and the twins are sleeping so try to keep her quiet for me."

"Okay Mr. Knight. I'll go in there with her right now."

"Thanks Tab. I appreciate you," I grabbed my keys and walked out. My baby didn't know how much I missed her, but she was going to find out real soon when I pull over and make her ass climb on top. Her warmth was calling my name. I swear she had fairy dust between her thighs. I ain't never been this strung out or pussy whipped.

I pulled in front of the Delta terminal exit and she ran out of the sliding doors of the airport.

"I missed you sooooo much," she smiled from ear to ear.

"I bet I missed yo' ass more," I kissed her and grabbed her ass. "Let me get this stuff so we can go," I shot her a look and she bit the corner of her lip.

We both hustled to put her stuff in the car and then hopped in.

"You have fun?"

"So much fun baby and everyone got along. God is good because I never thought I would see the day that all my sisters would cordially be in the same room."

"That's great baby. I'm happy for y'all," I dipped off on the first street away from the airport and parked. I let my seat back and she already knew what time it was. She damn near jumped into my lap. She lifted her Maxi dress and slid down my rod within seconds, causing us both to moan.

"Shiiiiit Jax, ride that mafucka Ma." Yet again she was showing the fuck out and delivery shots that had me zoned out. I matched her rhythm and before I knew it, she was shaking, and I was bustin' hard as hell inside of her.

"Ughhhhh," I squeezed her legs, holding her in place.

"Shit Baeeeee," she laid her head on my shoulder as she caught her breath. We were both feeling the aftershock of the session and chilled for a second before we moved. When she was ready, she kissed my neck and climbed back over the center console. "Oh, how I missed you," she smiled and licked her lips. "Get me home. I need more and I miss my babies."

"Yes ma'am," I laughed and pulled off.

That year away from each other had us insatiable. We couldn't turn the shit off or down. It was crazy. We even started fuckin' in our people crib. I bent her ass over in my granny's kitchen last week and she rode me in Kabrina's living room a few days prior to that. Shit was crazy but a nigga was happy as fuck too. This bond was unbreakable, and it felt good as fuck to know I had a woman that I could genuinely trust.

"Why is the front door open?" She asked as soon as we pulled up.

"Fuck! Stay here."

"Hell naw," she hopped out with me and we ran in the house.

"Tabitha!" I called out and she didn't answer.

"Tab." Jaxsyn called her and looked in the kitchen but still no response so we hauled ass upstairs to the kids' room. The rooms were ransacked but Jeniah was sleeping like a rock. There was no sign of Nevaeh, Junior, or Tabitha. We went in each room and finally we got to the basement. We both drew in a deep breath as our eyes landed on Tabitha's body lying in a pool of her own blood. Her throat was cut, and my heart dropped.

"Where the fuck are my babies? Oh my God Messiah! Please God no. Where the fuck are my babies Siiih?" Jaxsyn dropped to her knees and cried loud and hysterically. It was a DVD on the table next to Tabitha's body that said, "Press Play". Knowing two of my kids were missing made me almost nervous to see what the fuck was on it, but I had to.

"Go upstairs for me Baby. I don't know what's on it and I don't want you to see this Jaxsyn."

"Just put it in," she gasped for air and held her chest. "Hurry up!" She yelled and I put the DVD in the player.

242

"I know you don't know me, but I definitely know you." A nigga was talking to my security camera at the gate. "Let me start off by saying both you and your bitch don't know who the fuck you've crossed," he hit his blunt and smiled. "I can promise you on everything I know and love, you've never crossed a nigga like me before and I'll show you better than I can tell you." The video cut to him inside of our home. He snapped his finger while still wearing that same devious smile, "Abra Ca Muthafuckin Dabra my niggas. You thought that weak ass gate could keep a nigga like me out? Wroooong. No. Wait. Maybe you thought your tough ass maid was a match for me? Wrong, again," he held a knife to Tabitha's throat and slid across slowly while licking the side of her face. "You take from me bitch nigga and I take from you. Now to the best part." The DVD cut to him tiptoeing into our kids' room one by one like you see cartoon characters do. This nigga was joking around, and I felt my fuckin' skin start to crawl. "So precious at this age huh? I think so too. Watch this mommy. He took Nevaeh out of her crib and dropped her.

"Jesus!" Jaxsyn was beside her self and I couldn't fuckin believe it either. She started crying and he stepped right over her and went to our son's room and did the same thing. He laughed and then picked him up. "The *little* heir to your *little* throne. Awwww. I think I'll take this one, and end the bloodline after I kill you two," he went back to Nevaeh who was now standing in the hallway crying her heart out and calling out for her mommy. He smiled sadistically. "And I guess I'll take the only connection that you have to your dead ass brother too," he picked her up and took both kids downstairs. "Take them," he passed the kids to someone and then looked back at the camera. "I'm taking those two because they're the most important. You take something from me, and I take everything from you. It's not a nigga or a bitch walking this earth that I can't touch. Remember that shit. Now come find me pussies so I can dump this hot lead in both of you hoes." The DVD turned off and Jaxsyn hadn't stopped crying the whole time.

"My fuckin babies are gone Messiah," she took off running upstairs. I knew she was going to get Jeniah and I completely understood. My fuckin blood was boiling, and I called the only person that I could trust to handle some shit like this with me.

"Gizmo I need you ASAP nigga."

"What's going on?"

"Somebody got my fuckin kids cuz. Get out here right the fuck now. Just go to the airport and I got you."

"On my way cuz," he hung up and I looked over at Tabitha's limp body. I felt responsible for her death and I was going to avenge her death just like I was going to get my fuckin children back. This nigga was not going to get away with this shit. I hit play on the DVD again and watched his every move. I was going to find this nigga and kill his ass with my bare fuckin' hands.

Zionna

The travel agent messed up my ticket and booked all four of our departures going to Detroit. I didn't mind because that was extra time with my sisters even if we did sleep most of the time. I was shocked when Sih called me out of the blue and told me he needed me to not board my plane and come straight to their house. I had no fuckin clue why but when I showed up and found out, my heart broke into pieces. I couldn't believe what the fuck he told me, and I cringed the entire time I watched the DVD.

Jaxsyn was an absolute mess and it wasn't shit that could be said to her to snap her out of it. She cried uncontrollably and she wouldn't let either of us hold Jeniah. She wouldn't let her out of her sight at all. I tried my hardest to console her, but she rocked and cried, rocked and cried, and rocked and cried. I had no idea how to help my sister or Sih for that matter, so I sat next to her and just became a presence for her.

Every day that the kids weren't found, Jaxsyn slipped deeper and deeper into a depression that was far worse than the one that I had allowed myself to slip into after Nash was killed. She locked her and Jeniah in her bedroom and only came out for food for her daughter. She wouldn't talk to any of us and she cried constantly. Messiah's heart was broken, and he barely came home. Him and Gizmo were hitting the streets day and night trying to find the kids and kill the crazy ass nigga that took them, but they kept coming up empty handed.

"Messiah I have to at least tell my dad so he can tell Becca. Jaxsyn really needs help."

"I said no and don't ask me that shit again. Becca is going to think she's lost her got damn mind and that momma shit is going to become a professional opinion on whether to admit her or not and I'll die first."

"I don't think they would do that to her Sih. Rebecca loves her."

"Look at her Zionna," he snatched me up hard as hell by the collar of my shirt and dragged me to the kitchen where she was. "Actually, look at your fuckin' sister right now Z," he said through gritted teeth and I was almost scared of him, but I looked. She had Jeniah strapped to her chest in a baby carrier that was too small, her hair was matted to her head, her face was puffy from crying, she was dirty, she honestly looked deranged, and she was talking to herself about God knows what. "Now tell me with one look at her if Becca don't recommend a program or treatment facility. I don't give a fuck how long it's been since she washed her ass or what she's in there talking to herself about. She has every right to look like she looks and chant whatever the fuck she's chanting. Her babies are gone, and I've failed her again. Don't call no fuckin body on my wife and I mean that shit. Let her do whatever the fuck she wants to do in this bitch," he stormed of out the front door and slammed it behind him. She jumped and turned around.

"That was just Messiah leaving sweetie. It's okay."

She stared at me and I didn't know what the hurt that consumed her felt like but the pain in her eyes nearly broke me. I simply opened my arms and she finally allowed me to embrace her. It was almost as if the door slamming loudly woke her up in some way.

"I have to keep reminding myself to breathe Z," she cried loudly and from the depths of her soul. I had no idea that's what she had been chanting to herself this whole time. For days I had been trying to figure it out and now I was replaying it in my mind; *Keep breathing for Jeniah, Jaxsyn. Just keep breathing.*

"They're going to find them Jaxsyn. You know Sih is not going to rest until your babies are back in your arms where they belong. He's been combing the streets with no sleep for days."

She ignored me and grabbed a bottle of Patron out of the cabinet. Jeniah was sleep but she was clean, and her hair was combed so my sister wasn't that far out of it.

"Can I hold her Jaxsyn?"

"No!" She turned up the bottle and slowly strolled back upstairs. I had never seen her like this, and I think Messiah may be wrong about not calling the rest of the family, but I was going to stay in my lane… For now. The last thing I was going to allow, is for her to follow down the path that I'm still trying to recover from. Drinking to survive every day is not the way to go and I refuse to allow her to make the same mistake I made.

Messiah

Gizmo and I was racking up a body count that was obscene, but I didn't give a fuck about the nigga's that we left leakin'. I had to get my kids back and I had to do whatever the fuck it took to do so. I was silently losing my mind and my fiancée. Jaxsyn was going fuckin' crazy right before my very own eyes and I had to save her from herself. She drank constantly and I hadn't held my daughter in days. She wouldn't allow me to come near them like I was the enemy. I can't lie, that shit hurt bad. We went from living a dream life to a fuckin nightmare within seconds.

"I need to watch that video again bro." Gizmo said as we rode around another night with no fuckin clue.

"I'll try to get it back from her."

"Can I try?" He looked at me and I nodded my head. They had become close while I was locked up so if he thought he could get through to her, then he could damn sure try. I had run out of all options and for the first time in my life I had no fuckin clue what to do. I was filled with a rage that consumed me and a pain in my heart that was far greater than when the streets took my brother. This shit was next level, and nothing could have prepared me for it.

We pulled up to the house and sat out front for about twenty minutes while we finished the blunt that he had rolled to ease my mind.

"I can't believe this shit cuz. I swear I can't," I looked at my house and all the security cameras around it. "Somebody violated me and my family in a major fuckin way and I'm so fuckin stupid for thinking that this type of shit wouldn't ever happen to us."

"Stop blaming yourself. Shit like this happen everyday son and we just have to handle this shit head on. I'm about to shoot in here and holla' at Jax," he got out and I stayed in the car. It was a long shot and I wasn't in the mood for another let down. I stayed away from her because the look of pure hate that she had in her eyes when she looked at me was far more than I could handle under the circumstances.

Jaxsyn

I looked over at the clock on my dresser and it was 5:49 am. I didn't know why Gizmo was knocking on my bedroom door, but I got up anyway.

"What?" I opened the door and he stormed pass me.

"Close that," he pointed to the door. "Now put her down and come holla at me in this bathroom," he went in there and leaned against the sink. For some reason unknown to me, I did what he said.

As soon as I got to the bathroom, he snatched me up and shook me hard.

"I want you to wake the fuck up and shake this shit off. This shit ain't you my nigga. I watched you torture three muthafucka's for hours without flinching or blinking an eye. It's a fuckin beast inside of you and this is the time to unleash that bitch. This is the time to let loose," he punched me in my chest so hard he took my breath away. "These hoe ass niggas came in y'all fuckin' crib and got your fuckin' babies and you're held up in this bitch like he's just going to bring them the fuck back. You're smarter than this Jaxsyn, it's time to wake the fuck up, and I mean now. Ain't no bitch in yo' blood. I've seen your heart and it can turn black and cold as ice. I need that muthafucka to surface right the fuck now. Your kids need you and yo' nigga is breaking the fuck down mentally. He can only take so much B so step the fuck up like I know you can so we can get y'all shit back in order. The babies need to be home in they fuckin' bed and they need us all to make that shit happen," he turned me toward the mirror. "Look at you. You look mad crazy Ma and everybody's fuckin worried that you're going to off your fuckin self in this bitch any day now. Hop the fuck in that got damn shower and come watch this footage with me. You have an eye and ear for this shit. Listen to everything this nigga says and everything the nigga don't say. Watch how he moves and pay attention to every got damn thing going on around him. Take your emotions out of it for a minute and really pay attention Jaxsyn. Give the baby to Sih and meet me in the basement after your shower. He misses her and it's some real hoe ass shit to keep her from him under the fuckin circumstances. You already fuckin' know that though, so I shouldn't have even had to say that shit bro. Real spit," he pushed pass me hard as hell, knocking me into the counter, and I was at a loss for words. I stared at myself in the mirror and he was one hundred percent right across the board. I had completely fuckin lost it and got caught up in my grief. Sih was an afterthought to me for the last few days even though he's the only one in the world that knew how I was feeling. We were in this together and I was fuckin' up.

I turned on the shower and hopped in. I let the hot water beat down on my back as I cried, and the water washed my tears away. I washed myself thoroughly because it had been days and then got out. I slipped into my black jogging suit with my black Timb's and put my hair in a messy bun. I felt a little better and I damn sure smelled better.

Messiah was sitting on the couch with his head laid back and his fitted over his face. I placed Jeniah on his chest and he jumped. He moved his hat and looked down at her. Tears welled up in his eyes and I kissed his forehead. I was wrong for keeping her away from him and I felt like shit. I walked away without saying a word and I went to the basement with Gizmo. I guess the cleaners had come to the house because there was no sign of Tabitha anywhere.

I put the DVD in and for well over two hours, me and Gizmo picked the video apart inch by inch.

"Wait. Go back, go back," I stopped him, and he rewound it.

"Abra Ca Muthafuckin Dabra nigga," I had heard that shit somewhere, but I couldn't place it. I took the remote from Giz and kept rewinding it over and over until it hit me like a ton of fuckin bricks.

"Ollie," I stood up. "He fuckin knows Ollie. Ollie is the connection. I told you Ollie was the small fish, and this is the shark we've been looking for."

"My nigga. I knew it was in you," he pushed me playfully.

"Remember when we finally found Ollie and that nigga was talking shit to him and-"

"Ollie came out with the burner and said the same shit. Ol' boy didn't think he was strapped."

"Exactly," I nodded my head. "Now we just need to know how he's connected to him."

"I'm on it cuz. I told you it was a fuckin beast in there. This is guerilla warfare baby and we need you present," he hugged me and ran upstairs. I followed behind him and I felt slightly better that we were one step closer. He said something to Messiah and left out the door.

"What did y'all find?" Messiah looked over at me and his tone was dry.

249

"Hopefully a connection," I shrugged, and he directed his attention back to Jeniah. "I'm sorry for-"

"Stop Jaxsyn," he stroked Jeniah's face as she slept peacefully in his arms. "We're not about to fight and argue because we're both hurting and what's happened has taken a toll on us both. This shit is enough to drive anyone insane. Let's just leave it at that."

"I love you."

"I love you too Baby," he looked back towards me and I walked over to him. I sat down and kissed him deeply. We shared a moment that we both needed and tears rolled down both of our faces.

"I don't want you to suffer through this alone Ma."

"I know. I had a moment but I'm back," I kissed him again and then looked at our sleeping daughter. "I swear I'm back."

"Good. We have to find these muthafucka's and make them pay. I have a few more of my cousins coming out here because I don't trust none of these muthafuckas now. None."

"I'm ready for whatever will get our kids back safe and sound," I laid in his arms and I could feel his anger radiating off of him. Clearly this nigga had a beast inside of him too. You don't fuck with people kids. The line had been crossed and we were war ready.

Messiah

Jax and I stayed up all night thinking of how this shit could play out and what moves we needed to make. We agreed that Jeniah had to go somewhere safe and the safest place for her was with my people in New York. We told Zionna we needed her to hold us down and take her out there with my cousin Shawn. We could tell she was nervous, but we needed this and she knew it.

I held Jaxsyn in my arms as we watched my cousin and her sister drive away with the only baby that we had left. My heart and stomach were in knots for both of us, but it was nothing else that we could do. I had to protect my baby girl and I know my fam wouldn't let a hair on her head get harmed. For the first time in a long time I had no doubt in my mind that we made the right decision.

"Let's get in here and map this shit out ma. Gizmo said he has more information," I wiped her face and she nodded. My whole living room was family and she had no idea when I said they were coming that it was going to be this many. It was nineteen of my closest cousins and they were all ready for whatever, whenever.

"Thanks to Jaxsyn I know who the fuck we're looking for." Gizmo put his picture in the middle of our living room table and my cousin Fresh spoke up first.

"I know this muthafucka," he rubbed his head. "His name is Dominic. They call him Gato which is cat in Spanish. He's the leader of the Vargas Cartel and he's notorious for being vicious but he plays with his prey which is why they call the nigga Gato. This nigga is heavily guarded, but he goes rogue every now and then."

"Cartel? How the fuck did we cross paths with this muthafucka?" I looked at Gizmo.

"Stepped on his toes one too many times, I'm guessing. Apparently, he was fuckin your girl Mariah behind your back for years. We popped that bitch then we killed his little brother Ollie for killing Nashon. His cousin Rodney was The Knight that y'all caught trying steal from y'all and you and Nash handled his ass too. I'm assuming Tone knew Ollie through him coming around with Dominic while he was fuckin' Mariah."

"Wow. So, was these niggas coming for us through that nigga Rodney or was that some fluke shit?"

"I'm still working on that, but it seems like it was all a part of a plan. This couldn't be that much of a coincidence," I rubbed my hands over my face and the reality of my actions hit me all at once. My kids were kidnapped and caught in the middle of my bullshit. Now they're telling me that not only does this lunatic that has my babies have cartel connections, but this shit may be even deeper than we originally thought. I killed that nigga Rodney almost two years ago and now this shit is coming back at me. They were trying to infiltrate our shit all the way back then. I knew that shit felt bigger at the time, but I couldn't figure this shit out and today I wasn't any closer.

"The shit gets a little worse cuz." Gizmo looked at both me and Jaxsyn.

"Nigga," I shook my head.

"Look who he passed the kids to on the video," he sat down the blown up still frame from the video. I couldn't believe my eyes and Jaxsyn look like she was about to throw up.

"Sandy?" Tears rolled down her face. "That's how the nigga knows so much about us. He could go after anybody next to hurt us even more," she took her phone out and called Zionna.

"Please answer the phone," she paced. "Hello."

"Yeah."

"Have you talked to Sandy?"

"Not in a few days."

"Good. This bitch was with him when he took the kids Z."

"What?" She yelled into the phone.

"Yeah. Do not tell her anything. She's probably feeding this nigga all kinds of information on us."

"Who the fuck is he and why would she be helping him do some shit like this?"

"Somebody named Dominic and I don't know. Drugs, money, her granddaughter that she didn't want me to have in the first place. Who fuckin knows with her?"

"Let me talk to her," I snatched the phone out of Jax hand. "Sis call her. See if she gives you any information. Y'all say she likes to run her mouth so make her believe that you're on your way back to Arizona and you got into an argument with Jaxsyn. Call her now on the three way."

"Can you pull over?" She asked my cousin Shawn. "I have to get out the car Messiah. Jeniah has been crying since we left."

"Okay," she briefly paused and then I heard the phone ringing.

"Hello."

"Hey ma."

"Hey baby. Where are you?"

"On my way back to Arizona. You know I went on that vacation with Jaxsyn and her sisters."

"Did that bitch treat you right or she was actin' funny like I told you she would?"

"Actin' funny. You were right about her once again and I shouldn't have gone. Where are you?"

"That dusty bitch doesn't know any better. Look at who raised her. I told you she's not family."

"You were right too. Where you at?"

"You wouldn't believe me if I told you," she laughed.

"Try me."

"Arizona."

"Did you come to visit me?"

"Not really, but I do have a surprise for you if you can keep a secret. Hold on." We could hear her walking and then the door closed. "Hello."

"Yeah. What's the secret?"

"I can get your baby back from Jaxsyn if you still want her."

"I definitely want her. You know she belongs with family, right?"

"Right. The light bulb finally fuckin' came on for you girl. She's ours. Our blood. Not that fake ass wanna be sister." Sandy whispered and we all listened on speakerphone.

"So how are you going to get her back? I signed her over ma."

"Fuck them papers girl. I got her already, but you can't say shit Z. Not a fuckin' word bitch. This nigga crazy as hell. I mean the real kind of crazy Z so just keep your mouth shut and I got us. Shit, I think he killed Kabrina the other day so the nigga ain't nothin to be played with. Don't say shit," I looked over at Jaxsyn and she had a blank expression on her face.

"What?"

"Yeah. I'll explain all that lil shit later but listen to this, he says I can keep her if I do what I have to do. He wants Jaxsyn and her baby daddy dead so if I give him what he need, he said I can keep her."

"Good." Zionna's whole demeanor had changed and I hoped that Sandy didn't pick up on it because we all started to look around at each other.

"Alright baby. I'll be back in Detroit tonight. He wants us to show him where Jax baby daddy grandmother lives and then yo' no good ass daddy is after that. Once that's done, I can take the baby and go."

"So, should I stay in Detroit and wait for y'all?"

"Yeah. Just stay there and meet me at my house. That way we can all go back to Arizona together as a family."

"Okay. Bet."

She hung up and Zionna started crying.

"Tell Shawn to bring y'all back," I hung up and held Jaxsyn. My baby was suffering, and it was all coming at her from different angles. I swear I hope her mother is still alive and this nigga didn't do that shit.

"We have to get granny out of that house. This nigga is coming for straight blood and he's not stopping." My cousin James said through gritted teeth.

"Take my family and your family to the house in the woods. We know for a fact no one knows about it but us, so they'll be safe there." Jaxsyn wiped her face and stood up. "Half of us go post up at my dad's and the other half of us go post up and Granny Knights house. We don't know if he has the babies with him, but we have to hit him before he hits us again and this is the only way. What we do know is that he's in Arizona, so we have the upper hand right now. He's bold so he's going to want to be the first one out and we make our move from there. Did y'all hear her say he wants 'us' to show him. It's more people or another person. Ugh, this shit is crazy."

"Yeah I heard that shit," I nodded. My head was pounding.

"Are we killing this nigga on sight or are we taking him for information." Fresh asked.

"Information. I need to find my children if he doesn't have them with him and from the sounds of all this, it's getting deeper. We need to eliminate everyone involved."

"Bet." Everyone started moving and I looked at Gizmo. He had a lot of confidence in Jaxsyn and now I see why. She was a leader and even I didn't mind following her plan. I looked around the room and I knew that I may lose some of these people tonight but unfortunately, I didn't have any other choice, my kids' lives were on the line.

"Oh," Jaxsyn said and everyone stopped. "Can somebody please go check on my momma?"

"We got you Ma." One of my cousins said as they walked out, and I texted the address. I kissed her and we followed everyone else out of the door.

Jaxsyn

The coldness that Gizmo knew my heart held had surfaced and all I could think about was revenge. Revenge for Nash, revenge for my nigga going to jail and missing out on the first year of our children's lives, revenge for the betrayal that was lurking so close to us, revenge for Tabitha, revenge for how these bitches did my babies, revenge for turning our whole world upside down. I wanted Dominic's blood on my hands. I wanted him dead in the worst kind of way, but I needed him to suffer first. A quick death was too good for him.

This nigga took my kids from me and now he's probably killed my fuckin mother. She just got her shit together and was out here doing everything in her power to right her wrongs and this bitch ass nigga stole her from me. I couldn't even remember the last time I told her that I loved her, and it was bothering me. All she wanted was for me to call her momma and she never even got to hear me utter those words, but I swear I felt it. She really stepped up these last few years and I loved her ass so much for it.

I wiped the tears that fell just at the thought of what he took from me. He was walking around thinking shit was sweet, but I was willing to go to hell and back to avenge the people he stole from me and the shit he's put us through. Fuck his brothers' bitch ass, that hoe Mariah, and his shady ass cousin Rodney too. All they asses deserved what they got and he's next.

We couldn't give our families much information, but we made sure they knew it was imperative that they didn't use their phones for anything and that they stayed in The Spot which was the safest place for them at the moment. My daddy tried to give us a hard time because Rebecca was at work, but I assured him that as soon as she turned her phone back on, we'll make sure she's brought to him. After about five more minutes of worrying he gave in and went with Messiah's cousins. He knew me well enough to know I wouldn't allow anything to happen to her.

When Zionna and Shawn got back we had him take her and Jeniah there too. We had to make sure that this shit played out like it was supposed to and we didn't lose anyone else.

"You ready for this Tink?" Messiah looked over at me while we sat across the street from his grandmother's house and I nodded my head yes.

"I want this nigga dead Baby."

"Me too." His eyes were dark and filled with hate.

"I can't believe our fuckin lives just changed this drastically."

"I know. We can't catch a fuckin break," he shook his head.

"Not one. Nashon died and then everything went downhill. Sometimes I feel like I'm dreaming."

"This is a fuckin nightmare Tink. A long ass fuckin' nightmare, and now we're going after Freddie Krueger," he looked across the street and we both peeped a van pulling up slowly. It rode pass the house and we ducked all the way down. A few minutes later the same van pulled back around and parked in front of the house.

I said a silent prayer to myself that we both make it out of this situation safely but also that Dominic was the one to step out. They sat there for about five minutes as we watched in silence and then my heart started pounding so loud that I thought Sih could hear it. There he was, in the flesh. The first fuckin one to step out just like I said he would. That was one of the first things that I peeped when I watched the footage from our home. He didn't have back up. Fresh said he's normally heavily guarded but it was only him and the person that he passed my babies to which we now know was Sandy. He's cocky and think he's untouchable. Little did he know, we ain't to be fucked with and it was a group of nigga's waiting for him in the house.

Dominic finally slithered his snake ass out of the van and snuck around the back of the house. A few seconds later we saw the living room light come on and we knew his ass was caught. That was our cue. Me, Messiah, and two of his cousins snuck over to the van and peeped that he had a passenger. Messiah snatched the door open and his cousin hit his ass one time and put that nigga to sleep. They carried him across the street and tossed him in the trunk while me and Sih crept around to the back of the van. We looked at each other before snatching both doors open at the same time. Never in a million years was I prepared for who was in the back with Sandy. Before I could even wrap my head around what the fuck was happening, Messiah raised his gun and she raised hers too. Sandy rocked my daughter back and forth with a smug smirk on her face.

"Rebecca?" Tears of confusion filled my eyes as both her and Sih squeezed the trigger at the same time!

To be continued...

AFTERWORD

Hey readers! Thank you so much for taking this journey with Messiah and Jaxsyn. This is just the beginning for them, and this is just the beginning for US! Part two is going to be crazy. The betrayals are unforgivable, and the lies have stacked up so high, a few people are stumbling over them... You don't want to miss what's coming next!! Please stay tuned for the release date and a sneak peek.

Fueled By Revenge: Friend or Foe
The Conclusion

COMING SOON

Please take a moment to leave a review on Amazon and tell me what you think! Reviews are important and appreciated!!

Personal Connections
Instagram: @bb_the_author
Twitter: BB_The_Author
Website for Monster Ink Publishing Coming SOON: @monsterinkpublishing.com

THANKS AGAIN!

www.ingramcontent.com/pod-product-compliance
Lightning Source LLC
Chambersburg PA
CBHW032031240626
47154CB00003B/863

www.ingramcontent.com/pod-product-compliance
Lightning Source LLC
Chambersburg PA
CBHW032030240626
47154CB00003B/846